FINAL EXAM
A Legal Thriller

Terry Huebner

Published by Thunder Road Publishing

ISBN 13: 978-1470108366
ISBN 10: 1470108364

For all those over the years who inspired me and made me believe that this was really possible.

1

Wednesday January 2, 2002

Gordon Hyatt carried himself with the easy, relaxed manner of one who has spent his life contemplating the battles of others, while never quite engaging in any of his own. At this moment and during all moments really, he appeared to the world to be exactly who he was - a Professor of Law at the Chicago College of Law. Blessed with a glint in his eye and a Virginia drawl, Professor Hyatt could dress down an unsuspecting student without any hint of venom or animosity. The student would dig himself a hole and not realize he was in over his head until he saw the grin on Hyatt's face and heard the murmuring of his classmates.

Hyatt pointed the key fob at the shiny, black BMW and the locks clicked shut. He stood there and admired the car as a rogue snowflake floated down and landed on the hood. He wore a brown leather jacket, worn buttery soft and unzipped for the short walk, and carried an old leather briefcase slung over one shoulder. His shaggy brown hair and his beard were just beginning to show flecks of gray as he advanced beyond his early-fifties. He reached the end of the parking lot and stepped over a low metal parapet onto the sidewalk beyond. He looked up Adams Street toward the river as a strong, cold wind blew in his direction. The street was virtually deserted. Then he crossed in the middle of the block and took a sip of his Starbuck's, letting the hot steam drift up to his nostrils in the cold air. He took another sip of the coffee as he pushed through the revolving doors at the front of the school.

Hyatt nodded at the security guard as he passed by and made his way to the elevators. Upon reaching his office, he unlocked the door and pushed inside. He set his coffee on the desk and dropped his jacket and briefcase on a chair next to the door before moving around the desk and plopping down in his chair. In front of him sat the last stack of final exams from his first-year Property class. Hyatt glared at them and growled. He looked at his watch – 9:15. Then he fired up his computer and surfed the web for fifteen minutes before feeling the pull of the exams. He glanced over at them, sighed, then pulled the top one off of the pile. By ten minutes of eleven, he needed a break. He put down his pen, pushed back from his desk and stood, straightening his back and yawning. The coffee had gone right through him. He swore he peed twice as much as he did ten years ago. This must be the curse of the middle-aged man. Can't hold your liquids any longer. Or your liquor. He looked at the remaining exams sitting in a pile on the corner of his desk. Probably an hour-and-a-half or so to go, he thought. He could finish up here and be home in time to grab a late lunch. He would take the exam scores home with him and figure out a grading scale tonight while watching the Fiesta Bowl.

He eyed a note sitting next to the phone. Last week, he had received a voicemail message from Dan Greenfield about a law review article he had written years ago which briefly touched on the constitutional implications surrounding the use of DNA in child custody matters. Hyatt rummaged through a file cabinet behind his desk and pulled a copy of the article out of an expandable file folder. He would stop at the bathroom, then pop down to Greenfield's office on the 6th floor and leave a copy of his article on Greenfield's chair, along with a note offering to discuss the matter over lunch any time next week. He tucked the article under his arm and set off for the washroom. A moment later, he strolled past the elevator and toward the stairwell at the end of the hallway. As he reached the doorway to the 6th floor, Hyatt pulled a keycard out of his wallet and stuck it in the slot next to the doorway. The door clicked, Hyatt pulled the handle and stepped from the stairwell.

The first thing he noticed was the smell. It hit him like a slap in the face - a sick, rotting, metallic kind of smell. He looked down the hallway toward Greenfield's office, then back to the right toward the main entrance of the 6th Floor near the elevators. He hesitated, then turned and headed toward Greenfield's office. The smell grew stronger as he neared Greenfield's door at the end of the hall. He thought he was going to gag. The door was slightly ajar. He knocked, pushing the door open with his shoulder and called out, "Dan, are you in there?" Hearing no response, he entered the room only to be greeted by the strongest, foulest odor he had ever encountered. He turned involuntarily back toward the door and closed his now tearing eyes.

Hyatt forced himself to turn back in an attempt to identify the source of the smell. The wall, bookshelf and credenza in the back corner were splattered with blood. He took several short, hesitant steps around the desk. Daniel Greenfield lay in a heap on the floor, his body partially obscured by his desk and chair. His skull, or what was left of it, had been crushed.

Hyatt gasped for air. Lying across Greenfield's legs, covered with blood and pieces of Greenfield's skull and brain matter, was a baseball bat. Hyatt staggered back as the reality of the scene hit him. He tripped over the leg of one of Greenfield's guest chairs and fell awkwardly against the wall next to the door, striking his head. He gagged and began to retch. Then he stumbled to his feet and backed out the door. He raced down the hallway, around the corner, through a set of double doors and past the elevators to the men's washroom. He bolted through the doorway into a stall, where he vomited. Several minutes later, drenched in sweat, his peaceful existence now a distant memory, Hyatt found a phone on the desk of one of the secretaries and called security.

2

By the time Detective Scott Nelson pushed through the circular doors at the front of the building less than an hour later, the crime scene had already been secured and the police techs were well into the process of gathering evidence. Nelson was a short, stocky man in his early forties, about five foot seven and weighing almost two hundred pounds, depending on lunch. He kicked the snow off of his black leather boots on the mat inside the door and unzipped his parka. Sipping on a Diet Coke from the McDonald's drive-thru, he ambled over to the security desk, where he found a nervous, too-young looking security guard apparently awaiting his arrival.

Running his hand through his thinning and often out-of-control crop of sandy brown hair, Nelson leaned over the security kiosk and spoke to the young security guard in a soft voice. "Excuse me. I'm Detective Nelson. Would you please locate your chief of security for me?" Getting no response other than a blank expression, Nelson continued. "Whosoever in charge will do. As soon as you can, if you don't mind. Thanks."

"Sure," the guard muttered, grabbing his radio and placing a call to his boss.

A moment later, a tall, lean man dressed in a denim shirt and jeans rounded the corner carrying a walkie-talkie. The tall man extended his hand to the detective. "I'm Roger Tierney, can I help you?"

"Sure can," the detective answered. "Are you in charge here?"

"Well, yes, at least for today anyway. I'm Deputy Chief of Security. My boss, Steve Sanborn, is the Director of Security. But he's out of town on vacation until Monday. You know, we're between terms here. We usually don't expect this kind of commotion."

"No, I wouldn't think so," Nelson said. Tierney looked over Nelson's shoulder and could see across the way that a small crowd was gathering on the sidewalk and looking through the glass windows at the front of the building. Following the taller man's gaze, Nelson turned and glanced back at the front of the building before returning to Tierney and saying, "Why don't you take me upstairs and show me where it happened, Mr. Tierney."

"Of course, right this way."

Tierney led Nelson around the corner to a bank of elevators. "Detective Cole arrived a few minutes ago and is already upstairs," Tierney said as the elevator arrived. The two men walked inside and Tierney pressed the button for the 6th floor. Tierney turned to face the detective expecting more questions, but Nelson said nothing. He merely looked straight ahead and up at the numbers over the door as the lights changed. A bell sounded. The elevator slowed to a halt and the doors opened.

As he stepped across the threshold, Nelson turned to Tierney and said, "Thanks Mr. Tierney. I'll let you know if I need anything else."

He had been dismissed. Disappointed and slightly put-off, Tierney stepped back into the elevator, watched the doors close in front of him and rode it back downstairs. Nelson stepped through a pair of glass doors into a small reception area. A uniformed officer greeted him. The officer gestured down the hallway to Nelson's left. "The victim is located down the hall and around the corner to the right, sir."

Nelson looked in the other direction, down the hallway to the right. He turned back to the officer. "Can I get there if I go around this way?"

"I believe so."

"Thanks, I think I'll take the scenic route." Nelson appeared like a man out on a Sunday stroll, sipping his Diet Coke as he traveled down the hallway. The floor appeared to consist of offices on the outer perimeter of the building, but it was unclear what was on the inside. All he could see so far was wall. When he reached the end of the hallway, he turned left. He saw a somewhat shorter hallway in front of him with offices again to his right along the outside of the building. About a third of the way down on the left-hand side, he saw a glass door. Next to the door was a long string of windows. When Nelson reached the windows, he stopped and looked inside and the floor plan became suddenly clear. He could see an endless string of tall bookshelves running down the middle of the room, which appeared to cover the entire middle portion of the 6th floor. There were long tables on either side of the shelves and workstations scattered throughout the room. This was the library, or at least part of it.

Nelson paused for a moment and scanned the room in front of him. No one inside studying at the moment. As he moved a few steps further down the hallway, he could see the entire expanse of the library, all the way to similar windows at the opposite end. He could see police officers and evidence technicians working on the other side. When he reached the end of the hall, he turned left again. To his right was a large, metal door marked, "Stairs." Down at the end of the long hallway in front of him, he could see more evidence technicians and a uniformed officer. Next to the uniformed officer, he recognized a tall, powerfully built black man - John Cole. He was also a detective.

Cole turned when he heard Nelson approach and called out, "Hey Scott, how's it going?"

Nelson nodded. "What have we got here, John?" Nelson said with a sigh.

"Deceased white male," Cole began, "early to mid-fifties."

"ID?"

"Daniel Greenfield - one of the professors here at the law school."

"Who id'd him?"

"One of his colleagues, another professor, stopped by the office to drop something off and, well, he walked in on a pretty bad scene."

"Cause of death?"

"Blunt force trauma to the head."

"Blunt force trauma to the head?" a voice cackled from inside the office. "He got his brains beat in with a baseball bat. That you Scott?"

"Yeah, sure is, Ham. Happy New Year."

"Not for this guy," the voice replied. A moment later, the Deputy Assistant Medical Examiner, Dr. Hammed Akhter, emerged and faced the two detectives. He was a thin, studious-looking man, who had come to America from his native India in 1970 to attend medical school. He began to extend a gloved hand, stained with the victim's blood, but then drew it back. "I'd offer to shake hands, but I don't think you'd want to."

"Probably not," Nelson agreed. "You say beaten with a baseball bat?" he continued. "That's some way to start the new year."

"This guy never made it to the new year," Akhter replied. "By the state of the body, I would say he's been there a few days already. Depending upon whether they had the heat on over the holiday or not, I would place the time of death at probably Saturday, maybe even Friday. Friday would be what, the 28th? Say the 28th or the 29th. I'll know more after I look into it a little."

"So, he's been just laying there in his office dead for four or five days, that's what you're telling me?" Nelson asked.

"Sure looks that way. See, it's not really that surprising. What with the holiday, this being a school, no students around, he might have been the only one here when he got it."

Nelson nodded. "Not quite the only one. When can we come in and look around a bit?"

"Well," Akhter said stroking his chin with the top of his wrist, "I'd give these guys a while yet, but you can probably peek your head in the door and get the general gist of things."

Nelson and Cole followed Akhter to the office, staying in the doorway as the medical examiner went inside. Nelson took one look at the far wall and let out a long, low whistle. "I guess someone was pretty serious about this, weren't they?" he said after a long pause. "He's back there behind the desk?"

"Yeah," Akhter said pointing.

Nelson stuck his head as far into the left side of the doorway as he could, craning to try and see the body behind the desk. He could see the victim's left arm and part of what was left of his head. Nelson stood straight up and looked at the wall again for a moment. Then he briefly scanned the rest of the room and stepped back out into the corridor. Cole followed him. Nelson looked down at his feet. Water from the melting snow on his boots stained the carpet. He took another step away from the office and looked up to catch Cole's eye. "Well, this looks like it's going to be a while," Nelson said. "Anyone been notified yet? Wife? Family? Anything like that?"

"No, not yet. The guy who found him, Professor Gordon Hyatt, said he was divorced a couple of years or so ago, and that his wife lived up in Evanston."

"You mean ex-wife."

"Yeah, that's right. Anyway, she lives up in Evanston. Somebody was trying to find an address or a phone number for her up in Evanston. The Dean was working on it. I think his office is down on the 2nd floor if you want to take a stroll."

"Yeah, sure," Nelson replied, taking one last look inside the office before following Cole down the hallway. "We've got to keep a lid on this thing," Nelson said to Cole as they reached the elevators. "This guy's got a wife, or an ex-wife, and probably has some kids too. For all we know, he's got a girlfriend or something. We don't want these people flipping on the TV this afternoon and finding out that the old professor here got his brains beat out and nobody told them about it."

"It looks like it's going to be a heater," Cole said just as Nelson was thinking the same thing. Partners were like that. They could read each other's minds.

"A heater," Nelson repeated in a pained voice. Inside the department, a "heater" was a case that drew a lot of heat, either from the press, the public or the brass at headquarters, sometimes even City Hall. No one wanted to catch a heater. "I can feel the tan already."

8

Cole slapped Nelson on the back. "Thank God you're in charge," he said with a humorless laugh. "Do you want to send somebody to the wife's house?" Cole asked after a long moment when the weight of the immediate future began to settle in on both of them.

Nelson made a face, like he just smelled something bad and it wasn't the dead guy in the office. "Nah, I'll do it myself. We're not going to be able to get in there and look around for awhile yet anyway. Evanston's not that far. If I leave pretty soon, I should be able to get back later this afternoon to take a look around. Besides, I'd kind of like to see what her reaction is when she finds out. You never know, she might be involved."

It only took a few minutes for Detectives Nelson and Cole to find out what they needed to know in order to inform Greenfield's next of kin of his untimely death. The Professor and his wife, Sylvia, divorced three years ago, although Professor Greenfield really didn't want the divorce and tried to do everything he could to prevent his wife from going through with it. They had two daughters, both in their late teens - one a junior in high school and the other a freshman at Northwestern University. Sylvia Greenfield got custody of the girls, the house, the dog and most everything else from what Nelson and Cole could tell from their few minutes with the Dean and Samuel Dorlund, another professor at the law school who burst into the Dean's office five minutes after the detectives got there.

It was a quarter past one when Nelson merged onto northbound Lake Shore Drive and headed toward Evanston. Nelson would inform Sylvia Greenfield of her ex-husband's demise, with Cole handling things back at the crime scene. Nelson wanted to get back before traffic got too heavy, so he quickly punched the blue Taurus up to fifty-five and turned on talk radio.

3

Following directions given to him by Professor Dorlund, Nelson found Sylvia Greenfield's home on a nice, quiet tree-lined street about five or six blocks from the Northwestern University campus. It was a red brick Georgian built sometime in the first half of the 20th Century, with a large detached garage and a big yard. The house appeared to be well-maintained, and Nelson imagined from first glance that Daniel Greenfield would have had a hard time leaving it. From what Professor Dorlund told him earlier, Greenfield moved from this house to a small apartment near Wrigley Field, primarily chosen for its obvious convenience in attending Cub games during summer afternoons.

Nelson parked the Taurus across the street and made his way up the front walk. Despite at least a foot of snow on the ground, the walkway was clear and dry. Nelson rang the bell and turned to survey the surrounding neighborhood. Nice older homes, mature trees and big yards complete with Christmas decorations. Getting no response, he turned and rang the bell a second time. Still nothing. Eyeing the heavy brass knocker in the shape of a lion's head on the large wooden inside door, Nelson pulled open the screen door and banged it sharply four times. Positioned on either side of the front door were sidelights, long rectangular windows covered in sheer curtains. Nelson peered through the one on the right and could vaguely see all the way through to the back of the house. There was no sign of life or activity anywhere. Although Dorlund said that Sylvia Greenfield didn't work, it was possible that she was out running some errand. Nelson turned to take the walk over to the driveway where he would wander toward the back of the house and check if there were any cars parked in the garage.

Just as he reached the driveway, a tan Volvo station wagon pulled in, passed in front of him and drove slowly down and parked in front of the garage. Nelson followed down behind it. When he was about halfway down the drive, a woman emerged from the car and threw a gym bag over her shoulder as she slammed the door. Seeing Nelson coming in her direction, she called out in a non-threatening yet insistent voice, "Can I help you with something, sir?"

Not wanting to scare her or give her the wrong idea, Nelson stopped and reached into his pocket for his credentials. Holding them out he said, "Yes, Ma'am. My name is detective Scott Nelson with the Chicago Police Department. I need a few minutes of your time if you don't mind." He paused and then added, "You are Sylvia Greenfield?"

Eyeing him suspiciously, she approached him until she could see his badge and identification. She looked slowly from the picture on his ID to his face and back again, confirming that he really was who he said he was. Finally she looked him in the eye and said, "Yes, I am. Chicago Police Department? What's this about?"

"Ma'am, I think it would be better if we talked about this inside," Nelson said putting his credentials back in his pocket.

Not appearing to like this idea, but sensing that she had no real alternative, Sylvia Greenfield turned and said, "Of course, follow me." Nelson followed her across a flagstone patio and up three steps to the back door. They entered into the kitchen. To the left was the working area of the kitchen - black granite countertops flecked with gray, immaculate white cabinets, stainless steel appliances and a large island in the center of the room. To the right was a generous eating area, which housed a rectangular kitchen table in dark wood surrounded by four Windsor-backed chairs. Across from the table stood a built-in desk and small, cushioned chair. Everything seemed to be neatly stored away in its respective cubbyhole. A white cordless telephone hung on the wall. A brown leather address book, a clean white pad of paper and ballpoint pen lay neatly on top of the desk. The room smelled of fresh coffee and waxed hardwood floors. It could have come right out of *Good Housekeeping* magazine.

The woman took off a brown leather car coat and hung it in a closet opposite a set of stairs that went down to the basement. Nelson watched her closely. She was a fairly tall woman, about five-foot-seven, slim and very attractive, even without smiling. She had medium-length blondish hair, somewhat reminiscent of the Jackie Kennedy style of the mid-1960's. She wore a dark brown turtleneck, tan-colored tweed pants and brown suede slip-on shoes. She closed the closet door and turned back to him. "Now, what can I do for you, Detective?"

All business, Nelson thought. Yet he couldn't take his eyes off of her. She was indeed a very attractive woman, probably in her late-forties or early-fifties, and she carried herself with a sense of authority. He took a deep breath and exhaled, never losing eye contact with her. "It might be better if we sat down, Ma'am."

Suddenly, concern crossed her features. "What? What do you mean? Why are you here? Did something happen to my girls?"

"No, no Ma'am. It's not about your daughters. As far as I know, they're both fine. Please Ma'am. Please come over and sit down," he said gesturing to the kitchen table. He unzipped his coat, slowly pulled out a chair at the kitchen table and sat down. After a moment, she reluctantly joined him, moving slowly across the kitchen and pulling out the chair next to his before sitting down, her hands in her lap.

"It's about your husband," Nelson began.

"What about my husband, Detective? What's happened?"

She looked directly at him. After a moment, he continued in a soft, calm voice. "I'm sorry to inform you, Ma'am, but your husband, I mean ex-husband, Daniel Greenfield, was found dead earlier this morning." She took a deep breath, looked down at her hands, but said nothing. "He was found in his office at the law school by another professor. I'm sorry to have to come here like this and give you this kind of news, Mrs. Greenfield, but I didn't want you hearing in some other way. I didn't want your daughters finding out in some other way that their father was dead. I wanted

12

to make sure that you had the opportunity to give them that news yourself at the time and in the way that you thought was most appropriate."

Sylvia Greenfield nodded slowly, but did not look up. They sat in silence for a moment before Sylvia Greenfield finally asked, "When did it happen, Detective?"

"We're not quite sure, Ma'am," he said quietly, shading the truth. "We're still looking into those things right now. It's really too early to tell. There will have to be an autopsy and so forth before we really know the exact circumstances." They sat in silence for another moment or two before she finally looked up. There were no tears in her eyes. "Did your husband have any other family of any kind that needs to be notified?" Nelson asked.

"Just an older brother who lives in Florida now," she replied. "Daniel's parents died some time ago, and it was just he and his brother left. Of course, he has a few cousins here and there, but I can notify them. I'll also get in touch with his brother."

"Can I assume that you will be the one handling the arrangements?"

She looked almost surprised. "Yes. I suppose I would have to be," she said finally.

"Let me give you my card," he said taking one from his pocket and handing it to her. "It may be a few days before your husband's body is released for burial. I'm not quite sure how long it will be. But in the meantime, of course, you can call me directly on the number listed on my card. I will probably be the one in the best position to provide you with any information you might need."

She looked puzzled. "Why would it take so long, Detective?"

"Because in addition to the autopsy I spoke about, there will also be an investigation into your husband's death. You see, Ma'am, your husband did not die of natural causes. Daniel Greenfield was murdered."

13

4

Benjamin Lohmeier pulled into the parking lot at Tuscany and dropped his car with the valet. Tuscany was a popular spot located in an Italian neighborhood on Chicago's west side. The dining room wasn't large and was invariably quite crowded, particularly on Friday and Saturday nights. But this was a Wednesday, so reservations were fairly easily had. Ben pushed through the door and found his friends sharing a glass of wine in the bar.

"Hey, here he is," Bowden Flynn called out just as Ben walked up.

"Took a wrong turn," Ben said smiling.

"Wrong turn my ass," Bowden answered. "You're just on Lohmeier time."

A few moments later, a hostess led the group to a small round table for four in the back of the room. Shortly thereafter, a waiter who didn't look old enough to serve alcohol approached the table and asked Ben if he wanted anything from the bar. "How about a nice Chianti?" he answered.

"Red wine," Fran Fischer joked, "how unusual."

"Oh," Ben answered, "I guess I'm just trying to broaden my horizons. I'm handling some criminal matters for a couple of Italian guys who love to drink red wine, so ..."

"Criminal matters? I thought your office didn't do much criminal work?" Fran asked.

"We don't," Ben replied, "or at least we didn't. We're starting to get more in though; mostly existing clients or referrals from

14

existing clients, that sort of thing. I've had a couple of reckless homicides, an aggravated assault and even an attempted murder in the last few months. I'm trying to grow the criminal practice, but without all the drug cases. I hate drug cases, but there's a bunch of them out there. It's a welcome break from a lot of the civil stuff."

The four of them, Benjamin Lohmeier, Bowden Flynn, Fran Fischer and Megan Rand, became close friends during law school when they were assigned to the same first-year section, although Fran and Megan met a couple of years earlier as older undergraduate students. Ben and Megan sat next to each other in Professor Daniel Greenfield's Criminal Law class, where Ben served as a buffer while Megan, like many of the women in the class, lived in fear of being called on by Professor Greenfield to give some sexually explicit detail in one of the myriad of cases involving rape, murder and other various perversions. The more perverted the case, the more it seemed that Greenfield called on a woman to either describe the facts or dissect the various legal issues involved.

As their first year moved along, the four grew close and spent a great deal of time together. They studied together, ate lunch together and simply bullshitted together. Like many law students, they formed a study group, usually just the four of them. They were a little older when they started law school. Ben and Megan were almost thirty; Fran and Bowden almost forty, and they carried themselves with the seriousness that greater life experience tended to provide.

Fran had spent a couple of years early in her marriage living with her family in Israel, while Bowden had joined the Peace Corps and lived in a variety of exotic locales, including Tehran. While many of their colleagues displayed the cocksure, smartass attitude of young college graduates who knew they were on their way to big-money success as famous litigators, these four knew differently, and this knowledge coupled with their relative age and experience, drew them together and made them friends. While their paths after law school took them in four decidedly different directions, they tried hard to keep the group together, gathering for dinners such as this one every month or two, coupled with the occasional phone

15

call in between. As is often the case, one of them, in this case Fran, organized these little events and fought to make sure that everyone attended.

Following law school, Ben took a job with the Cook County State's Attorney's Office where he spent four and a half years moving up the prosecutorial ladder. Before he left to pursue greener pastures and more money in the private sector, Ben served as first chair in countless drug cases, aggravated assaults, rapes and murders. He knew he couldn't handle those kinds of cases forever, and he also recognized that he likely lacked the political skills required to climb the supervisory ranks. Nevertheless, the Cook County State's Attorney's Office had provided him with valuable experience and made him feel at home in a courtroom.

Fran Fischer experienced similar frustrations while following an entirely different career path. Having graduated near the top of her class, Fran grew frustrated by her inability to land a job with one of Chicago's top law firms during the tight job market in the early 1990's and ultimately settled for a job with a small law firm in the northwest suburbs specializing in school law. She left after two years to join her father's labor law practice downtown where her pressures were purely self-imposed.

Megan Rand never really understood why she went to law school in the first place. She didn't have a burning desire to practice law or prove herself in any real way. Her husband was a successful personal injury lawyer downtown, and they didn't need the money. She only entered law school because she needed something to do with herself, it seemed interesting and Fran was going too. On the eve of her graduation, she found herself unexpectedly pregnant and unable to take the bar exam with the rest of her class. She finally took it the following winter, passed it, and took a job her husband arranged for her as a law clerk with Justice Michael Sullivan of the Illinois Appellate Court. But for a brief stint as a hearing officer handling domestic relations and custody cases in Cook County, she had been there ever since.

Of the four, only Bowden Flynn knew exactly what he wanted when he entered law school and never for a moment wavered from his planned career path. Every course he took, every job he

16

accepted and every book he read in his spare time was designed to prepare him to become a public interest lawyer. During the years following graduation, Bowden Flynn was largely responsible for the closing of incinerators that polluted neighborhoods, for the funding of programs to help the underprivileged and for numerous downtrodden finally getting their day in Court. Homeless families found food and a place to sleep because of him, and the forgotten masses of the urban poor found a tireless voice to tell their stories of silent suffering. In short, he made the system work just a little better for those for whom it had never worked before.

Dinner began with the four devouring two plates of fried calamari and a basket of warm bread. By the time they finished their salads, a second bottle of Chianti arrived. Ben ordered chicken and Bowden chose fish, while the women veered toward pasta - linguini with clam sauce for Fran and cheese ravioli with marinara for Meg. As they waited for the main course, they turned their attention to the obligatory discussion of what had been going on in their lives since they last met for dinner a couple of months before. Nothing really spectacular was going on with any of them, save for the occasional new case worth noting or a funny story or two about one of their kids. They talked about classmates they had run into and vacations they were planning.

Finally, half way through the main course, Ben got down to business. "So," he said putting his fork down and looking directly into Meg's eyes. "What's up with the asshole?"

The question, made almost matter-of-factly in a tone that suggested not answering was not an option, came with the glare. Meg finished a bite of ravioli, took a sip of wine and looked first at Fran, then at Bowden, both of whom looked back in her direction. She did not want to meet the glare. While Benjamin Lohmeier was not a physically imposing man, he stood only five-feet-eight- inches tall and weighed barely one hundred forty-five pounds, he possessed a magnetic, dynamic and sometimes hypnotic personality. He learned at an early age the effect he had on those around him, and used it to his advantage.

Although capable of great warmth, he could also burn ferociously with frightening intensity and then suddenly cause chills with his sudden coldness. He could be friendly and inviting and intimidating all at the same time. Once you were out, you never got back in again. Meg slowly raised her head to meet the glare, as his friends called it. "He's fine," she said hesitantly.

"Hmmm, he's fine," Ben replied slowly. "I'm glad to hear it."

Both Fran and Bowden glanced back at Ben seeking to determine whether a follow-up was in the offing. It was. As Meg looked away, Ben met their gaze and raised his eyebrows with a slight smile.

"When you say fine," Ben continued, "do you mean the divorce is moving along?"

"It's moving along."

"How's his health?" Ben asked with a wicked smile.

Meg shot him a dirty look. Her husband, a prominent personal injury attorney in town, was much older than she, almost seventy. They met when Meg was in her early-twenties and working as a clerk in his small Chicago law office. Soon the relationship was more than professional, and Meg eventually moved into his brownstone on the near north side. Eventually, they got married and even had an unexpected child, a son born shortly after Meg graduated law school. As time passed, they slowly grew apart, their age difference serving as an anchor helping force the marriage under. Things hadn't really been right with them since law school. He really wanted a trophy, not a partner, and Meg's willingness to seek a place of her own in the legal world challenged and threatened him.

Truth be told, the divorce wasn't really going anywhere. Meg more or less dropped it under his pressure. Ben learned this from Fran long ago. Nevertheless, Meg and Joe lived separately, Meg in a high-rise condominium near downtown and her husband in his Gold Coast brownstone. They shared custody of their son.

Ben leaned back in his chair and glanced over at Fran who shook her head no. He decided to back off. His heart really wasn't in it tonight anyway. "So," he continued after a lengthy pause, "how's Anthony handling all of this?" Anthony Joseph Cavallaro, or A.J. as his parents often called him, was Meg's nine-and-a-half-year old son.

"He's good, he really is," Meg answered looking relieved for even the slightest change of subject. "He seems very comfortable with the way things are right now. I mean, he sees both of us all the time, just like before."

Fran steered the conversation away from Meg's marriage and toward children and families and parents and work. Ben let the conversation drift in that direction and poured another glass of wine. This was already his fourth or fifth glass, and he had a pretty good buzz on. He had handled enough DUI's as a prosecutor to know that he had better shut it down pretty soon or driving home could be an adventure he did not want. Unlike some lawyers, he did not want to use himself as a test case to argue the merits or lack of same in Illinois' drunk driving laws.

For the next half hour or so, they talked about their families, the holidays and even a little current events and whatever tension hung over the table melted away. Meg seemed pretty quiet during this time, apparently content to listen to her three friends tell stories of their lives. Finally, during a lull in the conversation, she turned back to Ben and said, "You said before that you are doing more criminal work now. How's that going?"

"Oh, I don't know," Ben said shaking his head. "Pretty well, I guess. We seem to be doing a little bit more of it and even bigger cases too. It's always different being a defense attorney rather than a prosecutor, but really, being in a criminal courtroom is a lot like it always was. If you've never done it, it's kind of hard to explain. There's a different feeling in the air, a different tension and, obviously, a different clientele than you usually see in a civil courtroom. I kind of like it actually."

A little while later, everyone was ready to hit the road and go home. They grabbed their coats from the coat check room and gathered outside the front door on the sidewalk. Ben pulled his overcoat closed at the neck and looked up at the sky. It had cleared, but the temperature was dropping steadily. They stood there shivering. Ben looked at his watch - ten forty-five. "Shit," he said to himself. He hadn't planned on being out nearly this late. "I've got to get going."

19

"Well, Fran," Meg said, "we should get going too. It is kind of late."

Bowden and Ben waited for the women to reach their car and then turned toward the parking lot. They reached Bowden's car first. "Say," Bowden said, "Meg sure wasn't in any kind of a mood to talk about the asshole, was she?"

"No, she sure wasn't," Ben agreed. "But then, she never really is, now is she?"

"No, she's not, but it seems to me she was even stranger than usual about it tonight. Or maybe it's just that she seemed quieter in general," Bowden said.

"Yeah, maybe," Ben said. "Fortunately, with Fran at the table, you don't need much help keeping the conversation going."

Bowden laughed. "Well, gotta go. See you next time," he said.

"Yeah, you too," Ben said.

Ten minutes later, Ben accelerated down the ramp onto the Eisenhower Expressway heading west, waiting for the heat to kick in. He turned on his book on tape, but clicked it off again after about two minutes. He just wasn't in the mood. He tried sports radio, nothing good there, and cruised the radio stations looking for a good song. Nothing doing there either. So he spent the rest of the ride home in silence thinking about the evening and wondering what was really going on with his three friends. It was always good to see everybody, he thought as traffic slowed around Austin as it always did. Pretty soon it picked up again and at the split, he veered toward the entrance ramp to southbound 294 going eighty. Before he knew it, he pulled into his driveway on Walker Avenue in Clarendon Hills just as he realized the car was finally warm.

He pulled the car into the garage, walked across the driveway, up the steps to the deck and unlocked the door to the kitchen. He found his wife, Libby, asleep under a blanket on the couch in front of the TV.

"Hey Lib," he whispered, kissing her on the head, "wake up, I'm home."

Startled, she jumped slightly and opened her eyes with a confused look on her face. A few seconds later, she regained her senses and slowly sat up rubbing her eyes. "I must have fallen asleep," she mumbled. She looked up at him. "Did you have a little garlic with dinner?"

"Just a little," he answered.

"A little or not, you stink," she replied with a mock frown. "Make sure you take a shower before you crawl into my bed tonight."

"Oh, it's your bed tonight, is it?" he said leaning over the couch and putting his arms around her while nibbling on one ear.

"It's my bed every night," she said. "You're just a guest. And sometimes an unwelcome one when you smell like that," she said wriggling herself free from his grasp.

"Just as long as I'm the only guest."

"How was everybody?" she asked.

"Pretty good, I guess. Meg seemed a little weird though."

"Well," Libby said clicking off the TV and standing up to stretch her back, "you're the lawyer. I'm sure you'll get to the bottom of it. While you do that, I'm going to bed. You coming?"

"Yeah, I'll be up in a few minutes."

She walked around him and back through the kitchen toward the front stairs as he admired her from behind. Looking over her shoulder with a smile she said, "Don't forget about that shower. And brush your teeth while you're at it."

He laughed. "I wasn't counting on getting anything anyway."

She kept walking. Without looking back she added, "Maybe not, but you know you'll have no chance unless you do what you're told."

5

Ben pulled into the parking lot of the office after completing the long drive back from the Lake County Courthouse up near the Wisconsin border. Once inside, he stopped in the kitchen to see who was around. There he found Brian Davenport, one of the other associates in the office, glancing at the *Chicago Sun-Times*. "Hey, what's up?" Ben said as he walked in and grabbed the sports section of the *Chicago Tribune*.

Brian looked up. "Court today?"

"Yeah, Waukegan."

"Ha," Brian laughed, "lucky you."

Ben liked Brian. On his surface, he seemed to be a smart guy, quiet and unassuming. He had the reputation in the office as a guy who always flew under the radar. He never seemed to get noticed much except in a positive way and rarely did anything that appeared to make him stand out. Everyone respected him as a good lawyer, but not everybody realized that he possessed a wicked sense of humor. He could be cutting and humorously opinionated when he wanted to be. With short, brown hair, an Irish complexion and a stoic public persona, he sort of reminded Ben of an airline pilot.

"Say," Brian said pointing to an article in the paper, "did you hear about Greenfield?"

"Greenfield? Do you mean Professor Greenfield at school?"

"Yeah, the one and only."

Both Ben and Brian attended the Chicago College of Law, Ben graduating in 1992 and Brian not until 1996. "No, what about him? What did he do?"

22

"He died, that's what he did."

Ben looked up from the paper. "Died? What do you mean died?"

"Died. You know, died as in dead. Look here at the article. See for yourself." There was a small article in a box on page 10 of the *Sun-Times*. The small headline read, "Law Professor Found Dead." Ben leaned over Brian's shoulder and read the article aloud.

> Police sources confirmed late Wednesday night that the body of a local law professor, Daniel Greenfield, age 54, was found in his office at the law school on Wednesday morning by one of his colleagues. Neither the cause nor the date of his death were immediately available. Greenfield had been a professor at the Chicago College of Law since 1978. He specialized in criminal law and criminal procedure. A spokesman for the Cook County Medical Examiner's Office indicated that further information would be available upon completion of the autopsy.

Ben looked up at Brian. "Holy shit. That's awfully weird, don't you think?"

"Yes I do," Brian replied. "I wonder how he died. You think maybe he had a female student up on the desk and had a grabber?"

"Who knows?" Ben said with a shrug, "but jeez, he wasn't that old, 54. That's kind of young to have a grabber, don't you think? I mean, it's not like he was a big, fat slob or anything."

Brian nodded. "You had him for a teacher, didn't you?"

"Yeah," Ben answered. "Both Criminal Law and Criminal Procedure. I had him for both. Except for my grades, I thought he was pretty good. His classes were fairly interesting, and he wasn't, you know, a big asshole or anything."

"No, I kind of liked him too, actually."

Ben put the paper down. "You know, it's kind of funny really. Here we are making comments about him and female students.

And, of course, that was his reputation while I was in school and, I guess, while you were in school, but to tell you the truth, I don't think I ever knew of anybody that he actually had sex with, or hit on, or anything."

"Maybe not," Brian replied, "but there was a story going around that he and Dorlund both had been called on the carpet by the administration over these kinds of allegations. I don't remember the details, but the story was that they got into quite a bit of hot water over stuff like that."

Ben looked surprised. "I hadn't heard that. Both of those guys have been there forever. I'm surprised the school would really do much of anything to them. But then, I don't hear much of what's going on there anymore, so how would I know?"

"Me neither, but the story is the law school came down on them pretty hard. In fact, I think Greenfield even stopped having those lunches with students that you had to have every semester if you wanted to get a decent grade."

"Hmmm," Ben said scratching his head, "I wonder how they got caught. I wonder if they hit on some student who didn't like it or whether they made a successful pass, but the girl didn't get the grade she was hoping for." He paused. "I really wonder how he died." Ben grabbed the *Tribune* sports section again, took a brief look at it, then tossed it back on the table. "What are we doing for lunch today? I'm getting hungry."

Brian shook his head. "Don't know. Never know 'til we get there."

6

Ben didn't have Court on Monday morning, so he dropped the kids off at school and finally pulled into the parking lot of the office at about nine-fifteen. His secretary, Nancy, heard him reach the top of the stairs on the way to his office. "Ben, is that you?" she called from her office across the way.

"Yeah, what's up?"

"I just got a call for you from your friend, Megan. She seemed kind of upset. She said she'd call back."

Ben reached the door to her office as she finished, and she turned and handed him a note with Megan's name and phone number on it. "Any idea what that's about?" she asked with a mock suspicious raise of her eyebrow.

Ben took the note and shrugged. "Not a clue." He turned and headed for his office while repeating, "Not a clue." Ben called her back and found out.

"Megan, my dear, what could possibly be troubling you this fine morning?" he asked when she picked up.

"What's troubling me? What's troubling me is the police. That's who." Ben sat up. "They've been asking me all sorts of questions about Greenfield's death." She spoke frantically. The words seemed to gush out of her like a water balloon with a hole in it. "They came here unannounced. They called me up on the telephone. They have all sorts of questions. They must think I know something."

Ben was confused. "Hold on, hold on, just hold on a second, will you please?" he said trying to slow her down. "Now, I don't know what in the world you're talking about. So why don't you take a deep breath, maybe two deep breaths, and start from the beginning." He could feel her exasperation even over the phone.

She sighed and said, "Okay, okay. I'll try to explain it to you. It started when they called me on the telephone."

"Okay," Ben said, "just relax a second. Start from the beginning like I said, but I need to know when, and how, and where these things took place, so don't leave anything out."

"Okay, okay. It started on Friday. I was at work, you know, then I went to lunch about eleven-thirty. These two detectives stopped by at work while I was out to lunch. Can you believe it? They came looking for me."

"I'm assuming they did that, Megan, because that's where they expected to find you. But wait a second. We don't even know how Greenfield died yet. At least I don't. It wasn't in the paper. Did they tell you anything?"

"Well, no, they didn't, but they came and asked for me in front of all the people I work with. Do you know how that looks?"

"Not yet. Go on," Ben said. His spider sense was tingling. He didn't like where this was heading.

"Well, like I said, I wasn't there, but they called back at about three. They asked me if I knew Professor Greenfield and if I knew that he was dead."

"When you say 'they,' who do you mean? Who asked you about Greenfield?"

"It was a detective with the Chicago Police, a Detective Nelson."

"Scott Nelson?" Ben asked.

"Yes, I think so. Why? Do you know him?"

"Yeah, maybe." Ben rubbed his forehead. This wasn't going to get any better. Nelson was a homicide detective. Greenfield must have been murdered, or at least may have been murdered. The heart attack theory looked unlikely now. "I had a couple of cases with Scott Nelson when I was a prosecutor. So yeah, if it's the same guy, I do know him. He's okay. What else did he say?"

"Well, he acted like he was trying to be nice and reasonable, but I didn't like it at all. He started by asking if I knew Professor Greenfield. Of course, I said that I did. I had him as a professor in law school years ago. Then he asked me if I knew that he was dead and, of course, I knew that too. You know, Fran called me two seconds after she found out. Also, it was on TV and it was in the newspaper, so how could I not know?"

"I'm sure," Ben said, "that he wasn't expecting that you wouldn't know, nor do I think he probably read anything into the fact that you did know. Anyway, go on."

"Well, he asked me a few more questions about how I knew him, about Professor Greenfield in class, things like that. Then he tells me that my name is on some notes in Greenfield's office where they found the body."

"Did he tell you anything about how Greenfield was killed, I mean, died?"

"No, not at that point. Wait, you said killed. Do you think someone killed him?"

"No, not necessarily. It could be a lot of things." Ben didn't really believe that, but could feel her freaking out on the phone. "What else did he say?"

"Well, we talked for a few more minutes and then he asked me if he could stop by at some point to ask me some more questions. What am I supposed to say? He's a police detective. I can't just tell him no."

"No, probably not," Ben agreed.

"So, of course," she continued, "I'm a nervous wreck about this all weekend, then yesterday afternoon, he just shows up here unannounced. Just knocks on my door."

"Here? Where's here? Are you at home?"

"Yes, I'm here at the condo."

"Didn't you work today?"

"Yes, but then I came home. I'm too upset. So, like I was saying, they just showed up here yesterday afternoon about three. Thank God A.J. was gone. He was at his father's. They just knocked right on the door. I suppose since they're the police, the people downstairs just let them in. So much for security."

Ben shook his head. Normally you wouldn't need security from the police, he thought, but said nothing. "Go on," he finally said.

"Well, I opened the door and there they stood, the two of them. That Detective Nelson that you must know and a tall, black man named Cole, another detective. They just stood there right in front of my door. What was I going to do?"

"Let them in?"

"Well, yes, of course I let them in."

"What happened next?"

"Well, they had more questions. You know, more of the same. All these questions about Greenfield, how I knew him, when did I know him, when did I see him last, stuff like that."

Ben was puzzled. "Why would they ask you things like that? I'm assuming you haven't seen him in years. I'm not sure I've seen him since graduation."

"Exactly," she responded, "I told them I couldn't remember when I saw him last."

"He said they found your name in his office. What was that all about?"

"I don't know. They wouldn't really say. I got the impression that I may have been on the reunion list."

"Reunion, what reunion?"

"You know, since this is now 2002 and we graduated in 1992, they're planning reunions for the summer. I got dragged in to be on this Reunion Committee. I've been getting stuff from the administration about class lists and, you know, we're in the beginning stages of planning for this reunion. Apparently, from what I could gather, Greenfield had stuff about the reunion in his office with notations with my name on it."

"That doesn't sound terribly unusual. I'm sure they're just following up on loose ends they may have, just trying to gather information, things like that."

"No, no. It was much more than that. They started asking me about, like where I was on New Year's Eve, where I was the Friday

28

before New Year's. What did I do on New Year's Eve. Where did I go. Who was I with. Things like that."

"Is that when he died? New Year's Eve?"

"I don't know. No, well, I don't know. I don't think so. I got the impression they think he died on like Friday or Saturday, but the body wasn't found until, I don't know, the 2nd or 3rd, or something."

"It must have been the 2nd," Ben said, remembering the newspaper.

"I don't know," she said, her voice shaking. "I'm just so upset about this. I've never been questioned by the police before. This is unbelievable."

"Look, Meg, just relax. I'm sure they weren't trying to upset you or anything like that. They were just trying to gather information. I'm sure it was nothing more than that." Ben tried to get the focus off of Meg. He needed to talk her off the ledge. "So they didn't tell you how he died?"

"No, in fact, I asked, but they didn't answer. They kind of changed the subject."

"Hmmm, that's interesting. It doesn't sound like anything. But the thing you've got to remember, you can't tell them anything that isn't true. They always seem to find out in the end. Now, tell me, do you know of any other reason, any reason at all, why they would be questioning you about this other than what you've told me?"

"No, of course not."

Ben sighed. "Okay, then. Look, you've got to remember, if we find out that Greenfield didn't just drop dead at his desk, if you really and truly believe they think you're involved somehow, you shouldn't talk to them again without an attorney present. If you want, call me, and I'll be there when they talk to you. But remember, you don't want to say anything, even inadvertently, that may unduly cast suspicion on you, okay? I'm not trying to upset you. I just want you to know how these things work." There was a long pause. "Meg? Do you understand?"

"Yes."

"I'm sure it will turn out to be nothing."

"I hope you're right."

"Again, I don't think it means anything, but still, be careful. These guys build cases through people saying the wrong things at the wrong time."

They talked for a few more minutes. Ben could sense that she was calming down a little bit and really needed to get this out of her system more than anything else. Nevertheless, he couldn't believe that she could really be a suspect in a murder, assuming it was a murder. It just didn't make any sense.

"Ben," she finally said, "if it came to that and I needed a lawyer to represent me in this, would you help me? Would you represent me if I needed help?"

Ben flushed. "Of course I would," he said, "but I'll be honest with you, I don't think you're going to need anyone's help. I think you just misunderstood what they were trying to find out. I'm sure it's going to be nothing."

A moment later they hung up and Ben sat in his office for a minute staring silently at the phone. Scott Nelson. That had to mean something. His secretary, Nancy Schulte, poked her head in the door. She must have heard him hang up the phone. "So, what was that all about?" she asked. Nancy had been with the firm for more than twenty years, and had more or less been Ben's secretary since he arrived several years before. Something of a refugee from the Sixties, who only became a legal secretary when she didn't know what else to do, Nancy was fast, efficient and almost never made mistakes. Ben considered her the best legal secretary he'd ever known and he liked working with her.

She also served as the unofficial gatekeeper for the firm. She often had the task of breaking in the new people to ascertain whether or not they were truly competent to practice law with the firm. Once they had passed this threshold and thereby earned her respect, a woman who at first glance appeared very difficult, suddenly became very easy to work with. Ben crossed over that bridge fairly early in their relationship so that any hazing period he had experienced with her was relatively short.

The only problem with Nancy from Ben's perspective was that Nancy also worked for Phil Luckenbill, the firm's managing partner. That occasionally put her in an awkward position and necessarily tended to divide her loyalties. Ben appreciated this fact and found a way to work around it without ever forgetting it. She sat down opposite Ben on the bench that served as the guest chairs in Ben's office. "So, tell me, what happened?"

Ben sat back in the chair and took a deep breath. "Well, it appears that our Megan is being questioned regarding the death of one of our former law professors."

"You mean that guy in the paper?"

"That's the one."

"What did she say?"

"Well, not too much. I really don't think it's anything. They just wanted to get some facts. We don't even know how he died. They found her name on something in his office. Probably nothing."

"So that's what you told her?"

"Yeah. I told her I didn't think it was going to amount to anything."

She noted that he wasn't making eye contact, unusual for him. "But you don't really believe that, do you?" she said suspiciously. He didn't answer. Scott Nelson. Homicide detective. He merely looked at her, a gaze which spoke volumes. "Holy shit," Nancy said. "Does she want to hire you?"

Ben nodded. "If she needs to, I suppose."

"And you think she's going to need to, don't you?"

Ben paused. "Is Phil going to come in today?" he asked avoiding the question.

"I doubt it," she answered. "He's got redistricting meetings all day downtown. You can probably catch him on the cell phone if you want to badly enough though."

Ben nodded getting to his feet. "I'll go over to the other side to talk to Casey. I'll be back."

"A murder case," she said to herself as Ben walked by.

As he reached the door, he turned, "Nance?" She turned to face him. Ben simply put his forefinger across his lips in the universal symbol for silence. She nodded.

Ben was the last one left in the building that night. He looked at his watch and yawned. It had been a long day and he was tired.

31

He got up and walked downstairs and grabbed a beer out of the fridge in the kitchen. It had been one of those days where he had been busy from the time he got into the office, yet what he had accomplished didn't seem to amount to much. Some days it seemed as though he could work for twelve hours straight and only bill for six. Other days, far less frequent, he could work for six hours and bill for twelve. Ben liked those days better.

He had Court in the morning in Wheaton and needed to get his stuff together before he could go on home. As he took a long swallow of his beer, he couldn't get Megan Rand out of his mind. He couldn't possibly fathom what evidence the police could have that caused them to link Megan Rand with the death of Daniel Greenfield, however that may have occurred.

He thought back to the day he first met Meg and Fran. It was late August of 1989 when the Class of 1992 at the Chicago College of Law began law school. Their first class was Property with Professor Gordon Hyatt. Their second class was Criminal Law with Daniel Greenfield. When Ben got to the classroom on the 4th floor of the old building on Wacker Drive, many of the seats were already taken. Greenfield hadn't arrived yet and the students were milling about and engaging in quiet conversation. Ben saw a seat on the aisle at the end of the second row and sat down. A few minutes later, Megan Rand and Fran Fischer came in together. Ben did not know either of them. Meg took the lone empty seat next to Ben, while Fran took a seat in front of them in the first row. It was apparent that the two women knew each other. After a moment of small talk, Fran introduced herself. "Hi. I'm Fran Fischer. This is my friend, Megan Rand. We went to undergrad together."

"Nice to meet you," Ben said quietly with a nod.

A few minutes later, Professor Greenfield arrived and they began their study of criminal law. It didn't take long before they realized that all of the rumors were true - the more prurient and sensational the subject matter of a criminal case, the more likely that Professor Greenfield was to be interested in it and discuss it in class. Thus, his class focused on assaults, rapes and murders, the more brutal and graphic, the better. They also noticed Professor Greenfield's habit of beginning his lectures by starting with a student seated at the end of a row and working down that row, class after class, before moving on to another row. Although Greenfield was fairly Socratic in nature, he wasn't particularly difficult to students, unlike some of the other professors in the law school. He usually allowed students to embarrass themselves before moving on to the next person. He apparently didn't feel the need to pile on.

Many of the women in Greenfield's class were embarrassed both by the subject matter and his need to hear them recite the specific facts of the crimes described in that day's cases. It was about three weeks into the semester and Ben and Meg's row had yet to be called on in class. They had been talking about it for days and knew that it was coming sooner or later. One bright Wednesday morning, their time came. They were talking about one particular case before class, and Meg was hoping that this would not be the day. It was a case before the United States Supreme Court, a Justice Brennan opinion involving sexual assault. Professor Greenfield introduced the case and turned to face them. "Mr. Lohmeier," he said, "can you give us the facts of this case, please?"

Megan groaned as Ben began describing the facts in some detail and squirmed uncomfortably to his right while he continued. After a few moments of this, Greenfield turned to Meg and asked a follow-up question.

Without hesitating and before she could speak, Ben cut in and began to answer. Greenfield stopped him. "I'm sorry Mr. Lohmeier, I meant that question for Ms. Rand, but since you've already started, why don't you go ahead and finish." Megan sighed in relief. Ben finished his answer and continued to answer all of the questions Greenfield posed until they were done with the case. Greenfield did not turn his attention back to Meg until the next case, one largely devoid of lurid details.

From that date on, the friendship between Benjamin Lohmeier and Megan Rand was set in stone. Ben's performance that day not only got Megan off the hook, but also had the unforeseen benefit of inoculating them somewhat from these kinds of cases. Because he realized that Ben could handle a case like this without any difficulty and throw whatever he dished out right back at him, Professor Greenfield tended to shy away from them in situations like this. Instead, he preferred to give them cases with more difficult legal issues, not more prurient fact patterns. And Megan Rand couldn't have been more grateful.

7

When Ben dragged himself out of bed on Wednesday morning, he peered through the blinds of his bedroom and saw a smattering of snow flurries falling harmlessly from the sky. By the time he left his house and headed for Court, more than two inches of fresh snow covered the driveway. It was twenty-five minutes past eight and he had to be in Wheaton by nine. "God damn it," he said to himself as he pulled out of the driveway. He knew there was no way he would make it on time.

Ben arrived at the Courthouse twenty minutes late, but managed to take care of his two status calls without serious difficulty. His route back to the office took him down Bloomingdale Road, past the former house of Senior Partner Jim Schulte. He checked his speed as he headed down the hill toward Schulte's house because he knew that the Ithaca police often hid on the side streets off Bloomingdale Road in order to catch unsuspecting drivers who had not slowed sufficiently as they cruised toward downtown. As he passed Schulte's old house, once known as the Pig Farm, he saw a handful of Schulte's old plastic pigs dotted throughout the front yard, partially obscured by the falling snow. He eased his way into downtown, circled around Usher Park and turned left at the Tree Top Pizza Inn and coasted back toward the office.

Irving Park Road is a highly trafficked thoroughfare bisecting downtown Ithaca. The office was set back off the road west of and slightly behind the pizza place and its adjoining tavern. Further up

Irving Park Road to the west stood the Ithaca Train Station, where commuters would take the forty minute trip to downtown Chicago. The train tracks angled behind the office and its parking lot and were so close that they could make telephone conversations difficult when the numerous commuter and freight trains rumbled by. The office also sat smack dab in the landing pattern for O'Hare Airport to the east and jumbo jets flew deafeningly low over the building all day long.

The original part of the office was a white frame Victorian house built in the 1890's. To this structure, some twenty or so years before, Jim Schulte had attached a storefront grocery store originally found around the corner in downtown Ithaca. The grocery store served as the main entrance to the building. On the other side of the grocery store, Schulte built a two-story addition, which housed additional offices for both the firm and for a handful of renters, primarily other lawyers. Facing the railroad tracks, Schulte built a structure that appeared to be a modest-sized garage, complete with an old gas pump on the east side and what appeared to be the entrance to a barbershop on the west. The garage served as the building's library and conference room.

Clients coming to the office for the first time would turn off of Irving Park Road onto First Street and drive back behind the tavern, where they would encounter the new addition on the east side of the building flanked by a row of parking spaces. Continuing back, they would come to the garage and the gas pump jutting out from the main entrance of the building at a right angle toward the railroad tracks. If there were no parking spaces on the east side of the building, clients would circle around the garage, where they would find a back entrance to the building and four more parking spaces. Proceeding around the corner of the white frame house, six or eight more parking spaces ended at a sidewalk that paralleled Irving Park Road. A short walk down this sidewalk across Walnut Avenue brought the commuters to the Ithaca train station.

Finding no parking spaces near the main entrance, Ben pulled around the garage and found an open space next to the back entrance at the corner of the house. Ben grabbed his briefcase and shuffled through the snow, past a telephone box and a small stone fountain, and up the six wooden steps to the back entrance of the building located in a small porch. He kicked the snow off his shoes as he entered a small hallway, which housed the restrooms. At its end, a doorway led down a couple of steps into a hallway and out to the garage. To his right, the bookkeeper's office sat opposite the copy room.

Ben walked through the copy room and stuck his head into a small, oddly-shaped office where he had spent the first couple of years of his time with the firm and Dan Conlon now called home. The office had a large window which looked across the open yard to the pizza place and tavern beyond. Conlon was on the phone and Ben gave him a quick nod before heading left toward the lobby and dropping his briefcase and coat on a long, wooden church pew against the wall on the right. The main entrance to the building under the Matt's Grocery sign stood opposite the church pew. There was no identification for the law firm or any of its tenants anywhere.

The lobby also contained a large wooden reception desk, fax machine, and two rocking chairs flanking a small table. One corner opposite the door held a large wooden credenza complete with book shelves, while the other contained an open icebox dating from the 1940's with artificial food inside adding to the rustic country feel of the room. A rustic chandelier hung from a white, ornate trey ceiling made of faux plaster. Beyond the lobby and a stairway filled with political posters and photographs, a perpendicular hallway formed the new part of the building, a two-story structure with a row of offices on each floor.

Behind the church pew and opposite the main entry was the kitchen. A modest room with a wooden table, sink, microwave and refrigerator to go with a small amount of counter space and a few cabinets, the kitchen was largely a tribute to Jim Schulte's late father, an assistant fire chief in a small town in Wisconsin. The walls were ordained with framed newspaper clippings, photographs celebrating his career and even his fire axe and helmet. A sense of casualness permeated the atmosphere of the office, where lawyers seldom wore suits unless a Court appearance or formal meeting required it.

James Schulte came to Ithaca in the 1970's when most lawyers still practiced in downtown Chicago and DuPage County was wide open and there for the taking. He and a handful of others established a foothold in DuPage County, where they could bridge the gap between the silk stocking practices of downtown Chicago and the more rural collar counties. His firm broke apart in the early 1990's, with several of his more senior people leaving to set up their own firm in Ithaca and taking some of Schulte's business with them, without much of a protest. Phillip Luckenbill, then an associate only four or five years out of law school, decided to stay and was named a partner in the new firm, Schulte & Luckenbill.

Thereafter, Schulte became even less interested in practicing law, ceding much of the management duties of the firm to Luckenbill, and spending increasing amounts of time at a rustic home he was building on a large piece of property outside of Hayward in northern Wisconsin. By mid-1997, he more or less quit the practice of law, giving away all his suits save for one and even renting out his own personal office in the building. Within two years, the Pig Farm on Bloomingdale Road was also on the market and he was spending essentially all of his time in Hayward. He would come back occasionally to handle the odd matter or two, but for the most part, Jim Schulte's large ego and unusual presence were largely confined to the north woods, where, among other things, he raised buffalo.

Law firms, particularly small and mid-sized ones, are often oddly managed enterprises, for some of the best lawyers are also the worst businessmen. It is not uncommon for small and mid-sized law firms to operate both fiscally and otherwise as little more than the alter egos of their founders. This typically results in a chaotic and often despotic management structure. Within the confines of Schulte & Luckenbill, Ben defined the management structure with something he liked to call the Pie Chart of Power.

The Pie Chart was really very simple. It was a traditional pie chart, where the size of an individual's slice of the pie corresponded with his or her degree of power within the hierarchy of the firm. The size of the pieces of pie might vary from time to time and according to the particular issue involved, but generally speaking, Phil Luckenbill possessed approximately sixty percent of the pie, while Jim Schulte's share had dwindled to twenty percent.

The remaining twenty percent was divvied up in what at first glance would be unusual proportions. Nancy Schulte, the secretary to both Phil Luckenbill and Benjamin Lohmeier, held about seven percent of the pie, reflecting her longtime status as the firm's gatekeeper and a major power behind the scenes. Newly-minted Senior Associate Casey Gardner also held seven percent. Dianne Reynolds, Jim Schulte's secretary and the firm's office manager, had seen her share shrink to three percent with her boss's semi-retirement. The remaining support staff members combined for approximately two percent. That left a meager one percent share of the pie for all the remaining attorneys in the firm combined.

Unusual though this may seem on the surface, small firms often see the support staff possessing much more power and control over the operation of the firm than even the vast majority of the lawyers themselves. Several factors explain this reality. First is longevity. Support staff members typically stay with the firm for many years, so long that they accumulate increasing levels of autonomy and control. Conversely, many young lawyers move around a lot in their early years trying to find a niche that best suits their skills, interests and temperament. Moreover, autocratic senior partners view new lawyers as somewhat fungible commodities. They can always move mid-level attorneys out, or make them want to leave, and replace them with newer graduates who make less money and suffer fewer expectations. Finally, and most significantly, it is a matter of control. Senior partners do not want to share power with the underlings. This is, after all, not a democracy. No, this is a dictatorship with one, or maybe a couple of occasionally benevolent despots. One means of ensuring this control is to empower the support staff and use them against the younger lawyers. Because senior partners typically have great demands placed on their time, they are frequently unable to efficiently keep an eye on things themselves.

In the case of Schulte & Luckenbill, this is why Casey Gardner had been named the Senior Associate for the firm. His job, among other things, was to handle some of the more routine decision-making and provide an element of management and control over the other attorneys during Phil Luckenbill's frequent absences. Luckenbill also utilized the support staff as a kind of mini-intelligence service, not unlike the CIA, who would keep him informed of events in the firm when he was away. Some might call this spying, and they'd be right. Others might call this keeping in touch with your employees, and to some extent, they would be right too. Whatever you called it, however, it served to frequently drive a wedge between the attorneys and the staff members who were supposed to support them. Nancy Schulte probably handled these issues better than most. Even though she was at all times aware that her loyalties to Phil Luckenbill superceded all others, she didn't tell him everything, only those things he truly needed or really wanted to know.

Megan called again on Friday afternoon at four-thirty just as Ben was getting ready to go home. If anything, she was even more upset than before. The police had come again, this time with a search warrant. The hope that Greenfield had died from natural causes had pretty much vanished now. They searched both the condo and the brownstone, concentrating mainly on winter clothing. They took a wool coat, a couple of wool scarves, some gloves and a hat. They were looking for trace evidence of some kind, Ben figured, blood or fibers that could tie Megan to a crime scene or Greenfield to Megan. He tried to make light of it to her even as he became increasingly convinced that she was indeed a prime suspect. Finally, Meg asked him to represent her and he quickly agreed. She needed a lawyer now, that much was certain. Everything else couldn't be more unclear.

8

After Ben hung up the phone, he turned the case over and over again in his mind. From a couple of cases back when he was a prosecutor, Ben knew that Detective Scott Nelson was both thorough and very good. There was no question now that Meg was a suspect and that the police were trying to build an evidentiary case against her. Yet he couldn't understand the connection between Meg and Greenfield. She insisted there was none, and he didn't know of any reason to disbelieve her, yet her denials notwithstanding, Nelson had to have something connecting the two. He wished he knew how Greenfield died. That would make it a little easier at least. The uncertainty gnawed at him. Perhaps he could check with some sources he still had in the department; poke around a little bit, see if he could find out anything. Or maybe he could just call Nelson directly. Tell him that he was on the case now and that any communications with Meg had to go through him. He would do that, he decided. He would call Nelson in the morning.

The following day, as he pulled his car around the back of the office after returning from Court, he saw Phil Luckenbill's black Lexus parked in the first spot next to the garage. When he got inside, he headed upstairs. He walked through the open area where Dianne Reynolds sat and entered his office. It was a long alley-shaped room that formed the northwest corner of the old Victorian house. The door was located at about the mid-point of the interior wall. A large wooden desk sat in the far point of the room in front of a spacious double-hung window cut into the north wall. Along

41

the western wall stood four more double-hung windows with lace curtains consistent with the style of the building.

Ben dropped his coat and briefcase on the bench opposite his desk and sat down in his brown leather chair. To his right and under the first of the four double-hung windows on the western wall sat a computer table with Ben's computer on it. To his left and filling the interior wall from the corner of his office to the doorway were built-in bookshelves filled with law books, assorted knickknacks and files. Beyond the doorway were some more built-in shelves. Opposite the bookshelves, and up against the windows, stood a small round conference table flanked by four chairs.

As Ben sat at his desk, he looked directly into Phil Luckenbill's office, the two rooms separated by a set of narrow French doors, currently closed. Phil's office took up the remainder of the western wall of the house and ran largely perpendicular to Ben's office along the southern side of the house. A large bay window faced out of Phil's office to the west. Without shades or window treatments of any kind, this window supplied continuous daylight and brutal afternoon heat, particularly in the summertime. Phil either didn't notice, didn't care or was too cheap to do anything about the problem. After a moment, Ben decided to go in and tell Phil about Meg.

Phil Luckenbill was a tall man, about six-foot-five, with an athletic build growing slightly paunchy as he neared forty. He had dark olive skin, dark hair and dark eyes inherited from his mother. He was not a particularly outgoing man, and he suffered through terrible mood swings, frequently ranging from dark to darker. On his darker days, he tried to avoid inflicting his mood on other people in the office, unless it simply couldn't be helped. Being a natural introvert, a perfect day for Phil probably meant that he didn't have to deal with any of the other attorneys or staff members at all. Sometimes, though, dealing with Phil was unavoidable, and Ben all too frequently found himself in the line of fire because of his close proximity to Phil's office. Since Phil rarely ventured to the upstairs at the other end of the building, those stationed there were rarely the victims of a spontaneous combustion.

Ben stuck his head through the French doors and said, "You got a minute?"

"Yeah, sure," he replied without looking up, "come on in."

"My friend, Megan, appears to be getting unwanted attention in my old law professor's death." Phil looked up and arched an eyebrow. Ben continued. "They showed up at her brownstone over the weekend with a search warrant and took some clothing, coats, things like that. She wants to hire us."

Phil leaned back and stuck the end of his pen in his mouth contemplating the news. "Do we even know he was murdered?"

Ben shrugged. "Not for sure, but is sure seems like it. I know the detective. I was going to call him later today."

Phil stared at him for a long moment. "You sure you really want to do this?" he finally asked. Ben nodded. "Okay then," he said with a sigh, "how do you think we should set this up?"

They agreed on an arrangement that sounded workable, assuming Megan actually got charged with something. Two fellow associates, Dan Conlon and Brad Funk, would help out as needed. Another former associate, Ken Williams, currently the Public Defender in one of the collar counties, would provide behind-the-scenes assistance. Finally, if a trial was to take place, Ben would recruit Mark Schaefer, an old friend of Ben's with significant criminal defense experience to serve as co-counsel on the case since the firm couldn't afford to devote half the lawyers in the office to just one case.

Just then Nancy's voice came over the intercom. "Is Ben in there?"

"Yeah, go ahead."

"Joseph Cavallaro is on the phone for you."

Ben and Phil made eye contact and Phil arched his eyebrows again. "Here it comes," he said. "Probably doesn't like his wife's choice of lawyers."

"Voicemail," Ben called into the speakerphone and Phil gave him a questioning glance. Ben responded, "This guy's an asshole. He's got to be handled or he may be a pain in the ass the entire time we're in this case."

"I hope you know what you're doing."

Ben returned to his office and left messages for Mark and Ken and got Nancy working on the preparation of the retainer agreement. He spent the next hour at his desk brainstorming about the case with a notepad and pen. At three, he hunted down Scott Nelson's number and left him a message saying that he would now be representing Megan Rand and any further communications with her now had to go through his office. He also told Nelson that he would like to get the lay of the land in light of all the contacts between Meg and the police. Nelson called him back a short while later and confirmed for the first time that Professor Greenfield had been the victim of a homicide and that Megan Rand was being investigated in connection with the murder. In light of their previous relationship, Nelson agreed to meet Ben the following afternoon in the main lobby of the law school.

Mark Schaefer called late in the day and Ben briefly laid out the facts and invited him to come aboard and join the defense team. Mark quickly agreed and they decided to meet the following day for a quick bite to discuss the case before heading downtown. Ken Williams called a little while later and told Ben that he would help out any way he could. At six-thirty, Ben looked at his watch and thought about calling and leaving a message for Joseph Cavallaro at his office. He decided not to.

9

"This is quite a place," Mark Schaefer said as he shook hands with Ben in the lobby of the office. "There are no signs or anything. I thought I was lost."

"A common reaction," Ben replied putting on his coat. "Let's go out and grab something and bring it back, then we can talk in the conference room."

Twenty minutes later, after a quick stop at a greasy spoon down on Irving Park Road, Ben led Mark down a couple of steps, through a hallway jammed with old typewriters and even a pinball machine and out to the garage. Mark laughed as he entered the room. "And I thought the lobby was something."

About the size of a normal two-car garage, the garage had tall ceilings that reached a peak in the center. A beam ran across the room parallel to the peak on which stood various military helmets and headgear of the last century. On the far wall, underneath a set of smallish windows, sat two barber chairs and an old shoeshine stand. The wall on the left contained an entrance from the parking lot masquerading as an entrance to a barber shop, complete with a barber pole on the outside wall. The near wall heading to the right contained built-in bookshelves where the firm housed much of its law library. In the corner stood a five-foot high cast iron antique bank safe, which didn't house much these days. The wall opposite the outside entrance held a stained glass window highlighting the scales of justice.

A large wooden library table, approximately ten feet long and stained in light oak, dominated the middle of the room, surrounded by wooden library chairs. As if this weren't enough, the truly distinguishing feature of this room was the series of stuffed animal heads mounted and hung on the walls - deer, elk and even a razorback. All of these were actual trophies from Jim Schulte's hunting days. In the corner above the old-fashioned safe hung a stuffed horse's ass. Schulte commissioned this trophy and presented it to a friend of his, who also happened to be a local judge, complete with the caption *"Res Ipsa Loquitur"*, Latin for "The Thing Speaks for Itself".

Mark's reaction was fairly typical - wide-eyed amazement. He let out a long belly laugh. "I like this."

"Yeah, I do too," Ben said. "I think it's my favorite room in the building. It's a great place to work when you're by yourself. And it's really a great place to take depositions. I think it intimidates witnesses."

They sat down to a quick lunch. Mark had gyros, fries and a Diet Coke, while Ben ate a burger, fries and a chocolate milkshake. Grabbing a handful of fries, Mark said, "I think I can feel my arteries hardening as we speak."

Ben nodded. "Mine too, but the fries are good and the chocolate shake is extremely good. I think all the grease helps you clean out your system."

"That's one theory, I suppose," Mark replied. He looked over at a potbelly stove that sat against the far wall between the barber chairs and the shoeshine stand. His eyes traced the metal grating as it vented through the roof. "Does that thing really work?"

"Yeah, it does, but Jim Schulte and Ken Williams were the only ones who ever really used it. After Schulte rented out his office, and before he moved north to Hayward for good, he spent a lot of time out here and used the garage as his office, which really sucked for the rest of us who wanted to use it as a conference room or a library. As he was going through all his shit trying to decide what to get rid of, he used to shove old law books in the stove and burn them up. The fire would get so hot you could look out from the second floor balcony and see flames and black smoke shooting out of the stack. Then with the fire raging, Schulte would just go off somewhere and not come back. We're probably lucky he didn't burn the place down."

They talked about the case as they ate and Ben told Mark everything he knew, which wasn't much. "So what do you think?" Ben asked.

"Well," Mark said pushing back from the table and taking a long drink of his Diet Coke, "my view is probably the same as yours. She's clearly a prime suspect, a 'person of interest' they call it these days, and they must have found something in that office or somewhere else which caused them to think that. Clearly, there's a lot more that we don't know than we know." Ben nodded. "So," Mark continued taking another drink, "you say you know this Nelson guy?"

"Yeah. I had a couple of cases with him when I was a prosecutor. He's a pretty good guy for a cop. He's a pretty straight shooter."

"There aren't many of them," Mark answered.

"Spoken like a true defense lawyer."

"Well, as you well know, I was never a prosecutor so I would have to acknowledge that my view of the police and the prosecutors is somewhat jaundiced."

Ben looked at his watch. "We should probably get going. It's getting late and we may catch some traffic going in."

They pulled into the parking lot across the street from the law school at one-thirty. After paying the attendant, the two men weaved their way through the parked cars toward the back of the parking lot, which faced the law school building across Adams Street. They hopped the metal parapet and crossed in the middle of the block, pushing their way through the revolving doors ten minutes early. "There he is," Ben said nudging Mark and pointing to a man standing next to the main stairway with his back to them.

"Detective Scott Nelson," Ben called out as they approached.

"Counselor," Nelson said as he wheeled to face them. "Good to see you again," he said extending his right hand, which Ben took in a warm greeting.

47

"This is my colleague, Mark Schaefer," Ben said gesturing. "Mark, this is Detective Scott Nelson. He's one of the good guys."

"You say that now," Nelson said with a laugh. "You may not be saying that by the time this thing is over with."

Ben patted him on his shoulder. "Don't underestimate yourself, Detective."

Although Ben genuinely liked Nelson, he also knew that his prior relationship with the Detective could ultimately prove beneficial to him and his client. He hoped that it would cause Nelson to cut him a break now and then. All he really wanted was some consideration. Defense lawyers didn't usually get much of that.

"Why don't we head upstairs?" Nelson said as he turned for the elevators.

"This looks like a pretty nice building," Mark said to Ben as they entered the elevator. "Did you go all three years here?"

"No, just my last semester. We were supposed to be in here for my entire third year but, you know, with construction, they never get things done on time. It was a lot nicer than the old building over on Wacker, which is gone now."

Nelson looked over at them. "I didn't realize you went here. You must have known Greenfield then."

"I had him twice - for Criminal Law my very first semester of law school and for Criminal Procedure my last semester. Of course, I didn't do as well as I should have either time. He definitely took a hit on my GPA. I suppose that probably makes me a suspect too."

All three of them laughed. "Have you ever been to his office before?" Nelson asked as they got off the elevator.

"Yeah, I guess I have. I came to see him after my Criminal Procedure grade came. I thought he kind of screwed me so I came to his office to talk to him about it. Didn't get anywhere though. I think I was just venting. I wonder how many people actually do that. Quite a few probably."

Nelson looked over his shoulder as he turned the corner toward Greenfield's office. "A very good question," he said.

48

The whole area around Greenfield's office was surrounded by yellow police tape and a security guard sat in a chair outside the door. The sickening smell associated with rotting human remains grew stronger as they approached the door, but it was a mere echo of the scene more than a week before when Professor Hyatt discovered the body. The three men navigated the police tape and found themselves at the door to Greenfield's office.

Turning to Nelson, Ben asked, "Now that we're here, what happened?"

Nelson didn't answer at first. Instead, he took a key from his pocket and unlocked the door. He opened it slowly and stepped inside, Ben and Mark following him. He didn't feel the need to warn them that what they were about to see would be most unpleasant. He knew this wasn't the first murder scene for either man. Not knowing in advance how Professor Greenfield died, neither Ben nor Mark knew exactly what to expect, yet probably expected the worst. Nelson stepped to the center of the room and placed his hand on one of the guest chairs. Ben stepped around Nelson to the left and got his first long look at the carnage in the back corner of Greenfield's office. Mark stood next to him also taking in the scene.

The eyes of the two men moved quickly from the floor to the side wall, to the back wall, to the ceiling, to the desk and back and forth. They said nothing. The head and body of the outline prepared by the medical examiner stuck out from behind the desk. A large circular bloodstain extended out from beneath the head of the outline and blood splatters covered the credenza, back wall, side wall and file cabinet. Ben stepped forward to get a better look behind the desk, where he found more unmistakable evidence of blood splattering.

After a long moment, he turned to his right and looked at Nelson. "Bludgeoned?" he asked softly.

Nelson nodded. "A baseball bat, an autographed Sammy Sosa model in fact," he said finally. "Left at the scene."

Ben turned his attention back to the area behind the desk. "He was a huge Cub fan," he said to no one in particular. The men surveyed the office for a few more minutes in complete silence.

The scene took on a somber, almost reverential tone. No one spoke for a time. Over the years, each of them had been involved on one side or another in society's evaluation of violent death committed by one human being upon another, and witnessing a scene such as this invariably took something from each of them that they probably couldn't even put into words.

Ben stood for a moment looking out the window at the street below, his hands stuffed in the pockets of his overcoat. Then he turned on his heel and looked down at the outline of Greenfield's body lying on the floor. He studied it for a moment and looked back up at Nelson. "So," he said, "I take it that you believe you can tie Megan Rand to this?"

Nelson nodded. "I'm afraid so."

Ben fixed his gaze directly on Detective Nelson, who felt the heat and intensity he had witnessed previously during the two trials the men had been involved with years before when Ben was a prosecutor. Sensing the moment, Mark stepped in and said, "I think we've seen all we need to see for today. Why don't we go back outside." His words seemed to break the tension, and the two men looked at him and nodded. Nelson led them from the room.

No one said a word until they reached the elevator and were sure they were alone. Ben looked around. Seeing no one, he asked, "You have physical evidence?"

"Yes. Physical and otherwise."

Ben looked puzzled. "What do you mean?"

"I can't say right now, but you should know soon enough, I suppose. We hope to have some tests done fairly soon. That should help us with the investigation."

"Do you anticipate anything happening soon?" Ben asked.

"Quite possibly."

Ben nodded thoughtfully and the elevator doors opened. The men stepped inside and the doors closed behind them. "You're aware, I'm sure, that Megan Rand has a young son?"

"Yes."

"I would prefer, if at all possible, that we not traumatize him needlessly."

"I agree."

"So, if it comes to that, if you feel like you need to do something, and you're ready to do something, please call me and I'll be ready to make the necessary arrangements. I'd rather bring her in myself than deal with some sort of a media circus."

"Why don't you let me know where I can get in touch with you," Nelson said.

Ben reached into his pocket and removed one of his business cards. He took a pen from his briefcase and scrawled two phone numbers on the back of the card, handing it to Nelson. "If you need to get in touch with me, my office phone is on the front and my home phone and cell phone numbers are on the back."

The men got off at the third floor and headed for the main landing. Extending his hand, Nelson shook hands with both Ben and Mark. "Mark, it was nice to meet you." Mark nodded. "Say, Ben," Nelson continued, "you never said how you like it on the other side."

Ben smiled. "It's different. I'll definitely say that. Now I'm on the side of the angels."

Nelson laughed softly as he turned and headed for the stairs. "So they say, so they say. I'll be in touch."

Ben and Mark stood at the railing and watched the Detective descend the stairway down to the first floor, then out the main entrance and down the sidewalk out of sight. Mark turned and looked in the windows of the school cafeteria. "Hey, let's go in here and get something to drink." He noticed the sign, "Makrateria" over the door. "What's this 'Makrateria' thing?"

Ben replied, "Professor Makra allegedly donated the money to upgrade the cafeteria so they call it the 'Makrateria'".

Mark laughed. "Isn't Makra that funny bald guy with the glasses that does a lot of the bar review lectures?"

"Yeah, that's him. He's pretty funny and he's actually a pretty good professor too."

They each grabbed a drink from the fountain, went through the cashier line and found a deserted table in the back corner of the room.

"So, what'd you think?" Ben asked as they sat down.

Mark shook his head in a study of contemplation. "Well, given that we didn't know anything to start with other than the victim died in his office, we at least learned how he died, better said, how the police think he died."

"True enough," Ben agreed, "but it's probably also how he did in fact die. It would seem implausible that somebody would bash his brains in after killing him another way. They can certainly figure that out quickly enough."

"True, if they're looking for it. Given the nature of the scene though, did that really seem like something that a woman would do to you? I mean, can you really see our client committing an act like this? From what you've told me about her, this doesn't seem to fit."

Ben shook his head, "No, it doesn't. I can't imagine her doing something like this at all. It would be completely out of character for the person I know."

"We have to ask ourselves," Mark said, "what this crime tells us. In my view, bludgeoning someone to death with a baseball bat strikes me, no pun intended, as a very personal act. This isn't like poisoning someone or shooting someone even. To hit somebody over the head with a baseball bat, you have to get right in there and do it. That doesn't sound much like a woman to me, but I may be wrong. I'm sure there are women out there who could do it. My wife probably could have done it. Also, if the bat was there in the office already, that probably means that it wasn't a planned murder. That would seem to indicate that something happened that caused the murder to take place."

"More of a spontaneous act," Ben said.

"I think so. It seems a little bit farfetched to me, although I didn't know the victim, that someone would come there planning to kill him and count on the baseball bat being there and having the opportunity to use it. Unless, of course, it was a fairly well-known trophy."

"You would almost think that he must have been taken by surprise, although we don't know the extent to which there were other wounds, you know, defensive wounds on his hands, arms, whatever."

"Let's face it," Mark said with a shrug. "We don't know a hell of a lot more than we did before we got here. We're really just speculating here. They cleaned that office out pretty good. We don't know what may have been in there, what documents may have been in there, what he may have been working on at the time, or even whether or not the killer might have taken something from the office. All this really tells us is that we have a lot more questions than we did before."

"We do know one thing though," Ben said in a low voice, leaning in close so only Mark could possibly hear. "We know that they think they can tie Megan Rand to this killing. What did he say, 'physical and other evidence', something like that? That means they either found something at the scene they could link to her or found something at her house that they can link to the scene. Maybe they have other stuff too. Who knows what that could be? But they're not just fucking around. They think they know who did it and when some of these tests come back and confirm what they think they already know, they're going to move pretty fast."

Mark gave a resigned nod. "You are undoubtedly correct about that."

10

"Which way?" said Casey Gardner. They were all piled into his Acura on the way out for lunch. Gardner was driving, Ben was in the front seat, and Brian Davenport, Dan Conlon and Brad Funk were jammed into the Acura's too small back seat. Gardner was just pulling out of the parking lot and he stopped at Schiller Street, which veered off to the left. If he turned here, they would eventually head down Irving Park Road toward Wood Dale. If they continued up to the corner, they could also turn right and head through downtown Ithaca in the opposite direction.

The inevitable response came from Davenport. "Go up to the corner." Essentially, they postponed the lunch decision another thirty seconds. This happened virtually every day.

"Hey," Funk complained from the backseat, "you guys told me we were going to 'Smoky Mexican'."

"We lied," Gardner said with a laugh.

On most days, Funk brought his lunch from home, a cornucopia of healthy selections, usually including a salad made by his wife, Sue. He had taken to eating healthy in an effort to reduce his chronically high cholesterol level. All those days of eating rabbit food for lunch had only reduced his cholesterol by about one point. Nevertheless, he soldiered on. Not that he didn't have weaknesses. Funk would occasionally join the guys for lunch if they were going out for either Chinese or Mexican food, or, of course, if Phil was going along.

54

Gardner pulled the Acura to the corner and turned left into traffic. "Where're we going?" Ben asked.

"I guess I could do Mexican," Gardner said.

After the grumbling in the backseat subsided, they agreed they would indeed go to "Smoky Mexican". It was one of three Mexican restaurants they regularly visited, all more or less fast food places with small sit down areas inside for those so inclined. "Smoky Mexican" got its name because it was always hazy and smoky inside and was located about ten minutes from the office in a small strip mall that didn't have enough parking. After waiting for five minutes, Gardner pulled the Acura into a vacated space at the end of a row and the five of them piled out. They placed their orders and Gardner and Ben stepped out of the interior fog and into the fresh, cold air, while Conlon walked over to the 7-Eleven three doors down to pick up a Big Gulp.

"Hey," Gardner said with a nudge suddenly remembering something, "did you see the thing on the internet on that Professor's murder? I tried buzzing you earlier, but you were on the phone and then I forgot about it."

"No, I didn't see it. What was it?"

"Well, I was on the *Tribune* website and the police or somebody must have released a statement indicating that an unidentified former student at the law school was being questioned as a person of interest in the case. I'm assuming that's our client, right?"

"Fuck," Ben said, "so much for keeping this under wraps. They didn't mention her name, did they?"

"No, just an unidentified former law student, that's all they said."

"I better call her. If she finds out about this before I get in touch with her, she'll probably freak."

"Good idea."

A few minutes later, Funk was the last to emerge from the restaurant and Conlon stepped out to let Funk climb back into the middle of the backseat. "Why do I always have to sit in the middle?" he complained.

"Because you're the one with the twenty-five inch inseam," Conlon quickly retorted.

There's always a guy in every office that takes a lot of shit from all the other guys. At Schulte & Luckenbill, Brad Funk was that guy. A feisty man in his mid-thirties, Brad Funk stood five-foot-seven with heels, had short brown hair and wore glasses. Born and raised in central Indiana, Funk was also a bit of a redneck and a longtime member of the NRA. He liked to go target shooting and hunting in his spare time, for which he received immeasurable grief from the rest of the guys in the office. His political views were wholly consistent with his status as a gun owner and NRA member. And he always seemed to have at least a couple of running feuds going on with opposing counsel on his files.

His combative nature was one of the two things you just had to know about Funk. The other was that he had a pathological need to be important. Some felt this Napoleon complex stemmed from his obvious lack of height, while others figured he was just trying to keep his wife happy. In any event, his cases were always the biggest and most important, and he always absolutely, positively had to see Phil right away. Phil knew this, of course, and avoided Funk whenever possible, even going so far as to move Funk's office to the opposite end of the building so as to provide himself with a larger buffer zone and more opportunities to come and go unnoticed. This often left a frustrated Funk with little choice but to pepper Phil with voicemail messages, e-mails and bothersome calls to his cell phone.

Despite these seemingly negative traits, Ben actually liked Funk. They would spar over who was better, Ben's Packers or Funk's Bears, and Ben thought that Funk had a pretty good sense of humor and was a good sport most of the time. He also worked hard and was a pretty decent lawyer on top of it all. Nevertheless, you couldn't help but give him shit.

Halfway through lunch, Dan Conlon looked up from the *Sun-Times* and said, "Hey Funk, I see in the paper that some guy in Congress wants to regulate how much money groups like the NRA can spend on political advertising."

"Fucking Commies," Funk said with a laugh. "They just don't understand all the good things the NRA does for society."

56

"Yeah, like make sure nuts like you have weapons," Casey Gardner said.

"You just don't realize and fully understand the benefits of a well-informed, well-armed society," Funk replied not altogether joking. "You know, they've done studies. Places where they allow concealed weapons have lower incidences of crime."

"That's because self-defense shootings probably don't count in the statistics," Ben interjected, "and everything, I'm sure, is considered self-defense. Oops, a guy knocked on my door. I better shoot him. Self-defense."

"Oh ye of little faith," Funk said. "One day you'll find yourself in a situation where you'll wish you had a gun on you."

"Shit," Ben answered, "that happens pretty much every time I run into you in the hallway." People continued to pick on Funk for the rest of lunch.

Half an hour later, Ben was back at his desk reviewing some cases Conlon had pulled regarding bail issues. He recognized some of the cases from back in his prosecutor days; others were simply new takes on familiar themes. These were little more than general recitations on the current state of bail law. What Ben really wanted, and didn't have yet, was fresh research on the appropriateness of bail under Meg's specific circumstances, an upper class woman with no history of crime and a young son to care for. He reasoned that something was going to happen sooner or later, probably sooner, and he wanted to have something ready to go when the time came.

He was in the middle of reading one of the cases when Dianne Reynolds stuck her head in the door. "I've got Joseph Cavallaro on the phone for you," she said.

Ben looked up, hesitated for only an instant and said, "Tell him I'm in a meeting."

"He seemed pretty insistent."

"Good. Tell him I'm in a meeting."

"You must really not want to talk to him."

"I'll talk to him eventually, just not now."

Although it was always possible that Cavallaro had something significant to convey, Ben didn't really believe it and didn't regret putting him off. He waited until a quarter to seven, just before he went home, to call Cavallaro back. He knew Cavallaro wouldn't be there. As expected, he got the firm's answering machine and left a brief message. He hung up the phone, flicked off the table lamp and headed for the door.

11

Nothing happened over the following weekend. Ben kept his cell phone handy and jumped every time either that or his home phone rang. He didn't hear from anyone. He tried to keep himself busy to keep his mind off things. It didn't work. Meg's pending arrest and the connection between her and Professor Greenfield gnawed at him the entire time. It kept turning up unwanted like his least favorite cousin - when he shoveled snow, when he folded some laundry and when he vacantly watched a movie with his wife on Saturday night. He just couldn't drive it out of his head.

He didn't have Court on Monday so he stopped at Jiffy Lube on the way into the office for an oil change. It snowed overnight and traffic moved much slower than usual. He didn't hit the office parking lot until almost ten. In deference to the weather and the forecast for more snow later that afternoon, Ben wore jeans, a black sweater, brown suede casual slip-on shoes and his brown bomber jacket. He ran into Nancy on her way to the bathroom as he kicked the snow off his shoes just inside the back door. "Where have you been?" she asked, pausing when she noticed his clothing. "Whoa, casual day today, huh?"

Ben nodded. "Yeah, well, it's shitty out there."

"It's shitty in here too," she said. "That husband's been calling non-stop. He's probably called four or five times already. You're right. He is an asshole."

"Why? What did he say?"

"It wasn't so much what he said. He was just rude and obnoxious to both me and Dianne. I don't know who he thinks he is."

"Oh, I can tell you who he thinks he is," Ben said, "and I can also tell you who he actually is. Did he leave any messages?"

"At least one."

"Well, whatever you do," Ben said, "don't give him my cell phone number. Tell everybody. Just be civil to him and offer him my voicemail. But don't, under any circumstances, give him my cell phone number unless I tell you to ahead of time. I want to be in control of when I talk to him, not the other way around."

Ben listened to his voicemail messages even before he took his jacket off. The only message on his system was one from Joseph Cavallaro, who was indeed belligerent and berated Ben for not returning his calls in a timely fashion. He also said that he needed to see Ben as soon as possible. Ben deleted the message, took off his jacket and threw it over the bench opposite his desk.

A few minutes later, Nancy joined him. "Well, was he an asshole or what?" she said.

"Of course. I'm sure he got worse every time he called."

"What does he want?"

"I think he wants me to cater to him more and he's probably pissed off that she hired me at all. Oh, and I've been summoned."

"Summoned?"

"Yeah, he wants to see me at his office."

"What are you going to do?"

"I'm going to go."

"Are you going to call him first?"

"No, I'm just going to show up. If he wants to see me that bad, he shouldn't complain when I show up unannounced." Ben rubbed the side of his nose. "I've got to call Mark and Ken and talk to Funk and Conlon," he said. "In the meantime, print me two copies of the Retainer Agreement. Put them in a manila folder."

Both Mark and Ken were in Court so he left messages. He met Dan Conlon and Brad Funk in the garage for a quick update on their research projects. Ten minutes later, after putting on his jacket and stuffing the Retainer Agreement into his briefcase, he headed for the door.

The SUV cut through the remaining snow and slush with relative ease. Cavallaro's office was located in a mid-story office tower downtown that overlooked the Chicago River. Ben found a parking garage down the street and parked. He eased through the revolving doors at the north end of the building and strolled up to the automated information screen in the center of the lobby and punched in CAV at the prompt and touched Enter. A second later, Joseph Cavallaro & Associates, Suite 2050, lit up the screen.

Ben picked his way through the growing crowd of office workers on their way to lunch and located the correct elevator bank. A bell rang and an instant later, the middle door opened, releasing two men and three women to the corridor. Ben stepped on, hit the number 20 and the doors closed in front of him. He had considered his course of action carefully while driving downtown from Ithaca. The elevator reached the 20th floor and the doors opened. Ben stepped into a small lobby area and looked to his left, then back to his right. There, on the other side of an intersecting hallway, stood two ornate wooden doors on which the words "Joseph Cavallaro & Associates, Ltd., Attorneys and Counselors at Law" were emblazoned in gold letters.

Ben pulled the door open and walked quickly inside. A pretty blond girl in her early-twenties sat at a reception desk and looked up as he entered. "Hi, can I help . . ." was all she got out before Ben interrupted her.

"I'm here to see Mr. Cavallaro," he said without breaking stride. He turned to his left and strode down a long hallway with secretarial stations and offices on his right.

"Hey, you can't go down there," the blond said from behind him.

"That's okay," he said over his shoulder as he kept walking, "he's expecting me." Ben reached the end of the corridor and found another blond sitting at a secretarial station. This one was maybe ten years older than the first, but no less attractive. Seeing Ben coming and hearing Blond #1's attempt to slow him down, Blond #2 stood up and made a weak attempt at blocking his path.

He quickly stepped around her and said, "Excuse me," as he grabbed the doorknob, opened the door and stepped inside.

There he found Joseph Cavallaro holding court behind a large, ornately carved mahogany desk the size of a small boat, his feet propped up on the stern and a telephone receiver wedged between his left shoulder and left ear. He was filing his nails. Cavallaro looked dumbstruck. Ben fixed him with a firm gaze, his green eyes blazing. After a moment, he looked down to his immediate right, where a bookish-looking brunette sat on a black leather sofa with a yellow notepad and a gold Cross pen. This one was a lawyer, Ben thought to himself. He looked at her and said, "You can leave now." She neither moved nor replied, a shocked, mouth-open look on her face.

Right then, Blond #1 and Blond #2 stumbled through the door behind him. Sensing a pending disaster, Blond #1 stuttered as she tried to compose herself. "I'm, I'm sorry, sir. But this man just, just went right by me." Ben gave her a deadly glare. Cavallaro, still on the telephone, waved her off with his right hand, still holding the nail file as he sat up. The two blonds didn't know whether they should shit or take notes until Cavallaro mouthed the words, "Go, Go" and again waved them toward the door. The two blonds stepped back outside and closed the door behind them.

The bookish brunette didn't move. Ben looked down at her again and she stared back, eyes transfixed. He lowered his head until it was almost at her level and said in a much louder voice as though he was talking to someone who was hard of hearing, "I said you can leave now."

He turned back toward Cavallaro, who was still on the telephone, although paying more attention to Ben than he was to the person on the other end of the line. Ben took two steps in his direction and said, "Hang up the phone." At this, the brunette rose slowly from the sofa and slipped quietly from the room. Ben ignored her. He continued to stare directly at Cavallaro, whose expression morphed from shock to disbelief to confusion to anger in a matter of seconds.

Getting no response, Ben moved to the front of the desk and leaned over and pushed the button on the receiver, disconnecting the call, never taking his eyes from Cavallaro's. He repeated, much softer than before, "I said hang up the phone." Ben turned and walked slowly back to the couch as Cavallaro slammed the handset back down on the telephone. "Who the fuck do you think you are coming in here like this?"

Ben ignored him and sat down, crossing his legs and putting his hands in his lap as though a priest patiently awaiting the report from one of his altar boys. Cavallaro rose to his feet, a fury building within him. "I said, who the fuck do you think you are?"

Ben didn't say anything for a moment and Cavallaro appeared to struggle to find stronger words with which to make his point. Ben continued to look directly into his eyes. "I believe you summoned me," he finally said. A knock came at the door and a tall man poked his head in. "Apparently they're worried about you, Joe," Ben said with a sly smile.

Now Cavallaro was embarrassed in addition to angry. He tried to compose himself. "It's ah . . . it's okay. We . . . ah . . . have an important meeting here that we need to attend to. I just . . . ah . . . I just didn't know that Mr. Lohmeier was coming right now. That's all. That's all. You can leave us now. Thanks." Cavallaro waved the man out, while Ben continued to smile at him.

"Now that you've summoned me and I've come," Ben said, "what is it that you'd like to talk about?"

Cavallaro, all five-foot six of him, attempted to pump himself up like a third world dictator, his reddening face a marked contrast with his thick gray hair. Ben always thought Joseph Cavallaro looked like Eddie Arcaro, although he had never seen the famed jockey in such a state. "I don't know who the fuck you think you are," Cavallaro said, "but I've got a god damn wife on death row practically and you stroll in here and pull this bullshit? I should come around this desk and kick your ass."

The smile vanished from Ben's face and he continued to look Cavallaro straight in the eyes. "I would have thought," he said finally, "that you would be too busy allowing your wife to speak with the authorities without the benefit of counsel to kick my ass. Particularly an experienced advocate like yourself. I would have thought that the mother of your youngest son would have merited a bit more concern from the great Joseph Cavallaro than to allow her wade helplessly into a thicket with the police and perhaps even implicate herself in a capital murder. Nevertheless, I'm quite sure that you had your reasons for what you did. But never mind, we're beyond that now. Thankfully, we have extricated Megan Rand Cavallaro from those people who appear more interested in implicating than exonerating her." Truth be told, Ben couldn't really hold Cavallaro responsible for Megan's conversations with the police. They had appeared out of nowhere with questions Megan couldn't comprehend. Not much damage was done. Since Cavallaro had never practiced criminal law, Ben thought he could use that fact to his advantage.

"Who do you think you're talking to?"

"Oh, I know full well who I'm talking to. But I can't imagine that this is why you brought me down here," he said, gesturing at the wide expanse of Cavallaro's office, "to discuss your apparent proficiency in helping the police gather evidence against your wife. So I repeat my question, what is it that you want to talk about?" Ben continued to remain perfectly still.

This contrasted sharply with Cavallaro's ranting and raving, something not lost on the older man. Uncomfortable with Ben's placid demeanor, Cavallaro smoothed his pants and sat back down. He seemed to consider the possibility that he had not served his wife well. "What I want to know," he said trying to regain his footing, "is what you're going to do to keep my wife from being charged with a murder she didn't commit."

Ben nodded slightly as though weighing his answer carefully. "The unfortunate truth of it," he responded, "is that I'm not going to do anything to prevent that. There's nothing I can do to prevent that. The police are under the serious impression that they have enough evidence, or are about to have enough evidence, to bring her in and charge her with Daniel Greenfield's murder. In fact, I'm a bit surprised they haven't done so already. But rest assured, the day is coming, and soon, probably."

This news seemed to hit Cavallaro hard, and he slumped in his chair. "Then what do we do now?" he rasped.

"We wait, and we start preparing for the things we have to do after she is arrested. For example, we've already begun researching and preparing a brief to be used at her bail hearing. We've also discussed surrendering her to the authorities so as to avoid your son having to witness his mother being led off in handcuffs and the ensuing media circus that would undoubtedly follow. I've also visited the crime scene."

"The crime scene?" Cavallaro interrupted. "What do you know about the crime scene? What do you know about how he was killed?"

"He was bludgeoned," Ben said. He watched Cavallaro closely as he said these words. Cavallaro exhibited no visible response. If the manner of Greenfield's death surprised him, he didn't show it. Feeling Ben's eyes upon him, Cavallaro swiveled in his chair and looked out the back window of his office at nothing in particular, his right hand slowly rubbing his chin. "So what am I supposed to do?" he asked without turning back, "Just sit here?"

"No, you need to prepare for when the call comes. We should get a heads-up, but you still should prepare for having your son stay with you for a while." Cavallaro nodded in apparent agreement, still looking out the window. Ben continued. "The two of you should come up with some sort of story - Mommy has to take a trip, that kind of thing. But you're not going to shield him from this forever. He's got to go to school and, as you know, kids hear things and then they talk about them. You don't want some snotty-nosed kid spilling the beans in the middle of the cafeteria one afternoon.

"Hopefully, we'll be able to get bail. We should be able to, but you never know. Some judge might think that you're rich and more than able to skip town, perhaps even leave the country. At least that's what the prosecutors are going to tell the Court. You can bet on it. If things go well, we should have her out of there pretty quickly. If things go well."

Cavallaro turned back to him. "So you're convinced they're going to arrest her," he said as a statement rather than a question.

"Yeah, I am," Ben answered. "Detective Nelson as much as told me that it's coming. I don't see any reason to doubt him."

Ben pointedly didn't ask Cavallaro about any possible connections between Megan and Daniel Greenfield. He knew he couldn't trust anything Cavallaro would tell him.

"So what else am I supposed to do," Cavallaro asked with a sarcastic edge in his voice.

"What are you supposed to do?" Ben asked as he opened his briefcase and grabbed the manila folder inside. "What you're supposed to do is play the dutiful, supportive husband at all times and make sure all the expenses are properly paid. Toward that end, here's a Retainer Agreement," he said tossing the manila folder down on the desk in front of Cavallaro, who lowered his eyes to look at it, but did not touch it. "I'll give you forty-eight hours to review it, sign it and get it back to me with the retainer check. And another thing, you better start thinking about arranging for the bond. It will probably be a big one if we get one at all."

"Just like that?" Cavallaro asked looking up at Ben who stood impassively above him.

"Just like that. And one more thing," Ben said slinging his briefcase over his right shoulder, "don't summon me again. If you do, or if you continue to treat my staff like dirt under your five hundred dollar loafers, I will wait until this case is over and Megan is freed and then make her divorce from you my life's work. And I'll succeed." He turned and headed toward the door. "I'll see myself out."

Cavallaro didn't respond.

All eyes were on Ben as he walked back down the hall past the receptionist's desk and out the wooden doors. He reached the elevator doors just as two people got off. As the doors to the elevator closed leaving him alone, he shook his head and said, "What a prick," under his breath.

Rather than go directly to his car, Ben decided to go for a walk and grab a char dog at Gold Coast Dogs on State Street. It wasn't too cold outside and the exercise would do him good. As expected, the hotdog hit the spot. On his way back to the car, at the corner of State and Kinzie, in front of Harry Caray's Restaurant, Ben's cell phone buzzed. Ben extricated it from the clip on his belt and looked at the display. He didn't recognize the number. He flipped it open. "Benjamin Lohmeier," he said.

He immediately recognized the voice on the other end of the line. "Ben, this is Scott Nelson."

12

As soon as she answered, Ben started right in. "Nance, it's me. I just got off the phone with Nelson. D-Day is here," he said all in rush.

"Oh, no," she said, "I was hoping . . ."

"Yeah, me too," he interrupted, "but we're hoping for other things now, I guess. We're going to work the surrender at eight. I want to be back down here by seven, seven-thirty."

"Where are you?" she said. "Are you outside? What's all that noise?"

"Yeah, I'm on my cell phone. I'm walking over to Meg's office."

"You mean you haven't told her yet?"

"No, I just found out. I'm going to walk over and talk to her in person."

"Okay," she said, "what do you want me to do?"

"I've talked to Mark already, and he's going to call Ken, and they're going to meet over there later this afternoon. Mark's going to have some motions and stuff to put on the system so we can get them ready and on file ASAP. Dan should be working on the brief for the bail hearing. That should take place tomorrow morning."

"Yeah, I think he's already working on that. He's got a draft pretty well done. Dianne is already typing it."

"Good. I've got to stop back at the house after I talk to Meg so I can change into a suit. I don't know what the fuck I was thinking dressing like this today, but I've got to have a suit on later.

I should be back there sometime this afternoon. Put me through to Conlon."

"Oh, by the way, how did your meeting with the asshole go?"

"Kind of fun actually. I'll fill you in later."

Nancy transferred Ben to Dan Conlon, who said that the first draft of the brief had indeed been completed and was being typed at that very moment by Dianne Reynolds. Conlon also pulled copies of the key four or five cases cited in the brief and would make extra copies for the Court and the prosecution. Convinced that things were under control back at the office, Ben signed off and continued over to Meg's office.

Ben found her in a hallway on her way to the bathroom. They both stopped in their tracks when they saw each other. She knew instantly why he had come and her shoulders sagged. Tears welled up in her closed eyes as she fought to compose herself. Without saying a word, Ben went to her, took her softly by the arm and led her to a small conference room at the far end of the corridor, closing the door behind them. They sat in silence for several minutes before Ben relayed the details of his brief telephone conversation with Detective Nelson. Nelson would be coming by the townhouse around eight to pick her up. She would then be transferred to a local stationhouse on the near north side for processing before transferring to the main lockup at the Cook County Jail.

Their entire conversation lasted only a few minutes and Ben rose to leave. "I'm sorry. I have to get going. I have a lot of things to do before I get back to your place."

She nodded. "I'll be alright. Just get going. I'll see you later."

"Would you like me to take you home?" he asked.

"No. No. I'll be okay. I'm just going to sit here for a little bit and get myself together. Then I'm going to talk to Joe. You go ahead."

She got up to say goodbye, and he put his arms around her in a long embrace, an uncharacteristic move for him. "Trust me," he whispered into her ear. "We'll get through this. We're going to beat this."

She nodded. "I'll be okay. Now you go ahead."

He opened the door, took one last look at her, then closed the door behind him and was gone.

Traffic on the Eisenhower was light and he was back in his driveway in less than forty-five minutes. He decided to grab a quick shower before he changed. After he finished, Ben went around the corner to the walk-in closet and picked out a charcoal gray suit, white shirt and conservative blue tie. He couldn't believe that he was dressing with TV in mind.

As zero hour and Megan's arrest rapidly approached, Ben felt himself enter a sort of zone with respect to the case. While in this state, Ben's intensity level and focus would skyrocket, while he subconsciously drove all extraneous matters, including people, from his thoughts. He had experienced this single-minded sense of purpose at various points throughout his youth and it grew increasingly prevalent during his college and law school years. During these periods, people frequently found him short-tempered and difficult.

At first, he didn't even notice the changes in himself. It took Libby, after they had been together for awhile, to point out where and how these transformations, some little, some not, occurred. Over time and with his wife's assistance, Ben became more acutely aware of these periods and the profound effect on his moods. This zone or "there," as his wife often described it, reached its zenith while Ben was a prosecutor. As he began handling more violent cases - aggravated assaults, rapes, and even murders, and his anger and highly competitive nature more and more got the best of him, Ben went "there" with increasing frequency. Although Ben never thought that it ever seriously hindered his performance as a prosecutor, he nevertheless recognized that it negatively impacted his physical and mental well-being, not to mention his personal relationships. Recognizing the circumstances when they existed certainly helped, as did the fact that he now had more and more outlets than when they first got married, not the least of which were his children.

Six weeks premature and weighing just four pounds at birth, Ben and Libby's first child, a son named Matthew, was born in October of 1993, the day before his father's birthday. Physically,

70

Matthew resembled his father, but with straight brown hair and brown eyes. Almost four years after Matthew was born, the Lohmeiers welcomed a little girl into the world in the late summer of 1997. Strong willed and opinionated, Natalie Lohmeier had blond hair and green eyes like her father and appeared to spend every waking moment seeking to wrap him around her little finger, usually succeeding.

Between the two of them, Matthew and Natalie provided Ben with an indispensable escape from "there" or that zone, whatever it was called. His other salvation occurred when he decided, with Libby's strong encouragement, to leave the State's Attorney's office and enter private practice. As a prosecutor, Ben served as a necessary point man in society's desire to avenge the victim and punish the guilty. In civil practice, unlike criminal practice, there are few great truths to unearth or wrongs to right, personal injury and class action lawyers notwithstanding. At least these crusades didn't pop up in the commercial practice Benjamin Lohmeier found himself in these days. One way or another, it always boiled down to a battle over the money.

In the past couple of days, the TV news and the newspapers had started calling this the "Law School Murder" and Ben figured that the name would probably stick. They were on the verge of a lot of media attention, Ben knew, because of the nature of the crime, the nature of the soon-to-be accused and the fact there wasn't another big media case out there at the moment to seize the headlines. Although Ben's competitive nature made him want to win every case very badly, nothing in his day-to-day existence as a civil practitioner ever stoked his fires as hot as they used to get in the old days. That's why he was startled to feel himself drifting down that lonely path to a place he had not visited in so long. Maybe getting back into an important criminal case caused his reaction. Maybe seeing Megan Rand as a defendant did it. He didn't know for sure. His self-awareness had limits after all. Whatever the cause, Ben recognized the scenery and understood where this path might eventually lead.

13

Ben returned to the office at about three. Mark was already there and Ken was on his way. Ben called for a meeting of the defense team at three-thirty in the garage and checked his voicemail messages - nothing of significance. On his chair, he found the draft brief Conlon had prepared, together with a couple of motions Mark had slapped together. He turned to the brief first and buzzed Conlon. "Hey, you down there?" he asked.

"Yeah, what is it?"

"Is this brief pretty much in final form?"

"Yeah, it is. I think it's pretty good, but you might want to spruce it up a little bit."

"Okay," Ben said, "I'll take a look at it before the meeting and get it back to you." Then he was gone.

The brief read like something drafted by a prosecutor, as Conlon had been, competently prepared, covering all the bases, yet lacking in anything really special. Good enough for government work, but certainly improvable. Ben knew many of the cases cited in the brief and liked the way Conlon incorporated newer opinions to buttress his claim that Megan deserved a reasonable bond. Ben decided that all it really needed was tinkering. He smoothed out the analysis, punched up the introduction and strengthened the conclusion to make it sound less neutral and more authoritative. Satisfied, he dropped the brief on Dianne Reynolds' chair for revisions and headed downstairs.

He ran into Funk in the copy room and followed him down the short corridor into the garage. Mark and Dan were already sitting at the far side of the conference room table talking about bail. Funk took a spot opposite them and Ben climbed into one of the barber chairs next to the potbelly stove. Just as he began, he heard a door slam and footsteps coming down the steps and paused. They all turned and Ken Williams made a grand entrance into the room.

"Greetings all," he said, strolling to the end of the table and pulling out a wooden chair. He turned the chair sideways and looked over at Ben to his left. "So, today's the day?"

"Yeah," Ben replied.

"It sucks to be her," Ken said.

"Yes, it does," Ben said. "I'm going to leave here about six to meet her."

"It sucks to be you too. So what did I miss?"

"Not too much," Ben said. "I just sat down and was about to start when I heard you coming in. Well, for everybody I haven't talked to, here goes."

Ben gave them the lay of the land and briefly summarized his conversation with Nelson. "You know," he continued, "we've all seen this Law School Murder stuff on TV, and I think once word gets out that Megan Rand has been arrested, things may get pretty crazy around here. My point is simply this - don't talk to any media people. Be polite. Be respectful. We don't want to piss anybody off, but any comments to the media will go through me, not that I want to be a big shot, but we have to make sure that we speak with one voice and that we don't say anything that we don't want to say. Obviously, we don't want to mention anything about Ken's involvement here. We don't want to piss off the people out in DeKalb County."

"No doubt about it," Ken chimed in. "It's like I'm not even here."

"Just like when you worked here," Ben said. Ken gave him the finger. "All right, Dan and Brad you can go. Ken and Mark and I have a couple things to talk about yet. Dan, make sure that Dianne's on that brief. I need it by the time I leave with all the cases and stuff. Thanks."

"So are we having fun yet?" Ben said as Funk and Conlon left the room.

"It's only just starting my friend," Ken said. "I think you're right. I think this could be a pretty big media case."

"We may even get Geraldo out here," Mark said with a laugh.

Ben leaned forward in the barber chair and rubbed his temples. "I think one thing we need to do is set up some sort of a division of responsibility. First, we have to start thinking about expert witnesses. I think at the very least, we're probably going to need some sort of a blood splatter guy to try and figure out what Greenfield may have been doing when he got whacked. Now, Mark and I have visited the scene, and I don't think what we saw down there is consistent with a woman, a smaller woman at that, smacking a relatively tall guy upside the head and then finishing him off. It seems to me the height thing may have been a problem. You agree, Mark?"

"I do," Mark said. "My view is that given what you've told me about our client, I don't quite see how she could have pulled that off if the victim had been looking right at her when it happened. We'll just have to see how that plays out."

"Yeah, that's right," Ben said. "A blood splatter guy for sure. I'll have to wait and see after, you know, we get a look at all the evidence. Speaking of which, I'd like Mark to focus on the evidence when it comes in. Ken, we'll also get you a copy of the reports and things so maybe you and Mark can look at it independently from each other. That way, one of you could catch something the other one missed and vice versa. Ken, if you could get us some more motions that you think we might need, maybe some briefs, stuff that we could cut and paste, that would be good. I haven't been doing much criminal stuff since I left the prosecutor's office so a lot of my stuff isn't as current as I would like."

"I can do that," Ken said. "I've got a lot of good stuff. My people scan everything that comes in from defense attorneys. Some of it's damn good. Not that I would ever admit that."

"We'll know a lot more after we know what the evidence is, but I think we can assume certain kinds of motions may be appropriate. And get them over here so we can put them on the system."

"What about a speedy trial?" Ken asked. Ken referred to a demand made by a defendant for a speedy trial.

Ben sat back in his chair and clasped his hands behind his head looking vaguely into the middle distance. "Somehow I would tend to doubt it," he said after a moment. "I think we're going to need some period of time here to conduct an investigation, to figure out what happened. I think we're going to have a lot of people to talk to about this. I think he's divorced, or he was divorced, so we're going to have to look at the ex-wife. It could be a student. How many students has he had over the years? He's given bad grades to some of them. Hell, he gave bad grades to me. Plus, if it's true that he was chasing students all over the place, that might mean there could be a boyfriend or spouse involved. Who knows? Which reminds me, I think we're going to need to have at least one good investigator, if not more. I know one I've used in the past who's pretty decent. Either of you know anybody?"

"I do," Ken said. "I've got a guy who I used to work with who's great. His name is Stan Disko. I've got his address and phone number at the office. I'll call you with them."

"I know him," Ben said, "Casey Gardner uses him to serve people. He's pretty good. We can always use my guy too if we have to. As far as interviewing people and stuff, I'll probably do a lot of that myself. I get a better idea when I can look somebody in the eye and hear what they have to say, rather than always relying on reports other people give me. I'm going to start down at the school. I haven't been back there much in the last ten years, but I still know some of the professors and their reputations. I guess now that I think about it, Ken, you went there too, so you may have some contacts you can help me out with as well."

"Not a problem," Ken said.

Ben continued. "Mark, while we're at it, why don't you get some subpoenas ready for the law school. Make them pretty broad. We're going to want lists of all Greenfield's students - names, addresses, grades for the past, say, ten years. We also want Greenfield's personnel files. Brian tells me he got called on the carpet for fooling around with students a few years ago. If that's true, there may be something in there that could prove helpful. I'll try and get them to be cooperative, but if they're not, let's just hit them with a subpoena and not fuck around with it. Any other thoughts?"

"No, that pretty much covers it, I think," Mark said without looking up as he scratched notes on a yellow pad in his heavy hand.

"You know," Ben said as he got down and noticed Mark taking notes, "you don't have to press so hard on the paper, do you? I mean, you're not trying to typeset here."

"It's just the way I write."

"You know, I'll talk to Phil about that empty office down the hallway by the men's bathroom. It's not the best location in the world, but at least it's an office and it's pretty private. I'm sure he won't mind if you work in there."

"That would be great," Mark said.

"It'll be great," Ken said, "until somebody comes along and takes a dump in that bathroom. Mark my word. You'll see."

14

Ben went back upstairs to his office, checked his voicemail and e-mail and sat down to work on his presentation for the bail hearing. At about five-fifteen, Dan Conlon brought him the final draft of the motion for bail, supporting brief and the stack of cases cited therein. He dumped them on the bench next to Ben's briefcase. Fifteen minutes later, Nancy stuck her head in to tell him she was taking off for the night. "You need anything else before I go?" she said. "I can stay if you want me too. I don't have any plans."

Ben looked up at her with a vague expression of not having heard a word she said. "No. That's okay, you go ahead," he said finally. "I think I've got everything I need here."

"Well, okay," she said, "good luck tonight, tomorrow too. You think this is going to be on the ten o'clock news?"

Ben shrugged. "I hope not, but it wouldn't surprise me."

She wished him luck again and was gone.

Ben pulled a copy of the bail brief out of the pile and reviewed it once again, not that he could make any changes anymore at this point. A pretty good effort, he thought to himself, as he put it back in the pile. He looked at his watch - it was almost six. He had to leave. He grabbed a fresh notepad and stuffed it into his briefcase and stood there for a second thinking about whether he'd forgotten anything. Deciding that he hadn't, Ben put on his suit coat and overcoat, slung his briefcase over his shoulder and grabbed the stack of pleadings for the Court, shutting his light off on the way out.

As he passed the office at the top of the stairs, he nodded in at Marc Swift, another associate, who was on the telephone. He was always on the telephone. He ran into Casey Gardner in the copy room, on his way back from the bathroom. "Good luck," Casey said slapping him on the shoulder as they passed each other. "Hey," Casey said as he stopped in the doorway of the copy room right outside Dan Conlon's office. Ben stopped at the opposite end of the room and turned to face him. "What do you think? Did she do it?" Casey asked.

Ben gave a gesture that was partway between a shrug and a shake of the head. "It would be hard to imagine . . . No, I don't think so."

"Well, somebody did."

"Yeah," Ben said, "somebody did."

"Well, anyway, good luck."

"Thanks," Ben said as he turned and headed for the door.

Ben pushed through the back door and stepped out onto the porch. He stood there for a moment and watched the wind blow swirls of snow off the roof of the garage. A tall lamplight stationed on the snowy bank beyond the parking spaces and driveway illuminated the area and gave a faintly Christmasy feel to the scene. Then the light went out. It did that a lot, Ben recalled. He often looked out at this light from the window behind his desk and noticed that it went off and on and off again with surprising frequency. He could be sitting and working at his computer and catch the light going on or off out of the corner of his eye and was always somewhat startled by it.

Occasionally, he would look out the window to see whether anything caused the light to go on, such as a passing car or a commuter walking through the parking lot from the train station, but was never able to come up with anything. Ben shrugged, shook his head and headed down the steps toward his car.

***

Almost thirty miles away, Megan Rand Cavallaro watched her husband and son move away down the corridor. When they reached the elevators, she turned and went back inside her condominium. She leaned against the closed door and listened

78

silently until she knew they were gone. When would she next be able to take Anthony in her arms and tell him that she loved him? She slid down the door to a sitting position and buried her head in her hands as tears began to well in her eyes and drip down on to the knees of her pants.

What if they didn't believe her? What if she were found guilty? Thoughts like these swirled around her head leaving her dizzy with fear. What if Joe died while she was in prison? Who would take care of Anthony? Who would go to Anthony's high school graduation? To his wedding? Who would make sure that he always knew how much his mother loved her only child? She couldn't know.

After a while, the tears slowed, the cathartic release having done all it could, and Megan rose to her feet and began preparing for Ben's arrival and that which lay ahead. First, she decided on a quick shower, not knowing when she would next get another in the comfort and quiet of her own bathroom. As the hot water cascaded down her back, she studied the sounds, scents and sensations around her as though for the first time. The smell of the soap and shampoo and the feel of the thick bath towel wrapped around her brought fresh tears to her eyes. She fought to compose herself as she wiped the steam off the mirror with her hand and gazed at her own reflection, both from the front and the side as if composing her own mug shot. She looked like hell, her eyes puffy and red.

Meg removed a pair of gold, heart-shaped earrings and set them softly on the counter next to her watch. She would need neither where she was going. After fumbling in the medicine cabinet for some Visine, she clumsily put two drops into each eye. She reached for her make-up, then hesitated, figuring there wasn't really any point. She didn't use much make-up anyway so she applied a little mascara and some moisturizing cream and left it at that.

Meg stepped out of the bathroom and into the coolness of her bedroom and walked over to the closet to pick out something to wear. What do you wear to an arrest? She didn't know. She settled on a black sweater, jeans and a pair of suede casual shoes.

As good as anything. After she finished getting dressed, she tidied up the bedroom and threw her dirty clothes into a hamper. She found her cell phone on the dresser and turned it off.

Coming into the kitchen, Meg noticed the clock on the wall and realized that Ben wouldn't be there for a while. She rinsed off the dishes and placed them into the dishwasher with some Cascade she found under the sink and started the machine before wiping off the counter with a wet sponge. For just an instant, she thought about changing the message on her answering machine before realizing that anyone who wished to speak to her would undoubtedly know that she couldn't come to the phone and why.

When Meg finished in the kitchen, she pulled the vacuum out of the hall closet and did a quick once-over on the living room carpeting, moved the magazines from the coffee table to a pile on a buffet against the far wall and straightened up the cushions on the sofa. With nothing else left to do, she curled up on the sofa and waited quietly for Ben to arrive, taking in the small details of the room, her fate and her future pressing in on her from all sides.

***

The drive downtown took almost an hour. Ben left his car in valet and pushed through the revolving doors at the entrance to the building. Having been alerted to Ben's pending arrival, the security guard sent him upstairs with barely a cursory glance.

Ben took the elevator up to the 22nd floor and found Megan's unit at the end of the corridor on the right-hand side. She opened the door before he even had a chance to knock, the security guard downstairs having called a moment before.

"Hi, come on in," she said in a soft voice.

Megan led him from a smallish entryway into a good-sized living room. Ben had never been here before, though he wasn't terribly surprised at what he saw in his first look around. The room was light and airy, very feminine looking, a sole table lamp illuminating the entire room. The carpeting was off-white, as were the walls, and a large, formal Chippendale coffee table stood in the middle of the room flanked by a pale yellow overstuffed sofa and matching wing chairs in a soft chenille fabric. A glass vase with a dried flower arrangement sat on the coffee table, and Ben noticed a

80

similar one on a buffet table against the wall. Inoffensive modern art, mostly geometric shapes in pastel colors, dotted the walls. Although tastefully decorated, the room felt sterile and almost non-lived in. Ben noticed that he could still see the marks the vacuum cleaner had left on the carpeting. He thought he could smell lemon furniture polish.

"Can I take your coat?" Meg asked.

"Sure. Why don't you just leave it on the chair? We'll be going in a little while."

She took the coat from him and rather than drape it over the chair, hung it up in the hall closet. Everything has its place, Ben thought. He walked into the room and sat down in one of the wing chairs. Meg stopped in front of the sofa and said, "What do you think of my arrest outfit?" holding her arms out and posing before taking a seat across from him.

Ben eyed her carefully. He decided to play along. "Very nice," he replied. "Sweaters are always good. Perhaps you can come out with your own line. I don't know, maybe add some stripes?"

She laughed a little. "Thanks a lot."

"I'm always here to help."

They sat there awkwardly for a few moments, Meg sitting very still, leaning slightly forward, her feet together and her hands folded in her lap.

"So," she said with a slight smile and a shrug of her shoulders.

Ben fidgeted in his seat and surveyed the room. "This seems very nice," he said finally. He had never been to Megan's condo before.

"Thanks. What am I thinking?" she said, "Would you like anything to drink?"

"Water would be fine, thanks."

"I'll go get some for you. I'll be back in a second," she said rising to her feet.

Ben got up too. "I'll go with."

He followed her through a doorway at the back end of the room and into a formal dining room. Next to the dining room and behind the living room was the kitchen. Meg turned on a light as she led him into the kitchen and took a glass from the middle shelf of one of the cupboards over the sink. The room was also light and airy, even at night. Beyond the kitchen and separated by a half-wall was a nicely-sized eating area. The dining room, kitchen and eating area all afforded spectacular views of Lake Michigan between the buildings to the east.

Ben walked through the kitchen and into the eating area and stood before a large window facing the lake. Light from the kitchen struck him and cast his profile in shadow on the wall to his right. He gazed down at the dark water below, the lights of the City appearing as sparkles on the water lapping against the shore wall. "This is quite a view," he said, without looking back, as she entered the room behind him. "I'll bet it's really something in the morning when the sun's out."

"It is, even too bright sometimes, but I like it."

He turned and she handed him a glass filled with ice water. "Thanks," he said taking it. An awkward silence fell between them, and Ben turned and took another long look out at the lake. "Well," he said finally, "why don't we go back into the living room. We have a couple of things to talk about."

She nodded and he followed her out another door, past a long corridor and back toward the living room. "I take it the bedrooms and stuff are down that way?" Ben said with a gesture of his head.

She stopped. "Yes," she said coming back to him and pointing down the hallway. "The master bedroom is down at the end of the hall on the left with a master bath. Next to that, in this direction, is A.J.'s room. There's a bathroom across the hall from his room and a small family room and another bedroom down at the end of the hall on the right. I use that as a home office."

"Sounds real nice," Ben said.

"It's really very comfortable. It's not a huge amount of space, but we have a lot of room at the other house, so we don't need as much space here."

Ben nodded and said nothing. He led them back into the living room. The place looked like its owner was about to embark on a long sabbatical across the European continent. All it lacked were suitcases sitting by the door. Ben felt a sinking feeling in his stomach. He hoped that Megan's time away from this place would be short and not extend from days, to weeks, to months or longer.

They resumed their seats in the living room and Ben found that words which often came so easily floated out of reach. He could not summon the necessary detachment to describe the events that lay before them in the clinical fashion they required. His personal relationship with her, forged long ago in the fires of common experience, rendered this impossible. But he was more than simply her friend now, he was her lawyer; he was the man entrusted to do his best to protect her, protect her from the grinding, endless wheels of justice, protect her from those who did not believe in her, and ultimately to protect her from herself if need be. He leaned forward, his elbows on his knees and looked down at the carpeting to compose his thoughts. Although their relationship had now changed, he nonetheless had to be himself. Looking up into her eyes, he said, "So, I take it you've been sitting here alone in the semi-darkness stewing about this?"

She held her hands out at her side, palms up, as though to say, "And what else could I do?"

"Well," he said, "I can't blame you, but this isn't the beginning of the end. This is just the beginning of our fight. It's just an unfortunate step we have to go through right now."

"I know," she said without convincing him.

She seemed disheartened, dispirited. He understood it and didn't like it. "Look, did you kill him?" He didn't know where that came from. He hadn't intended to ask her that. It just sort of came out. Defense lawyers didn't do that because the answer didn't matter.

"No," she answered without hesitation.

"No," he repeated, feeling like a weight had been removed from him. "Of course you didn't. And we will fight, and fight, and keep on fighting until everyone understands that, especially until a jury of your peers understands that, if we have to."

"What about my reputation?"

"Don't worry about your reputation. We'll start with the jury, and then we'll worry about your reputation after the jury's convinced. Look, everyone who knows you, who understands you as I do, will realize and understand that you could never do such a thing. Everybody else, people you don't know, people you don't care about, you can't worry about what they think. You can't prevent them from thinking whatever they want to think, so why worry about it? Trust me. If you listen to me, do what I say and trust me, we will beat this thing." He said the words slowly and firmly. He was beginning to feel a little better.

"I believe in you," she said, "really I do. But you have to believe in me too. You have to understand, really understand, that I didn't do this."

"I do. I do understand that. But right now, we have to talk about what's going to happen in the next twelve to eighteen hours."

Ben spent the next few minutes explaining what was going to happen next. All the while, she sat quietly, occasionally nodding as he explained something to her. She asked no questions.

"We're going to be ready to hit the ground running," Ben said. "Just look at tonight and tomorrow as the first step toward clearing your name."

"Clearing my name," she said with a laugh. "It's funny, nobody knows my name. Nobody knows I'm being charged yet, and now I'm worried about clearing my name. Soon, it'll be like *Cheers*, where everybody knows my name."

Ben knew it wasn't funny at all. "Don't worry," he said, "we'll get it done. Now, I take it you and Joe made arrangements for A.J. okay?"

"Yes. Joe's been really good about that. They left an hour and a half or so before you got here. We talked for a long time about what to tell A.J. and we finally figured the best thing to do was just tell him the truth. We told him that I was being wrongfully accused of doing something I didn't do, but that we hoped to have it sorted out and behind us as soon as we can. He seemed scared, but I think we convinced him that everything would be okay. I just worry about what's going to happen at school. I hate to think about that. Between that and the TV coverage ..." Her voice trailed off.

"I can't imagine," Ben whispered. He paused and then forced a smile. "Let's just assume that A.J. won't have to be without his mother for long. That's our goal."

The phone rang, startling both of them. They looked at each other for a second before Megan started to get up.

Ben held up his hand. "I'll get it." She sat back down and Ben walked over and grabbed a portable phone off the side table. He fumbled with it for a second and it continued to ring before he found the button to answer the call. "Hello," he said.

The security guard was on the other end of the line. "Oh, I was looking for Mrs. Cavallaro."

"I'll take a message for her."

"Oh, right. There's a Scott Nelson and a couple of other guys down here to see her."

"Okay," Ben said, "tell them we'll be right down." He hung up, turned and said, "They're here." She had already gotten up and was heading toward the closet to get their coats.

A couple of minutes later, they were on the elevator heading downstairs. Ben put his arm on her shoulder and leaned in close to her. "One thing I want you to remember and never forget is that you will not talk about this to anyone. I don't care who they are or how friendly and supportive they seem. You will not talk about this to anyone. The only people you talk to about this are your lawyers. Not Joe, certainly not A.J., not anyone but your lawyers. You cannot trust anyone but us. Unless Fran files an appearance, you don't talk to Fran either. Same with Bowden. You have to assume that the prosecution is going to try anything to convict you. We can't help them out. Do you understand?"

"Yes sir," she said and gave a mock salute.

"Good. Things are the way they are, but we are looking out for you. We're not going to let this get to you. And another thing, no matter what, we will always act like nothing bothers us. That includes you. Especially you. You have to assume that from this moment forward, you are on public display at all times, and you want to put your best face forward whenever someone may be watching. Okay?"

"Okay," she said.

"And when you talk to Joe, make sure he understands that no one talks to the media except me. I'll tell him too. If we think it's a good idea, then we'll suggest something else, but we don't want anybody saying anything that may hurt the case."

The bell sounded and the elevator slowed to a halt on the first floor. As the doors opened, he leaned over and whispered in her ear, "You can do this. Knock 'em dead." She gave him a curious look and he shrugged. "So to speak," he said with a slight grin and a twinkle in his eye.

"Thanks a lot," she said smacking him on the back. They turned the corner and entered the lobby as though on a Sunday stroll. The tension had momentarily eased. At the security desk stood Detectives Nelson and Cole and a third man Ben didn't recognize. None of them were wearing uniforms. Nelson stepped forward and shook hands with Ben. Detective Cole did likewise.

"Ms. Rand?" Nelson said with a nod. She nodded back. "Why don't we step outside?" Nelson said. The five of them pushed through the revolving doors.

They gathered under the canopy and a valet approached. "Would you like me to pull up your car, Mrs. Cavallaro?" he said to Megan.

"No thanks," Ben responded, handing the man his ticket, "but you can get mine." The young man took off around the corner toward the parking area leaving the five of them alone under the canopy.

Two unmarked cars stood in the small circle driveway at the front of the building. Both cars were running, and a driver sat in the first one. "We'll take Ms. Rand in the first car. The second car will follow, and you can follow that car. We'll wait for them to pull your car up," Nelson said to Ben. "We're going to the stationhouse over on North Avenue, just past LaSalle."

"I know where it is," Ben said.

"You can park on the side. You shouldn't have any trouble there." Detective Cole pulled a set of handcuffs from his coat pocket. Nelson waved him off. "I don't think we'll be needing those right now, John." Somewhat surprised, Cole returned the handcuffs to his pocket. Nelson read Meg her Miranda rights and she said she understood them just as the valet emerged from around the other side of the building with Ben's car. Nelson nodded and led Meg to the first sedan.

Cole opened the door and Meg got in one side, while Nelson walked around to the driver's side and got in the other. Cole climbed into the front seat. The third man got into the front seat of the second car, and Ben took three dollars from his pocket and handed it to the valet before climbing behind the wheel of his SUV.

It was only a short five minute drive from Megan's townhouse to the police station. Ben parked on the west side of the building in a small parking lot and walked inside. Megan was standing inside the front door with Detectives Nelson and Cole and two uniformed officers. When Ben arrived, Nelson led her through a set of metal doors and down a long corridor toward a processing room near the back of the building.

The whole thing took about an hour. Megan was searched, fingerprinted and photographed. Her belongings were inventoried and she was forced to change out of her clothing and into an orange prison jumpsuit and dingy tennis shoes without laces. When they were done, Nelson brought her out to a small corridor where Ben waited.

"Can I have a couple of minutes alone with her?" Ben asked.

"Sure," Nelson said, "why don't you go in here. Just knock on the door when you're done."

They went into a small conference room with a square table and four metal chairs. They didn't sit down. Ben faced her and put his hands on her shoulders. "You're doing a great job," he said. "I'm very proud of you."

She laughed a mirthless laugh. "Proud of me the way I'm handling my first arrest? I can hear it now. 'Gee Mom, you should have been there when I had my fingerprints taken. You would have been proud of me.'"

"Okay, okay," Ben said. "If you're going to do something, you may as well do it right." He smiled and shook a finger at her. "And don't talk to anyone. Even here. You never know who may be listening." She nodded. "You can do this. I know you can," Ben said. "I'll see you in the morning for Court."

"Can you call Joe later and check on A.J. for me?" she asked.

"Of course. I was going to call him and let him know how things were going anyway. Don't worry about that. We'll take care of everything out here and hopefully by this time tomorrow, you'll be back at home sitting in your freshly vacuumed house with the lights out."

She shrugged. "About the only thing worse than getting arrested, I figured, was getting arrested and coming home to a messy house."

"Well, if it's any consolation to you," Ben said, "you've probably got the neatest house of anybody who got arrested tonight." As he said this, he put his arms around her and held her long enough so she would know he really meant it. "All right. Now take care of yourself. Don't talk to anybody and I'll see you in the morning," he whispered in her ear.

Ben knocked on the door, it opened and they stepped out into the hallway. Detective Nelson took Meg by the arm and began to lead her down the hallway toward the back of the building. As he did so, Megan grabbed Ben's hand and gave it a short squeeze. He nodded and said, "Take care of yourself," again and turned and headed in the opposite direction toward the front of the building. As Ben emerged from inside, he stood on the front steps and looked at his watch - eight-thirty. A cold gust of wind blew open the front of his coat, and he grabbed it and buttoned it, pulling his gloves from his pockets and putting them on. He looked around. No reporters. True to his word, Nelson had kept a lid on the news. Ben walked around the side of the building to the parking lot, clicked open the locks with his keyless remote and climbed inside. He took his cell phone from its belt clip and punched in Joseph Cavallaro's home phone number.

About an hour later, just as Benjamin Lohmeier pulled into his driveway, a news brief came on Channel 7, the local ABC affiliate in Chicago. "An arrest is made in the Law School Murder case. Details at ten," the talking head said.

***

The Protector sat in a small room paying bills, the TV serving as little more than background noise when the news brief came on.

It was over before the Protector could locate the remote and turn up the sound. The Protector quickly searched through the other channels looking for more local news, but couldn't find the story anywhere. I'll just have to wait until ten, the Protector thought.

The Protector was ready when the ten o'clock news began on Channel 7.

"Our top story tonight," the anchor began, "an arrest has been made in the New Years Eve murder of Professor Daniel Greenfield in his office at the Chicago College of Law. We go now to Channel 7 reporter, Randy Shaw at District 4 headquarters. Randy?"

The Protector sat upright, head cocked toward the television, the aroma of tonight's dinner still filling the air.

"Thank you, Ron. At about eight o'clock this evening, Chicago Police Department detectives arrested one Megan Rand Cavallaro, age 39, of 1200 North Dearborn in Chicago on charges of first degree murder in the death of Professor Daniel Greenfield of the Chicago College of Law. Ms. Cavallaro surrendered into police custody at that time and was taken here for processing.

"It is believed that she has already been transported to the main lockup at the Cook County Jail, where she will await a bond hearing at nine o'clock tomorrow morning. According to police sources, Mrs. Cavallaro, the wife of prominent Chicago personal injury lawyer, Joseph Cavallaro, is a former student of Professor Greenfield's at the law school, graduating in 1992. Police sources confirm that Mrs. Cavallaro has been tied to the crime scene through physical and other evidence. Authorities have still not confirmed how Daniel Greenfield died.

"The accused's husband, Joseph Cavallaro, has been unavailable for comment. A spokesman for Cook County State's Attorney, Richard McBride, told Channel 7 News just a few minutes ago that more details about this case will be available tomorrow morning after Mrs. Cavallaro's appearance in Bond Court. Back to you, Ron."

The Protector surfed the other channels, but could find no additional information. "Megan Rand Cavallaro," the Protector said aloud. "I wonder."

Meanwhile, Benjamin and Libby Lohmeier watched the same news report from the couch of their family room. Ben sat silent and still, his eyes fixated on the TV screen, a piece of cold pizza in one hand and a bottle of Rolling Rock in the other, as Randy Shaw gave his report. As the anchor began the next news story, Libby grabbed the remote, clicked the pause button on the Tivo and turned to her husband, who was still staring silently at the stilled screen. "So," she said, "when is the phone going to start ringing?"

He took a bite of the pizza and washed it down with a sip of the beer. "Soon," he said. "You'd better get used to not answering it."

15

The Cook County Criminal Courts building is an imposing dirty-white stone structure that is the kind of place where people go never to return again. Neither architecturally significant nor aesthetically pleasing, the Criminal Courthouse looks like exactly what it is - a brutish factory of waste and despair, churning out inmates every year by the thousands. Connected to its rear is the sprawling campus surrounded by circular rings of barbed wire that is the Cook County Jail. The jail complex contains more than ten different buildings, a couple of which were designed specifically to house female inmates. A separate building even provides maternity care for female prisoners in need of it. Ben tried not to think about Meg spending the night in one of the cells behind those walls.

Although Ben didn't necessarily realize it at the time, the dirt and grime that clogged the wheels of justice in Cook County infected all of those who worked there as well. No matter how hard you washed or scrubbed, you took a bit of the grime of the Cook County Criminal Court system with you when you left this place.

Ben and Mark made it through the metal detectors unscathed and found Megan's name and case number on a bulletin board outside Room 101.

"We're pretty far down the call," Mark said. "Why don't we go and check in? Sometimes they take the cases out of order if you check in early enough."

They pushed through the doors and into the large courtroom. On the near side of a wall of bulletproof glass, members of the media jostled for spots in the front row of the visitor's section. Across the way, at the table reserved for prosecutors, stood Bridget Fahey. Even with her back to them, Ben would know Bridget Fahey anywhere. Mark let out a low whistle. "Wow," he said under his breath. "They're bringing out the big guns for this one. This has to be for our case." Ben nodded in agreement.

Tall, slim and attractive, Bridget Fahey wore her reddish-blond hair straight and parted on the right, much like her current politics. She turned to grab something from her briefcase and they got a better look at her. Her dark gray suit looked professionally tailored, and her black heels freshly shined. Her pale blue eyes were covered in fashionable frameless lenses, probably just props, Ben thought, to make her look more intelligent.

"You know her, don't you?" Mark said under his breath.

"Yeah," Ben said, "we used to work together."

For a time, Ben and Bridget Fahey were fellow Assistant State's Attorneys assigned to Judge Patrick Maloney's courtroom. Bridget was the senior assistant in the courtroom at that time and, therefore, received most of the best assignments, leaving few plums for the less experienced prosecutors like Ben. Nevertheless, Ben got a few good cases now and then and managed to catch the attention of his wing supervisor. During the year or so they shared the courtroom, Ben and Bridget got to know each other fairly well. They handled a number of cases together, including some fairly significant prosecutions. Ben's skills in the courtroom earned Bridget's respect in those days, and Ben had to admit that she was a fine trial lawyer herself.

When he saw her, Ben realized that he should have expected that this case could draw Bridget Fahey back into the courtroom. Ben turned to Mark and slowly shook his head. "Don't bother checking in. With her here, you can rest assured that we'll be first on the call. Come on, I'd better go pay my respects."

Ben led Mark through the door and down the center aisle. They walked over to the counsel table, where Fahey was looking through a file, and Ben said in a loud theatrical voice just as they arrived, "Why, if it isn't the Honorable Bridget Fahey. Good to see you slumming this morning."

"Counselor," she replied looking up, "it's been a long time. Have you gained weight?" She gave him a thin smile and extended her hand, which Ben shook. Never one to be intimidated, she squeezed Ben's hand more firmly than necessary. Her hand felt cool and dry.

"No, just wisdom," he said. "Bridget, I'd like to introduce you to my colleague, Mark Schaefer." He gestured to Mark, who was now standing beside him. "Mark, this is Bridget Fahey, the First Assistant State's Attorney of Cook County."

"Nice to meet you," Mark said.

"Likewise."

They shook hands. Ben continued. "Mark's going to be helping me with this case. So, I can assume from your presence that this case is not quite big enough to draw Mr. McBride himself?"

She gave Ben a chilly glare. "Not at this point. Nelson told me you were handling this case. I guess that explains how you managed to surrender your client in the dark of night with absolute secrecy."

Ben feigned a look of amazement. "Why, I don't know what you mean? We brought her in as soon as we could. But look," he said getting serious, "she's got a little kid at home. I don't think it benefits anybody to have a little kid see his Mom dragged off in handcuffs."

Fahey considered this for a moment. "Perhaps not," she said finally. After another moment, she said, "I take it you'll be seeking bail for your client?"

"Of course," Ben said. "Toward that end, I have a copy of my appearance, motion and brief in support of bail." He handed a small stack of documents to her. "I also have a copy of all the cases we cited in our brief, if you'd like those."

"Please," she said taking the pleadings from him.

He handed her a three-inch stack of cases held together by a rubber band. "What's your position on bail?" he asked.

"We're opposed to it. Here, I've also written a brief on the subject." Hers was considerably thicker than his, Ben realized when he took it from her.

"Just slapped this thing together at the last minute, did you?" Ben asked.

"Something like that."

"So that's your position, no bail under any circumstances?"

"Unless the judge tells us otherwise."

"He will," Ben said.

"We'll see, Counselor. You haven't been here in a while."

"No, but I walk with God now. Are we going first?" he asked.

"What do you think?" she replied.

"Good," he said touching her lightly on the forearm. "Well, it's good to see you again. I'm sure this will be interesting."

She gave him that same cool smile. "I'm sure it will be."

Ben and Mark walked over and set their briefcases down on the opposite counsel table. "That was a little mating ritual of sorts," Ben said.

"You know her pretty well then?"

Ben looked at Mark and grinned.

The courtroom slowly filled as the time approached nine o'clock. Ben reviewed the brief prepared by the prosecutors, made thick by the attachment of excerpts from several of their key cases as exhibits. Pretty routine, off-the-shelf stuff, Ben thought as he finished and handed the brief to Mark without saying anything. "This really isn't anything special," Mark whispered in his ear a few minutes later. "Ours is better." Ben nodded.

At precisely nine o'clock, the clerk stepped out of the courtroom through a door behind the bench. Two minutes later, he returned and cleared his throat, which was a signal to all that he was about to speak. "All rise," he said, "the Circuit Court of Cook County is now in session, the Honorable Michael P. Quinn presiding. Please be seated and come to order."

A burly man in his early-sixties, with a ruddy face and a silver comb-over swept into the courtroom and up the steps to his seat behind the bench. "Good morning ladies and gentlemen," he said in a cheerful voice, scanning the courtroom and noticing that it was extra crowded this morning due to the presence of reporters and interested spectators. "Why don't we get started."

94

The clerk called the first case, "People v. Megan Rand Cavallaro."

The door at the left side of the courtroom opened and a sheriff's deputy emerged and escorted Megan into the courtroom. Megan looked awkward and uncomfortable in the orange jumpsuit. Her hair barely looked combed. As she entered, she glanced to her right at the gallery. Ben instinctively followed her eyes and noticed for the first time that Joseph Cavallaro sat in the first row. Clad in a dark blue suit, his gold cufflinks gleaming in the light, Cavallaro fixed his eyes on his wife.

Bridget Fahey stepped around the counsel table and strolled up to the bench as though she owned it. "Good morning, your Honor," she said without waiting for the others to join her. "Bridget Fahey, First Assistant State's Attorney, on behalf of the People."

Ben lagged behind for a moment until Megan could cross the courtroom and join him. He took her by the arm and led her up to the bench, gesturing for her to stand between himself and Mark. "Good morning, your Honor," he said in a calm voice when he reached the bench. "Benjamin Lohmeier and Mark Schaefer on behalf of Megan Rand Cavallaro."

"Good morning, Counselors," Judge Quinn said looking down on them with a slight smile. After a couple of minutes of preliminaries, Judge Quinn turned to Ben and said, "I take it you want to be heard on the question of bail, Counsel?"

"Yes, we do, your Honor," Ben replied. "Toward that end, we've prepared a motion and brief in support of our position." Ben handed his pleadings up to Judge Quinn, who took them with a raised eyebrow. "I've also attached copies of the relevant cases, your Honor."

The Judge looked immediately to his right at the prosecutor. "The People have prepared a brief as well, your Honor," Fahey said handing a copy up to the bench. The Court took the prosecution's filings and added them to the stack he'd gotten from the defense and evened out the stack with both hands.

"In light of this," he said, "I'm going to adjourn to my chambers for a few moments to review these and see what you have for me. Please remain seated." Judge Quinn rose and left the bench, exiting the courtroom from whence he came moments before.

As the Judge disappeared from view, Ben leaned over and asked Meg, "How you holding up?"

"Not so bad," she said with a shrug. "They had me in the maternity ward last night. I don't think I've seen the worst of the system yet."

"Probably not," Ben replied. A bailiff approached to take Megan back to the holding area. "It will just be a few minutes," Ben said.

Ben looked over at Bridget Fahey sitting at the counsel table. He couldn't help but notice that the other prosecutors in the courtroom kept their distance and did not appear at all interested in interacting with her in any way. She pretended not to notice. Instead, she took out the defense brief and began taking notes on a yellow pad.

Ten minutes later, the door behind the bench opened and Judge Quinn returned, the bailiff crying out, "Please remain seated," as the Judge ascended the steps to his seat.

"Counsel," he said looking down at Ben, Mark and Bridget Fahey, who had stood, calling them forward to the bench with a wave of his hand. A moment later, Megan joined them from the room on the left.

"Okay," Judge Quinn said when everyone was standing before him, "Mr. Lohmeier, you're the one seeking bond in this case, tell me why I should grant it."

Ben spent several minutes summarizing the arguments contained in his brief, focusing on her standing in the community and the fact that she was a mother of a young son. Judge Quinn listened intently.

When Ben was finished, Judge Quinn nodded and turned to his right. "Ms. Fahey?" he said.

"Your Honor, the People could not disagree more. In particular, we believe that the Defendant presents a serious flight risk. Not only does she have substantial resources, her husband is a prominent personal injury attorney, but it has also come to our attention that the Defendant and her husband own a residence in the Cayman Islands." Ben did not know this. Fahey continued for several more minutes succinctly summarizing the points made in her brief. Nothing too spectacular, Ben thought, yet she covered all the necessary points and provided Quinn with a basis for denying bail should he so choose.

Judge Quinn asked several questions and appeared genuinely undecided about which way to go. He sat quietly for a moment and stroked his chin. Then he said, "I'd really like to hear more about the issues regarding the Defendant's child. Obviously, because he is a minor, we have privacy issues, so why don't the lawyers and I adjourn to my chambers and take a few minutes to discuss these issues. Follow me folks." With that, he rose and led them out through the door behind the bench, and down to his chambers at the end of the corridor. They followed him through a small outer office where a woman sat working. She never even looked up when they passed.

Judge Quinn's chambers was a large, rectangular-shaped room, cluttered with files and dominated by a large mahogany desk somewhat the worse for wear. The Judge plopped himself down in his leather chair, still wearing his robe. The credenza and the wall behind him were dotted with photographs, honorary degrees and other memorabilia of a career spent in the law. Ben and Bridget Fahey each took one of the chairs in front of the desk, while Mark sat on the couch against the inside wall. The court reporter followed them in and took a seat on the couch next to Mark. The outside wall of Judge Quinn's chambers consisted of a series of large picture windows providing him with a panoramic view of downtown Chicago off in the distance.

As the court reporter began to get set-up, Judge Quinn waved her off. "That's okay," he said, "we're not going to need you to take any of this down." Somewhat puzzled, she stopped what she was doing. Then the Judge turned his attention to the lawyers. "Look, I didn't bring you in here to discuss the issues regarding the child. I want to know where we're going with this. Miss Fahey, I find Counsel's arguments here on bail to be pretty convincing. I'm familiar with these cases. I don't think you've shown me enough to cause me to lock up a mother of a young child with no previous criminal record for six months to a year until trial. That just doesn't seem reasonable. On the other hand, I know this is a big case and you have to take the position that bail is unjustified."

"But your Honor," Fahey started to say before the Judge cut her off with another wave of his hand.

"I know. I know," the Judge said interrupting. "I can sympathize with your position." He turned to Ben. "Mr. Lohmeier, although I do find your position meritorious, the State does have a point with respect to flight risk. Your client appears to have ample resources and the means to leave the jurisdiction and not come back. So, I think you need to give her something."

As Ben expected when the Judge called them into his chambers, Judge Quinn was seeking to broker a deal that would satisfy everyone and not make it appear that one side won and another lost. This was consistent with his reputation. He had never been known as a rigid authoritarian figure. Rather, he had the reputation among lawyers as a highly pragmatic judge, who preferred to avoid technicalities and let lawyers cut to the chase and try their cases on the merits. "Mr. Lohmeier, I take it your client would be willing to surrender her passport?" Judge Quinn asked.

"Of course, Your Honor. Mrs. Cavallaro isn't going anywhere. She looks forward to clearing her name, and the only way to do that is in a courtroom in this building."

"Very well," the Judge said, "she surrenders her passport. What else do we need here?"

"Might I suggest home confinement?" Bridget Fahey said. The Judge raised his eyebrows and turned to Ben.

"Frankly Judge, I think home confinement is a little extreme. There is no significant evidence of flight here. She has a child in school and significant ties to the community. I'm just not sure that's warranted."

"Perhaps not from your point of view," the Judge said, "but it doesn't appear to be terribly unreasonable either. Can you live with home confinement, Ms. Fahey?"

"If we must, your Honor."

"Okay then," the Judge said, "home confinement it is. Counsel," he said holding off Ben with a shake of his head, "home confinement isn't that bad. She'll still have some freedom to come and go if she can make a case for it and you clear it ahead of time. This will allow her to be with her son after school, things like that. That seems fair. Now we're left with the amount of bond. Ms. Fahey, what do you think?"

"The People would suggest ten million dollars, your Honor."

The Judge whistled. "I'm assuming you mean ten million dollars bail which means one million dollars in bond, correct?" Fahey nodded. "I take it you believe the Defendant and her husband have those kinds of resources?"

"We do, Your Honor."

"I can't wait to hear your reaction, Counsel."

"Well my reaction ought to be obvious, Judge. Ten million dollars is excessive in light of the fact that you're talking about home confinement. I mean, what are the odds that she's going to go anywhere now? You essentially have a tracking device on her. That should lower the amount of bail required substantially. I wouldn't think you'd need bail in excess of five hundred thousand dollars given the fact that you're talking about home confinement."

The Judge shrugged. "That means fifty thousand dollars bond, which isn't very much, even when you consider home confinement. But, Ms. Fahey, he does have a point." He considered it for a moment, then nodded. His decision was made. "Let's make bail at an even one million dollars, which means a bond of one hundred thousand dollars. Okay. That's enough. Why don't we go back in and put it on the record."

16

It took over two hours to effectuate Meg's release. Following much haggling and a great deal of pressure from her husband, Meg agreed to move back into the brownstone on Astor Street and stay there pending the outcome of this ordeal. After completing the paperwork in the clerk's office, Ben, Mark and Joe Cavallaro were ushered into a small room, where they were joined by Detective Nelson, a uniformed officer and eventually by Meg herself.

"You look like you survived okay," Ben said when he saw her.

She shrugged and seemed more interested in seeing Ben than her own husband, who made an excessive production out of being reunited with his wife.

As they were getting ready to leave, Nelson took Ben aside and said, "You might want to have somebody pull up her car. There are a lot of media types out there and it's a long way between the entrance and the parking garage."

Ben looked slightly puzzled. "What do you mean? There weren't that many media people in the courtroom, maybe ten or twelve," he said.

"Well, there are a lot more of them now," Nelson said. "Once they found out who was arrested, the story has taken on a new life."

They all looked at each other for a minute. Finally, Cavallaro spoke up. "I guess I've got to get the car. She's driving with me after all."

"You do that," Nelson said. "We'll let you pull up out front." He looked around. "You're going to have a hard time getting through all the reporters without making some sort of a statement."

Meg looked horrified. "I don't want to say anything."

"You're not going to say anything," Ben said. "I'll make a brief statement, proclaim your innocence, and we'll get you to the car."

"I'll be out there with a handful of uniforms to make sure nothing crazy happens," Nelson said.

"Thanks," Ben replied.

"I'll pull my car up behind Mr. Cavallaro's," Nelson continued. "We'll be following you over to your house so we can hook up all the monitoring equipment. It shouldn't take too long. Once we're there, I'll be able to give you a brief rundown on how things work. It's not that bad really."

Nelson led them through a series of corridors, up one set of stairs and down another, until they came out a side entrance to the building. Nelson looked back when he reached the doorway. "Once I open the door, you'll probably be able to hear the commotion out there. Are we ready? Okay, c'mon, follow me."

Nelson went first, followed by a uniformed police officer, Ben, Megan, Mark and then two sheriff's deputies. They went down along the side of the building and turned left and came out on the front steps. An army of reporters greeted them at the bottom of the steps near the street. Megan saw them before they saw her and whispered, "Oh my God," under her breath.

Ben, too, was slightly taken aback by the size of the throng and stopped, taking Meg by the arm and leading her out in the direction of the reporters. A couple of reporters saw them and cried out and the horde turned and rushed toward them. Nelson stopped and let them gather around, but did not allow them to get too close. Additional officers joined them in an effort to keep the crowd at bay. Cavallaro, who had parked his black Mercedes on the street at the bottom of the steps, circled around the reporters and pushed through the perimeter of uniformed officers to emerge at his wife's side. Ben stood on the other side of Meg, flanked by Mark. Nelson stood off to one side eyeing the crowd.

As camera lights half-blinded him and microphones wagged in his face, Ben realized that his mouth was dry. He worried for a second that if he tried to speak, no words would come. Reporters started throwing questions at them from all directions, most of which Ben couldn't understand in the jumble of competing voices. He held up both hands in an effort to quiet the crowd, the noise barely subsiding. An odd thought flashed through his mind - why didn't I comb my hair before we came out here?

"Good morning," he said in a tentative voice. The crowd grew quieter and pushed toward him. "As I said to some of you earlier, my name is Benjamin Lohmeier. I'm with the office of Schulte & Luckenbill in Ithaca. To my left is my colleague, Mark Schaefer." Several reporters shouted out questions toward Meg. Ben put up his hands again and said, "Hold on a minute. I'm sorry, but my client will not make any comment here this morning. I can tell you this, however," he said glancing to his right and noticing Joseph Cavallaro's expression, "Mrs. Cavallaro has the full support of her family and friends as she embarks on this ordeal. As you can see, her husband, Joseph Cavallaro, is here providing his full support."

Ben's voice grew more confident. "These charges are very serious, and we will approach them very seriously. Rest assured, Mrs. Cavallaro looks forward to her day in Court, for she knows that when a thorough and complete examination of all the evidence occurs, there will be no doubt whatsoever in anyone's mind that she is innocent of the murder of Daniel Greenfield. That's really all I have to say right now. Obviously, we'll know a lot more when we see what evidence the prosecution thinks they have."

He turned and took Meg's arm and a voice called out, "What's your reaction to the bail situation?"

"Bail?" he said, "I can only say that Judge Quinn is one of the most highly-respected judges in this division. Making decisions on the amount and the availability of bail is one of the most difficult decisions any judge has to make. While we believe that home confinement is not necessary under these circumstances, we respect the Court's decision and firmly believe that he did what he thought was right. We certainly accept that. Thank you very much folks."

With that, Ben raised his arm in almost a wave of goodbye and ended the short press conference.

Nelson and his men pushed through the reporters, who parted only grudgingly, and made their way down the steps to Cavallaro's car. Cavallaro went around to the driver's side and Ben held the door open for Meg to get in on the passenger's side. Before he shut the door behind her, he leaned in and said, "You did a great job. We'll see you back at the house in a few minutes." She nodded and smiled, every moment of the scene captured by cameras.

17

Later that afternoon, after getting Meg settled in at the brownstone, Ben rounded the corner and looked for Professor Samuel Dorlund's office. Finding it, he knocked on the door, which was slightly ajar. He pushed the door open only to discover that no one was inside. "Damn," he said aloud. Closing the door, he started to turn and go back toward the elevators when Professor Dorlund himself turned the corner and walked toward him. Seeing Ben standing at his office door, Dorlund said, "Hi, can I help you with something?"

"Yes, I hope so," Ben said. Dorlund walked by him and opened the door and entered his office and began putting his class materials on his desk as Ben followed him inside. "My name is Benjamin Lohmeier. I represent Megan Rand ..."

Dorlund turned at the sound of her name and gave Ben an angry look. "I know who she is," he said. "She's the one who murdered Daniel. I don't have anything to say to you."

"She didn't kill anyone," Ben said, "but obviously, I'd like to find out who did."

"I'm sure you would," Dorlund said. "Now if you'll excuse me."

"No," Ben said, "I'm not going to excuse you."

"I beg your pardon?" Dorlund said.

"Professor," Ben said holding up his hand, "just hold on a minute. I've known Megan Rand a long time. We were in the same section together at this law school. I also knew Professor

Greenfield. And most importantly, I know that Megan Rand did not kill Daniel Greenfield."

"Is that what you think?"

"That's what I know. Now, I also know that you and Daniel Greenfield have been close friends for a very, very long time, and I'm sure that you would very much like to see the person who did this caught and punished. One way to do that is by talking to me."

The two men stared at each other for several seconds before Dorlund realized that Ben would not take no for an answer. He relented. "Okay," he said, "Mr. Lohmeier is it? Sit down. I have a few minutes for you. What do you need to know?"

"Thank you," Ben said taking off his overcoat and placing it on a chair next to his briefcase. He sat down in another chair. Dorlund's office was cluttered and disorganized, books and papers everywhere. "I don't want to take up a lot of your time, Professor. I'm sure we're going to have a lot of opportunities to speak in the future. The first thing I'd like to know now though is who should I be talking to about Professor Greenfield? Who are the people on the faculty and staff of this place who could tell me about him, tell me about what was going on with him, what he was working on, that kind of thing."

Dorlund was a short, round man with a soft body that had long since gone to seed. He had dark curly hair that never quite seemed combed or washed, bushy eyebrows covering slightly bulging eyes, a large, flat nose and thick puffy lips that would make a catfish proud. He always seemed kind of sweaty. Amazingly, despite these physical characteristics and a less than winning personality, he still considered himself something of a ladies man, although few ladies shared this perception. He leaned back in his chair. "Dan and I have been friends for twenty years and as you can imagine, his death has hit me pretty hard. I don't think anyone is as close to him …" He hesitated. "Or was as close to him, in this law school or outside of it as I was. But if you want some other names, some of the professors who were here when you were here would probably be a good place to start. I can't think of anyone in particular."

"Okay," Ben said, "that's what I figured."

Ben spoke to Dorlund for about twenty minutes and Dorlund slowly opened up and grew a bit more cooperative. He told Ben that Greenfield and his wife had divorced about three years earlier, but that Greenfield seemed to be handling it better and better in recent months. Other than that, he knew of nothing in particular that had been troubling Greenfield recently, and suggested that Greenfield had been in a pretty decent frame of mind. Finally, Dorlund told him that Greenfield had seemed particularly excited about a new law review article he had been working on in recent weeks. The article concerned DNA testing and its use in criminal law, but Dorlund told Ben that he wasn't really familiar with any of the details.

The two men shook hands when Ben got up to leave and agreed to talk again when Dorlund had more time. Seeing that it was getting fairly late in the afternoon, Ben decided to forego a trip to Hyatt's office - he probably would be gone anyway - so he could get back on the road before traffic became too unbearable. As it turns out, it didn't matter. He'd waited too long. He didn't get back to the office until almost five and went directly out to the garage, where he found Mark working on some discovery matters.

"Hey," he said walking through the door.

"You've become quite the little celebrity in this part of the world," Mark said.

"Oh, really," Ben replied. "Isn't that just great?"

"Well, I don't know whether it's great or not, but the phone's been ringing off the hook. You've got reporters calling all over the place."

"Is Phil here?"

"I don't know, but I'm sure the secretaries are getting pissed enough."

"Okay, I'd better go upstairs and try to smooth things over."

Ben went to take his medicine. At the top of the stairs, he glanced to his right - Swift was on the phone again, but gave Ben a thumbs-up sign as he walked by.

"Hey, the celebrity is back," Dianne Reynolds said as he walked into the room. "We saw you on TV earlier."

106

Hearing that, Nancy spun around in her chair and came out of her office to join them. "Yeah," she said, "you were pretty good, not stiff or anything."

Ben shrugged. "I'll take that as a compliment, I guess," he said. "What were we on?"

"We saw it on WGN in Phil's office," Nancy said. "The story only lasted for a couple of minutes. They said who she was and that she lived downtown. Then they showed the part outside on the steps where you said that she looked forward to clearing her name, or something like that. You were good. You made a good impression."

Ben rolled his eyes. "I understand from talking to Mark downstairs that you guys have been getting a few phone calls."

Nancy growled. "A few?" she said. "The phone's been ringing non-stop."

"Well, today was the first day it was on TV. Maybe it will slow down."

"Hope so," Nancy said returning to her office.

"It hasn't been that bad," Dianne added. "It's actually kind of exciting."

"So what have you been doing?" Ben asked, "dumping them all into my voicemail?"

"Yes, but I think your voicemail box is full. A couple of people have called back in the last hour or so saying they couldn't get through, so we had to write down their messages."

"Great," Ben said. Dianne handed him two pieces of paper with the names and telephone numbers of two people he didn't know. He looked at them and went into his office. He dropped his stuff on the bench and sat down at his desk to check his e-mail. Only a couple of new messages, nothing urgent. "That's good," he said aloud.

He checked his voicemail next. The female voice intoned, "Your mailbox is full. You have nineteen new messages."

"Shit," he said.

He listened to each message - seventeen were from reporters or somebody asking for information about the case, while the other two concerned his other files.

Nancy's voice came over the intercom. "I've got Ken on the phone. He said he wants to talk to the TV star."

"Tell him to wait in line," Ben said. "Unfortunately, I probably need to talk to him. Tell you what, bullshit with him for a couple of minutes and then transfer the call to the garage. I'm heading down there right now."

"Okay," she said.

"Did you fix it?" Mark said when Ben entered the garage.

"Not really. They didn't seem too mad."

Mark laughed. "That's not the story I heard."

"My voicemail box was full. I had nineteen messages and seventeen were reporters."

"That's a lot," Mark said. "That's one of the things I think you're going to have to get used to on this case. Handling the press. That will take a lot more time than you think."

"Maybe," Ben said. "Hopefully it will level out after the first couple of days or so. I can't imagine that this case will be that big a deal for the entire time. Of course, I may be full of shit given that I've never really handled a case like this before."

"It may depend on what the evidence is. If Bridget Fahey starts alleging something really spectacular, the media could get all over this thing."

"True," Ben said. Then the phone started ringing. "That's Ken. I'll put him on speaker." Ben punched the button for the speakerphone and said, "Hey, Ken what's up?"

"Hey, Perry Mason, can I have your autograph?"

"Sure, anything for the Public Defender of DeKalb County. Of course, I charge twenty bucks a pop now that I'm famous. By next week, it'll be up to a hundred."

"Well worth it. So, I hear you're quite the TV star now. I didn't see it myself, but a bunch of people here did, and I heard all about it. It sounded pretty good."

"Yeah, I guess it went okay. I didn't drool on myself or anything. I would have preferred avoiding the home confinement, but the judge wasn't going to go for that."

"Yeah," Ken said, "sounds like he didn't want to appear on Geraldo, so he gave a little something to everybody."

108

"Pretty much," Ben said. "He basically called us into his chambers and told us what he wanted to do. I think he'd made up his mind before we ever walked into Court this morning."

"Figures. Did we learn anything new today?"

"No, not really. I didn't have much chance to talk to the prosecutor. The First Assistant, Bridget Fahey, showed up. I knew her from when I was back in the office. She's a ball-buster."

"Most of those female prosecutors are," Mark chimed in.

"True enough," Ken said, "but given that our client is a woman, they probably figured they needed to throw a woman prosecutor in there just to even their odds up with the jury."

"You're probably right," Ben agreed, "although Bridget Fahey isn't exactly the type that would automatically appeal to women. Not that she's not a good trial lawyer, but she can be a bit on the cold side. I know her pretty well, or at least I did years ago. You can't turn your back on her, that's for sure."

"Say," Ken said, "did you hear any of McBride's press conference?"

"No," Ben answered, "I'd forgotten all about it. I went over to the law school and the McBride thing pretty much slipped my mind."

"Well," Ken said, "I didn't hear it either, but I guess he put on a big dog and pony show without giving any details. You know, they can link her to the murder scene and shit like that. He promised they wouldn't try the case in the media, which means they're probably about to try the case in the media."

"I'll have to make sure I get home in time for the news tonight," Ben said. "Did you hear we got Wilson as the trial judge? We're in front of him a week from Friday."

"No," Ken said, "I hadn't heard that. He's about the best judge they've got down there in that division, so I'm not surprised he got the case. I never have appeared in front of him though. You know him, don't you? That should probably be good for us. You wouldn't think he'd recuse himself, would you?"

"No, I don't think so," Ben said.

Ben knew Judge William Wilson from his days in law school when he was a member of the Chicago College of Law Trial

Advocacy Team. Judge Wilson served as the director of the Trial Advocacy Program at the law school and personally coached many of the trial teams as they prepared for various competitions. Ben made the trial team at the law school in the fall of 1991 and spent a good two months working almost every day with Judge Wilson and some other former team members as they prepared for a competition.

"I haven't really kept in close contact with anyone from the team like I probably should have. In fact, I don't think I've seen Judge Wilson since I was a prosecutor. I appeared in front of him a few times when I was subbing for other guys in the office back then, mostly on status hearings, and he never recused himself then. You know, it's not like I'm close to him or anything. I know other people have appeared before him over the years and I don't think he ever recuses himself. Besides, he's not the kind of guy to give anybody any breaks if they don't deserve them. He is the straightest of the straight shooters. If we have any edge at all, it's in that he trained me as a trial lawyer and I know how he likes a case to be tried. That's how I like to try cases anyway. That, and because he was probably the best criminal defense lawyer of his day, you know a defendant in his courtroom is going to get a fair shake. He knows the law backwards and forwards, no doubt about it."

"What do you think about the possibility of a preliminary hearing?" Ken asked.

"I don't know, probably not," Ben said. "I honestly can't imagine that McBride and Fahey are going to let us go to a preliminary hearing. Don't you think they would seek an indictment first?"

Under Illinois law, a defendant could request a preliminary hearing, sometimes called a probable cause hearing. The standard of proof for the prosecution in such a hearing isn't a major stumbling block. All it requires the prosecution to present is sufficient evidence to enable a judge to rule that there is probable cause that the defendant has committed the crime in question and should be bound over for trial. Defense lawyers like it, even if they don't expect to win, because it essentially gives them a free crack at some of the prosecution witnesses. It also gives the defense lawyers a good opportunity to lock in some of the testimony that the prosecution will ultimately need at trial.

Prosecutors have the option of bypassing the preliminary hearing stage by going directly to a grand jury and seeking an indictment. Although the standards are basically the same, grand jury proceedings fall under the direct control of the prosecution. Potential defendants are not allowed to participate, unless they are called as witnesses, and even then, they cannot be accompanied into the grand jury room by their attorney. Grand juries are viewed by knowledgeable members of the defense bar as little more than rubberstamps for potentially overzealous prosecutors.

"Yeah, I would probably seek an indictment," Ken said. "I think that's what would happen out here. What do you think, Mark?"

"My view is the prosecutor isn't going to let a case go to a preliminary hearing when he thinks he can get an indictment from a grand jury. They've got to be convinced they have something to gain from holding a preliminary hearing, and I can't think of what it would be in this case. We don't have to put on any evidence or call any witnesses, and we get a free shot at their witnesses. I don't think they're going to make Megan Rand look any more like a murderer by making her sit through a preliminary hearing. I think she's probably a pretty sympathetic figure. No, I would think they would indict her."

"Yeah, I think that's right," Ben said. "I stopped by the law school today and we're going to have to subpoena all the records we can think of relating to Greenfield and every student he's had for probably ten years. We should go back at least as far as when Meg and I were students there. I think the police have already taken some of his files, but I think we're ultimately going to have to look at not only his personnel records, but also examine the grades he gave all of his students, whether he gave anybody any grades that cost them a scholarship, an award, or maybe even kept them from graduating. I know that's a lot of shit, but if you think about it, there's a lot of possible motives for some student to whack him. Not to mention the fact that there always could have been stuff

111

going on in his personal life. So, anything we can think of in that regard, we should probably put in the document rider. Mark, can you get started on that?"

"Sure," Mark said.

"Hey, by the way," Ken said, "how did she handle her night in the joint?"

"She said it wasn't too bad," Ben replied. "First of all, she didn't get there until pretty late. Then they put her in the maternity ward over at Cook County Jail. I think it's a separate building. She said she was in some sort of a dorm-type thing with a handful of other inmates. I don't think it was staying at the Ritz-Carlton, but I don't think it was nearly as bad as it could have been."

"No," Ken said, "doesn't sound like it. Sounds like the detective may have done you a favor."

"Yeah, I think he did. I think he figured she was getting out anyway, so why put her through the wringer just for one night. Not that home confinement is any bargain. I think that having that ring around your leg is no picnic. I think it probably has the effect of making you aware at all times that you're not really free."

They talked for a few more minutes, mainly just bullshitting, before Ken signed off. Ben sent Mark home a little while later and went back upstairs to work on some other stuff for awhile. He checked his voicemail again - four more messages from reporters. God, he thought, I hope they stop calling. It had been a long, long day and his brain felt fried. Meanwhile, many miles away, the Protector made plans.

18

Ben fumbled in his pocket for his keys and unlocked the door just as Libby headed toward him through the front hall and into the kitchen. The kids were already in bed.

"Hey," he said. "Did we make TV?"

"Oh, you've been all over the place," she answered. "You were on the six o'clock news, on all the local channels. I Tivo'd some of them for you, and you even made Fox News and MSNBC. Pictures of you at the Courthouse, but no sound, and MSNBC just talked about the story. It was kind of exciting."

"Did I look like a dufus, or what?"

"No, you looked pretty good. You sounded serious and intense, maybe a bit too intense. You might want to loosen up a little bit, but overall, I think it was pretty good. You'll see, I'll show you."

Ben walked over and pulled open the refrigerator. "What did you have for dinner?"

"Tacos. There's some left in the refrigerator."

He turned and scowled. He found the Tupperware container with taco meat inside and put it in the microwave on one minute. He chopped up some lettuce and grabbed a package of shredded cheddar cheese out of the bin on the middle shelf and laid it on the counter. He took the bowl out of the microwave, the meat was sizzling and spitting, and he dumped the lettuce and cheese in the bowl and mixed it up.

"Are you going to eat it right out of the bowl?" Libby asked.

"Yeah, if I feel like it. It's easier that way."

"Whatever."

He took a couple of bites and rummaged through a cupboard for the tortilla chips and a glass, which he filled with ice and root beer from a can in the refrigerator. Libby went back into the family room, and he joined her with his dinner a minute later. "What are you watching?" he asked as he sat down.

"I just finished watching the news. You were on there again, but it was the same stuff as before. Nothing new."

"Did they show any of McBride's press conference?"

"A little bit, yeah. I'll find it."

He stared at the screen as Libby replayed the news story from Channel 7 on Tivo. It started with a brief description from the anchor, then cut to maybe twenty seconds of the State's Attorney, Richard McBride, at his press conference.

"That's Bridget Fahey to his right," Ben said, his eyes not leaving the screen. After McBride, they showed a short clip of Ben outside the Courthouse, with Mark on one side and Megan Rand and her husband on the other.

After the story ended, Libby hit the pause button and turned to him. "Was that her husband standing next to her?" Ben nodded and put another spoonful of the taco concoction into his mouth. "He is old," she said. "He didn't look very happy either."

"He doesn't have a lot to be happy about," Ben replied while chewing.

"I can't imagine sleeping with someone that much older than me."

"No," Ben said after swallowing. "I can't either. I mean, he's older than your parents."

"Yuck," she said.

They spent the next half hour or so watching the other stories Megan recorded. They all pretty much showed the same thing. She tossed him the remote, which was typically his responsibility. He found *Hardball* on the Now Playing List on Tivo and hit the play button.

"You wouldn't believe the number of voicemail messages I got today."

"I bet the secretaries are loving that," she said.

"About as much as you'd expect. If this doesn't slow down, we're gonna have to figure out some other approach. Phil's been looking into that automated answering system for the phones, but I'm not sure he was quite ready to bite the bullet on that yet. But unless all these calls slow down, we'll have to figure out something or the secretaries will never get any work done."

"So how's Meg holding up?"

"Not bad. They stuck her in the maternity ward last night, so she had it pretty easy. Now that she's out, it should be a lot easier."

"Well, yeah, but she's got that home monitoring thing."

Ben explained how the system worked and that Meg would probably have a little bit more freedom than she might originally expect, especially if she cleared the trips ahead of time.

"Still, it's like being watched all the time," Libby said.

"Yeah. I suppose it is, but it's a pretty big house and the perimeter is big enough so she can go out in the yard and even down to the neighbors if she wants to. This time of year anyway, it's probably not as bad as it could be."

"You know, her husband is probably kind of glad she's got the home confinement because now she's stuck back living at home with him."

Ben looked over at his wife and scooped up the last remnants from the bowl and stuffed them into his mouth. That hadn't occurred to him. "Maybe you're right," he said.

"Is he going to be a problem?"

"Probably, but I'm trying to put him in his place right away by establishing some ground rules. I doubt he'll follow them."

"Guys like him never do."

19

Ben and the team spent the next few days getting the discovery requests together, focusing first on subpoenas and their document riders. Some of the subpoenas were duplicative. Greenfield's phone records, for example, were undoubtedly obtained already by the prosecution and should be produced during discovery, but Ben sought them anyway for a couple of reasons. First, he might be able to obtain them sooner by serving subpoenas himself. More importantly, it served as a check on Bridget Fahey and her willingness to produce evidence in her possession as required by the Code of Criminal Procedure. The subpoena to the law school included a very broad document rider designed, in part, to test the limits of the school's cooperation. Sensing some difficulties ahead, Ben decided to drive downtown and serve the subpoena on Dean Freeman himself.

He reached the parking lot at the law school by eleven-thirty. The attendant now recognized him and gave him a friendly wave whenever he arrived. Once inside, Ben went directly to the Dean's office to serve his subpoena. Finding no one in the Dean's office, Ben left the subpoena with Freeman's secretary.

Ben took the stairs back down to the first floor, where he found Charles Powell sitting at his station at the security kiosk. "Hello, Charles," Ben said reading the man's nametag and extending a hand. "My name is Benjamin Lohmeier. I represent Megan Rand in the Greenfield murder case."

Powell took his hand and replied, "I know who you are, counselor. I've seen you on TV. What can I do for you?"

"I was wondering if your boss is around. I'd like to speak to him."

A few minutes later, Roger Tierney emerged from around the corner and Ben greeted him with a handshake. A moment later, the two men were off to Greenfield's office on the elevator.

"Tell me about your security system," Ben asked as they got off on Greenfield's floor.

"Sure," Tierney said. "You were a student here, right?" Ben nodded. "Well, if you were a student here, things haven't changed much. Down on the first floor, there are only two entrances, one in the front and one in the back. People can enter and exit the building through the circular doors at the front on the Adams side. There's another entrance in the back of the building, but you can only leave through that door. It's locked if you try to get in from the outside."

"Unless, of course, you happen to come up when someone else is leaving and they let you in that way," Ben said.

"Yes, I suppose that's true too. Other than that, there's no other way to get in or out of the building. As you know, there are ten stories to the building, plus the concourse on the lower level. There's no outside entrance or exit from any location other than those I've just described. Other than the loading dock, of course, but there's no real public access to that."

"But you have security cameras," Ben said. "What do those cover?"

"As you may have noticed," Tierney said, "we have cameras posted at each entrance/exit, outside the elevators on every floor and at various locations on every floor of the building."

They reached Greenfield's office and stopped outside the door.

"Would there be a way to get to this office without being seen on one of those security cameras?" Ben asked.

"No, I don't think so, but I know what you're thinking, and the police have thought about it too, and the cameras don't help you."

"Why not?"

"Because, unfortunately, the cameras recycle in a seventy-two-hour timeframe, and the police have concluded, I guess in conjunction with the medical examiner, that Professor Greenfield was killed more than seventy-two hours before the discovery of the body and our accessing of the security tapes."

"In other words," Ben said with a grimace, "at any given point in time, the security cameras only have the last seventy-two hours of material on them?"

Tierney nodded. "That's right. As you recall, Professor Greenfield was found on January 2nd in the late morning. That means the security tapes only go back to that same time period on December 30th. By that time, the building was already closed for New Year's. Any video taken prior to that time was already taped over."

"Shit," Ben said. "Is that common knowledge? I mean, does everybody know that the security tapes only get the last seventy-two hours?"

"Don't think so. I'm not sure it ever came up before this. You see, security cameras are only designed for a kind of real time look at what's going on in the building. Also, we use it to try and protect against the theft of materials from the library. To tell you the truth, that's probably the primary concern. You don't expect much violence in a law school with a bunch of law students around."

"No, I suppose not," Ben said with sigh. "Still, it would have been nice. Like I said though, how many people would have known about the specifics of the security cameras?"

"Not very many, I wouldn't think. The security guards probably all know, but I'm not sure anybody else really does unless they happen to inquire about it. I think we had an issue several years ago when they thought they had some volumes missing from the library, but that was quite a while back. Nobody really suggested that we take any steps to change the cameras or anything," Tierney said defensively.

"Has anybody ever asked you about it? About how many hours of tape are stored in the cameras?"

"No, I don't think so. Like I said, it may have come up when we had the problem in the library, but I'm not even sure it came up then. I can't remember anybody asking me about it since then. Of course, that doesn't mean somebody didn't ask one of the guards on duty. I don't spend that much time sitting at the security desk downstairs. You might want to check with them."

"I'll do that," Ben said. "I just wonder if the killer got lucky or if he knew that by the time anybody found the body, the tapes of him or her getting on this floor would be taped over."

"That's a good question," Tierney said.

"Tell me about the locks on the doors," Ben said. "I seem to recall something going on with them."

"Well, as you may remember, the offices on the 6th, 7th and 8th floors of the building are on the outside perimeter of the building with the library on the interior. The professors can access the library through the doors on either end of the hallway, but students in the library can't get out to those floors. They have to go back out and leave through the main entrance to the library on the 9th floor."

"So basically," Ben said, "the professors can get in and out of the library without having to go up to the 9th floor, but the students can't get out without going to the 9th floor."

"Exactly."

"I assume the professors have a key of some sort to go from the library to the office part of those floors?"

"Yes, they do. Here, let's walk around to the door around the corner here and I'll show you," Tierney said. The two men walked around the corner to a door that accessed the library.

"Of course," Ben said, "just like the main entrance, if somebody let you in from the library to the office, then you wouldn't need the key."

"No, you wouldn't. No system is perfect, I guess. The main principle is, again, that we're trying to keep a handle on materials leaving the library and make sure that they come and go through the main entrance on the 9th floor."

"Unless, of course, a professor takes them?"

"Yes, unless a professor takes them," Tierney said.

Ben looked around and surveyed the area. "So which camera would cover this entranceway?"

Tierney looked around for a moment as well, then pointed to the far end of the corridor. "I believe the one down there at the end of the hallway."

"Way down there? I wouldn't think you could get much of a view of this location from way down there."

"Of course," Tierney said, "there are additional cameras by the elevators as well."

"Yeah, but if you went back and forth through this doorway, say with a key card, there wouldn't appear to be much of a view of you coming and going."

"I'm not sure. We would have to go downstairs and see what kind of view there is."

Ben nodded. "Okay, then, let's do that."

The two men returned to the first floor, where they found Charles Powell sitting at his station. "Charles, let me slip in here for a second, will you?" Tierney said. Powell got up and stepped aside as Tierney sat down and began punching a few codes on the keyboard. "Here it is, right here," he said pointing to the screen at the far right of the panel. "This is the view down the hallway from that camera."

Ben leaned over Tierney's shoulder and studied the screen. "That's not much of a view is it?" he said. "Sure, you get a view of the doorway right in front, but the one at the end of the hall, the one closest to Greenfield's office, you can't really tell much of anything. I'm not sure you could tell whether someone went in or out of that door. Plus it's so close to the corner that you could be in or out of it and around the corner in just an instant."

Tierney didn't like the implication that the security system was flawed, but he couldn't disagree with Ben's logic. "You may be right," he said finally, "but it really doesn't matter anyhow since the camera only goes back seventy-two hours, and we don't have a shot of whoever may have done it. Whether it was your client or not," he said trying to put Ben back on the defensive.

"It wasn't my client," Ben said, "but just because we don't have a picture doesn't mean that the killer knew we weren't going to have a picture. You could probably get in or out of that door and around the corner in less than what, a second or two? Unless

Charles here, or whoever was on duty, was looking at that exact picture at just the right moment, he would have missed it. Not that he could tell much from that view even if he had been looking at it."

"Maybe not," Tierney said, "but the fact remains we don't have a picture."

"No, no we don't," Ben said scratching his head. The two men spoke for another couple of minutes before a call on Tierney's radio took him back upstairs to the library, leaving Ben alone with Charles Powell. Ben studied the screen for another minute and then stood and stepped out from behind the kiosk. "Charles, let me ask you something. You've seen my client on television, I take it?"

"Yes sir, I have."

"Had you seen her before you saw her on television?"

"I think so."

"What do you mean?"

"I think I saw her here in the building. I'm pretty sure I did."

"I understand. When do you think you saw her?"

"I think it was around Christmastime, right around the time the Professor was killed or maybe a little bit before."

"How many times did you see her?"

Powell thought about it for a few seconds. "Oh, I would say twice, maybe three times at the most," he said.

"What makes you think it was her?"

"Well, for starters, it looks like her. Another thing, she didn't look like a student. You tend to notice when someone comes in here and doesn't look like a student or isn't one of the professors. Plus, she didn't come in here during one of the between class times when it's all crowded and everything."

"Okay, so you say you think you saw her coming in the building. Did you ever see her leave?"

"Yeah, I did, at least once. She went around to the elevators and came back just a few minutes later."

"So she wasn't upstairs very long at all."

"Nope."

"Now, again, how many times do you think you saw her, Charles?"

"I would say twice coming and once going, sir. I don't remember seeing her leave the second time."

"So the first time you saw her, that was the short visit?"

"Yes, I think so."

Ben nodded. "Okay, Charles, that's fair enough. Let me ask you something else. Did she ever stop here at the desk and look at any of these video screens?"

"No, nothing like that."

"Has anybody ever done that, stopped and looked at the monitors?"

"Oh sure, every once in a while a student will stop by and ask me if I'm seeing anything. You know, joking around stuff. Every once in a while, someone will ask me if I've ever spotted anything on these cameras."

"Has anyone ever seemed more curious about the security system than they ought to be?" Ben asked.

"No, I don't think so. Mostly, people are just wondering why there's a guy sitting down here looking at these cameras all day long. You know how it is, after a while you get to know some of the students a little bit, and you get to talking to them, and they ask you questions sometimes. But do I think anyone was casing the joint? No, I can't say that. Mostly just routine curiosity. I never thought nothing of it 'til now."

"No," Ben said, "I could see why you wouldn't. Has anybody asked you about the security around here who wasn't a student?"

"No, I don't think so, except maybe for some professors or staff. Some of them ask occasionally about how we make sure their offices and stuff are protected."

"Really," Ben said, "like who?"

"Mostly women. Some of the lady professors are a little concerned about security and stuff."

"Do you remember any of the women professors in particular?"

"Oh, I don't know," Powell said rubbing his chin, "let me think about it. I seem to remember Professor Harper asking me about stuff once or twice and I think maybe Professor Berman did too. Other than that, I'm not sure I can remember, but I'll think about it for you if you'd like."

"Thanks, Charles. I'd appreciate that."

The following day, Ben met with three of his former professors at the law school - Richard Seagram, Gordon Hyatt and Thomas Makra, and found all three very cooperative. Ben and Seagram talked over lunch down the street from the law school and Seagram gave Ben a better idea of the politics at the law school, including the reputations Greenfield and Dorlund had as skirt chasers, a trait not completely lost on Seagram himself.

After lunch, Ben found Professor Hyatt in his office and they discussed the circumstances surrounding Hyatt's discovery of the body. Other than that, he didn't have much to offer. Makra, on the other hand, was a wealth of information. As Ben suspected, he knew where all of the bodies were buried at the law school. He gave Ben the names of two of the students who had made accusations of impropriety against Greenfield, both had also taken Makra's classes in the Uniform Commercial Code, and even described a loud argument between a first-year student and a professor on Greenfield's floor shortly before Christmas. Whether the argument involved Greenfield himself, Makra couldn't say. Makra also told Ben that there had been strong rumors circulating in the law school for years that Greenfield may have enjoyed some recreational chemicals from time to time. None of the three professors, however, could envision a scenario where Sylvia Greenfield had killed her ex-husband. They agreed that she was much too cold a fish for something like that, particularly now, several years after her divorce. Given the unanimity of their analysis, Ben reluctantly moved her name off of his top list of possible suspects. He wouldn't eliminate her altogether until he had the opportunity to meet her and assess her personality himself. When that would be, only time would tell.

20

Ben looked up to find Mark staring at him. "What?" Ben said.

"Oh, I don't know," Mark replied. "Do you have to use the red pen when you review that? It makes me feel like I'm back in grade school."

Ben was reviewing some discovery requests that Mark had drafted. There were edits and additions all over every page, written in precise red ink. "It's easier for them to read," Ben said. "I don't want them to miss any changes. You're lucky I'm not grading it. Next time you write something, you should try using a crayon. It would be more fitting."

Mark's eyes narrowed. He knew Ben was kidding. At least he thought so.

Ben finished the last page and handed it to Mark with a sly grin. "Don't worry, it wasn't too bad. I just had some things I thought of that you didn't include. No big deal. Make sure Nancy gets the corrections made so we can take it to Court tomorrow."

"You know," Mark said, "I used the form I got from Ken and made a few additions . . ."

"Hey," Ben interrupted, "don't worry about it. It was fine. No big deal."

"Ben, Mr. Portalski is here," a voice said over the intercom.

"I'll be right out," Ben said. "Take this up to Nancy and I'll go get Portalski." Ben pulled on the door that led back to the main part of the building from the garage. He found Ed Portalski in the kitchen looking at a copy of the *Chicago Sun-Times*.

"Ed," he said and slapped him on the back.

124

"Counselor, how's it going?" Portalski said in a gruff voice. Ed Portalski was a stocky man in his early-fifties with greasy hair that looked like it hadn't been washed in two weeks. He combed it in a modified pompadour.

"Hey, I like the new do," Ben said. "What is that, chestnut?"

Portalski rubbed his hand self-consciously through his hair and said, "Yeah, I had to cover up the gray. I was tired of looking at it."

"Follow me," Ben said and he led Portalski out toward the garage. A former sergeant with the Chicago Police Department, Edward Portalski left the force under mysterious circumstances about ten years before to become a private investigator. Ben first met him when he was a prosecutor and he knew Eddie Portalski to be thorough and well-equipped to dig up information often found in the seedier parts of town. He was also very well-connected with his former colleagues in the Chicago Police Department and Ben had taken advantage of this fact several times over the past few years.

Noticing his fingernails, Ben said, "Are you still fixing cars?"

"Na, not too often, only when a friend needs something. A buddy of mine needed to have a new starter put in on his Buick, so I was working on it last night."

"Take off your coat," Ben said as they pushed into the garage, "make yourself comfortable."

Eddie took off his green parka to reveal a stained blue denim work shirt with the sleeves rolled up to reveal severe eczema on both forearms. He never felt fully confident in Eddie Portalski's hygiene. Portalski looked around at the stuffed heads looking down on him.

"I always get a fucking kick out of this place," he said. "So what's the deal this time?"

"Hold on, I'll tell you when everybody gets here. You're not the only guy that's going to work on this one. Do you know Stan Disko?"

"Sure, Stan and I go way back. I haven't seen him in years though."

At that moment, the door to the garage opened and Mark entered, a large bald man trailing in his wake.

"I met Mr. Disko out front," Mark said.

"Eddie," Disko said, "I didn't know you'd be here too."

"Stan, Ben Lohmeier," Ben said sticking out his hand. "We met a while back when you were in here doing something for Ken Williams."

"I remember, counselor, good to see you again." Disko said.

"Now that we're all here," Ben said, "why don't we sit down and get started?"

Stanley Disko was also a private investigator and specialized in more upscale matters and insurance cases. He didn't do much surveillance work anymore, but could be persuaded under the right circumstances and for a handsome fee. Ken Williams had used him for years and Ben had met him a couple of years earlier when he was helping Ken out on a case involving one of the firm's contractor clients.

Ben sat down in one of the barber chairs, while the others grabbed spots around the large conference table. Then Ben gave them a brief summary of the events that brought them together.

"It doesn't sound much like a woman's crime," Disko said when Ben finished.

Ben shook his head. "No, I don't think so either. On the other hand, there must be some evidence connecting Megan with this crime or she wouldn't have been arrested. We don't know what that evidence is since they haven't turned any of it over to us yet. The client insists there is no real connection other than she was one of his students many years ago, but that doesn't seem to add up either. We have to get to the bottom of what happened with her and the Professor, both together and separately, if we want to get a better handle on this.

"Eddie, I want you to focus on the victim, Daniel Greenfield. Find out what he was into and who he hung around with. I can give you a couple of tips, and write this down." Portalski slid a note pad from the center of the table and pulled a pen out of his pocket. Ben relayed what he knew about Greenfield's divorce, before moving on to the situation with the students. "One of the students was a woman named Hinkle, while the other's name was Wexler. I don't know much more about them than that. See what you can dig up. There is also another student that the professor apparently had a fairly significant relationship with. I don't know her name. We're trying to find that out. Try and dig into this without making too much of a scene at the school. I will concentrate on talking to most of the professors and staff myself. I know some of them and should be able to get some answers. Approach it from the outside in.

"Finally, I hear tell that the professor had a little problem with tooting the white powder. So look into that angle as well. His closest friend at the law school and anywhere else for all I know is a fellow professor named Samuel Dorlund. I have already talked to him once and I'll be talking to him again. Look into that a little bit too, but don't talk to Dorlund directly. That's pretty good for a start."

"I'll say," Portalski said.

"Now," Ben continued, "as for you, Stan, I want you to focus on a couple of other avenues. First, I want you to look into the husband, Joseph Cavallaro."

"The husband?" Disko said. "Why are we looking into him?"

"We're looking into him because I don't trust him as far as I can throw him. Yeah, he's footing the bill because he has to. He and the client have had some marital problems over the past few years, he's quite a bit older than she is, and he's doing whatever he can to try and keep the marriage together when she would just as soon get out. Look into him pretty carefully, you know, see if there is any connection between him and the Professor. Look into his law practice, see if he has any financial problems, that sort of stuff. He has already been a problem and I want to see if there is anything floating around out there about him that I don't know about.

"Next, I want you to check out some of the professors at the law school. See if anybody has had problems with Greenfield in the past, particularly the women, although I suppose they all have husbands as well. Try and be discreet about it. Like I said before,

I'm going to be talking to a lot of them, so be careful how you poke around."

They talked for a few more minutes as Ben told the detectives what he knew about the case and some of the people who could be involved. Then he got to his feet and said, "Look, if you guys have any other questions, you can give me a call or you can talk to Mark too. I'll talk to you guys later."

Ben went back upstairs and checked his messages. They were still rolling in at an incredible clip and he was starting to get nasty looks from the secretaries in the office. Then he called Sylvia Greenfield. There was no answer so he left a message. He spent the rest of the day scrambling to put out fires that were beginning to erupt in some of his other files, and around six he began preparing for Court the following morning.

Later on, Ben found himself staring out his window at the dark parking lot, the light on the pole at the opposite end occasionally going on or off according to its mood. Ben felt out of it and recognized that the odds of him getting any significant work done tonight had grown slim so he decided to pack it in for the night. After he loaded his briefcase, he pulled the chain to turn off the light in the ceiling fan over his desk. A lone figure hidden below in the shadow of a pine tree watched the scene transpire. By the time Ben reached his car in the parking lot, the figure had gone.

21

The following morning dawned clear and very cold. As he showered, Ben pondered his upcoming Court appearance before Judge Wilson. Particularly when coupled with the media throng that would undoubtedly be present in the courtroom, the thought of it left Ben feeling nervous and a bit jittery. He got dressed and went downstairs, where Libby and the kids were already getting ready for school. The kitchen smelled liked fried bacon and Ben stole a bite out of the bagel on Natalie's plate, squishy not crunchy, just the way she liked it, but his heart wasn't in it. He felt too uptight to eat.

Rinsing off a pan in the sink, Libby turned and asked "Is Meg going to be there today?"

"No."

"What time do you think you'll be home tonight?"

"No idea."

"Should I save dinner for you?"

"Probably not."

Although she certainly didn't appreciate his surliness, Libby understood the pressures Ben was under and didn't make an issue of it.

"Well, good luck today," she said as she rubbed him softly on the back.

He seemed to take the slightest comfort in it and said, "Thanks" in a soft voice.

"Daddy, I want to go uppy," Natalie said as she came over and reached up toward him while swallowing the last bites of her breakfast.

"Okay sweetheart," he said reaching down and grabbing her. "You know your Daddy can't resist you." He picked her up and balanced her in the crook of his left arm. Her head was the same height as his and she rested it gently against his temple. He kissed her twice on the cheek and she returned the favor. "Unfortunately my dear, I have to go to Court." He kissed her again on the top of the head and then set her down.

"Daddy, why do you have to go to Court?"

"Because that's what I do. Sometimes lawyers have to go to Court."

"Do you have fun in Court?"

"Sometimes."

"Are you going to have fun today?"

"Probably not."

"Well, I hope you have fun in Court, Daddy."

"Thanks sweetie." He tousled her hair and then went back into the front hall and took his overcoat off the hall tree. He grabbed his briefcase, slung it over his shoulder and headed outside. "I'll see you guys tonight," he said. He then paused on the deck and took a deep breath through his nose. The air felt clean and fresh and the sky looked unusually blue this morning. He hoped the fresh air would calm his nerves.

Mark arrived a minute later and Ben backed the car out to the end of the driveway, while Mark parked his car on the street and lumbered over, tossing his stuff in the back seat of the SUV before wedging his large frame into the front seat.

"Morning," he said putting on his seat belt. "Are we ready for a good day?"

"Hope so," Ben answered.

Like Libby, Mark too sensed that Ben was not in a talkative mood and the two drove for a while in relative silence. Traffic was spotty, but not too bad. As they neared the exit at California Avenue, Mark turned and said, "I've got a place where we can park.

I use it all the time. We'll be able to get right out when we're done."

Mark directed Ben to a parking lot just past the Courthouse, next to a Popeye's Chicken stand. They dropped the SUV off with an attendant that Mark knew and headed to the Courthouse. They walked past the original entrance to the old Courthouse and up the steps to the current entrance, stuck between the old Courthouse to the north and the tall narrow administrative tower to the south. They stood for a long time in the cattle call that was the line through the metal detectors, made that much worse by the events of September 11th. Because he had a Cook County pass, Mark pushed through the metal detector without being searched, while Ben had to remove his coat and all of the metal on his person, including his belt, and he still set the metal detector off. He stepped through and over to the Sheriff's Deputy, who gave him the once over with a wand, while Ben held his arms straight out at his sides.

As Ben slipped his belt back through the loops of his pants, Mark said, "You really should get a pass. It saves a lot of time and trouble."

"Yeah, I know it." Ben replied. "I half-thought they were going to do a body cavity search there for a minute. The pass I had when I worked down here expired years ago. Remind me on the way out and maybe I'll stop and get one. At least get the picture taken."

The two men pushed through the crowds and around the corner past Courtroom 101 where they were last time. On the bulletin board opposite that courtroom, they found Meg's name on the computerized printout of the daily call.

"Here we go," Ben said when he found it on the wall. "Courtroom 700. Let's go."

Ben and Mark wound their way through the corridor and into what was once the main lobby of the old Courthouse. Although not very large by modern standards, the lobby was nevertheless grand and ornate in a style not seen in public buildings constructed today. The front doors looked down a set of steps and across the street to a small grassy square complete with a fountain now walled

131

off by iron gates. The front half of the lobby evoked a feeling of a time long past, from the days of Al Capone and Leopold & Loeb to Richard Speck and John Wayne Gacy. Each of them had met their fate here. The floor was pale stone, the walls trimmed in rich woods and the ceiling an intricate pattern of multi-colored tiles. A granite staircase rose at the far end. Muted lighting added to the reverential feeling. People spoke only in whispers. Ben and Mark walked through an archway flanked by large marble columns and into the area housing the elevators.

The old Courthouse held seven floors of courtrooms - those on the bottom three floors displayed a modern touch, small and cramped with bullet-proof glass separating the gallery from the bench, jury box and counsel tables. Video monitors transmitted the proceedings to those crammed into the gallery. When Ben and Mark stepped off the elevator on the 7th floor, they may as well have stepped back into a bygone era of American justice. The elevators opened into a large open area where lawyers, court personnel and reporters milled about. Each floor housed four courtrooms; two sat opposite each other on each end of the building. Courtroom 700 was on the northeast corner of the building and as they approached it, a couple of reporters came up to them and asked for comments on the upcoming events of the morning.

"I'm sorry. I don't want to talk right now," Ben said. "I'll have a brief statement after we're done here."

It occurred to him that he had not considered what that statement might be. Mark pulled the door open and they stepped inside. As he entered, Ben felt like he had just walked into a cathedral, the hushed tones of those inside reflecting the solemnity of this grand space. They stopped just inside the door and savored the moment.

Mark leaned over and whispered, "Are you nervous?"

Ben nodded. "A little," he said. An ornate ceiling of blue and gold tile framed in dark wood with recessed lighting rose high above a terrazzo floor. Seven rows of mahogany spectator benches stretched like pews on either side of the wide aisle that led to the center of the courtroom. Rising well above them like a pulpit at the far end of the courtroom was the large carved mahogany bench, occupied by the judge and his clerk, as well as the witness box and a seat for the court reporter. The round seal of the State of Illinois was affixed to the front of the bench. Ben and Mark slowly walked up the aisle toward the counsel tables. Against the wall to their left stood the jury box framed in more dark mahogany, housing individual cushioned chairs for twelve jurors and two alternates. On the opposite wall to their right and directly facing the jury box stood the counsel table used by the defense. In the center of the courtroom, perpendicular to the jury box and the defense table, and directly facing the bench, stood the counsel table used by the prosecution. Bridget Fahey sat there now, along with one of her minions.

As they reached her, Ben tapped her lightly on the right shoulder and said "Good morning, Bridget." She looked up, her face pale and drawn.

"Good morning, counselor," she returned.

Ben took solace in the fact that she too appeared somewhat nervous and ill at ease. He looked at his watch - they were fifteen minutes early. Ben and Mark sat down at the defense table and Ben pulled his briefcase up on his lap and removed the discovery requests they had prepared for today. He walked over and placed a small stack next to Fahey and said, "Here is a copy of our discovery requests."

"Thanks," she said without looking up.

He returned to his seat and tried his best to appear nonchalant and completely at ease, which of course, he wasn't. Sunlight filtered in over his shoulder from the small row of windows stretching across the paneled wall behind him. Unlike the courtrooms downstairs or the countless civil courtrooms downtown at the Daley Center, Courtroom 700 gave off the formal hushed air reminiscent of Federal Court, largely populated with silk stocking lawyers and their Ivy League pedigrees.

Ben glanced to his left at the rapidly filling gallery. There appeared to be only a handful of other lawyers in the courtroom so Ben concluded that the spectators were here for what the press was now calling, the "Law School Murder." He looked back to his right and up at the bench. Behind it were two doors: one led to Judge Wilson's chambers, the other was used by court personnel. This was the door through which defendants in custody would be brought to the courtroom, usually still wearing the jumpsuits issued at the Cook County Jail next door.

Ben turned and noticed a woman in a blue business suit entering the courtroom and moving down the aisle to take a seat in the second row of the gallery. She looked very familiar and he struggled to place her for a moment before it dawned on him. She was the woman sitting in Cavallaro's office when he barged in. Now she was here, sent by Cavallaro to keep tabs on him. Not surprising. He expected as much. Ben let his gaze linger on her just long enough so that she knew he had both spotted and recognized her. When she looked up and they made eye contact, she quickly looked away. Ben did not. A few seconds later when she raised her eyes again, he was still staring at her. Only then did he look back at the bench, where a clerk now entered the courtroom. The brief episode seemed to put Ben at ease.

A moment later, a sheriff's deputy emerged and called out, "All rise."

At that very instant, the other door behind the bench opened and the Honorable William Wilson emerged, walked up a handful of steps and took his seat behind the bench. Ben did not hear the rest of what the deputy said, for his eyes were glued on Wilson. Despite being an average-sized man, Judge Wilson presented an imposing figure. With his gray balding crew cut and stern, almost expressionless demeanor, Judge Wilson carried himself with the bearing of a Marine drill instructor. Known as the best defense lawyer in Chicago before he ascended to the bench, Wilson intimidated lawyers in his courtroom just as he intimidated students in his classroom. After having the opportunity to watch the Judge up close as a member of his trial team years before, Ben concluded that Wilson did it without even trying. Whether it was his reputation, or his manner or his obvious skill as a lawyer and judge, Ben did not know. He just knew that he had to be completely prepared and fully professional at all times. As everyone in the courtroom took their seats, the Judge gave a quick good morning and called the first case. Theirs was the fourth and last case on the call. When Wilson called the case, Ben and Mark rose from their seats and walked up to the bench.

Bridget Fahey seemed to race from her seat to be the first one there and said, "Good morning, your Honor. Bridget Fahey for the people," before Ben and Mark had even arrived.

Ben gave her a quick glance and said, "Good morning, your Honor. Benjamin Lohmeier and Mark Schaefer on behalf of Megan Rand Cavallaro."

"Good morning, Counsel," the Judge said with a short nod. As he looked down at them, there was no sign of recognition. "This case has been assigned to me from downstairs," the Judge began. "Before we get started, I'm sure it's no secret that I knew the deceased in this case personally by virtue of my position of an Adjunct Professor of Law at the Chicago College of Law and my having served for many years as the Director of the law school's Trial Advocacy Program. While I did know Professor Greenfield personally, I did not know him well, nor did I ever work with him closely despite his being a Professor of Criminal Law. Consequently, I do not feel that there is any reason why I could not thoroughly and objectively handle my duties in this case. Of course, if Counsel believe otherwise, or believe that a conflict exists such that I should recuse myself in this matter, please let me know and I will be happy to do so."

Bridget Fahey spoke first. "Your Honor, the people see no reason why you should recuse yourself at this time."

The Judge looked at Ben. "Your Honor," Ben said, "we agree. We see no reason why a recusal should be required. We believe you are more than capable of being fair and objective in this matter and we will not be seeking a recusal."

"Very well," the Judge said. "I understand we have some discovery matters to discuss this morning," he said, wasting no time. "Mr. Lohmeier, what information are you seeking from the State?"

Ben took a moment to outline the discovery he was seeking. After he finished, Judge Wilson looked at Bridget Fahey and said,

"Ms. Fahey, this all seems pretty routine and reasonable. How much time will it take you to produce the information requested?"

"We would like at least twenty-eight days, your Honor. Not all of the scientific reports and medical analysis have been completed as of yet."

"That is too long, counsel. You have had enough evidence in your possession to arrest the Defendant and take her before a grand jury, you should be able to provide defense counsel with this information within fourteen days."

"But your Honor," Fahey interjected, "as I said, we still have not received all of the reports yet."

"Fine. Produce everything in your possession that is responsive to both Defendant's discovery requests and the applicable rules of discovery within fourteen days. You can supplement your responses as additional information becomes available. Let's get the information out there and get this case moving. I will see you back here in twenty-eight days," he said looking at his calendar. "That will be March 1st at nine-thirty. Ms. Fahey?"

"Yes Judge?"

"When do you anticipate getting a decision from the grand jury?"

"Your Honor, we hope to have the grand jury return an indictment against the Defendant by the next Court appearance."

"Very well," the Judge said. "Before I let you go, I want to emphasize the dictates and requirements of the rules of professional conduct, though I am sure you are aware of them. I will not institute any gag order with respect to the media at this time, however, I fully expect all of the lawyers in this case to strictly adhere to the rules of professional conduct, particularly with respect to providing information and commentary to the news media. I recognize that this is a case of some degree of public interest, but I will not allow this case to be tried in the media." The Judge looked down at them and nodded.

"Very well, your Honor," Ben said.

"Okay then," the Judge concluded, "that will be all."

22

Citing Judge Wilson's admonition about the rules of professional conduct, Ben's conversations with the reporters on the front steps of the Courthouse was necessarily brief. He frankly appreciated Wilson giving him some cover so he could avoid dealing with the media the way lawyers in so many of the high profile cases do. This was his first big public case and he wasn't yet comfortable with the public relations aspect of it.

When they crossed 26th Street and reached the parking lot next to the Popeye's, Ben stopped when he saw the cars parked wall-to-wall in the modestly-sized lot. "Oh shit," he said. "We're never going to get out of here."

Mark laughed. "Don't worry, it'll be fine. I guarantee it. These guys take care of me, you watch." Mark maneuvered through the cars and headed toward the shed in the middle of the lot. Ben followed at his heels. When Mark reached the chief attendant, he pulled a twenty dollar bill out of his wallet and placed it in the palm of his hand and shook hands with the attendant.

"Counselors," the attendant said, stuffing the money into his pocket, "did you have success this morning."

"Not too bad," Mark said, "not too bad. Where are we?"

"You're over there in the back corner. The SUV, right?"

"That's right," Mark said.

The attendant waved his arm to a young man standing near the back of the lot. "He'll show you where it is."

"Thanks a lot, my man," Mark said slapping him on the back. "We'll see you next time."

"Have a good day now," the attendant said.

Mark led Ben between cars until they reached the back corner, where an alley cut through behind the lot and the Popeye's store to reach 26th Street. There, in the far right hand corner, parked right up against the alley, stood Ben's car. All they had to do was hop in, pull out and go.

Ben nodded. "Nice job," he said with true admiration.

"I told you they take good care of me. It's worth the extra money to be able to get in and out when you want to."

"Can't argue with that," Ben said. "We'll be coming here enough." They climbed into the car and in thirty seconds they were gone.

Fifteen minutes later, they pushed through the revolving doors at the law school and headed off to the elevators. Ben got off on the 5th floor and Mark went up to the library on the 9th floor to do some research. The door to the office was open, but Ben knocked anyway. The woman behind the desk jumped.

"You startled me," she said.

"Sorry about that," Ben replied. "Professor Berman, I was wondering if I could bother you for a few minutes?"

The woman looked away and considered the request for a few seconds. "Sure," she said, "come in and shut the door."

Ben did so and sat down on the lone guest chair. He glanced around the office and found it not particularly inviting. It gave off a strange, almost sterile air that seemed designed to avoid saying anything personal about its inhabitant. Professor Sally Berman was a nervous, almost mousy woman full of all sorts of personal idiosyncrasies. Ben could see instantly that the ten years since he had last spoken to her had not diminished any of her quirkiness.

A tall thin woman in her late-thirties, Sally Berman came to the Chicago College of Law from a brief career in a big New York law firm, one for which she was no doubt ill-suited. She specialized in torts and Ben's first year section was also the first class she taught after she joined the law school. Her fidgety manner, quivering voice and refusal to make eye contact often overshadowed a sharp intellect and biting wit. She was definitely an acquired taste. By the end of the first year, most of her students had gotten used to her mannerisms and actually liked her and enjoyed her class.

"So, how have you been?" Ben asked remembering that Professor Berman's manner often made him uncomfortable as well.

"I've been well, thank you," she said looking to her left at nothing in particular. Ben subconsciously found his eyes traveling in the same direction. "You seem to be doing quite well yourself," she continued. "I certainly wish you the best of luck in your defense. Ms. Rand certainly does not seem to me to be the kind of person who could kill someone."

"No," Ben agreed, "she's not. I guess that's why I'm here. Having been here awhile now, I was hoping you could help me shed some light on some of the goings on here at the law school."

She cocked her head. "I'm not sure what you mean."

"What I mean is I'm certainly aware of the rumors that had been circulating around here while I was a student about Professor Greenfield and female students. I was wondering if you could shed any light on that. In particular, I was hoping you could give me some perspective as a fellow professor, especially since you are a woman."

"Ah," she said looking down, "so that's the rub." She paused for a moment to gather her thoughts. Then she looked up at him and directly into his eyes. Ben found this surprising and somewhat disconcerting. "This is somewhat awkward," she began.

Everything about you is awkward, Ben thought.

"Professor Greenfield was after all a colleague of mine for many years," she said. "On the other hand, he is a dead colleague now and your task in defending Ms. Rand seems somewhat more significant than my discomfort over discussing this." She hesitated before continuing. "So I will tell you simply that Daniel Greenfield was a pig."

"That is kind of a broad term," Ben said, "and it conjures up all sorts of images. What exactly do you mean by pig?"

"I mean pig in every real sense that a woman can describe a man as a pig. If it's fair to so describe a man, it is fair to describe Daniel Greenfield that way. Daniel Greenfield was a chauvinist of the worst kind." Professor Berman's eyes never left Ben's and he noted a surprising intensity in her manner. "In Daniel Greenfield's world," she continued, "women were mere objects, playthings put on this planet for his amusement and to satisfy his personal proclivities. It is amazing to me that he managed to find a woman who would marry him, bear him children and stay with him as long as she did."

"Perhaps he was different outside of law school," Ben offered.

"I doubt it," she responded. "I simply don't believe he was capable."

"Obviously I heard stories back when I was a student and I've heard more stories in the last few days, but do you know any specifics that might help me?"

"Of course, I don't know what you know or don't know, but it's pretty simple that he was having relationships with students for many years and somehow or another, he finally got caught. I couldn't give you and names or specifics because I am not privy to those or simply don't recall them, but I would hope that it's all a matter of record in his files and you should be able to obtain those at some point."

Ben nodded in agreement. "What about other teachers? Do you know of any situations like this between Professor Greenfield and other professors?"

She took a deep breath and let it out very slowly. Her body appeared to stiffen. "Yes, well, there've been a number of circumstances that probably don't add up to much. You see, with men like Daniel Greenfield, the normal condescending attitude of a male chauvinist is more or less a given and must often be accepted as a matter of course. So we'll put that aside, because every woman who works in this building probably dealt with that at one time or another. I'm sure what you're referring to is something more significant that may have ultimately led to his very unpleasant demise."

"Something like that," Ben said.

"Well, I don't think he hit on fellow professors nearly as often as he did his students. There could be several reasons for that, I suppose. First of all, most of us aren't the young and nubile types that seem to attract men like Daniel Greenfield. Second, the sheer number of female students and the willingness of a select few to improve their grades any way they can made them more willing targets. Also, not very many women who are teaching law school would put up with that kind of thing, if for no other reason than we would be presumed to know how to protect ourselves legally. I'm sure there are other reasons. Having said that, it doesn't mean that Professor Greenfield confined himself to young female students. He was known to make inappropriate comments and suggestive proposals to certain professors as well."

"Did he ever say anything like that to you?"

"To me? No," she said appearing almost relieved. "There were some, but I'm not sure I really want to get into who they were and what I know. Most of it is second and third-hand as you might expect."

"Look," Ben said, "I'm not here to gossip. Somebody killed Daniel Greenfield and there are all sorts of possible motives as to why they did it. I've got a broad area of possibilities here and I just want to figure out if there is somebody on the staff that disliked Professor Greenfield enough to kill him, whether it's provoked or not."

"I appreciate your predicament," she said. She looked down and fiddled with the corner of a law journal laying open on her desk. Ben could see her calculating her options and trying to decide the right course.

Ben sought to put her at ease. "I would never reveal your name and what you told me unless I couldn't do it any other way."

"I believe that," she said. She took another moment to collect her thoughts. "As I said, I'm not sure there are many women in this building who shed any tears over Professor Greenfield's passing, myself included. I would even go so far as to say that many of the slights and insults and behavior that the women in this building suffered through at his hands over the years were probably not even directed personally at any of us. He just didn't know any better. That was who he was and his chauvinistic attitude was just a part of his personality. But I did know that he made several inappropriate comments to fellow professors, in particular, to one fellow professor, which resulted in quite a bit of animosity between the two of them."

"Who was the professor?" Ben asked.

She paused. "Angela Harper," she said finally. Ben sat back and raised his eyebrows. That one surprised him. Angela Harper did not seem at all Greenfield's type. "I can see you're surprised."

"You're right, I am."

"Nevertheless," she said, "there were a couple of incidents between the two. I believe the first may have appeared harmless, but then on subsequent occasions, Professor Greenfield was more insistent on his desire to have a more personal relationship with Professor Harper. He even went so far as to make suggestive comments to her at a law school function at which Professor Harper's husband was also present. Eventually, there were some words between the two men. Afterward, it was fairly clear that Professor Greenfield and Professor Harper were never going to be close friends, if you know what I mean."

"Did you witness this yourself?

"I did and I've talked to Angela about it, although not recently. I saw the incident at the party mostly from afar, but eventually voices were raised and you couldn't help but witness it."

"When did this take place?"

"Oh, maybe three or four years ago, I suppose. I don't remember exactly."

Ben left Professor Berman's office at ten minutes to twelve. He thanked her for her time and her candor and she promised to keep in touch and let him know right away if she thought of anything that might prove helpful to his defense. As Ben took the elevator back down to the third floor, his head whirled with possibilities. He got off the elevator and walked straight into a crowd of students just getting out of class. He joined the group and bumped his way along to the Makrateria, which was now filling with the lunchtime crowd. A moment later, Mark trudged around the corner with another group of students.

"Any luck?" Mark said as he approached Ben outside the entrance to the Makrateria.

142

"I don't know, maybe, but we can't talk about it here obviously. Why don't we go in and get a quick bite?"

After a quick lunch and a conversation devoted largely to football, Mark went back up to the library and Ben went looking for Angela Harper. He found her leaving her office on the way to her next class. A tall, thin African American woman in her early-forties, Angela Harper wore glasses and had her curly reddish hair pulled back behind her ears with barrettes. She brushed past Ben as he introduced himself.

"I would like to talk to you about Professor Greenfield," he called after her.

"I'm sorry, I don't have anything to say about that subject. Please don't bother me again," she said turning slightly.

"If you would rather speak to me in a crowded courtroom filled with reporters that would be fine too," Ben called as she reached the corner of the hallway. She turned again and glared at him, saying nothing. Then she disappeared around the corner toward the elevators. Ben laughed, taking her rejection in stride. So that's how it was going to be. He would talk to her eventually.

Professor Harper taught Constitutional Law at the law school and always appeared to Ben to be more than a bit full of herself. Although Ben had never taken any of her classes himself, he had heard numerous times through the student grapevine that Professor Harper spent much of her classes spouting liberal orthodoxy combined with a steady dose of shrill harangues against conservative Supreme Court Justices and Republican politicians generally. Ben really didn't know her, yet he didn't like her at all.

Ben took the elevator back down to the 3rd Floor, where he ran into Martin Beileck, the school Registrar. "Excuse me," Ben said as they collided.

"Counsel," Beileck whispered as he grabbed Ben's arm, "meet me in the library on the 10th floor in ten minutes." Then he walked away leaving Ben standing there puzzled.

Beileck? What could he want? Ben thought. He took a deep breath and forced himself to think. Beileck had not been someone that Ben even considered talking to previously. But the more he thought about it, the more he realized that Beileck should have been at or near the top of his list. As the School Registrar, Beileck had his fingers in almost everything that went on in the law school. He was one of the few people to interact with the students, the staff and the faculty on a regular basis. More than a bit of a nebbish, he overcompensated for his lack of stature with an affected, overly aggressive persona that made him the frequent butt of student jokes. As Registrar, Beileck possessed all the thankless jobs that no one else wanted, yet needed to get done.

Ben entered the library through the main entrance on the 9th floor and walked up the stairs to the 10th floor. The 10th floor of the library was a largely ceremonial space, with large cherry tables and bookshelves rising high near the top of the twenty-foot ceiling. The north wall of the main room was devoted entirely to windows and a balcony overlooking the city. Ben walked over to the window and looked out. Only three students studied at the tables and not a sound could be heard. The room felt more like a church than a law school. Martin Beileck arrived exactly on cue. As he approached Ben, he pointed to a door in the corner of the room. Ben followed him into a small room which housed several rows of additional shelves containing library materials. When Beileck closed the door behind them, they were alone.

"Good to see you again, Counsel," Beileck said as he approached Ben and the two men shook hands. "I give you a lot of credit for what you're doing here. You're starting to really stir the pot and I want you to know there are things here that are worth investigating." There was a small table against the near wall with two chairs and they sat down. "We don't have a lot of time," Beileck said. "I don't want people to know I'm cooperating with you. It'll make it easier for me to help you out."

"Why do you want to help me out?"

"Because Daniel Greenfield was a friend of mine. I know he had problems here and there, but he always treated me decently and I will never forget it."

Ben nodded. He could imagine that being treated decently by a school full of arrogant law professors didn't happen very often, particularly to someone like Martin Beileck. "Okay, I guess I understand. What do you have for me?"

They spoke for a few minutes and Ben outlined what he had learned so far, which wasn't much. "I think you're on the right track with Professor Harper," Beilick said. "It's no secret that they haven't gotten along for years. There was a rumor circulating that they had a big argument shortly before Christmas and you may not know it, but she can be a real . . . I mean, she can be very difficult."

"I've always had that impression. Are you telling me you wouldn't be surprised if Professor Harper were involved somehow?"

"I'm telling you that nothing would surprise me about Angela Harper."

"Do you know of anyone else with problems like this with Greenfield?"

"Well, I don't think any of the female teachers or staff liked him very much. You probably know his reputation. But I don't think anyone had the animosity for Daniel the way Professor Harper did. I would definitely look into her very closely."

"I'll do that. What about some of these students? I understand there were some complaints made from students."

"You'll find most of that stuff in the files. I think there were a couple of others previously that may have been purged from his files."

"Purged from his files? When?"

"Not recently. Things were just sort of swept under the rug at the time and kept out of his files. You know, Daniel was here a long time and the Administration didn't want to see anything happen to him, or to the school for that matter, on their watch."

"I understand."

Beileck appeared nervous and was looking over his shoulder constantly to make sure no one was coming in the door. "I don't want to be seen talking privately to you. That way I could be of more help to you. Sometimes I hear things. Look, I've gotta go. I'll be in touch."

23

Ben spent an uneventful weekend with the family, while Meg's case percolated in the back of his mind, never far from the surface. Ben spent all day Monday trying to catch up on the work he had neglected and preparing for a Forest Preserve District meeting the following day. When he returned to the office from that meeting at about eleven-thirty on Tuesday morning, Ben ran into Dianne Reynolds by the fax machine. "You'll never guess who called," she said. Ben shrugged. "The wife." Ben had been trying to get in touch with her for days, without success.

"Really," Ben said. "What'd she say?"

"I don't know. Nancy talked to her."

Ben went upstairs and into Nancy's office before even taking off his coat. "So what'd she say?" he asked.

Nancy spun around in her chair to face him. "Well, she wasn't very friendly, for starters. She said that she understood that you wanted to talk to her and she wanted you to call her back as soon as you got back to the office. She said she was free this afternoon if you wanted to meet with her."

"This afternoon? That's quick."

"Yeah, I thought so too."

"Did she say anything else?"

Nancy shook her head. "Not really. I don't think she wanted to talk to a lowly secretary."

"Can't blame her for that," Ben said. Nancy scowled. "Any other calls?" he asked.

"Tons, but isn't that enough?"

"Maybe too much."

Ben went to his office, hung up his overcoat and suit jacket and dialed the number on the piece of paper Nancy had just given him.

"Hello," a woman's voice answered.

"Hello, is this Sylvia Greenfield?"

"Yes it is."

"Hello Mrs. Greenfield, this is Benjamin Lohmeier. Thank you for calling me back."

"I understand that you want to speak to me. Would this be better in person, or can we do it over the telephone?"

"I would prefer if we did it in person, if you don't mind."

"I suppose that would be okay."

"Are you free this afternoon?

"Yes, I suppose so."

"What time is good for you?"

"How long do you think this will take?"

"Oh, probably less than an hour."

"Okay then, can you meet me here at one-thirty?"

"That will be fine."

"Do you know where I live?"

"Yes, I do."

"Do you need directions?"

"No, I think I can find it okay."

"Okay, then, I'll see you later. Goodbye." She hung up.

That was a strange conversation, Ben thought. It had all the impersonal charm of scheduling a dental appointment. Ben decided to skip lunch and prepare a brief outline of subjects he needed to cover. With the help of directions he got off the internet, Ben found her house without difficulty. As Ben pulled onto her street, he thought that her neighborhood reminded him somewhat of his own; gracious older homes situated on mature, tree-lined streets. Evanston was decidedly more urban than Clarendon Hills to be sure, and Ben knew that Evanston was a much larger and more racially and ethnically diverse community. Ben parked across the street and walked up to the front door.

Ben didn't know what to expect as Sylvia Greenfield answered the door wearing a white blouse and tan twill pants. Ben found her

147

surprisingly attractive, in a princess sort of way, much more attractive than he figured Greenfield deserved.

"Mr. Lohmeier?" she said in a business-like voice. Ben nodded and she said, "Please come in," stepping aside to allow him to pass. She didn't extend her hand and Ben didn't offer his own. She led him through a center hallway to the back of the house and into a family room. "Can I get you anything to drink, Mr. Lohmeier?"

"No thanks, I'm fine."

"Okay then, why don't we sit down." She took a seat on the couch and Ben sat in a leather club chair.

"First of all," he began, "I want to thank you for agreeing to meet with me. I can imagine that this has been a very difficult experience for you and particularly for your daughters. Although I don't want to intrude on your privacy, there's certain information that I do need in order to provide an adequate defense for my client."

Sylvia Greenfield sat very upright and still, her hands folded across her lap. "I understand, Mr. Lohmeier," she said. "Obviously, Daniel was involved in criminal law from the time I met him in school, so I believe I have naturally become more sensitive to the needs and protections afforded criminal defendants in our system."

"I hadn't thought of that, but I'm sure that's true," he said.

"The police obviously think your client killed Daniel."

"Yes, I suppose they do, but I don't know what causes them to think that way."

"Do you consider me a suspect, Mr. Lohmeier?"

The question took Ben completely off-guard. And he was sure that he looked quite startled hearing it. He looked closely into her eyes before answering, trying to get behind the question to ascertain what her true motives were. He figured she had planned that broadside in advance. "I don't really know, to tell you the truth," he said finally. "I don't know enough about you or your relationship with your ex-husband to know whether that theory is reasonable or possible. I certainly wouldn't rule it in or out at this point."

"Fair enough. I wouldn't expect that you would. In case you were wondering though, I didn't kill my husband." Her features remained impassive as though she were telling him where she took her dry cleaning.

"Could you tell me a little bit about your marriage?"

"For a long time, we had a good marriage. Everything was good in the beginning. Daniel was, at least as far as I know, a good husband and a good father. He loved his girls very much. I can never take that away from him. But as he grew older, I think spending so much time in the presence of attractive young women became too tempting. I don't know when he began having relationships with students, but I suspect it was some time ago. I got suspicious, but tried not to think about it."

"What made you suspicious?"

"Little things mostly. He wasn't where he was supposed to be. He would disappear and I wouldn't know where he was or when he would be back. And I would begin to notice that he smelled of perfume. As I said, I tried not to think about it and when I confronted him with it, his denials were quite plausible. I mostly tried to put it out of my mind. He still treated me and girls very well and I just hoped it was something that he would get over and stop doing."

"What brought about the end of the marriage?"

"More of the same." She looked down at her hands and appeared to consider her words carefully. Ben waited patiently trying not to put words into her mouth. It would be better to just let her talk. Although dredging up these memories couldn't be pleasant, she still maintained a certain detached civility that Ben found interesting. "I think what hurt the most was when he seemed to lose interest. Before, his little conquests didn't seem to affect our relationship that much except for the fact that it was obviously quite demeaning." Ben sensed that she didn't want to make eye contact with him. Perhaps she didn't want to see pity in his eyes. "Eventually though," she continued, "he seemed to be just going through the motions."

"Did the accusations by students at the law school affect it in any way?"

"Of course. That was very embarrassing, both for Daniel and for me, but that didn't tell me anything that I hadn't already known for a long time. He denied it at first, but that was no good."

"So, are you familiar with the students involved?"

"Familiar? No, not terribly. One of them was named Hinkle, I think. I remember the name Hinkle. I don't remember her first name, nor do I remember the name of the other student. I don't think the school wanted to pursue the matter, to be honest, so Daniel wasn't seriously disciplined, at least not as seriously as you might expect."

"So, you're saying that really wasn't the cause of the end of the marriage?"

"No, not totally." She looked up at him now. "What really hurt the most was when I found out that he had been having a long-term relationship with one of his students even after she graduated. Apparently they had been together for almost three years."

"Do you know the name of the student?"

"Nora. I believe her name was Nora. I don't remember her last name."

"When did this take place?"

"I found out about four years ago. I found a strange note in Daniel's pants in the laundry and I confronted him with it and he more or less admitted it. That was pretty much the beginning of the end. It was one thing when he had these little conquests. It was quite another when he was carrying on a long-term relationship with another woman probably half his age."

Ben had not heard of any of this. He couldn't quite understand the difference between a one-night stand and a long-term affair and didn't think Libby would either. "What happened then?" he asked when it became clear she wasn't going to continue.

"I basically threw him out."

"How did he react to that?"

"He didn't want to leave. He didn't want to lose the image of his family and especially his girls. They took it rather hard."

"Of course," Ben said not knowing what else to say. He searched for the right question before asking, "What happened with your husband and this Nora?"

"I have no idea," she said. "I got the impression that it was over sooner rather than later. Perhaps she threw him out too."

Sounds like wishful thinking, Ben thought. "Was he living with her?"

She shook her head. "No, not that I know of."

"Do you know where she lives now?"

"I have no idea."

"How would you describe the divorce?"

"It was pretty bad. We didn't fight over things like the house or money or anything like that. It was just that I couldn't bear to be in his presence any longer and he didn't want the divorce, so our personal interactions were not always very civil."

Ben looked at her closely and didn't feel like he could get a good read on her yet. While he understood the idea of her being something of a cold fish, he couldn't tell whether this reflected her true personality or was simply an affectation to deal with his questioning. "When was the last time you saw your husband?"

"It had been quite a while, before Thanksgiving, I think. We spoke on the phone once or twice after that regarding the holidays, but we didn't see each other very often lately because it just seemed to work better that way. He talked to the girls quite a bit, but we didn't speak that often."

"Did he ever tell you of any threats or anything like that?"

"No, never. I know over the years that he would have occasional disagreements with students over grades and that sort of thing, but I think any person in his position has that given the pressures of law school and the importance of grades and the like."

Ben nodded. "Do you know of any problems with other professors?"

"Nothing unusual that I can remember."

"What about Angela Harper?"

A small cold smile crossed her features. "Angela Harper never seemed to me to be a particularly friendly woman, Mr. Lohmeier. Although I met her only a few times, my encounters with her at

151

school functions were fairly consistent with Daniel's opinion of her, which wasn't very good. I don't recall Daniel ever saying anything about having any personal problems with her, however. Are you suggesting that maybe Professor Harper killed my husband?"

"No, no nothing like that," he said shading the truth. "I'm just trying to get to the bottom of what may or may not have been going on at the law school, that's all. I have just heard that perhaps Professor Harper and your husband didn't get along very well. My attempts to talk to her about it have proven unsuccessful."

"That doesn't particularly surprise me," she said.

Ben rubbed his chin and considered his next question. "If you don't mind my asking, when were you last at the law school?"

She looked away and appeared to think carefully about her answer. "I'm not sure I've been there in more than three years, maybe even since Daniel and I separated," she said.

"Where were you on December 28th? That was a Friday."

She looked directly into Ben's eyes. "Is that when they think he was killed?" Ben didn't respond. "Yes, that must be why you asked. I believe I was shopping. I had dinner that evening here with my daughters." She looked almost defiantly at Ben.

"Were you ever aware of your husband being involved with drugs of any kind?"

The question startled her. It was the only time during their conversation when Ben thought he had caught her unaware. "Drugs? I can't imagine such a thing. I don't believe my husband ever used drugs in his life, not even in college. Where did you hear that?"

"Just something that came up in a conversation I had with someone. They suggested that perhaps your husband used some recreational drugs."

"I wouldn't believe that and I would appreciate it if you didn't spread that rumor. It would be very hurtful to my daughters."

"I'm sure that it would. It's not my intention to spread any rumors. As far as your daughters are concerned, I would prefer not to speak to them unless I had to."

"I don't see any reason why you would ever have to."

"Well, I don't know about that," Ben said. "But I won't contact them without telling you first. I'll only do it if I think I really need to." She appeared unconvinced. "If I needed to speak to someone who knew what was going on with your husband, who should I talk to?"

"That's easy," she said, "Samuel Dorlund."

24

Ben didn't know quite what to make of his conversation with Sylvia Greenfield. He didn't know whether he should take her at face value, or view her as someone relentlessly trying to protect herself and her children. He found it a little far-fetched that she would be willing to put up with a series of meaningless sexual encounters between her husband and his students, while objecting to a more serious relationship between them. He didn't know of any wife who would put up with either - certainly Libby wouldn't. He also had trouble buying the fact that she didn't believe he was capable of drug use. If Makra was correct, there was no doubt about it, yet she seemed convinced that it wasn't possible. He agreed with Seagram's assessment that she was a cold, seemingly impersonal woman, but was far from ready to conclude that she wasn't capable of killing her ex-husband. Revenge is, they say after all, the dish best served cold.

When he got back to the office, he called Martin Beileck to track down the student named Nora, whom Sylvia Greenfield suggested ultimately caused her divorce. On Tuesday morning, Beileck called and left Ben a message telling him that Greenfield's girlfriend was likely a woman named Nora Fleming, who had graduated three years earlier. He could locate no other Noras or even Eleanors that would fit the profile and the right time frame. After proving unable to locate her in the Chicago area, Ben gave the information to Stan Disko and asked him to start looking. Early Friday afternoon, Disko called with the news that he had found her.

154

"She's now Nora Scott," Disko said on the telephone.

"So she got married then?"

"Yeah, it appears so, about a year ago according to one of her friends. She married a guy, Andrew Scott, who graduated from the law school the year before she did. They live in Florida."

"Florida? Whereabouts in Florida?"

"A place called Ocala."

"Where the hell is Ocala?"

"It's a small town in horse country about forty or fifty miles north of Orlando."

"Do you have an address?"

"Yes, but no phone number."

"Okay, give it to me."

Ben decided he would make the trip to Ocala himself to talk to Nora Fleming. He would go unannounced and try to surprise her. He got on the internet and discovered that there were no direct flights between Chicago and Ocala, Ocala only had a small municipal airport, so he booked a flight to Orlando and then rented a car for the hour or so drive north to Ocala. He made reservations for Monday and called Libby, who didn't hide her displeasure over the trip. Ben figured it wouldn't be too bad if he could go down Monday morning and come back Tuesday night.

The limo arrived on time at seven in the morning. Libby took a sobbing Natalie out of her father's arms, while Matthew, on the other hand, thought the whole limo thing was quite cool indeed. The car dropped Ben at the Departures terminal at twenty minutes before eight and the check-in and extra security measures resulting from September 11th took about twenty minutes or so.

Ben sat in the lounge outside the gate and waited for the plane to board. He passed the time by watching his fellow passengers gather for the flight. There were a handful of businessmen and women dressed in suits, a few families leaving on vacation and even a couple of trashy-looking teenage girls who apparently hadn't looked in the mirror before leaving the house that morning. Ben watched the human traffic pass by hoping all the while for a little bit better atmosphere. At ten minutes to nine, the Delta airlines staff started boarding the airplane and by nine o'clock sharp, Ben was in his seat between the wings. He pulled the airline guide from the pouch on the seat in front of him and paged through it looking for the diagram of the airplane. This particular plane had three seats across on either side of the center aisle. Ben took the seat on the aisle and there was no one else in his entire row. The plane was barely one-third full.

Ben didn't consider himself a bad flyer or afraid of flying. Nevertheless, he knew that most crashes occurred right around take-off or right around landing causing him to pay special attention at those points in his infrequent flights. The take-off was uneventful and the plane settled into a nice cruising altitude and Ben took a deep breath and pulled out a book for a good read. Ben lost himself in the exploits of Lucas Davenport as the plane cruised southward. He looked up and put the book away as the plane started to descend. He paid close attention to the landing and considered it an unqualified success when the tires of the airplane touched down on the runway without incident. The connecting flight from Atlanta to Orlando sat on the runway for half an hour before returning to the gate to repair a burned out bulb, or at least that's what they said it was. The resulting delay caused them to land about an hour late in Orlando, another successful take-off and landing, and Ben was now firmly behind schedule.

He took the tram from the arrival gate to the main terminal and tried to find the rental car place. Lugging his carry-on bag and briefcase with him, he went downstairs and located the main rental car vendors in a row along the wall - Avis, Hertz, Budget, everyone but Thrifty. He cursed himself for picking the wrong rental car company. He dragged his things outside and set them on the sidewalk. Tall palm trees and flowering plants graced the parkway and the leafy branches of overhanging trees shaded the service drive separating the terminal building from the parking area. Even though he began to perspire under the dark blue wind shirt he used as a jacket, Ben liked the way the warm air felt when contrasted with the bitter cold he had left in Chicago.

After a few moments, he got the lay of the land in the rental car area and concluded that he merely had to find the right shuttle bus

156

to take him to the place where he could pick up his car. He wandered down the row of parking spaces until he found the light blue Thrifty sign. As if on cue, a blue and white shuttle bus pulled into the space in front of him and a young Hispanic man got out. Ben climbed the steps and took a seat in the air conditioned shuttle, stowing his bags in the bin next to him.

Ten minutes and a couple of stops later, the shuttle eased up a ramp and out of the airport, eventually pulling into a Thrifty Rental Car location a half mile or so away. Ben got off and headed around the corner to the entrance. As the automatic door whirred open, a blast of air conditioning hit him in the face and blew his hair back. It felt good. He now wanted to get rid of the wind shirt. Ben walked through the rope maze and up to the counter stopping at the lone open clerk, a big-boned blond who looked as though she hadn't spent much time doing her hair that morning.

"Good afternoon sir," she said with some level of sincerity, "welcome to Thrifty Car Rental. How can I be of service today?"

Ben pulled his reservation from his briefcase and placed it on the counter. "I have a reservation. The name is Lohmeier. L-O-H-M-E-I-E-R."

"One moment," she said, "let me see if I can locate your reservation." She punched in a series of keys and then another and then another before finally locating his reservation in the system. "Sir, we have you with a four door, midsize sedan. Is that correct?"

"I think so."

"We could upgrade that to a convertible for an extra twelve dollars a day."

"A convertible?" Ben said. "What kind of convertible?"

"A Chrysler Sebring." Twelve bucks wasn't that much considering he wasn't paying for it. He turned and looked out the glass doors for the parking lot, hoping to spot one of the convertibles. Noticing, she said, "You see it? It's that red one in the first row right by the sidewalk."

"Yeah, I see it," he said. "Okay, that's fine. I'll take it."

Five minutes later, he peeled off the wind shirt and tossed it in the back seat of the red Sebring, pulled his sunglasses out of his briefcase and climbed inside. He took a couple of minutes to figure out how to lower the top and pretty soon, he was ready to roll.

Following the directions he received from the woman behind the Thrifty counter, which seemed slightly different from the directions he had printed off the internet while back home, Ben took a couple of turns, got off one expressway, got back on another, paid more tolls than he could count and then finally hit the ramp for the exit pointing in the direction of "North Turnpike". Ben spent twenty minutes fumbling for a good radio station. He never really found one - only occasional good songs. Unlike northern Illinois, where a driver is lucky to find dead grass in the middle of a divided highway, the Florida Turnpike, apparently now known as the Ronald Reagan Turnpike, came replete with palm trees, flowering plants and other lush vegetation, and even a pine forest or two along the way.

Ben kind of liked the Sebring. It handled well and had good acceleration, and Ben enjoyed the feeling of his wispy blond hair flying in the breeze. He pushed the case and the reason for his visit to the back of his mind and concentrated on the heat of the sun, the roar of the engine and the speed of the Sebring as it blew past scenery heading north up the Turnpike in excess of eighty-five miles per hour. About twenty miles south of Ocala, Ben split off onto I-75 North and ten minutes later, as he slowed to a more respectable seventy miles per hour, he began to see horses grazing with the cattle in the pastures by the side of the highway. Just south of Ocala, he spotted a small group of buffalo, maybe six or eight. He didn't know what groups of buffalo were called grazing there in a semi-circle. He always liked buffalo. They seemed to be such powerful, almost regal animals. He thought of Jim Schulte raising buffalo in Hayward, Wisconsin and shivered despite the heat. Since Jim Schulte was just about the last person he wanted to think of blazing up the Ronald Reagan Turnpike in central Florida, he turned the radio up for the rest of the trip, which wasn't long.

He flew down the ramp at the Ocala/Silver Springs exit and took a hard left onto College Road. Passing through the underpass, he saw the hotel, a Marriott Courtyard, just up on the right. He parked the Sebring out front and went inside to check in.

A small lobby greeted him with a restaurant/lounge at the far end. A glass case stood against the wall next to the front desk filled with New York Yankees memorabilia - autographed hats, balls, pictures and gloves. This puzzled Ben a little bit because he didn't think that Ocala was a spring training town. He couldn't understand the connection to the Yankees until he noticed a gold plaque on the wall which proclaimed, "This is a Steinbrenner-Company Hotel." That explained it.

He found his room at the end of a corridor not far from the laundry. The room was nice and clean, with a single king-size bed and a small sitting area consisting of a love seat and a Williamsburg-style desk. Good enough. Ben tossed his stuff on the bed and pulled the curtains open to crack the window and let some fresh air inside. He shuffled through his briefcase looking for the map to Nora Fleming's house. According to Yahoo, the house was about twelve miles from the hotel with an approximate travel time of twenty-nine minutes, which seemed long.

Ben looked at his watch - almost five o'clock local time. He didn't want to call ahead and tip her off that he was coming, but he didn't know what time she would be home either. He decided that one way or another he needed to find her house. He would set off now and if she was there, great. If not, he could grab some dinner and try back again later. At least he would know where the house was. He made sure that he had a couple of business cards on him and set out.

He pulled the Sebring out of the parking lot and turned right onto College Road with the top down and the radio on. College Road appeared to be one of the main drags through Ocala and Ben assumed there must be a college or university associated with it someplace. The road moved generally from northeast to southwest and Ben headed southwest, apparently away from town. After a mile or so, College Road became Southwest State Road 200 with the usual assortment of car dealers, restaurants and the ubiquitous vacation property sales offices. After about seven miles, Ben took a sharp left on Southwest 103rd Street, which appeared to be largely residential in character. The homes were nothing to get excited about, mostly one-story ramblers made of cement block construction in a slightly Spanish style motif. Occasionally, he'd see some odd-for-Chicago colors like turquoise blue, pale pink or lime green.

After about four miles, the houses began to thin somewhat and the area became less developed. He looked at the map. He had to be getting close. He had gone about the right distance. He saw a sign for Ocala Waterway Estates, which looked promising at first, but didn't pan out into anything. He took a right and went down a small road that led off toward a row of scrub trees in the distance, then abruptly stopped. He paused at the intersection beyond which Ocala civilization seemed to cease. To his left, a teenage girl in cut-off jeans and a halter top showing way too much skin for someone her size washed an SUV with a garden hose. He looked back at the map.

"God damn it. It should be right down here," Ben said aloud. The roads he saw on the map should be right in front of him, but all he saw was open landscape. "There must be a way to get back there," he said. The sun was beginning to sink low in the sky. He took a left and sped along looking for a road where he could cut in on his right hand side. All he found was more trees. Several blocks down, he saw a bulldozer parked off to the side of the road as though road construction was about to commence. He continued a few more blocks and reached a dead end in the road. Now the undeveloped land stretched in front of him and to his right. The only houses were to his left and back behind him. "Fuck," he said.

He spun the Sebring around and headed back in the other direction. Maybe he could go back down the other way and then find another crossroad and come back at it from the other side. Ben reached the intersection he had stopped at a few minutes earlier and pulled the car to a stop. The area where he needed to be was now on his left, but he was at least three or four blocks away from it. The problem was he had no way of getting in there. He decided to keep going.

About three-quarters of a mile later, Ben hit a two-lane road and took a left. The road seemed to bisect several developments in various stages of completion. On his right, there was a

160

development with mostly paved roads and a smattering of houses. A sales trailer sat near the main entrance to Norwood Estates. He had to be close now. Up ahead on the left, he saw what appeared to be a road. When he got there, he concluded that the term "road" was more than generous. It seemed to be more of a path made out of packed-down dirt, somewhat like the precursor of a paved road. It looked like the roads had been plotted, just not built yet. Off in the distance, Ben thought he saw a small house. The last thing he wanted to do was get the rental car stuck back there so he took a long, hard look down the path. It appeared solid enough to support a car and wide enough for two cars to pass in opposite directions. He looked in the rearview mirror - nothing coming behind him and nothing in front of him. He could sit here and think about this for a minute. He glanced to his right - the sun was setting now and daylight rapidly began to fade. Ben could feel the air growing cool and damp. If he was going to find the house, it had better be soon.

He eased the car off the road and onto the path. It inched along for about a quarter of a mile before he came to a house on the left, a one-story, lime green job quite reminiscent of the ones he had seen earlier. He looked at the number on the mailbox. He was about two blocks away. He crept along until he came to another larger house on the right. This one was set back in a grove of trees. The driveway was packed dirt just like the path. Next door, a new house began to rise up out of the ground, its cement block foundation sticking out of the dirt.

Ben came to something of an intersection, where another fairly wide dirt path crossed this one. He looked in both directions, but did not see any houses. Further up on the left-hand side, he saw a mailbox sticking out behind a small clump of trees. As he approached, he could see the name Scott painted in red on the black mailbox. "Bingo," he said. He moved the car forward until he was even with the mailbox and his heart sank. There was nothing there, just the mailbox, behind it a stand of scrub trees and wild overgrown bushes. There was no house anywhere.

25

Ben leaned against the hood of the Sebring and pulled out his cell phone. The car was running and the driver's door open, the headlights illuminating the trees in the distance. The sun had fallen behind the forest off to the west and daylight quickly slipped away.

"Where the fuck am I?" Ben said into the phone.

"How do I know?" Disko answered from back in Illinois.

"You gave me the address and the directions. The only thing this place lacks is alligators, oh yeah, and roads. This is the place they go to to dump the body so no one will ever find it." Disko didn't answer. "Okay, well, it's obvious that I'm not finding anything else out tonight. It's almost dark here, so check it out and I'll try and call you when I get back to the hotel. I'm hungry. I need to get something to eat."

Ben took one long last look around, thankful that he was alone, and climbed back into the car. Ten minutes later, he was back on State Road 200 heading in the direction of the hotel. When he reached the hotel, he kept going down College Road looking for a place he could find a decent meal. About a mile past the hotel, he came to a large glass complex lit up like the Fourth of July against the night sky. He spotted a sign - Central Florida Community College. That explained College Road. A bit further up on the right, Ben saw the sign for the Lone Star Steakhouse.

"Good enough," he said and pulled the Sebring into the lot and parked under a lush green tree. He had only been in Florida a few hours, but had already gotten used to the weather. The warm sun, blooming flowers and soft breezes sure beat the hell out of Chicago in February. He struggled with the roof of the Sebring for a few minutes trying to get it latched before finally heading inside. He was seated at a table in the middle of the room. He ordered a draft beer which came in a frosted mug. Just the right temperature, he thought savoring the first sip. He ordered a rib eye steak, medium rare, baked potato, tossed salad with Italian dressing and ranch toast and considered his options while waiting for his meal to arrive.

He thought he remembered that Ocala was the county seat for whatever county he was in and he decided to head out to the county government complex in the morning, he assumed they had one, to poke around the real estate records if Disko didn't come up with a better address by then. Having done a little real estate investigation work on a few of his Forest Preserve District files, Ben knew he should be able to dig something up from either the property transfer records or the tax assessor's office.

After he finished his meal - the steak was large, tender and cooked just right - he asked his waitress for the name of a local watering hole where he could grab a beer. He needed to kill a couple of hours and maybe blow off some steam. She directed him to Cal's, about a half mile away on the other side of the Community College.

"You should be able to find whatever you want there," she said with a knowing smile. Ben didn't think she understood quite what he was looking for, but decided not to set her straight. He paid the check, left her a nice tip and headed back to the Sebring.

Cal's proved that all college bars are pretty much the same - lots of loud music, cheap beer and guys looking to score. Ben almost didn't find the place at first, but once he did, he realized he felt really out of place, about like he expected. Cal's occupied two stories next to a Foot Locker store on a busy corner just north of the Central Florida Community College campus. Clearly the local hang-out for the students, the place was hopping pretty good for a Monday night. Ben grabbed a Rolling Rock long neck and took a slow tour around the first floor and then up to the second. He felt a little like a parent doing a reconnaissance mission for an Oprah show on wild teens.

163

He found a spot up against the wall on the second floor and sipped his beer. The room was hot and Ben began to sweat. He couldn't hear much of anything above the din and probably didn't need to. He had enough to look at. Girls in mini-skirts and thin halter tops bumped and grinded with their boyfriends, or at least Ben assumed they were their boyfriends. Guys danced with girls, girls danced with girls, groups of girls danced with groups of guys. Guys didn't dance with guys, at least not here. This was sensory overload for a guy Ben's age. When he decided to come here, he hadn't factored in the whole Florida weather thing, the fact that girls could dress this way all year round in Florida's warm and sunny climate. Back home, even the best looking college coeds would be all covered up this time of year.

Ben finished his beer and ambled over to a bar along the near wall for another. An hour or so later, after fending off two perky college roommates who tried to convince him to go back to their apartment with them to party a little, a shocked, but relieved Benjamin Lohmeier headed back to his hotel. Although he thought the girls were probably just toying with an older guy to try and make him feel good, he nevertheless did wonder about what might have been.

He called Disko back. Nothing new on the address front. Then he called home before turning in. He left out the part about the roommates. Nothing good could come from that. Ben had a pretty good night's sleep. The great thing about hotels is that you can always get the room cold enough and dark enough, both of which Ben liked when he slept. He slept until almost eight local time and then took a quick shower. On his way out, he stopped at the front desk and got directions to the County Complex. It was only about fifteen minutes away, roughly two miles east of the County Courthouse, located in downtown Ocala. Ben took a left on College Road and headed back in the direction of the Community College, which seemed larger and newer in the light of day. As community colleges went, it looked fairly impressive. A couple of miles further down the road, he took a left on Pine Avenue, which took him right into downtown Ocala. After about half a mile, he took a right on Silver Springs Boulevard heading east. As he turned the corner, he saw what looked to be the Courthouse a couple of blocks up and over to his left.

The County Complex was on 25th Avenue, a couple of miles down Silver Springs Boulevard. He turned into the Complex at the first light and came to a fork in the driveway. Signs pointed in every direction. Geographic Information Systems, Building, Zoning and Property Management, Museum, Green Clover Hall, Property Appraiser, Tax Collector, County Attorney, County Administrator, County Commissioners. The sign looked like the totem pole on *M*A*S*H*. Ben took a minute to figure out where he was going and chose the Property Appraiser's and Tax Collector's offices, both of which seemed to be housed together in a large building just off to his right.

He parked the Sebring in the lot not far from a vendor selling pretzels. As he strolled up the walk to the building's entrance, Ben noticed that the cement walkway and rambling single story brown brick structure looked almost new. He couldn't decide if that was a function of the climate or whether the building was in fact new. He figured that the harsh climate of the north, complete with wild temperature fluctuations, snow and salt, probably aged buildings before their time. Inside, he discovered that the building was essentially split in two - the Property Appraiser's office was located on the left side of the building, with the Tax Collector housed in a much smaller space to the right. He chose the Property Appraiser first and pushed through a set of glass doors into a large open area with countless desks arranged in rows. The room was fairly dark and they had the air conditioning turned up high to guard against the coming afternoon heat. Ben walked up to the first desk, where a Hispanic woman in her early-fifties sat behind a sign that read, "Information."

"I was wondering if you had any public access computer terminals?" Ben asked.

"Yes, we do," she said, gesturing to a long counter on the near wall which housed eight to ten PC's. She led Ben over to the first computer and got him set up. Within a couple of minutes, he was able to perform rudimentary searches on county real estate records. He figured out how to do name searches and punched in Nora

Fleming and Nora Fleming Scott. He confirmed that Nora's husband's name seemed to be Andrew and that Andrew seemed to buy and sell quite a bit of real estate. Ben assumed that Andrew Scott probably worked as a real estate developer or was otherwise involved in rental properties. Ben located their likely residence, a warranty deed transferring the property from a land trust to Andrew Scott and Nora Fleming Scott, husband and wife, in tenancy by the entireties. The deed gave an Ocala address on Northwest Palisades Parkway. Ben had no idea where that was. After a few more minutes of searching failed to uncover anything new, Ben decided to go across the way and double-check what he had discovered with the Tax Collector.

When he reached the counter at the Tax Collector's office, a middle-aged woman who reminded him of everyone's Mom greeted him with a smile and provided him with all the information he needed. She even knew Andrew Scott from some estate work he had done for her a while back. Apparently, Andrew had taken over the Scott Law Offices from his uncle, who was semi-retired now. The firm had been a fixture in Ocala for years and the woman gave Ben directions to the office, located in a one-story, red brick building a block or two from the courthouse.

Ben walked out of the Tax Collector's Office with a sense of accomplishment. Maybe he should be the detective and not Stan Disko. He turned left on Silver Springs Boulevard and headed back toward downtown Ocala. As he passed through the intersection at Pine Avenue, he looked to his left and saw a large white gazebo on the lawn in front of the City Hall. Following the instructions he received at the Tax Collector's office, he took a right at the next intersection and a block down drove past the entrance to the Marion County Judicial Center, a nondescript gray stone structure that looked more like a prison than a County Courthouse. Attached to it was an equally unattractive parking garage. Ben was a little disappointed. Ocala was kind of a charming little town with a nice City Hall. He even liked the gazebo. The Courthouse, on the other hand, looked like a Sixties-era mistake.

Like the woman at the Tax Collector's office suggested, he kept going a block or two before making a right and heading back toward Pine Avenue. There on the near left corner, he saw a one-story, red brick colonial structure with a white sign in front. "The Scott Law Offices. Established 1927."

"There it is," he said aloud.

Ben parked up the block, slung his briefcase over his shoulder and headed down the sidewalk. The building appeared much larger on the inside than it had from the outside. The small lobby was nicely appointed with traditional furniture and artwork depicting the American Revolution. The walls were painted a periwinkle blue and the floors were dark wood with several Oriental area rugs scattered throughout. On the wall behind the dark mahogany reception desk the name, "Scott Law Offices" was etched in gold lettering. Beneath it in smaller script were the names of seven lawyers beginning with Henry L. Scott. He must be the uncle, Ben thought. Andrew W. Scott and Nora Fleming Scott came next. A pretty receptionist with long blond hair smiled as he approached her station.

"Hi, can I help you," she asked.

"I hope so," Ben replied. "I'm looking for Nora Fleming Scott. I need to speak to her regarding a legal matter."

"Do you have an appointment with Ms. Scott?" she asked. She looked and sounded like a southern belle. She even batted her eyes.

"No, I'm afraid I don't," Ben said. "I do need to speak to her though."

"May I ask your name, sir?"

"Sure, my name is Benjamin Lohmeier."

"Well, I'm sorry Mr. Lohmeier, but Ms. Scott isn't in right now."

"Do you expect her back anytime soon?"

"She's in Court this morning. We expect her back before too long."

"Maybe I can help you." A tall, blond-haired man in his early-thirties entered the lobby from the corridor to Ben's right. "I'm

Andrew Scott," he said in a firm voice extending his hand, which Ben took.

"I'm Benjamin Lohmeier."

Scott's white dress shirt looked so heavily starched it made Ben feel uncomfortable in his yellow golf shirt and khaki pants.

"Now what can we help you with?" Scott asked.

"Well, I'm not sure you can help me. I need to speak to Ms. Scott about a legal matter."

"Can I ask what this refers to?"

"I'm afraid I can't discuss it. I need to discuss it with Ms. Scott."

"Well, Nora is my wife," he said insisting. "I'm sure you can discuss it with me. I'm a lawyer and the managing partner here."

"Oh, I'm sure you're more than capable," Ben said. "It's just that it's not up to me whether to discuss it with you."

Andrew Scott looked more than perplexed. Finally he said, "Rather than stand out here, why don't we go back to my office and see?"

Just as Ben started to respond, a tall slim woman with shoulder length brown hair came through the front door and joined them in the lobby. She wore a tan suit with a satchel over her right shoulder and she carried two brown expandable file folders in her left arm. All eyes turned to her as soon as she entered.

"Hi, what's up?" she said, slightly out of breath and looking from one to the other. Ben deferred to her husband.

"This gentleman says he's here to speak to you about a legal matter."

Ben stepped forward and introduced himself. "Hi, I'm Benjamin Lohmeier," he said sticking out his hand. He caught a glimmer of recognition on her face as she hesitated for an instant before taking it.

"Nora Scott," she said not quite looking him in the eye.

"Now that my wife's here, perhaps you can tell us what this is all about," Andrew Scott said.

"As I told your husband, Ms. Scott, I have a legal matter I would like to discuss with you if you could spare me a few minutes.

Unfortunately, it's not the kind of thing we should discuss out here in the lobby."

For just a second, Nora Scott looked Ben's way and their eyes met. In that second, Ben sensed that she knew what he was talking about and more significantly that she knew that he knew that she knew it. Nora stepped forward.

"That's okay, Andrew," she said putting her hand on his arm. "Mr. Lohmeier is right. Why don't we just go back to my office where we can talk privately."

"I'm not sure . . ." Andrew Scott said before his wife cut him off.

"No, that's fine. Mr. Lohmeier, follow me." Nora led Ben out of the lobby and into an open area dotted with secretarial stations. They passed several offices on the right, each of which had a window outside to the street. A couple of them appeared to be vacant. The hallway appeared to end at the corner of the building then turn left and continue down the far perimeter, where more offices were undoubtedly located. Nora's office was the second to last one before the end of the hall. Across from it sat a large conference room enclosed in a glass wall. Its blinds opened to reveal a large mahogany conference table surrounded by ten cushioned chairs. As he entered Nora's office, Ben turned and looked back toward the lobby to find Andrew Scott standing there in the distance glaring at him.

Nora's office seemed surprisingly stark for a woman, particularly one whose husband ran the place. It gave Ben the impression of someone who hadn't fully moved in yet and had yet to make up her mind whether she was ever going to. The furniture consisted of standard office issue, plain and not very expensive. Generic landscape artwork hung on the walls, but no diplomas. Six or eight files sat haphazardly in the near corner. A small vase of freshly cut flowers, one or two days old, stood on the credenza behind the desk next to a lone wedding photograph depicting the happy couple cutting their wedding cake. Ben glanced down and noticed a sizeable diamond on her ring finger.

Nora placed her things on one of the two cloth guest chairs, while Ben took a seat in the other. She moved around the desk and sat down. "So, Mr. Lohmeier," she said not quite looking up, "tell me, where are you from?"

"I'm from Chicago, but I have a feeling you know that already, don't you?"

"I am familiar with you, yes. I take it you came to see me about Daniel Greenfield?"

"That's right. I understand you had a relationship with Professor Greenfield?"

She steepled her fingers and looked out the window toward the street. "I'm sorry to disappoint you, Mr. Lohmeier, but that's not an area open for discussion."

"I'm afraid I can't accept that."

"I'm afraid you'll have to."

"If you know who I am, Ms. Scott, then you know that I represent Megan Rand, who is currently being charged with the murder of Daniel Greenfield. You should then understand why I need to speak to you."

"Actually, I wasn't aware of that at all, Mr. Lohmeier. I'm aware of Professor Greenfield's passing, but I didn't know the circumstances of your involvement in the matter."

Now Ben was confused. She looked back and saw it on his face.

"Mr. Lohmeier," she said with the slightest of smiles, "is it true that you once caused a witness to flip on cross-examination in a trial competition just by staring at her?"

Ben shrugged. "More or less, but it was a he, not a she."

"Ah, I stand corrected. You see, Mr. Lohmeier, I was a member of the trial team several years after you. Your reputation and exploits precede you."

"Good, I hope."

"Mostly. Now, if you only went to the trial team reunions, we would probably already know each other and perhaps you wouldn't have felt the need to fly down here for nothing."

"You're right," he said. "I didn't know you were on the trial team. But I don't know that I came down here for nothing."

"I don't have anything to talk to you about."

"Sure you do, you're just refusing to do it."

"Nevertheless, I'm not going to speak to you about my relationship with Daniel Greenfield and staring at me won't help."

"It might if you actually made eye contact," Ben said. Now he was smiling.

She forced herself to look at him. "Mr. Lohmeier," she said, "if you know enough about me to know that I had a relationship with Professor Greenfield and you know that I was recently in Chicago, then you should know that I was back in Ocala before he was killed."

Ben cocked his head. He didn't know any of that, but didn't let on. "When exactly did you fly back to Ocala, or better said, fly back to Orlando and drive to Ocala, as I have discovered this week?"

"I flew back on the afternoon of the 31st and was home in time for New Year's Eve."

"That's all very well and good, but Daniel Greenfield was murdered in his office on the 28th of December, maybe the 29th."

Ben hadn't really thought in terms of Nora Fleming being a potential murderer, but the news that she was in Chicago at the time of Greenfield's death and seemed strangely unwilling to discuss her relationship with him forced Ben to put her name into the mix. In any event, there was more information to be had here, whether or not he could obtain it directly from her. She took a moment to process things and gather her thoughts. Ben studied her and then followed her eyes to the doorway to find her husband standing there.

"I think it's time we end this conversation right here, Mr. Lohmeier," Andrew Scott said.

Ben put his right forefinger to his lips. "Why would that be?" he asked.

"Because I don't believe my wife needs to be harassed by you, that's why. Not that my reasoning is any of your business."

Ben shook his head. "I don't understand why everyone has so much to hide around here. I've barely asked any questions at all. You folks seem awfully defensive about something."

171

Andrew Scott took a step into the room. "What are you suggesting? Are you saying that you think my wife had something to do with his death?"

"I'm not suggesting anything. I just think you're acting strangely, that's all. For all I know, you killed him," he said gesturing at Andrew Scott. "I mean, did you come back from Chicago with your wife? Maybe you still resent the old boyfriend."

"That's it. We're done," Scott said moving another step toward Ben. His fists were clenched.

Ben held up his hands. "Fine, I'll leave voluntarily. I certainly don't want to be the next victim in this case." Ben took a business card from his pocket and a pen off of Nora's desk and wrote on the back of it. "I'll tell you one thing before I leave," he said. "I haven't done anything to you folks to cause this reaction. Could I have called first? Sure. But I had trouble finding you and it's a lot easier to say no and hang up the phone than it is to turn someone away at your door.

"But keep this in mind. As far as I know, no one else has been down here to see you except me. That means nobody really knows about you except me. I haven't sicced the authorities on you and I haven't sicced the media on you either. Do you know how many calls I get from media people every day? More than you can imagine. If I really wanted to ruin your lives, all I would have to do is pick up the phone and say, 'Geraldo, here they are. This is the relationship. Start digging,' and you'd have a swarm of people down here doing proctological exams faster than you can say 'rental property'.

"I could do any number of things to make your lives miserable. I could haul you into Court and make you out to be material witnesses. I could leak you as possible suspects. But rest assured, it won't take much before you won't be able to go out of your house at night to walk the dog without an escort consisting of three microphones and two cameras.

"All I'm asking is an opportunity to talk to you and ask some questions. I've got a woman back in Chicago, a good friend of mine as a matter of fact, who's being accused of murdering someone when I know she didn't do it. If you think I'm going to

172

stop following up on your relationship with Daniel Greenfield to avoid hurting your feelings, you can forget it.

"Here's my business card." He tossed it on the desk. "My cell phone number is on the back. I drive back to Orlando this afternoon and have a flight out at about six. Call me if you change your mind. If I don't hear from you, I can't promise how long I'll wait. But rest assured, if you have information, I'm going to find out what it is."

Ben rose from his chair and stood face to face with Andrew Scott, who was several inches taller and probably forty or fifty pounds heavier. Ben moved carefully around him to the door and turned back to face his wife. "It was nice meeting you, Ms. Scott. I hope to hear from you soon. I think I can find my own way out."

Ben eased out of the door and back down the hallway toward the lobby. As he reached the doorway to the next office, he heard the sound of Nora Scott's office door closing behind him.

Southern Belle gave him a sheepish smile as he whisked through the lobby and straight out the door. He stood on the front steps for a second pondering his next move. Nothing came readily to mind. A lavender Mustang convertible drove by and was gone. Birds chirped up on the eaves. He looked over at a clump of bushes in the bed to his left. He smelled the strong scent of lilacs, r at least he thought they were lilacs. Still nothing. He took out his cell phone and pretended to make a call. Still nothing. Finally, he moved slowly down the walk and then up the street to the car.

He took Pine Avenue to College Road and drove back to the hotel. As he drove, he contemplated what he could have done differently and concluded that not much else could have been done to salvage a hostile situation. Although he hadn't learned a lot, it hadn't been totally fruitless either. He learned that the Scotts had been in Chicago at the time of the murder and that something about that or Nora's relationship with Greenfield made them jittery, defensive and unwilling to talk. It may not have been much, but it was something, more than he had before he arrived.

With nothing but time to kill, Ben went back to the hotel and checked out before heading across the street to Steak 'n Shake for lunch. As he finished off his chocolate milkshake, he turned the case over in his mind. Still too many holes to fill and not enough pieces with which to fill them. He needed the records from the school and the physical evidence from the prosecution in order to really get going. He decided to put Disko to work on the Nora Fleming connection to see what he could turn up. Ben looked at his watch. It was after one o'clock local time, and he figured if he got back to Orlando early enough he could stop somewhere and pick up the required trinkets for his kids.

Ben paid the tab and went out to the parking lot and put the top back down on the Sebring. A couple of minutes later, he punched the gas and merged onto I-75 going about seventy miles per hour. He found *I Saw Her Standing There* by the Beatles on the radio and turned it way up letting the engine out. Just after he veered off onto the southbound Ronald Reagan Turnpike, he felt his cell phone vibrate in his pants pocket. He struggled to get it out and looked at the display. He didn't recognize the number. He flipped it open and said, "Hello, this is Benjamin Lohmeier."

"Mr. Lohmeier, this is Nora Scott."

26

The phone call was brief. Nora had thought about it and changed her mind. Now she wanted to talk. They agreed on an early dinner at the Lone Star Steak House, since it was a place that Ben knew. Ben turned the Sebring around and headed back up the expressway to the hotel. He even got the same room, now freshly cleaned. He changed his airline reservations to the following morning and got Libby on her cell phone to tell her that he'd be staying an extra night.

"Your daughter is going to be pissed," she warned. "You better call her later and beg for forgiveness."

Then he called Mark to see what was going on. Mark wasn't there so he talked to Dan Conlon instead. Dan told him that Mark had received a call from Bridget Fahey telling him to look out for a stack of documents, the first batch of evidence received from the State. He also said that they were scheduled to go downtown on Thursday to look at some of the files assembled at the law school.

"What'd you make of the girlfriend?" Dan asked.

"I don't know yet," Ben replied. "At least we know she was there at the time of the murder. I'm going to have Disko look into it. I should know more this evening. All I can tell you right now is that it's warm and sunny down here and I don't miss Chicago a bit."

"Fuck you," Dan said and hung up.

Ben arrived at the restaurant first, greeted by the same hostess as the night before, who raised her eyebrows when he asked for a table for two. Ben thought he saw her exchange a knowing glance and accompanying grin with a co-worker when Nora Scott arrived ten minutes later and they were led to a booth in the back of the dining room. As the hostess walked away, Ben laughed.

"What's so funny?" Nora asked.

"I think she thinks I got lucky."

"What do you mean?"

"I was in here last night by myself and now I'm in here tonight with you. I think she thinks I got lucky."

"In a sense, you did. Andrew wanted to come along, but I wouldn't let him."

"Just as well. I don't think Andrew and I hit it off very well this morning."

"No, you didn't."

Ben shrugged, then he asked, "What made you change your mind?"

"Oh, I don't know," she said. "I guess I thought about what you said and figured you could make it a lot worse for us if I didn't talk to you."

The waitress came and they each ordered a beer. Nora looked a little more relaxed than earlier that morning. Ben figured her husband not being there took a little bit of the edge off. He still sensed a bit of nervousness and hoped that a less formal setting would help put her at ease. She looked around to make sure that no one could hear and then said in a low voice, "Do you really think I could have killed him?"

Ben shrugged. "I don't know? Why not? I think you're probably as likely as anybody else. I think your husband probably could have done it too. Either of you two are at least as likely as my client is." Ben paused as he saw the waitress approaching with their beers. After she left, he continued. "Look, I'm just getting into this case. I'm trying to figure out who all of the players are before I form any conclusions. You seem like a decent enough woman. I hope you didn't kill him. Other than that, who knows?"

"How did you find out about me anyway?"

"The Missus."

"Sylvia told you? What did she say?"

176

"She didn't say much. She only knew your name was Nora and that you had a relationship with her husband for quite some time, one that apparently led to the break-up of their marriage."

"That's what she said? That's rich. I think the marriage had been broken long before I came onto the scene. It's just that nobody decided to pick up the pieces and throw them away until Daniel and I were together."

"Well, she acted like she didn't know who you were, just that your name was Nora and that you two had been fooling around for quite a while. She said that was the last straw. A bunch of conquests, as she put it, were one thing, but a long-term relationship with a student was another. She said that she couldn't accept that and filed for divorce."

"I suppose that's more or less true, although Daniel probably would have put a different spin on it. From what Daniel told me, Sylvia was very . . . well, very, very cold is how I'll put it."

"I'll take it he phrased it a little less delicately than that?"

"You might say that. Daniel thought she was just trying to stick it to him, both financially and with his daughters. I don't know whether that's true. I only know about Sylvia through Daniel. I never actually met her myself."

"If it's any consolation, I would agree that she's quite a chilly woman indeed. I'm not sure if it was a façade, obviously I don't know her that well, but warm and fuzzy she wasn't." Ben decided to get right to it. "So, how did you meet up with him?"

"About like you'd expect. I had him for Crim Law and went to see him once or twice about questions I had and one thing led to another and as you might imagine, he wasn't adverse to being with a student."

"That's his reputation anyway," Ben said.

"And it's probably well-deserved," she said matter-of-factly. "That was during the middle of my first year and things gradually got more serious until I moved into an apartment right downtown by the law school my second year and we spent loads of time together there."

"What did he tell his wife?"

"I have no idea. It's probably not that hard if you think about it. He could just say he had another class or office hours or something."

Ben nodded in agreement. "That's true. Plus he had all of those ball games to go to, right? He was a season ticket holder."

"Exactly. We missed quite a few ball games to go over to my apartment. That's one of the reasons I thought he was really falling for me, you know, because he managed to miss a lot of games."

"Was he with anyone else while you two were together?"

She closed her eyes and scrunched her nose as though recalling something unpleasant. Then she took a long drink of her beer. "Who knows? I don't think so, but looking back on it, I suppose anything is possible."

"Well, that's pretty definitive," Ben said.

"Sorry, that's all I've got."

"No, that's okay," Ben said. "I understand. So how did Sylvia come to find out about the two of you?"

Nora shrugged. "I'm not really sure. I think probably in the usual way. She had her suspicions and then confronted him, and then lo and behold, he didn't deny it. That's another way I thought we were serious, when he admitted to her that we were together and told her, at least he said he told her, that he wanted to be with me."

"But I thought he didn't want the divorce."

"He said he wanted it at first and then he changed his mind." She played with the coaster while she spoke. She appeared to be putting things into words that she had thought about for a long time, but never really discussed with anyone. Since she probably didn't really discuss this stuff with her husband, Ben assumed that the act of telling him about it may have helped her get it out of her system. It had the quality of something that had been ruminated about for some time. They sat in silence for a moment and Ben thought about where he could take the conversation. Just at the point it was starting to get awkward, the waitress came back to take their order. It gave him time to re-group and re-think his approach. Around them, the other tables started to fill and the restaurant got much noisier, thus assuring the privacy of their

178

conversation. Ben grabbed a warm roll out of the basket the waitress had brought and broke it in two, buttering each half.

"Was the divorce difficult for you?" he asked, swallowing a bite of roll.

She considered that. "Not at first. At first, it was what I wanted and what Daniel said he wanted. It only became clear later on that he didn't want a divorce at all. Of course, he couldn't say that to me because he had strung me along for such a long time and he didn't want to run the risk of losing both of us, which he eventually did."

"How did that happen?"

She got that far-off look again. "Well, it happened because it became obvious that he didn't want to divorce his wife and he didn't want to lose me either. He just wanted the status quo. He wanted both of us. But by that point, both of us wasn't good enough anymore. At least not for me and from the sounds of it, not for her either. I stuck it out for awhile to see if he might change his mind once it became clear that they would never get back together, but he didn't want me, at least not the way I wanted him to. So eventually I had to get out too."

"How did he take that?"

"Not very well because he was losing me on top of her and on top of losing his daughters, I guess. So he felt like everything was crashing in around him. Then you had the thing with those other girls at school and I'm sure he had a pretty hard time. I didn't care very much at that point though. I just knew I had to leave."

"How'd you wind up down here?"

"Andrew and I dated for a long time while I was in college and we had sort of broken up when I started seeing Daniel. We were still reasonably close and Andrew wanted to get back together and he kept telling me that my relationship with Daniel was a bad idea whether he got back together with me or not. I didn't listen at the time, although I suppose he was right. After my relationship with Daniel fell apart, he was there for me. I eventually came to realize that I wanted and needed him too." She smiled. "And I probably loved him in some way all along."

"That doesn't exactly feel like the movies, does it?"

179

"No, but is there ever such a thing really? I mean, I've thought about that a lot and have always wondered if there really is a person out there just for me, or for you. When I was younger, I thought maybe there was and that all you had to do was look hard enough and long enough and eventually you would find that person out there somewhere. Now, I'm not so sure that's true. At least not for everyone. Then I thought about what would happen if I let Andrew slip away. Now, I don't know if Andrew is the love of my life or not." She paused and then smiled. "I'll deny all of this if you ever repeat it. But I'm not sure that there's ever any such thing. Sure, for some people, maybe, but not for everyone. I know Andrew loves me very much and I love him too, and as you can tell, he's very protective of me."

"No question about that," Ben agreed.

"So, yes I love Andrew very much." She paused again, considering what she was about to say. "I know I may seem, what's the word, melancholy?

Ben nodded. "That would be a good description for it, I suppose."

"Okay, so I seem melancholy. But Daniel's death hit me pretty hard. Of course I was shocked to find out about it. Not that I wanted him back or I'm still in love with him or anything like that. It's just that I once cared for him so much that finding out that somebody murdered him was very difficult. I've been wondering what could've driven someone to do that. How could someone do such a thing? Daniel may not have been perfect, God knows that, but I don't think he was really capable of doing anything that would have made him deserve that. But to answer your question, yes I'm happy here. I'm happy with Andrew. And he's a very good father."

Ben was startled. "What do you mean?" he said.

She laughed. "Didn't you know? We have a son. His name is Brian and he's about to turn three." She could see Ben doing some calculations in his head. She leaned forward and whispered, "Yes, I was pregnant when I got married, but don't tell anyone." She laughed again. "It was just one of those things. Passion got the best of us and one thing led to another and … I'm sure you can figure out the rest. It's the best thing that's ever happened to me though."

Ben nodded. He certainly could figure out the rest. They talked about kids for a little while and Ben found himself liking Nora Scott in a strange way. And he couldn't quite convince himself that she was capable of murdering anyone. They sat there studying each other for several moments and Nora broke off a piece of roll and stuffed it into her mouth. "You never did answer my question," she said.

"Which one was that?"

"Do you believe there is someone out there for everyone?"

He exhaled. "Oh, I don't know. I'm just amazed sometimes that there was anybody out there for me." She laughed. "Really, I mean it," he said. "It's hard sometimes to imagine that somebody would want to spend the rest of their life with you. It's kind of a big commitment, don't you think?"

She nodded.

"No, I don't think I'm that philosophic about things like this," he continued. "I don't spend much time dwelling on whether or not I have found Ms. Right or even if there is such a thing. I'm just not that philosophic. That's just not concrete enough for me. I spend more time thinking about my own little section of the world and what I can do to influence it and shape it to my will. When I met my wife and got to know her, I knew I wanted her so I went about getting her and fortunately, she had more or less the same idea and everything seems to have worked out. The most I ever do is wonder sometimes when I meet a woman or get to know a woman whether or not she would have been fun to go out with. It never gets much further than that. At most, the whole exercise lasts about ten minutes until I decide to get back to getting what I want and I forget about the rest."

"So the whole thing for you is you see it, you want it and you take it?"

"Crudely put, but probably true." Ben took a long drink from his beer and then another, satisfied with his expression of his views on relationships. A moment later, the waitress came with dinner and they got caught up in their food for a little while before Ben

181

turned back to Nora's relationship with Daniel Greenfield. "When was the last time you saw Professor Greenfield?" Ben asked.

"Oh, I don't know. It's been a long time now, probably almost two years. I think I only saw him once, maybe twice after we broke up. He tried calling for a while, but I made it clear that I didn't want to have anything to do with him anymore and that the relationship was over. Eventually, I guess he got the message and stopped calling."

"Why did you come back to Chicago?"

"Just for Christmas. Both Andrew and I have family in Chicago. We came back to see them. We flew in on the 23rd and left around noon time on New Year's Eve."

"You didn't see or hear from Professor Greenfield during this period?"

"No, not at all. Daniel never crossed my mind, to tell you the truth. You may not believe this, but I'm very happy with Andrew and I'm happy here. This is a nice comfortable place to live. When Andrew got the opportunity to come down here and take over his uncle's law practice, a law practice that once belonged to his grandfather and his great grandfather, I was a little reluctant at first, I'll be honest. But after a while, I saw the opportunity in it and figured that we both needed to get away from Chicago. So we decided to come and we're glad we did. It's a more relaxed lifestyle down here and things are going very well. Not only do we have the law practice, but Andrew is involved with some real estate development as well."

"Yeah, I saw the lot in Ocala Waterways Estates. I wouldn't plan on moving there anytime soon."

She gave him a puzzled laugh. "What would cause you to go there? Bad address?"

"I guess."

"I'm not even sure I've been there. I take that back, I may have been there once with Andrew, but not more than that. I don't think he actually wants to live there. It was more of an investment property."

They ate their dinner and talked about Florida for a while and the differences between the Sunshine State and living in the Land of Lincoln.

"I'll tell you this," Nora said, "even being back there for Christmas, it's awful easy to get used to the nice weather down here. Sure I like the snow and stuff right around Christmas, but that's about it. Other than that, you can keep it. The weather down here suits me just fine."

Ben nodded in agreement as he put a nice piece of prime rib into his mouth. "I know what you're saying. I've enjoyed the weather the last couple of days myself. I'm not looking forward to getting back to the deep freeze. Hey, let me ask you one other thing," he said. "What do you know about Professor Greenfield and drugs? Did you ever know him to use drugs?"

She paused and considered the question. "Never with me. I can't say that I ever saw Daniel use drugs, but I know that he and Dorlund got high together periodically."

"What do you mean by high?"

"You know, they just smoked some dope now and then."

"Anything stronger?" Ben asked tapping his nose.

"Maybe. It's possible, but I can't say that I ever saw it myself. I suspected once or twice after he'd been with Dorlund that maybe they did more than just smoke a little pot, but I can't swear to it. Why? What have you heard?"

"Just a little rumor going around the law school that he may have been enjoying a little toot now and then."

"Hmmm," she said, "part of me would say I'm surprised by that, but then again part of me would say that I'm not. Like I said, I never witnessed it myself."

They finished their meal and talked for a little while over one last beer. Ben couldn't help but like her and wondered why a woman like this would be wasting her time with someone like Daniel Greenfield. He concluded that she was certainly better off without him even if part of her seemed to be settling for less than was possible. Ben walked her to her car, parked under a dark leafy tree in the back of the parking lot. The sun had set and the evening was pleasantly cool. It felt to Ben more like late-June or early-July in Chicago than mid-February in Florida.

"Thank you for dinner," she said. "It was good. It felt good to talk."

Ben noticed that she subconsciously played with her wedding ring as she spoke. This suddenly felt like the end of a strange date.

"Well, thanks for agreeing to speak with me."

"You know," she said, "you didn't tell me how Daniel was killed. All I know from friends of mine and from what I've been able to gather from news reports is that he was somehow beaten to death. Is that right?"

"Since you knew him as well as you did, you're probably better off not thinking about it," Ben said telling her the truth, but also not wanting to give away any details on the off-chance that she may have either been involved herself or known someone who was. "Let's just say he was bludgeoned and leave it at that."

She cringed and closed her eyes. "Daniel didn't deserve that," she said in a soft voice.

"No, I wouldn't think that he did," Ben agreed.

"Who's your client?"

"Her name is Megan Rand Cavallaro. We went to law school together."

"What makes the authorities think she did it?"

"I'm not sure. We don't have all of the evidence yet. In fact, we're supposed to be getting some of that tomorrow."

She extended her hand. "Well, I wish you the best of luck with your defense, I really do. It's hard for me to imagine a woman bludgeoning someone to death and you seem awfully convinced that your client didn't do it. I hope it works out for you."

"Thank you. You've never heard of my client, have you?"

"No, never."

"You never heard Professor Greenfield mention her?"

"No. I've never heard of her and don't know anything about her. What's her connection to Daniel?"

"Don't know that either other than we both had him for Criminal Law and Criminal Procedure. That hardly seems enough, now does it?"

184

"No, it doesn't."

"Well," Ben said, "I'll let you get back home now. I'm sure your husband is standing by the door waiting."

She threw her head back in a relaxed laugh, perhaps the first truly unguarded moment of the entire evening. "That's probably the truest thing you've said."

"Please," Ben said, "do me a favor and think about this a little and if anything pops into your head, anything at all, please give me a call even if it doesn't seem significant or important. You never know. I would greatly appreciate it."

"Sure. I'll do that." She put her hand on his forearm. "Have a safe trip home."

Ben walked back to his car parked in the front of the lot. As he reached his car, he turned and saw her pull slowly out of the parking lot and up to the corner before turning right on College Road, her tail lights disappearing into the night.

27

Ben took the morning flight from Orlando to Chicago. The plane was surprisingly crowded, but a safe touchdown at Midway made it a successful flight. The limo took him directly home, where he dumped his bags in the front hall before heading for the garage. After a couple of days in Florida, it seemed that much colder in Chicago and the heat in his car didn't seem to kick in until he was halfway to the office. He got there just about the time the guys were heading out to lunch. Casey Gardner originally intended to stay back at the office, but Ben enticed him along with the promise of an interesting story. Casey drove and Ben, Brian and Dan Conlon went along. Mark hadn't come in yet and Funk stayed back at the office eating rabbit food. They took the long drive to Friendly Mexican, another of their regular lunch joints, and Ben told them the story of looking for the Scott's house and winding up in the middle of nowhere as the sun went down. After they sat down and started eating chips and salsa at a table in the front window, Ben told them the story of the roommates in hushed low tones.

"Oh, this was your chance," Casey moaned. "Too bad it happened when you were married."

Back in college, Casey had a roommate who turned down a threesome offer because he didn't want to cheat on a girl he had just started dating. The girlfriend didn't last long and Casey's roommate regretted turning down the once-in-a-lifetime offer ever since. Casey had told the guys at the office about it at lunch a

186

couple of years earlier and they had been periodically debating it ever since. Now the tables were turned.

"I don't think it's the same thing," Ben insisted.

"What do you mean it's not the same thing?" Conlon said. "It's exactly the same thing."

"I don't think so," Ben disputed. "First of all, I'm married and he was just dating someone. In fact, he'd just started dating her. So that's one big difference right there. Second, and most important, it's not the same now."

"What do you mean?" Brian asked.

"I think back twenty years ago it was a bigger deal. Now everybody's doing it, except us, that is. I'm not sure it's even that hard to scare up a threesome anymore. It's kind of like steroids and baseball. It used to be that hitting fifty home runs was a big deal. Now everybody hits fifty home runs. According to Oprah, everybody's getting threesomes and random sex, especially teenagers and college students. I really think to have the same effect now, you have to be involved in a full-fledged orgy."

They sat around and contemplated that over chips and salsa the way medical ethicists would discuss the vagaries of stem cell research. When they got back to the office after lunch, they saw Mark through the window of the garage pulling documents out of a banker's box. Ben knocked on the outside barbershop entrance and Mark let him in.

"Hey, how was your flight?" Mark asked.

"Not bad. Did we get something in?"

"Yeah, a couple of boxes worth of shit."

"What's in it?"

"Not sure yet. I'm just starting to go through it. I'm not sure what it all means yet."

"Okay," Ben said, "well, take a look at it and I'll be down in a little while."

Ben went upstairs and checked his messages. Then he decided to call Meg and fill her in on his trip to Florida. He also wanted to talk to her before he knew too many details about the stuff they got from the State, so he wouldn't be in a position of keeping anything from her. He didn't call her every day. He didn't want her

187

devoting every waking hour to the next update from her lawyer. He hoped that her day-to-day life would take on a greater sense of normalcy instead. He found her in pretty good spirits, in marked contrast to several other times they had spoken recently. She seemed particularly interested in the details of his trip to Florida. He left out the stuff about the roommates at the bar.

He went back downstairs and found Mark with his head buried in a banker's box. Documents were arranged in loosely organized piles all over the conference room table and several of the chairs. Ben entered the room and took a deep breath at the sight. Organization had never been Mark's strong suit and Ben could envision this whole document review process spiraling out of control in a hurry.

"You do know what you're doing?" he asked.

"Yeah, yeah," Mark said. "I'm on top of it. Everything's under control."

"Yeah, right," Ben said. "It sure looks like it. So what have we got? Bad news first."

"Why don't you sit down."

"That bad?"

"Don't know yet. I'm not through everything."

Ben picked his way through the piles of paper and took a seat in the barber chair. "So," he said, "let's have it."

"Well," Mark said with a sigh, his eyes looking from one pile to another. He took another stack of documents off his lap and placed it on the table. "Keeping in mind that I haven't reviewed everything, not completely. What we have so far, and I'm sure this isn't everything, for example, we don't have any of the toxicology reports or even the autopsy report yet."

"Get on with it," Ben said.

"So far, I'd say there are three main pieces of evidence that are problematic. Namely, the State says they have hair consistent with the client's hair inside Greenfield' office."

"You can't match hair exactly," Ben said.

"No, but you can say it's consistent with a sample of the hair of the accused which is what they're going to do. But there's more. They have a thumb print and other partial prints near the label of

188

the murder weapon. And they have the victim's blood, two drops to be exact, on a scarf allegedly belonging to the client, which I believe was taken from the Astor Street residence."

Ben laughed a humorless laugh and looked out the window. "What? Is that all? Just blood and fingerprints?"

"Yeah," Mark said, "just enough to put her on death row."

28

"Right this way," Dean Freeman's secretary said as she led Ben and Mark down the corridor to a small classroom that she unlocked with a key. Ben recognized it as one of the small rooms used for meetings or seminars of ten to fifteen students or so. She opened the door and groped around in the dark for a light switch. She flicked it on and then turned and handed the key to Ben. "Dean Freeman told me to give this key to you." Ben took the key from her. "You aren't to leave this room unlocked unless one of you is inside. When you leave, you're to return the key to me. I leave at five so you need to get it to me before then. Any questions?"

Ben shrugged and shook his head. He felt like he was back in junior high. "No, I don't think so," he said. "Thanks for your help."

She nodded and left, leaving them alone. Ben turned and looked at the documents on the table. There was enough paper there to fill maybe one or one and a half banker's boxes. "Not very much is there?" he said.

"No," Mark agreed. "They probably shredded the rest already."

Ben nodded, not sure if Mark was kidding. "It wouldn't surprise me. I'll tell you what," he said, "why don't you get started. I want to go look for Dorlund." He gave Mark the key. "Don't lose it," he said.

Ben found Dorlund in his office reading the sports section of the *Tribune*. "Come on in and have a seat, Mr. Lohmeier," he said waving to a chair. "Just finishing up some heavy reading."

"I can see that," Ben said, "but you can probably find something in there that will fit into one of your tort lectures."

Dorlund laughed. "That's about all sports is nowadays - torts and breach of contract." He folded up the paper and tossed it on his desk. "So, what can I do for you?"

"Well, we haven't really had much of a chance to talk about Professor Greenfield's death."

"No, but from what I gather, you certainly have been talking to other people around here. You're creating quite a little stink."

"You gotta do what you gotta do," Ben said.

Dorlund nodded and ran a hand through his thinning curly hair. He wore a copper colored sweater with dark brown pants and well-worn leather shoes. He put his feet up on the desk and clasped both hands behind his head. The perfect picture of relaxation.

Dorlund didn't have a whole lot to offer. He insisted that he didn't know any reason why his friend would have been killed, although he had heard about the confrontation with Jason Hahn, the student identified by Professor Makra, he seemed to dismiss it. "That kind of stuff happens more than you'd think. There's a lot of pressure on these kids and sometimes they need to come in and vent when they don't do as well as they'd hoped. I'm not sure you can read anything else into it." Ben wasn't sure he agreed.

Dorlund also confirmed that there had been some friction among the faculty over recent changes in the curriculum, but downplayed those as being little more than routine office politics. Nevertheless, he did agree that Professor Greenfield never got along very well with Professor Harper. Dorlund suggested that Harper had problems with any man who didn't agree with her radical feminist approach to the workplace

Dorlund's open, easy-going manner surprised Ben, who always thought that Dorlund could be kind of an asshole. Perhaps he was misinformed. They talked for a few more minutes before Dorlund looked at his watch and said, "Look, I've got a class in about five minutes so I've got to get going, but we can talk again."

"Before I go," Ben said. "Do you know anything about my client, Megan Rand, that I need to know about?"

Dorlund rose from his seat and began gathering his books for class. He shook his head. "No, I don't think so. I don't think I ever had her as a student. All I really know about her is what I've seen on TV or the newspapers. Sorry."

"No problem. We'll talk again," Ben said. "Thanks for your time."

"My pleasure," Dorlund said as he slapped Ben on the shoulder on his way by. "I'll talk to you later."

Ben stood in the doorway of Dorlund's office and watched him make his way down the hall and around the corner. He seemed too willing to please, too happy-go-lucky. On his way back downstairs, Ben stopped off at Dean Freeman's office and got Jason Hahn's schedule and locker number from the Dean's secretary. She also gave him a piece of paper and an envelope so he could write Hahn a note and tape it to his locker, located up on the third floor.

***

Ben found Mark in roughly the same state as the previous afternoon in the garage. Papers were all over the place and Mark didn't seem to know which way was up. Ben stood in the doorway with a disapproving look on his face until Mark looked up and met his gaze with a sheepish grin of his own. "What?" he said.

"I see you're organizing things again."

Mark let out a guttural laugh. "It's what I'm good at."

"Found anything?" Ben asked.

"No, not really, not yet. It's a lot like looking through other people's mail."

"Isn't that what our job is?" Ben said. "Looking through other people's mail?"

"Pretty much. Did you find Dorlund?"

"Yeah, that was a bit on the strange side."

"Why's that?"

"He acted like he was my long lost uncle come back to the country to give me a check for a million dollars. The whole thing was kind of weird, to tell you the truth."

"What do you think his deal is?"

"No idea. Maybe he just doesn't want us looking in his direction? Who knows? I'm going to have to think about it a little more before I make up my mind. I also left a note for our friend, Jason Hahn. I told him to meet us down here. I think I'll let you give him the third degree."

"Love to," Mark said. "Always nice to knock a smart ass punk down a few pegs."

The room was set up in two levels of desks, arranged in semi-circles. Mark sat in the lowest level. Ben walked to the upper level and took a seat. "Are you doing this in any kind of order?"

"I was trying to look through it first to see what we've got. They just more or less dumped a load of shit on us."

"Did you expect anything less?"

"No. I've got a copy of Greenfield's personnel file." Mark said and let out a whistle. "He was making pretty good bucks for a guy who didn't work very hard and went to a lot of Cubs games."

"Hey," Ben said, "they don't sign up for this gig because they work you to death and don't pay you anything. Let me see that file."

Mark handed it over and Ben spent the next fifteen minutes or so looking at it in relative silence. Every once in a while, he let out a "Hmmm" or "I wouldn't have expected that." When he finished, he looked up and found Mark watching him.

"What'd you think?" Mark asked.

"Not much here. In fact, I'd say a surprisingly little amount. Do you think maybe the State has it?" Mark shrugged. Ben shook his head. "I don't know. We hear all about relationships with students and it's barely in here. A couple of women make accusations, they dig up a third and then he gets a slap on the wrist for the appearance of impropriety. It's got to be a big cover-up. I mean, come on, who would accept a reprimand when it's clear based on this that they didn't have any evidence of any wrongdoing in the first place. And what was the phrase in here? 'Insufficient

193

evidence of actual relationships with students.' That sounds like a load of bullshit too."

Mark laughed again. "That's the way I was looking at it too. My view on this is that everybody knew what was going on and for public relations purposes they figured they had to do something. Since none of the students he actually boinked were probably willing to complain because they got good grades and didn't want to get their reputations dragged through the mud, the school or somebody came up with this appearance of impropriety bullshit so they could slap him on the wrist and then slip the whole thing under the rug and hope everybody forgot about it."

"Sounds about right," Ben agreed.

At that point, a knock came at the door and a student in his early-twenties pushed inside, a blue backpack slung over his shoulder. He had shaggy brown hair and wore a black Public Enemy tee-shirt and dirty khaki pants worn low on his hips exposing the tops of his boxer shorts. "I'm looking for a guy named Lohmeier," he grunted with as much attitude as he could muster.

"That's me," Ben said. "You must be Jason Hahn."

"That's right."

"Why don't you come in and sit down."

"What do you want?"

"We'd like to talk to you about Professor Greenfield."

"What for? They found the person that killed him."

Ben leaned forward in his chair. "Maybe they did and maybe they didn't," he said. "Either way, we have a few things we'd like to talk to you about."

Hahn looked from Ben to Mark and then back again. He shook his head. "I don't have to talk to you guys."

Ben nodded. "Perhaps not, but we could always serve you with a subpoena and drag you into Court to talk about it. Hey Mark, that would look pretty good on his bar exam application, don't you think?"

"Sure would," Mark said.

Hahn thought about that for a minute and then took a couple of steps further into the room. "Okay, I'll give you a few minutes."

"Good," Ben said, "why don't you have a seat. No use standing. Mark, why don't you go ahead?"

Mark began slowly, using his "aw shucks I'm just a big boob" persona to lead Hahn from relatively meaningless anecdotes regarding Greenfield's first year Criminal Law class to Hahn's performance on the final exam, which he insisted should have earned him a good grade, perhaps even an A. Hahn appeared bored and disinterested through much of the twenty minutes or so it took Mark to get to the point, occasionally looking over at Ben, who sat and watched while saying nothing. Hahn said his grade on the final exam, a C+, shocked him because he knew the material inside and out and had been one of the best students in class from day one. He just knew that it had to be a mistake from the moment he accessed his grade from the computer.

At the Chicago College of Law, grades are posted on the computer as they are submitted by the professors so students can access their grades before the final grades are sent out. Hahn told them that he had made an appointment to see Greenfield shortly before Christmas and that things got heated when Greenfield insisted that his evaluation of Hahn's exam was accurate and that he saw no rationale for raising his grade.

"Look," Hahn said, "I thought he was full of shit, but I finally realized that it wasn't doing me any good to argue with him, so I decided to give it up and leave. I lost my cool a little bit, I admit that, and I shouldn't have yelled at him, but he was kind of an arrogant fuck about it, to tell you the truth, and it pissed me off. You know, this is my life. A C+ is a big deal."

Ben finally spoke up. "Not to interrupt, but I read your exam. You're lucky you got a C+. You didn't know what the fuck you were talking about."

Mark turned and looked at Ben and gave him a look that said, "What are you talking about? We haven't seen any exams yet." From where he was sitting, Hahn couldn't see the expression on Mark's face.

"Look," Ben continued, "you're not the first guy to come in here thinking you were hot shit only to discover that his class was filled with students just as smart or smarter than he is. You're just going to have to work harder, that's all."

Hahn's eyes blazed. "Fuck you," he finally blurted out. "You don't know what the fuck you're talking about. I did well on that exam. He fucked me over."

"You're just going to have to work a little harder next time," Ben said.

"Is that what you think?" Hahn said. He was now on his feet. Ben shrugged. "You don't know what the fuck you're talking about. I was one of the best students in that class, if not *the* best student."

"So you say," Ben said, "but you can't prove that by your exam."

"What makes you think you know what you're talking about?"

"You forget, Mr. Hahn, this is my business. I practice criminal law. I don't just watch it on TV."

Hahn took a step in Ben's direction. "Fuck you," he said again. "I don't have to put up with this bullshit from you or anybody else." He picked his backpack up off the table, turned and headed for the door.

"One more question for you, Mr. Hahn, before you leave," Ben said. "How'd you do on your other finals?"

As Hahn reached the door and yanked the handle he said, "Fuck you." Then he stormed from the room. The door closed slowly behind him and made a loud clicking sound as it latched.

"Thanks for stopping by," Ben said at the closed door.

Mark looked back at Ben and raised his eyebrows.

"That wasn't even very hard," Ben said.

"No, it wasn't."

"If I could do that in here six or eight weeks after the fact," Ben said, "think how easy it would've been for Greenfield to push his buttons a couple of days after he got his exam results."

The two men spent most of the afternoon reviewing grade reports. Dean Freeman had given them summaries dating back to 1989, when Ben was a student in Greenfield's first year Criminal Law class. Mainly, they just compiled lists of students who could have an axe to grind against Greenfield, either because they did poorly in his class, or because they did significantly worse in Greenfield's class than they did in others. They also tried to identify students who may have been particularly damaged by a Greenfield grade. For example, students close to some particular class honor or award could have taken a bad grade personally.

Painstaking and laborious work, document reviews rarely seemed to bear any fruit right up until the moment they did. After a couple of hours, Ben and Mark concluded that this work might be best performed by one of the younger guys in the office, leaving them more significant duties on which to focus. Nevertheless, they agreed to stick it out for the rest of the afternoon and make the trip as worthwhile as possible. At ten minutes past four, Ben got up and went down the hall to use the restroom. When he got back, he found Mark at the back of the room stretching his legs.

Hearing Ben come through the door, Mark turned and said, "I was just thinking, with this being Valentine's Day and all, you probably want to get going pretty soon."

Ben looked stunned. He looked down at his watch hoping the date would change, but it didn't. "Fuck," he said. "I forgot all about it."

"Damn. Even a total slug like me knows you can't blow off Valentine's Day," Mark said.

Ben shook his head. "What am I going to do?"

"Only one thing you can do - dinner and flowers. Did you get anything for her in Florida?"

"No, nothing. I got a little something for the kids, but nothing for her."

"That means nice dinner and nice flowers."

"Where am I going to go to dinner now? Every place is going to be booked?"

"You've gotta try man, you've gotta try."

Within five minutes, they had locked the door, dropped the key off and were heading to the parking lot. As they hurried across Adams Street, Ben said over his shoulder, "What am I going to do with the kids even if I can find a place?"

"Send them to the in-laws. That's what in-laws are for."

29

Traffic outbound on the Eisenhower Expressway couldn't have been much worse and Ben and Mark didn't arrive back at the office in Ithaca until five-forty-five. Fortunately, he managed to get a reservation at Les Deux Gros for the eight-thirty seating due to a last-minute cancellation. He got a hold of Libby's mother, who agreed to come over and watch the kids since Ben and Libby wouldn't be back from the restaurant until long after the kids should have been in bed.

As they drove out to the restaurant, Libby leaned over and said, "This should be nice. I figured you were so busy you'd probably just forget about Valentine's Day."

Ben flushed refusing to admit that she was correct. "Forget Valentine's Day? Never. I probably would've preferred earlier, but with the hours I've been working lately, I figured a little bit later was probably better than a little bit earlier."

She gave him a knowing smile. "The roses were also very lovely," she said. Ben stopped at the grocery store on the way home and bought Libby two dozen pink roses. "I hope the kids will be all right with Mother," she said.

"I hope your mother will be all right with the kids," Ben replied.

Dinner was very nice, just what they hoped for, and it even took Ben's mind off of the case for a little while. All in all, they enjoyed the restaurant very much and vowed to return on another occasion. While Libby would enjoy a meal like this perhaps once a month, Ben probably wouldn't be in the mood again for another year, or until he forgot about Valentine's Day again.

They returned home to find Libby's mother sitting on the couch watching Emeril on the Food Network. She gave them a good report on the kids. They watched a little television and had gone to bed early. Probably bored to death, Ben figured. By now, it was almost midnight and Ben wanted to get Libby up to bed before she got too sleepy. The only problems with their sex life were getting enough privacy and having the energy when they had the opportunity. After they finished, they lay in bed and talked for a few minutes before Libby drifted off to sleep first, which was her custom. A light sleeper himself, Ben got used to lying in bed and listening to the rhythms of his wife's breathing as she slept. Tonight was no exception.

Ben tossed and turned for a long time without falling asleep. He couldn't get the Greenfield case out of his head and now that more information had drifted in, his brain seemed to be working overtime processing it all. Ben lay in bed and looked at the ceiling before sitting up and leaning over Libby to check the clock on the nightstand – twenty-five after one. He groaned and flopped back down on his pillow. Then he got up and went to the bathroom. He decided to get dressed and go for a walk. Back when he was younger, long before he got married, Ben would take frequent walks, often in the middle of the night. He pulled on a pair of jeans and a sweatshirt and grabbed a pair of socks out of the drawer before heading downstairs. He took his leather bomber jacket off the hook in the front hall, found his gloves in the bin by the back door and stepped into a pair of suede Lands End moccasins.

He slipped out the back door, across the deck and down the steps to the driveway. He reached the end of his driveway and looked up into the now cloudless sky, stars twinkling brightly above him. He exhaled and his smoky breath disappeared into the darkness. Ben looked in both directions and turned toward town. Although cold outside - the temperature had probably dipped into the mid-twenties - the air felt crisp and clean and Ben found the fresh air invigorating. He had no particular sense of where he was heading even though town was only a couple of blocks away. He strolled along while the recent developments in the Greenfield murder tumbled over in his mind. Fingerprints, blood, hair, fingerprints, blood, hair. What did that mean? Did that mean she did it? Did that mean she killed him? Or did it just mean that she was in his office at some point? Could there be an innocent explanation to these facts, even if true? And what is the link between Meg and Greenfield? There has to be a link, some link, any link. Sure, she insists that there isn't one, but that can't be right. He didn't want to think about that link right now. It could only mean trouble. Eventually, he would know what the link was and then he could factor that into the equation. Until then, he had to look at it as just another unknown and push it from his mind. "Focus on what you know to be true and see where it takes you," he said aloud.

As he thought about all of this, Ben walked more or less aimlessly not focusing at all on where he was going. He looked up a few minutes later to discover that he stood in front of the Starbucks in downtown Clarendon Hills, now shuttered for the night. Ben scowled. He hated coffee and hadn't tasted so much as a drop in probably twenty years. He never understood how a place like Starbucks could succeed; three or four bucks for a cup of coffee. Who would pay that? Ben heard a noise and turned. A police car turned and moved away from him across the railroad tracks that bisected downtown.

He stood at the far south end of Clarendon Hills' small downtown and gazed up at the railroad tracks two blocks to the north. Those two blocks, with shops on either side, encompassed the entire central business district of this small bedroom community in the western suburbs of Chicago. They had a Domino's Pizza, an Ace Hardware, an ice cream shop, a barber shop, a small restaurant and, of course, the Starbucks. As the tail lights of the police car disappeared from view, Ben saw no signs of life anywhere. Ben liked downtown Clarendon Hills. In the winter, with snow on the ground like tonight, it sort of reminded him of Bedford Falls in *It's A Wonderful Life*. Maybe not that idyllic;

neighboring Hinsdale probably came closer to Bedford Falls, but still a nice, quaint little village.

Ben walked across the street to a small pavilion, really nothing more than a tiny wedge-shaped piece of land where Prospect Avenue cuts through downtown Clarendon Hills and then forms a fork. The remaining triangle of land contained a couple of benches and provided Ben with a ready vantage point from which to assess his surroundings and contemplate the puzzle that lay before him. He found an iron bench bare of snow, brushed free by a previous visitor, and sat down. He thought of Greenfield lying on the floor of his office, his skull in pieces, the mystery of his death still intact. What did he know about Greenfield? A womanizer who seemingly took advantage of every opportunity to bed students at the law school, so willing was he to score that he risked the break-up of his marriage to do so.

What of the scorned wife, the unfulfilled girlfriend and her current husband? What of the female professors at the law school or their spouses? What about Angela Harper? Could it be just a coincidence that the murder occurred at probably the one time during the year when the killer could conceivably come and go and not be discovered on the security cameras? Then there was the drug use. Did he have a problem or didn't he? Opinions appeared to conflict. Then we have Jason Hahn. What about him? Cocky and hot-tempered, could Jason Hahn or some other student flip out and kill a professor over the outrage and disappointment of a bad final exam grade? "Questions, questions," Ben said to his solitude, "I've got questions and no answers."

Ben sat in almost a trance-like state, his legs crossed, elbow on the armrest of the bench and his hand on his chin, looking sightlessly out into the stillness of downtown. After awhile, he couldn't say how long, he heard a noise behind him and turned to see a police car coast slowly to a stop alongside him. The driver's window came down and an officer who couldn't have been more than twenty-four or twenty-five said, "Can I help you?"

"No," Ben said, "couldn't sleep. I live over on Walker. Quiet night?"

The officer nodded. "Just the way we like them. Well, okay then, take it easy." The window slid back up and the officer pulled away.

Ben watched him drive to the end of the block and turn the corner. He rose to his feet and sighed. Still not sleepy.

30

Ben sat at his desk and yawned. The lack of sleep the night before took its toll the following morning. He looked at the clock on his desk, only ten-thirty and it felt like six at night. He went downstairs to the kitchen and took a Coke out of the office refrigerator and poured it over ice. Casey Gardner sat at the table sipping a cup of coffee and leafing through the sports section of the *Sun-Times*. He looked up when Ben came in. "Hey," he said, "what's up? Any luck?"

"I don't know yet. I'm getting more pieces, but I don't know what the puzzle's supposed to look like."

"What's with the Coke?" Ben was known for his affinity for root beer. He even kept frosted mugs in his freezer at home.

"Late night. I need the caffeine."

Casey nodded. "So you really think the whole threesome thing has been devalued?" he said in a whisper.

"Yeah, I think it has. I think it was probably getting worse and then Clinton started arguing that a hummer didn't count as sex and now pretty much everything goes. I've heard that girls in high schools give blow jobs at the drop of a hat and don't even think twice about it."

"Fuck," Casey said, "where were girls like that when I went to high school?"

"I don't know," Ben said, "but we both have daughters now and that puts a completely different spin on it for me."

"Agreed."

Ben heard someone come through the front door and stuck his head out of the kitchen to see Stan Disko shaking off the cold. "Hey Stan, come on in."

Disko walked into the kitchen. "Hey Case," he said, "how's it going?"

"Good," Gardner said without looking up. "Catch any cheating husbands lately?"

"No, not enough. I could use a few more like that. That's easy money."

"What do you have for me?" Ben asked.

"Not a whole lot actually," Disko said sitting down. "Have you talked to Portalski about the drug thing?"

"Yeah, I have. He says that his sources tell him that Greenfield was a recreational user who stuck mostly to pot and periodically splurged for some coke, but not that often."

"I kind of heard the same thing even though I wasn't looking into it really," Disko said. "I got a couple of things on some of the students though."

"I thought you said you didn't have anything?"

"Well, I've got a little, but nothing jumps right out at you. Nothing on Hinkle. She's one of the girls who filed a complaint against Greenfield about sexual harassment. She seems like a nice girl from the suburbs. Not much going on there. She is a looker though. Wexler's father is a rich orthopedic guy from the North Shore." Disko paged through some notes he had scrawled on a four by six-inch spiral notepad taken from his coat pocket. "Yeah," he said, "the father's an orthopedic surgeon up in Glencoe, pulls down some pretty big coin. She's Daddy's little girl. Only daughter after three sons, that kind of thing. People tell me that she's always bitching and complaining about something. She sounds like a spoiled rich brat. She was friends with Hinkle at law school. She may have pulled Hinkle into this thing against Greenfield. Hard to imagine her being behind something like the murder though. I don't think she has the gumption to actually get her hands dirty, if you know what I mean. This was a pretty personal crime from what you're telling me and it doesn't seem to fit her."

204

Ben nodded. "What about the Thompkins woman . . . what was her name, Marjorie Thompkins?"

"Yeah, I was getting to her. She's worth looking into, I think. She has a long history of making noise, complaining about being wronged, not getting her fair share, being discriminated against, that whole line of BS. She filed complaints against a couple of other professors, either unfair grading or not treating her properly in class. She really works the system."

"Not treating her properly in class?" Casey said as he looked up from his newspaper. "This is law school, isn't it?"

"Yeah," Ben said, "but we don't want to hurt anybody's self esteem."

Disko got up from his seat and went over and grabbed a mug off of a tray on the counter, filled it three-quarters full with coffee and then dropped in some Coffeemate powder. He stirred it with a spoon found in the drawer and took a sip.

"Go ahead, Stan, make yourself at home," Casey said.

"What?"

"I'm just blowing you shit."

"What about Hahn?" Ben asked, "Did you find out anything about him?"

"Yeah, I did." Disko set his cup down on the counter. "That Hahn is a real pistol. He's a smart kid and a pretty good student when he's in the mood, but he's a constant troublemaker."

"What kind of stuff?" Ben asked.

"Temper-related stuff mostly. A few fights in school, loud arguments, belligerent attitude - stuff like that. He's way too cocky for his own good."

"Hmmm," Ben said taking a sip of his Coke. "I saw that yesterday myself. I started pushing a few buttons on him and next thing you know, he completely blows his cool and storms out." Ben stood and scratched his head. "Well, I've got an appointment with Hinkle and Wexler this afternoon. They work together at some insurance defense shop downtown. Thompkins, on the other hand, won't take my calls and has basically been blowing me off. She works at Kenner & Black downtown. I'm thinking of showing up down there this afternoon and squeezing her a little. Try and make a point."

"She'll love that," Casey said. "Especially at a place like that."

"That's what I figure."

"Okay then," Disko said. "I'll keep digging. Keep me posted."

Ben met Kate Hinkle and Lucy Wexler for lunch at a pizza joint near their office in the Loop. Kate Hinkle stood about five-feet-seven inches with a nice figure, a pretty smile and light brown wind swept hair. She carried herself with the grace of an athlete and reminded Ben of a model in a chewing gum commercial. He liked her instantly. Lucy Wexler on the other hand, struck Ben as someone who would tell on you for cheating on an eye exam. Although dark and arguably attractive, she possessed none of Hinkle's charm and what good looks she had were marred by a surly, unpleasant disposition.

All he really got from the interview was a half-way decent personal pan pizza and the opportunity to wonder which lucky guy would wind up with Hinkle. Ben couldn't see either of them killing Professor Greenfield, however. Hinkle, because she was too nice and obviously didn't have it in her, and Wexler, because that would require too much effort and personal interaction that she undoubtedly found distasteful. Maybe she would hire someone, but never carry out the deed herself unless Greenfield were threatening her trust fund or make-up kit.

Ben thanked them for their time and walked north down State Street past the Chicago Theater and across the Chicago River to the IBM building, the home of Kenner & Black. Kenner & Black occupied roughly ten floors of the forty-seven story IBM building and even had its own bank of elevators. Ben found Marjorie Thompkins' name on the registry in the lobby and took the elevator up to the 44th floor. Kenner & Black's offices looked surprisingly stark and ill-suited for one of the top silk-stocking litigation firms in the United States.

Thompkins wouldn't see him at first, but when Ben told the receptionist to tell her that he was on his way to the *Chicago Tribune*, she changed her mind. Thompkins arrived a couple of minutes later and led Ben down a flight of stairs off of the reception area to the 43rd floor and a long conference room with a large wooden table that would seat twelve. She followed Ben inside and closed the heavy wooden door behind her. "Just who do you think you are?" she said.

Ben took a step toward her. "Everyone keeps asking me that. I know exactly who I am. I'm a defense lawyer in a capital murder case. I've tried to do the decent thing by contacting you on numerous occasions to set up an appointment at your convenience so we could sit and talk. You haven't even given me the courtesy of a return telephone call." He looked around. "So," he said, "here I am."

They sparred for a while. Ben suggested that in a firm like Kenner & Black, associates like her were a dime a dozen. She stared back at him, her arms folded across her chest as she seethed with resentment. Finally, when it became clear that Ben wouldn't go away easily, she relented through clenched teeth. "Look," she said lowering her voice to make sure no one outside of the closed conference room could possibly hear her, "Daniel and I had a brief relationship, but that was it. It was his idea, it was inappropriate and it was wrong. I shouldn't have done it, but I did. But we only slept together a few times and that was it. I haven't seen or talked to him in at least a couple of years."

They spoke for a few more minutes and Thompkins implored him to keep her indiscretion to himself. Ben made no promises, but came away from their meeting convinced of one thing - Marjorie Thompkins hadn't told him the entire truth.

31

Several days later, Ben sat in the garage reviewing some evidence summaries Mark had prepared for him when he heard the heavy footsteps of the man himself stomping down the steps. Mark came through the door loaded down with a box of documents, his briefcase over one shoulder and a large Federal Express envelope tucked under the other arm. He dropped the box on the conference room table with a thud and set the briefcase on a chair, then tossed the Federal Express envelope across the table in Ben's direction. "Here," he said, "this just came for you."

Ben pulled it in to get a better look at the label. "It's from Fahey," he said. "I wonder what she wants now?" He ripped the package open and pulled out a stack of documents about half an inch thick. Ben looked quickly at the top document. "Fuck," he said aloud. "Fahey has an emergency motion set for tomorrow morning. Filed under seal." Ben read a little further. After a few seconds, he stood, still holding the documents. "Fuck," he said again, this time in a slow, mournful tone.

"What?" Mark asked. Ben ignored him and kept reading. Then he looked at the next document and sighed. "What? What is it?" Mark asked again. Ben ignored him and kept reading. He looked to the end of the motion to find the prayer for relief, then scanned the attached exhibits. "Are you going to tell me what it is?" Mark asked, exasperated.

Ben paged through a brief and cases attached to the motion before tossing the whole pile back on the table. He looked up at

Mark. His face was a chalky white. Mark had never seen him like this before. "What is it?" Mark asked again in a low voice.

Ben paused and took a deep breath before saying, "A paternity test. Bridget Fahey wants a paternity test." Ben's words sucked all the oxygen from the room and Mark flopped down in a chair still staring at Ben, but saying nothing. Ben returned Mark's gaze and looked for the answers to the many questions spinning through his brain at that moment, yet he could find only more questions. "She wants to do paternity and DNA tests," Ben said after a long pause, "on both Megan and Anthony."

Mark whistled. "That certainly puts a new spin on things, doesn't it?

"Yeah," Ben replied, "it sure does."

"Do you really think he could be Greenfield's kid?" Mark asked.

Ben shrugged. "I hope not."

"To tell you the truth," Mark said, "the thought of them sleeping together had occurred to me. I mean, that seemed to be Greenfield's m.o. Admit it, you'd thought of it too."

Ben shook his head. "No, not really. Sure, it may have crossed my mind briefly, but I never really took that as a serious possibility. I know the people involved. I mean, I was around at the time. I would have picked up on it. It's really kind of hard to imagine." He paused. "Maybe I didn't want to imagine it."

"You know Fahey just didn't make this up out of nothing," Mark said. "She knows as well as we do that if she dropped this bomb and didn't have anything to back it up that Wilson would go nuts."

Ben nodded. "Yeah, he would." Ben thought for a minute. "I've gotta get her out here and get to the bottom of this right away."

"Good idea," Mark said.

Ben grabbed the phone and dialed Meg's number. On the fifth ring, he said to Mark, "She's not picking up. Where the fuck could she be? She's under house arrest for Chrissakes. She's wearing an ankle monitor."

"Maybe she's just in the shower or something," Mark said.

"Fuck," Ben said. "She better be." He slammed the phone down holding on to the receiver. He picked it up again and dialed Fran's number. "Fran, I need you to tell me the truth, no bullshit," he said when she came on.

"Okay," she answered tentatively.

"I want to know whether Megan slept with Daniel Greenfield." A long pause answered his question. "Fuck," he said again.

"Ben, I'm not really comfortable talking about this," Fran said. "You need to talk to Meg about it."

"Talk to Meg about it?" he said. "I shouldn't be finding this out in a Court document."

"What do you mean?" she asked.

"They want to do a fucking paternity test and a DNA test. On both Meg and A.J."

"Oh no."

"Oh no is right. And I've got a client who won't even tell me the truth. Tell you what Fran, I don't want to put you on the spot, but this is how it's going to be. I'm going to give her one last chance to come clean and then you're going to tell me everything you know."

"But Ben . . ."

"But Ben nothing. Do you want to see her in the penitentiary for the next thirty years?"

"No, of course not."

"Then I'm going to talk to her and if I need you to, you're going to tell me everything. Got it?"

"I guess so."

He signed off still seething. After he hung up with Fran, Ben tried Meg again. This time she answered. "I need you to get out here to my office as soon as possible," Ben said.

"Why? What is it?"

"I'll tell you when you get here."

"I was going . . ."

"I don't care what you were going to do," Ben interrupted. "I need you to get out here as soon as possible. I'll call Nelson and set it up. We need to talk. It's important. I'll give you an hour."

Ben gave her directions to the office and she arrived about an hour and fifteen minutes later. Ben and Mark were in the garage and saw her pull around and park in the back. "Why don't you go into the kitchen," Ben said to Mark. "I'll talk to her alone." Ben unlocked the outside door to the garage and held it open as Meg approached from the parking lot. If she didn't know already from the telephone call, Meg could see right away that something was very wrong.

"What's the matter?" she asked before even taking off her coat.

"Sit down," he said.

"Ben, what is it?" She sat down and he handed her the Court filings he received from Bridget Fahey. A moment later, she gasped and a hand went to her mouth and tears welled up in her eyes. She closed them in a vain effort to make everything go away. She laid the motion back down on the table without finishing it.

Ben climbed into one of the barber's chairs and sat there watching her for a couple of minutes saying nothing. Finally, he said, "Meg, you know crying isn't going to do you any good. I'm not even sure it's going to make you feel better." His voice held no trace of sympathy and the coldness of his tone made her look up at him. "I think it's time you leveled with me," he said slowly. "Now that we know what the stakes are, at least in the short term, it's time you told me the truth, the whole truth and nothing but the truth. You've been bullshitting me up until now."

Meg shook her head. "No, that's not true," she said her voice cracking and tears streaming down her face.

Ben seemed to be looking through her, not at her. Ben gestured at the documents on the table. "Why don't you tell me all about this," he said.

She shook her head again. "There's nothing to tell. I don't know anything about it."

Ben closed his eyes and rubbed his forehead. "Megan, don't lie to me. We've known each other much too long for that. I'm not just your friend, I'm your lawyer. You have to tell me the truth and tell me now. I don't trust Bridget Fahey, but I know she's way too smart to make this kind of stuff up without some evidence to back her up. Now tell me the truth. How and when did your relationship with Professor Greenfield begin?"

She looked deep into his eyes and found a hardness there that she'd never seen before, even when he'd been grilling her about her husband. She recognized that this was something he wouldn't let go of. Then she gave in to the inevitability of it. She tried to gather her thoughts. "I don't know quite where to begin."

"Just start by telling me when your relationship became more than just professor and student."

"Okay," she said. "I guess it started second year."

"You mean our second year of law school?"

"Yes," she said and Ben sighed. "I ran into Daniel while I was out getting lunch one day and we sat down and had a sandwich together. It all seemed innocent enough. I'd been fighting with Joe and we got to talking about our respective spouses and it seemed like we both needed to just let off some steam."

"Go on," Ben said.

Meg spent the next half hour or so telling Ben the story of their relationship from its beginning over that fateful lunch to its end a few months later. "We mostly just talked," she said under Ben's withering gaze. "He was a very good listener. But yes, we eventually started sleeping together." Ben realized how difficult it was for her to discuss these things and despite his anger, he tried not to make it harder than it needed to be. He looked at the ground. "The sex was kind of, well, secondary, if you can believe that. Joe and I weren't sleeping together very often and Daniel and Sylvia weren't doing it very much either according to Daniel and eventually we just sort of started." Ben continued to look down at his shoes. She paused, gathering herself to continue with the story. "We didn't sleep together very often or for very long for that matter. We probably slept together for the first time during the spring of second year and broke it off all together by the beginning of third year, right around Labor Day when we were back in school."

"When was Anthony born, Meg? July wasn't it?"

"Yes, July 11th."

212

"If you stopped sleeping with Greenfield in early September," Ben said doing the math, "that's cutting it kind of close, don't you think?"

"No, it's not," Meg said emphatically. Now it was Ben who didn't want to meet her eye. He looked up to find her staring directly at him. "Ben, you've got to believe me," she said. "Daniel Greenfield is not Anthony's father. He absolutely positively is not."

Ben wanted to believe her. "How do you know?"

"I just know. I know when he was conceived."

"How do you know that?"

"I just know, that's all. Women tend to know these things. He was conceived on a long weekend in Florida in October."

"You're sure?"

"Absolutely."

"Okay," Ben said. "Let's assume what you're saying is true. This still isn't going to look good and it's going to be mighty embarrassing for everyone involved, particularly you, your husband and your son." He paused again. "Does Joe know anything about this?" he finally asked breaking the silence.

"Yes, well, no not directly, but he knows there was someone for a time back then."

"Is there any way he could have found out?"

She shook her head. "I don't think so, but I don't know for sure."

"He's not going to like hearing about this, you can bet on that."

"No, but it was a long time ago."

"But it will be embarrassing and humiliating for him. Just like it would have been if he'd found out in the first place."

"What are you saying?"

"I'm saying maybe he did find out in the first place. Or maybe he found out recently."

"You're not suggesting that Joe had anything to do with Daniel's death, are you?"

"I'm not suggesting anything. I'm just raising logical inferences. The press is going to have a field day with this when it gets out."

"Why does it have to get out?" Meg asked. She pointed to the papers on the table. "This is filed under seal."

"That's all well and good, but you know in a case like this, there are no secrets. Obviously, we're not going to tell, but do you think you can trust Bridget Fahey? Of course not. Someone's going to find out sooner or later, probably sooner. That's assuming somebody in the media doesn't already know about it."

"We have to protect Anthony," Meg said.

"I don't know how we're going to do that," Ben replied. "It's going to come out eventually. The best thing we can hope for is that they do the test and your son is Joe's like you say he is."

"We can't let them do the test," Meg said frantically. She gave him a pleading look.

"Why not? The best defense we have is that he's not the father. Besides, I don't know how we can prevent the Judge from granting this motion. What better motive is there than killing a man who just finds out that your child is his? That's something worth killing for, don't you think? At least I might think that way if I were sitting on a jury. I wouldn't hold my breath if I were you. We've been wondering all along what the motive was for Greenfield's murder and now Bridget Fahey has tossed a perfect motive right in our laps. Now, you say that Anthony is not Greenfield's son and that you didn't kill him and I believe you, but we have to kill this thing once and for all and the only way to do that is to take the test and prove that the child is your husband's and not Daniel Greenfield's."

Ben scratched his head thinking and looked at her for a minute. "You're going to have to reconcile yourself to the idea that they're going to make you take these tests. Let's get back to your relationship with Greenfield for a minute. How did it end?"

"He broke it off," Meg said. Ben raised his eyebrows. "We didn't see each other much over that summer," Meg continued, "and I had a feeling at the time that he'd found somebody else and had more or less lost interest in me, at least from a sexual standpoint. We still talked after that, but not that often. It was really all over in just a few months."

"He found out you were pregnant, didn't he?"

214

"Well, of course. After all, I was still in school. I couldn't very well hide it."

"Did he ever question whether he was the father?"

"No, he never did. He knew he wasn't. He knew he couldn't be."

Ben got up from the barber's chair and slowly paced around the garage. He stopped in front of the door and peered out into the parking lot. Without turning, he asked her. "When did you last see him?"

"I don't know," she said haltingly. "It's been a long time, years probably."

"Years?" Ben said. "You know, Megan, there are phone records and witnesses and even security cameras." He turned and faced her again. "So, I'll ask you again. When did you last see him?"

She felt the full heat of his eyes boring into her and looked down at her lap. He took a step closer and paused. Tears continued to stream from her eyes. She sniffled. "I didn't kill him Ben," she said in a choked voice. "I tell you, I didn't kill him."

Ben took another step closer. "I didn't ask you whether you killed him. I asked when you last saw him."

She looked around the room, at the safe, at the stuffed animal heads hanging from the walls, anything but at him. Tears streamed down her cheeks. "He started calling me around Thanksgiving, I think," she said finally. "I didn't know what he wanted at first so I ignored him. Finally, he left a couple of messages on my answering machine, getting more and more insistent. He said he needed to see me."

"Did you go see him?"

"Yes," she said in a voice barely audible. She still couldn't look at him. "I went twice actually. The first time I didn't see him. I went to his office and he wasn't there so I left him a note that I'd stopped by."

"A note? In writing?"

She nodded. "Yes. Then he called again and left me another message and I went back to see him a second time."

"When was this?"

215

"Right before Christmas."

"Did you see him that time?"

"Yes. Just for a few minutes."

"What did he want?"

"I'm not sure. In fact, it was really kind of strange. His messages made it seem like he absolutely had to speak to me right away, but when I got there, we didn't really talk about much of anything."

"What do you mean," Ben asked a little confused.

"We more or less just made small talk. He asked how I was doing, about family stuff, that sort of thing. I asked him the same and he said things were going okay. It went back and forth like that for a few minutes, then we talked about the reunion coming up for a little bit and then he got a phone call and I left."

Ben couldn't believe that was it. He stood over her, hands on his hips and studied her for a minute. She looked up at him with pleading eyes begging to be believed. "There wasn't anything else?" he asked finally.

"No. Once I got there, he didn't seem that interested in talking to me."

"Do you know who called him on the phone?"

"No, I don't. But whoever it was, he didn't want me in the room when he talked to them. He told me that he had to take the call and he would be in touch, but that it was nice seeing me. It was clear he wanted me to leave, so I left. Once I shut the door behind me, I never saw him again."

Ben shook his head and paced some more. "Meg," he said his arms outstretched in a pleading motion, "there's got to be more than that. You have to tell me everything."

She shook her head hard. "I am telling you everything," she said, her voice rising.

"No Meg, I don't think you are." He pulled out a chair and sat directly opposite her, their knees brushing together. He looked directly into her eyes and said, "Meg, this is the most serious situation you'll ever encounter in your life. Your very life and future, and the future of your family, depends on our being able to successfully defend this case."

"I know that," she said.

Ben waved her off. "No, I don't think you do. These guys aren't kidding around. They've brought this case against you, not because of some sinister motive, but because they think you killed him." Ben said the words very slowly and emphatically. "Do you understand what I'm saying? They think you took a baseball bat and bashed Daniel Greenfield's skull in until he was dead. These people are true believers. They aren't joking around."

"I know that. I know what prosecutors are like," she said.

"You may think you do, but I can assure you, you don't. These are the most cynical, hard-nosed people you'll ever want to meet. How can I explain this to you?" he said. He looked around the room as though searching for a way to make her understand. "Okay," he said, "let me tell you a little story. Back when I was working for the office, I was already in felonies by that time, I shared an office with a guy named Ron Hirst. Ron was a good guy, a good prosecutor, but he was like everyone else in that office in that he took everything anybody said, especially defendants, with more than a grain of salt. He didn't take anything at face value.

"One day, I think it was before Court, we were sitting in the office looking at the *Tribune*. There was something in the paper about Mother Theresa," Ben said nodding. Meg nodded back. "Well, anyway, there was something in there about her. I don't know whether she was sick or making another tour of the United States. I can't remember.

"Ron looked up from the newspaper and said, 'Hey there's something in the paper here about Mother Theresa. What do you make of her?' I wasn't quite sure what he meant and said so. He said, 'What do you think her angle is?' I thought he was kidding. I looked at him and realized he wasn't. He was serious. I told him, 'What's her angle? I think she's a nun who's dedicated her life to helping the impoverished lepers in Calcutta.' He shook his head and looked me straight in the eye. 'No, really,' he said, 'what's her angle?'" Ben paused and let the message sink in. "And we were talking about Mother Theresa. No offense, Meg, I love you, you're a wonderful person, but you're no Mother Theresa. If they can ask

217

questions like that about Mother Theresa, what do you think they're asking about you?"

32

Meg left the office shaken, but guaranteed that she'd told Ben everything and vowed not to keep any more secrets from him. Ben watched her walk out to the parking lot, get in her car and drive away, not sure whether he believed her.

A few minutes later, Mark joined him in the garage. "What's the verdict?" he asked upon entering.

Ben smiled grimly. "Not the best choice of words, I don't think," he said. "She admits sleeping with him."

"Well, we knew that, didn't we?" Mark said. "That seems pretty obvious. The question is, is the kid his?"

"No," Ben said, "I don't think that's the question. I think the question ultimately is, does she think that the kid is his? Whether or not Greenfield's the father, if she thought he was, that supplies the motive for killing him."

Mark looked thoughtful, his hand on his mouth. "True enough," he said. "What was her answer?"

Ben turned and shrugged. "She says no, the kid is not his. She says there is no possible way he could be the father. She knows when and where the kid was conceived and Joseph Cavallaro has to be the father."

"Do you believe her?"

Ben shook his head. "I don't know. She seemed emphatic enough, but the last time she slept with Greenfield is close enough to when the baby must have been conceived for me to not feel very good about it."

219

"You mean she was sleeping with Greenfield at the same time the baby was conceived?"

"She says no. She says she stopped sleeping with Greenfield a month or two before that. Still . . ."

Mark finished the thought. "Still, anything's possible."

Ben nodded. "Anything's possible," he repeated. "The problem is, we now have a connection between Meg and Greenfield other than just student and professor."

Mark frowned. "Not necessarily," he said. "If we stick to our guns that this whole line of inquiry is bullshit, then a negative test proves the point." He eyed Ben. "I'm assuming she's gonna have to take the test. I don't see any way around it. It provides the motive if he's the father."

"Yep, sure does," Ben said. "I think we fight the test as hard as we can, act like it's ridiculous, and then when Judge Wilson makes us take it anyway, we hope like hell it's negative."

"Geezus," Mark said.

They spent the next few minutes playing out the various scenarios and Ben filled Mark in on Greenfield's phone calls and Meg's final meeting with him right before Christmas. "It just doesn't add up," Mark suggested.

"No, I don't think so either," Ben agreed. "I think we need to really hit on these phone records to try and establish when and where Meg may have talked to him."

Neither man said it, but both men thought that the phone records could also help them confirm Meg's story. Then the first phone call came. A reporter with the *Daily Herald*, a local suburban newspaper, called to see if Ben had any comment on unconfirmed reports that an emergency motion was due to be heard in Court the following day regarding proof of a link between the victim and the defendant. Ben didn't take the call. "Shit," he said to Mark, "they've already leaked it."

"Either they did, or somebody at the Courthouse did," Mark said.

Ben scoffed. "Or they had somebody at the Courthouse do it. God damn it," he said. "I'm getting out of here. I don't want to be around when these phone calls start coming. Just have

220

everybody say I'm not here. At least that's the truth. I'm going to go downtown and try and shake up Dorlund a little bit. Obviously, he hasn't been telling us the whole truth."

Ben found Professor Dorlund in his office sipping a Diet Coke from a Styrofoam cup. The room smelled like a mixture of bad cologne and fried food. When he saw Ben enter, Dorlund got up and said, "I'm afraid I can't talk right now, I've got a class in a few minutes."

Ben took a seat. "Sit down," he said. "You don't have a class for forty-five minutes. I've got a copy of your schedule." Ben smiled a mirthless smile.

Dorlund stuffed some papers into a briefcase. "I'm sorry, I really am. I can't talk to you right now, I don't have any time."

"You knew this was coming, didn't you?"

"I don't know what you're talking about."

Ben didn't look amused. "I'll tell you what," he said. "Either talk to me now or I'll subpoena you and we'll talk about your love life and drug habits in open Court in front of Judge Wilson. Dorlund looked up unamused. "Or," Ben continued, "I can stop by and have the same conversation with your wife. You pick."

Dorlund stood up and looked sideways at Ben, his features stiffening. "You'd do it too, wouldn't you?"

"Yeah, I would. And I'd enjoy it too. The problem, Professor, is you've been bullshitting me and that's gonna stop. Now sit down and tell me about the connection between my client and Daniel Greenfield."

Dorlund remained standing. "She's your client. Why don't you ask her?"

"Because I'm asking you. You knew Greenfield better than anyone. I want you to tell me what you know."

Dorlund finally sat down. "How do you think it would look if it got out that you came in here and were badgering a potential witness?"

"How would it look?" Ben said, looking at the ceiling. "Probably not as bad as you think, because all I'm trying to do is get you to tell me the truth. I'm not asking you to lie or make something up. I'm just asking you to tell me what you know.

Nothing wrong with that. So, if you want to get on the horn with Geraldo, go right ahead."

After apparently concluding that Ben was serious, Samuel Dorlund reluctantly began to relay what he knew about the relationship between Meg and Greenfield. His story didn't differ dramatically from the one Meg had told Ben earlier, nor did he really give Ben any reason to disbelieve him. According to Dorlund, they began a brief sexual relationship sometime during Meg's second year which lasted for several months before Greenfield broke it off. He also confirmed that he did not know Meg's name at the time, only that she was a student. In fact, he didn't even know it was her. He only learned Meg's identity years later.

"Why did he break up with her?" Ben asked.

"I don't remember exactly," Dorlund said. "He may have found somebody else, I'm not sure. I've been thinking about that ever since this thing happened and your client was arrested. I honestly don't remember."

"Do you know of any other students with whom Greenfield had a sexual relationship?"

"By name? No. I mean, I know there were probably others, but I preferred not to know who they were. I only really know about your client because Daniel told me about it years later. I didn't even know her name at the time."

"Okay," Ben said, "I assume you told this to the prosecutors?"

"Of course. If your client had something to do with Daniel's murder, I want to make sure she's caught and punished for it."

Ben nodded. "What about professors?" Ben asked. "Did Daniel Greenfield ever have any sexual relationships with other faculty members?"

"Maybe, but I'm not sure."

"What about Angela Harper?"

Now Dorlund laughed heartily. "Angela Harper?" He threw his head back. "I'm not sure Angela Harper has sex. I don't think Daniel seriously pursued any relationship with her, let alone had one. Like I said, I don't think she has it in her."

"Well, she is married, isn't she?"

222

"Yeah, I think her husband must be a eunuch. She wouldn't get near anyone who has any real balls. I can't imagine how they managed to have a kid together - artificial insemination probably."

"They have a child?"

"Yeah, a son, I think. Must be four or five by now, maybe a little older."

They talked until Dorlund had to leave for his class. Ben felt that Dorlund had more or less leveled with him, a healthy dose of skepticism notwithstanding. Although he probably hadn't told Ben everything, the basic story seemed about right. Ben wished he knew who that other woman was, even though he knew that she may not have had anything to do with Greenfield's murder. After all, that relationship took place almost ten years ago. The basis for the murder almost had to be something more recent than that.

After he left Dorlund's office, Ben pulled out his cell phone and called Mark. "It's a fucking zoo out here," Mark said. "The phone's been ringing off the hook starting about ten minutes after you left. The secretaries are really getting pissed. I heard them talking about bringing someone in just to answer the phones and charging it to this case."

Ben shrugged, "God damn it," he said. "I'm not sure we could even do that."

"We've gotta do something or better said, you've gotta do something. If you're not careful, there's gonna be a mutiny."

"Okay, okay, I'll think about it."

"Did you get anything out of Dorlund?" Mark asked. Ben described his conversation with Professor Dorlund telling Mark that Dorlund's story seemed fairly consistent with Megan's. "At least that's some good news," Mark said. While talking to Mark, Ben had made his way to the elevators. A bell rang signaling that the doors were about to open.

"Look," Ben said, "I'm about to get on an elevator, so I have to let you go. I'll talk to you later." The doors opened and Professor Sarah Berman stepped out.

"Mr. Lohmeier," she said with a sly grin, "your celebrity status grows by the day."

"Great," he said. "That's all I need."

223

She pulled him off to the side looking around to see if they were alone and spoke in a very quiet voice. "Is it true? What I heard on the radio about the paternity test?"

Ben groaned. "Shit," he said. "No comment. You can't believe everything you hear on the radio."

"That doesn't mean it's always wrong," she said.

"No," he agreed, "not always. Say, as long as I've got you here, I'd like to ask you a couple of questions if you've got time."

"Sure," she said, "why don't we go back to my office?" Ben followed her back to her office. She closed the door behind them and sat down behind her desk, while Ben remained standing. "So what is it?" she asked.

"Angela Harper," Ben said.

"Well, I think I told you before, Angela and Daniel did not get along, to put it mildly."

"Did they ever actually sleep together?"

She laughed. "I doubt that. I doubt that very much. He probably suggested it, but I can't see that it ever would've happened."

"So I'm told," Ben said. "Any other problems between the two of them that you're aware of?"

"No, not specifically. All I know is that he made a lot of inappropriate comments and they didn't really get along. It may have also been something to do with the law school, or it may have been something else, I just don't know. I'm sorry."

"Okay, I wasn't sure if you knew anything, but I figured it was worth asking. Would you keep your eyes and ears open for stuff like this, whether it's with Angela Harper or someone else on the faculty?"

"Of course, but I've got to ask you. I didn't like Daniel Greenfield either. You don't seem to think I could've had something to do with his death. Why is that?"

Ben reached for the handle on the door seeming to ignore her question. Then he turned and looked back at her as he broke into a broad smile. "Simple," he said, "you just don't have it in you."

224

33

Once again, Ben and Mark drove down together for the Court appearance, Ben not wanting to run the gauntlet of reporters by himself. As expected, a throng of media types in all shapes and sizes swarmed them as they approached the steps to the Criminal Courts Building. Mark led Ben through the crowds like a pulling guard leading a halfback through a hole, while Ben smiled coolly and muttered the occasional "no comment" as they ascended the steps. Once inside, the Sheriff's deputies helped keep the reporters at bay as Ben made his way through the metal detector, having still failed to get his pass. As Ben stood at the far end of the metal detector slipping his belt back into his pants, Bridgett Fahey approached from the south end of the complex where the State's Attorney's Offices were located.

"Good morning, Counselor," she said approaching civility. "I see you need to get a pass so you can skip the metal detectors."

"Yeah," Ben said, "I'll get around to it before trial." His eyes narrowed. "Nice job with all these reporters. What did you do, give them a copy of your motion?" Ben asked as they walked. Mark chuckled alongside him.

"I don't know what you're talking about. I hope you're not suggesting that I leaked anything to the media."

"Oh no," Ben said sarcastically, "you would never do something like that."

She stopped and faced him directly. "No, I wouldn't and I didn't."

"Pardon me, Bridget, if I don't believe you. Either you did it or one of your little minions did. I know you, remember? You know as well as I do that we certainly didn't say anything about it. I barely had the damn thing in my office before the phone started ringing." Ben started walking again. "I'd come up with a new story before Judge Wilson asks you about it though."

Ben and Mark strolled off ahead of her and grabbed the first elevator heading upstairs, leaving Bridget Fahey and one of her assistants lagging behind. Once in the courtroom, Ben and Mark went to their counsel table, while Fahey went to hers. There would be no other small talk this morning.

Judge Wilson came out on the bench and made them wait through his entire call before his clerk finally called the case. When counsel reached the bench, the Judge looked down on them and said, "I understand we have a motion here brought under seal by the State." His lips formed the slightest of smiles as he gazed over their heads out at the gaggle of reporters filling the gallery section of his courtroom. Point made, Ben thought to himself.

"I don't think we need to go into the details of this particular motion," the Judge continued, "nor do I really think that there is any kind of an emergency present here. Nevertheless," he said turning to Ben. "Mr. Lohmeier, if you'd prefer to address this matter now rather than come back again, I'll be happy to entertain this motion. It's your call."

Ben took the high road. "As long as we're here, Judge, I'd just as soon let them present it today."

"Fair enough," the Judge said.

Judge Wilson gave Ben fourteen days to file a written response to the State's motion and Bridget Fahey seven days thereafter to file a reply. The matter was scheduled for hearing in a month.

Ben and Mark walked quickly from the courtroom. As they pushed through the door and out into the hallway where a throng of reporters waited, a hand reached out and grabbed Ben's left arm. He jerked his head to the left and locked eyes with Sally Brzycki, another former classmate from law school.

"Ben, hi," she said. "Can we talk for a minute?"

Sensing an opportunity to avoid the reporters, Ben quickly agreed. "We'll walk and talk," he said.

Sally Brzycki was a tall woman, a shade under six feet and not particularly attractive. Her straw-colored hair was cut short just above the shoulders, which did nothing to soften her harsh, almost masculine features. In law school, she had displayed an aggressive and overbearing personality, likely to step over or on anyone who stood in her path. Ben always figured her lack of interpersonal skills merely masked long-held insecurities, at least he thought that when he was in a psychoanalytical mood. He had to admit, however, that she was a very good student. He had never liked her much and wouldn't have wanted to talk to her under normal circumstances. He nevertheless made a snap judgment that talking to Sally Brzycki seemed marginally preferable to fending off the crowd of reporters.

"How've you been?" she asked as they pushed their way toward the elevators. He shrugged and gestured toward the members of the media still peppering him with questions even as he ignored them.

"Not too bad, busy mostly."

When the elevator doors closed behind them, Ben turned to Mark and said:

"Mark Schaefer, this is Sally Brzycki. Sally, Mark Schaefer. Sally and I went to law school together."

"It's Sally Renfroe, actually. I'm married now."

"Oh," Ben said, "I didn't know that. Congratulations. Is this a recent development?"

"No, we've been married since not long after law school. My husband has a restaurant in Lincoln Park."

Sally and Mark shook hands. "Nice to meet you," Mark said.

"So, what brings you down here to the dregs of society?" Ben asked. "I didn't know you did any criminal work."

"I don't. I talked to Megan yesterday and I came by this morning to give her some moral support, even if she wasn't here herself."

Ben looked stunned. "You, you talked to Megan?" he stammered.

"Oh yes, Megan and I are quite good friends now. We talk all the time."

Ben had no idea. He talked to Meg too and he figured if they were such good friends, he probably would've heard about it by now. "Okay," he finally murmured, unable to hide his surprise.

"We've been pretty good friends for a long time," Sally said. "We've quite a bit in common. We both have sons, neither of us much liked the full time practice of law and . . ."

Ben interrupted her. "You've got a son too? I didn't know that either. Obviously."

"Oh yes."

"How long has it been since we've seen each other?" Ben asked. "I don't remember any of this stuff."

"It's been a long time, Ben. I found it too hard having a child and practicing law full-time as well. I just missed him too much. I went part-time and then I changed firms and now I'm working for one of the partners at my old firm. I mostly do research. It keeps me somewhat involved, but not too much."

They reached the first floor and got off the elevator and continued talking as they made their way through the winding hallways back to the main lobby of the Courthouse. Outside on the steps, they paused so Ben could make a brief statement to the gathered reporters.

"I'm sorry, but I'm unable to comment on any of the reports you've heard in the media," he said. "The motion filed by the State is under seal and I really can't say anything about it. Thank you very much."

They resumed walking and stopped at the corner.

"I'm parked this way in the garage," Sally said.

"We're down over here in a lot," Ben replied.

"If you need anything done, like research, or if you need a character witness, or anything at all, please call me," Sally said taking a card from her purse and handing it to Ben. "I know Megan couldn't have done this and I'd like to help out any way I can."

"Thanks," was all Ben could muster. He felt obliged to take a card from his pocket and hand it to her as well. They shook hands.

Mark said, "Nice to meet you," and watched her cross the street toward the parking garage before turning back to Ben, who was watching her as well. "That seemed kind of weird," Mark said.

"You have no idea," Ben answered.

Ben spent the next several weeks arranging for, attending and then worrying about the results of the Court-ordered paternity tests. On a raw spring day, Ben returned from lunch with the guys to find Nancy and Dianne sitting in the kitchen finishing their lunch.

"Have you been upstairs?" Nancy asked.

"No," Ben said.

"There's an envelope on your chair." Ben looked puzzled. "It's from the lab," Nancy said. Ben hurried upstairs, Nancy following behind him. Dan Conlon trailed behind Nancy. He found a priority mail envelope with the return address of the testing facility sitting on his chair. He picked it up, opened it and sat down. Nancy and Dan stood before him waiting eagerly. Ben took a deep breath and pulled a small stack of papers from the envelope. On top, he found a cover letter from the director of the testing facility. He paged through the remaining pages as Nancy and Dan looked down on him.

Ben looked up and smiled. "Joseph Cavallaro is the father."

"Hot Damn," Conlon said shaking his fist. "Never a doubt in my mind."

34

The Protector settled in behind a group of commuters and headed down the platform toward the sidewalk beyond. The group of five crossed Walnut and cut toward the edge of the law firm parking lot. Daylight Savings time was still a ways away and the sun had long since set. The glowing lights only showed two cars in the back parking lot and as the group passed the garage in silence, the Protector could see Ben working at the conference table inside. The group turned the corner at the far end of the garage and four of them split off in the direction of the commuter parking lot in the distance, while the Protector turned right, strolled through the front parking lot, which was empty, and toward the back door of the bar. The Protector mounted the steps and went inside, stopped in the restroom, walked through the bar, getting crowded now with people stopping in for a quick one after work, and cut out the front entrance onto the sidewalk running parallel with Irving Park Road.

The commuters had all filtered out of the station and found their cars for the ride back home when the Protector completed the circle and found a spot back beyond the back parking lot in the midst of a small clump of pine trees. From this vantage point, the Protector could see the two cars remaining in the parking lot, while watching Ben work at the table in the garage, oblivious to the surveillance.

About half an hour later, a tall lean man bounded down the steps and turned the corner from the back entrance of the office to the parking lot, getting into the black Acura parked across the way. As the car pulled around the back of the garage and disappeared, the Protector concluded that Ben was now alone in the building. The Protector looked up at a light shining in the second floor window above. That's his office, the Protector thought and continued watching. Fifteen minutes later, Ben rose from his chair and rummaged through a banker's box sitting on the other end of the table. Apparently not finding what he was looking for, Ben left the garage and walked back to the main part of the building. A minute later, the Protector saw Ben's shadow cross the window in his office.

The Protector knew from past experience that members of the firm were not all that scrupulous about locking doors when someone was still left working in the building. It was only a few minutes past seven after all, not terribly late, and what trouble could be had in downtown Ithaca? This wasn't the south side of Chicago. No, this was the western suburbs, DuPage County, the bastion of white bread Republicanism.

Seeing Ben's shadow appear to sit down at his desk, the Protector eased out of the hiding place and strolled casually around the garage toward the front of the building. The Protector walked up the steps to the main entrance and looked inside the glass door. The lobby was dark except for light coming from the kitchen and the hallway to the right. Gloves on, the Protector grabbed the handle and pulled softly and noiselessly on the door - unlocked. The Protector let the door silently close and walked briskly back down the steps out to front parking lot, completing the circuit through the bar and back to the hiding place in the trees within three to four minutes.

The Protector looked up at the window to Ben's office, no shadows now, then back to the brightly lit garage, still empty. Where was he? A moment later, the question was answered when Ben emerged in the corridor separating the garage from the main part of the building carrying a file. The Protector watched Ben settle back at the conference table and look through the file for a few minutes. Checking the surrounding area to make sure that no one was in sight, the Protector moved out from the hiding place in the trees and walked quickly into the parking lot heading toward the garage. Dressed all in black, the Protector looked like any other commuter strolling through the firm parking lot returning to a car. Nearing the garage, the Protector stopped for an instant and studied Ben, whose back was to the door. From what the Protector could see, Ben was reviewing some cases that had been pulled and copied. Probably the paternity issue, the Protector thought.

Not wanting to be seen, the Protector circled around the back of the garage once again and moved toward the front door of the building as though having every right to be there. The door was covered in darkness and its position in the building kept it somewhat hidden from view, especially at night. With no one present in the area, there was no chance the Protector would be seen entering the building. Without hesitating an instant, the Protector ascended the steps to the front door, opened it and went inside, letting the door close softly and silently. Moving quickly, the Protector passed through the lobby and turned right down the corridor past the copy room to the stairs heading up to Ben's office. The Protector took the steps two at a time, moving through Dianne Reynolds' office and into Ben's.

Although the lights were on, the blinds were drawn. No one will recognize me from the parking lot below, the Protector thought. The Protector quickly surveyed the situation. The round table to the left was empty. The Protector turned to the right and went around Ben's desk, pulled out his chair and sat down. There were several expandable file folders on the floor with Cavallaro scrawled on them and the Protector picked them up in turn, emptied them and quickly scanned their contents.

"Here we go," the Protector whispered pulling out a manila folder marked, "Legal Research", crammed full with notes and copies of cases. The Protector scanned the contents of the file and then stuffed it back into the expandable folder before placing the folder back on the floor where it had been found.

On the desk, the Protector found a memorandum from Dan Conlon to Ben Lohmeier regarding paternity issues, together with notes written on a yellow legal pad. The Protector paged through the memorandum stopping suddenly at the sound of a noise coming from downstairs. A door screeching open and then

232

slamming. Probably the door leading from the copy room out toward the conference room, the Protector thought. The Protector looked around and saw that the French doors leading to the next office were open. The Protector tip-toed across the hardwood floor as silently as possible, footsteps now sounding on the nearby stairs. Heart pounding, the Protector looked around for a place to hide. In the far corner of the room, the Protector spied an open doorway and eased over to it. It led to a long narrow closet used for file storage. The Protector slipped inside and out of sight. The Protector stuffed a gloved hand into the right hand pocket of the long overcoat and found the butt end of a 9 mm handgun. I'll do it if I have to, the Protector thought. Ben was in his office now and the Protector could hear him, but not see him.

Then the Protector heard Ben pick up the phone and start dialing. "Hey Lib, it's me," Ben said.

He's talking to his wife, the Protector thought.

"Yeah, I'm kind of tired," Ben said. "I'll only be here another half hour or so . . . yes . . . what'd you have for dinner? . . . Any left? . . . Okay, I'll see you in an hour or so … Love you too."

The Protector heard Ben hang up the phone, walk across the hardwood floor of his office through the carpeted outer office and back down the stairs. So close. A moment later, the sound of the door opening and slamming shut once again.

The Protector paused and considered things for several minutes before following Ben downstairs. In less than a minute, with a train rumbling by in the background, the Protector was back out the front door and gone.

35

As another dreary Chicago winter gave way to a dreary Chicago spring which quickly transformed into an early Chicago summer shortly after Memorial Day, Ben and the rest of the defense team worked hard on the collection and analysis of the evidence needed to make their case. Although the burden of proof beyond a reasonable doubt lay with the prosecution, the defense team realized that they nevertheless needed to propose an alternate theory of the evidence which would satisfy a jury and cause them to conclude that, at the very least, reasonable doubt existed.

Bridget Fahey didn't go out of her way to comply with the disclosure of discovery required by the Illinois Code of Criminal Procedure. Consequently, Ben used the media and his Court appearances before Judge Wilson to prod her into turning the evidence in her possession over in a more timely fashion. Fortunately, much of the evidence against Megan was also subject to differing and in some cases innocent explanations.

For example, since Meg conceded to Ben that she had in fact been inside Greenfield's office, something she had unfortunately denied in her interviews with the police, it came as no surprise that a blond hairs similar to her own could be found in the office. She further acknowledged that she had picked up the Sammy Sosa autographed baseball bat and briefly admired it while Greenfield was on the telephone. Thus, the presence of her fingerprints on the bat near the label would not be surprising.

It took Meg quite a while before she could explain how Greenfield's blood came to be found on a wool scarf taken from the brownstone. At first, Ben thought the blood on the scarf could have pointed to Joseph Cavallaro since Meg and her husband owned his and her scarves that were virtually identical. Further testing on the scarf, however, established that the scarf stained with blood also contained trace amounts of make up and perfume, which appeared to rule out Joseph Cavallaro. Then, one Monday evening in early May, during a telephone conversation with Meg, Ben told her about a rare nose bleed that he had suffered the previous weekend.

"That's it," Meg said excitedly. "That's it," she repeated.

"What?"

"The nose bleed, that's it."

Ben was confused. "I don't get it."

"That's how the blood got on my scarf," she said. "I just remembered. He had a nose bleed. Not a real bad one, but I remember handing him the Kleenex. I was standing by the desk when his nose started to bleed a little. The Kleenex box was right there on the desk in front of me, so I handed him a couple. It didn't stop right away, so I handed him a couple more. That must have been when the blood got on the scarf. You see, I was wearing my coat the whole time and never took it off. I'm sure I didn't take my scarf off either. He used to get nose bleeds all the time. That's probably why I didn't think it was anything significant enough to remember."

Ben thought this explanation seemed a little bit too convenient until he called down to Florida and Nora Scott confirmed the story. "Oh yeah, he used to get a lot of them, especially in the winter," Nora said.

"Did you ever suspect it had anything to do with drug use?" Ben asked. "You know, damage due to cocaine use?"

"No," she said. "He didn't have that many of them. My husband gets nose bleeds in the winter too and I can tell you for sure that he doesn't have a drug problem." Nora told Ben that she would be willing to testify about the nose bleeds at trial if he really needed her, although she strongly preferred to avoid getting involved at all.

Despite their best hopes, the files from the law school didn't yield much useful information. After extensive analysis, the grade reports only pointed to a handful of suspects, none of whom seemed to have any recent contact with Greenfield or any other connection that could be found linking them to the crime. Initial review of the final exams for Greenfield's last two classes brought similar results. A few possibilities, but not much else. The hot-tempered Jason Hahn hadn't been completely ruled out, for he had no real alibi for much of December 28th, the likely date of the murder.

The telephone records also proved to be a disappointment. They confirmed that several telephone calls had been placed from the law school to Megan's house and her office at the Appellate Court, but none of the other telephone records proved particularly interesting. They found a few telephone calls to several of the members of the Reunion Committee, but little else.

A review of the materials found in Greenfield's apartment and office only caused them to conclude that the Professor hadn't worked very hard. Other than a few old calendars which no one could explain, the only items of significance found in Greenfield's briefcase and office were some hand-written notes and a small amount of research, apparently for an article on the uses of DNA evidence in criminal prosecutions that Dorlund said Greenfield had been working on in the weeks prior to his death. From what they could tell, Greenfield hadn't begun writing the article since they could find no evidence in his office or on any of his computers that he had ever written a single word on the subject. Ben wondered if some of the missing work product might have been taken by the killer, but couldn't figure out why.

The only item of significance found among Greenfield's papers was a piece of note paper torn from a memo pad which had Megan's home and office phone numbers scrawled on it, apparently in Greenfield's handwriting. This only served to confirm that Greenfield was likely the person who made the telephone calls. Ben pressed Disko and Portalski to keep looking, keep digging for something, anything that might suggest that someone else may have been involved in the crime.

As part of their effort to attack the evidence, Ben retained several expert witnesses to poke holes in the State's case. Although very costly, none of the work done to date by the blood, fingerprint, hair and fiber experts hired by the defense had borne much fruit. Since much work remained to be done, Ben still held out hope that one or more of these experts could provide him with something he could use at trial.

Megan seemed to be handling the situation about as well as could be expected. She had fallen into something of a routine, particularly with Anthony, such that the home confinement did not appear as onerous as everyone first feared. Nevertheless, as summer and nicer weather approached, Ben could see that Meg's inability to get outside and really enjoy the outdoors was beginning to weigh on her. Other than that, Meg seemed outwardly confident that her innocence would be established and appeared pleased with the efforts that Ben and the rest of the team had taken in establishing her defense.

On a personal level, as the pressure surrounding Megan's defense grew, so did Ben's single mindedness of purpose. He now appeared to be focusing on little else. He came in early, stayed late and frequently missed meals. The guys in the office found him much more short-tempered and less willing to engage in the typical office banter. Even the staff, who had always found Ben to be fairly easy-going, now grumbled behind his back. He also found himself bringing his problems home and was occasionally guilty of taking his pressures out on his family. From time to time, he noticed that Libby and the kids were trying to avoid him after a particularly bad day. He fought the old urges and made a conscious effort to stay away from "there". He didn't always succeed.

One Friday in late June, Ben was still at the office at six when the phone rang.

"Enjoying the first day of summer?" Fran's voice said on the other end of the line.

"No, not really. I hadn't even noticed, to tell you the truth."

"I hope you remember that tomorrow is our ten-year reunion," Fran said.

"Shit," Ben said. "I'd forgotten all about it. Maybe I'll blow it off."

"No, don't do that. You've got to go. You've already paid for the tickets, if nothing else. Besides, you're now the most prominent lawyer in our graduating class. I can't wait to see the reaction."

"You know how much I care about that?" Ben asked.

"I know, I know, but a lot of those people will be pea green with envy. You've got to go."

"I suppose. I could use the night out, I guess."

"Good, we're getting there at seven. Don't be late."

36

The Roadhouse Tap was a yuppie microbrewery hangout just west of Harry Caray's restaurant on the near north side. Ben parked the SUV in an open air lot a block or two away and he and Libby walked over under bright blue skies and brilliant early evening sunshine. They walked inside and discovered a long line forming in front of the hostess. This would be a busy Saturday night. Their party was on the second floor and they were directed to a stairway around the corner next to a window displaying a series of gleaming silver vats, ostensibly used in the brewing of the establishment's prize product. Ben wondered as they passed the windows and headed upstairs whether the vats merely provided decoration and perceived authenticity or whether they had actually seen their share of hops or barley or whatever it was they used when making beer.

The upstairs party room was big and open, with a bar on one end and restrooms in the rear. The room was just beginning to fill and Ben could see Fran and her husband sharing a beer with Sally Brzycki and a tall man whom Ben assumed to be Sally's husband. Bowden was emerging from the restrooms off to the right and saw them come in. He walked up and gave Libby a hug saying, "Hey, you're early. We didn't expect you for an hour or so."

"Funny," Ben said.

"It's good to see you again," Libby said.

Ben leaned in and murmured into Bowden's ear. "I see Fran over there with Sally Brzycki. I hope we don't have to spend the entire evening with her."

Bowden laughed. "I doubt it," he said. "You'll probably be spending the entire evening fending off questions about Meg and her case."

"True enough," Ben said with a frown. "In that case, I better get a beer. Libby, you want one?"

"Sure, I guess I have to. You're pretty much obligated to have a beer here, I would think. Get me something on the light side."

"Sure," Ben said. "Bowden, you want anything?"

"I've already got one," Bowden said.

Ben grabbed two Pilsners at the bar and caught up with Libby and Bowden over by Fran and the rest of the crew. Sally Brzycki's husband was a tall man, about six-feet-four, with curly sandy brown hair, thinning in the front and kept relatively short, with a matching goatee. He wore a navy blue sport coat over a plaid shirt and dark brown pants. Ben noticed an empty earring hole in his left earlobe. He sort of reminded Ben of Art Garfunkle. He eyed Ben as he approached and both men appeared to look for a lull in the conversation to make their formal introductions.

Finally, the taller man stuck out his hand and said, "Hi, I'm Peter Renfroe, Sally's husband. You must be Benjamin Lohmeier. I've seen you on the television. Very impressive."

"Thanks. Nice to meet you," Ben said. "This is my wife, Libby."

"We've just met," Renfroe said. "Sally and I have been following Megan's case very closely. Of course, Sally has quite an interest in the result given her close friendship with Megan."

Ben nodded. "We all do," he said.

"Look," Renfroe said. "I know you don't want to spend the whole evening talking about the case, not that you can say much about it anyway. So, let's just hope that everything goes well and we get the right result." With that, he raised his glass as if to toast.

Ben joined him and said, "I'll drink to that. So, what do you do? I hope for your sake you're not a lawyer."

"No, far from it," Renfroe said with an easy laugh. "I have a degree in architecture, if you can believe that. But I've been in the restaurant business for years. For about fifteen years, I've owned the *Mad Hatter* up in Lincoln Park."

"Oh, that's right. Sally told me the other day that you owned a restaurant. I've heard of it," Ben said. "It's supposed to be a nice place. It's got kind of a Cajun theme, doesn't it?"

Renfroe tilted his head from side to side as if to contemplate his answer. "I suppose you could say it's Cajun-influenced. You and your wife should come and visit us sometime. We'll show you a good time."

"I'd like that," Ben said.

The group spent the next half hour making small talk as the upstairs room filled with more and more of Ben's former classmates and their significant others. A few professors from the law school came for the festivities, including some, like Richard Seagram, who were happy to see Ben, and others like Samuel Dorlund, who were not. Over the course of the past several months, Ben had run into each of them at one time or another during his long hours of investigation at the law school so that seeing him here did not provide the friendly reunion it would have under normal circumstances.

As Ben returned from the bathroom a little while later, he saw Angela Harper coming up the stairs with her husband, a white man several years younger than she and appearing equally unpleasant. Having still not graced Ben with an audience, Professor Harper made a point of acting like she hadn't seen him. Ben watched her head toward the bar only to be greeted by a handful of former students and kicked himself for not having pursued her more aggressively. She had been on his To Do List for some time, but he had never quite gotten around to forcing her hand like he had originally intended. As he watched the Harpers head for the bar, a voice draped in sarcasm whispered in his ear, "Aye, if looks could kill, Counsel, if looks could kill."

"That's a thought," Ben answered without looking away. Then he turned and broke into a wide grin. "Professor Seagram, my man. How goes it?"

Seagram laughed heartily, slapping Ben on the back. "Always good when I have a drink in my hand and so many pretty girls in the room."

"Can't argue with that," Ben said.

Seagram waved his beer in the direction of the Harpers. "She still giving you trouble?"

"Not so much trouble as nothing at all. She won't talk. I may have to hit her with a subpoena."

Seagram cocked his head, a twinkle in his eye. "There could be some fun in that," he said. "You could always go over later and bury the hatchet."

Ben raised his eyebrows as if to say, "Bury it where?" then said, "I don't think so."

"Well, my boy," Seagram said throwing an arm around Ben's shoulders, "things could always be worse. You've managed to drag yourself away from all of this unwanted media attention and come out on this fine Saturday evening for a good time with your old classmates."

"And professors," Ben added. Ben took a drink of his beer and let it settle. Finally he said, "One of whom may have killed another one of my old professors."

Seagram merely nodded. The two men studied the Harpers for a long moment and then decided to hit the appetizers. Although the selection was not terribly extensive, mostly typical fare, Ben enjoyed the marinated chicken breast on a stick, while Seagram gravitated toward the little spareribs and mini egg rolls. "You know," Seagram said stuffing an egg roll into his mouth and gesturing with his head toward the Harpers across the room, "you could always have a few more cocktails and start a fight." Seagram allegedly once punched a lawyer in a deposition. Ben didn't know if that was true or just another part of his legend.

Ben scoffed. "Oh, that would work out just great, wouldn't it? I can see that in the paper right now. Not only that, the guy is almost a foot taller than I am. I'm sure you'd be right there to hold my jacket."

Seagram looked serious. "No, not a foot. Five or six inches maybe," he said. "I still think you can take him. You're wiry, but you're mean."

Ben laughed a hearty laugh. "And probably motivated as well."

The evening passed by fairly quickly and Ben had to admit that he enjoyed getting together with so many of his old classmates, swapping lies and learning what the past ten years had brought each of them. Keenly aware of Megan's case, most offered their support and wished Ben the best of luck, while others hoped to get a little inside information, none of which Ben was providing.

The food turned out to be pretty good, even for a buffet, highlighted by tasty barbecued chicken and beef kabobs with onions, peppers, tomatoes and pineapples on metal skewers. The beer, of course, had to be good. There were lots of good choices, from light to dark and most of what you might want in between. Ben settled on a Pilsner early and stuck with it, except for an amber-colored lager he sampled during dinner, which he found more bitter than he liked. Given the amount Ben had to drink, Libby would most certainly drive home.

Later in the evening, sometime after eleven, Ben ran into Bowden standing at the urinal in the men's room. "Funny finding you hanging out in here," Ben said as he stepped to the next station.

"Yeah, that beer really runs through you."

"Say," Ben said, "what do you make of Sally Brzycki?"

"You mean Sally Renfroe. She sure has mellowed out. Back in school, she was like a bull in a china shop. Now she seems almost laid back."

"I don't know about laid back, but certainly easier to take. By the time we graduated, I couldn't even stand the sight of her."

"No, she wasn't very popular, was she?"

Back in law school, Sally Brzycki possessed the awkward knack for saying the exact thing that could offend you the most. She displayed an over-aggressiveness that was likely the by-product of insecurity, but that didn't make it easier to take. She was also more than a little impressed with herself. Ben remembered a time in class when Sally was bragging about her performance in the moot court competition the previous evening. As she droned on patting herself on the back, Ben concluded that some of the comments from the judges were backhanded compliments given Sally's transparent personality flaws.

The two men finished their business and retreated to the sink to wash their hands. "What'd you make of Sally's husband?" Ben asked.

"He seemed okay," Bowden said. "I hear that restaurant he owns is pretty good. I've been meaning to go there, but just haven't made it yet."

"He doesn't really seem her type though," Ben said. "It's hard to imagine her married with a kid."

Bowden reached around Ben and grabbed a paper towel. "It's hard to imagine you married with two kids," he said.

"That's probably true," Ben agreed.

On their way out of the men's room, Ben and Bowden ran smack into Professor Angela Harper. "Excuse me," Ben said without noticing who it was right away. "Oh, it's you," he said, "the woman who's been avoiding me at all costs. Did you know that Bowden? The esteemed Professor Harper here refuses to speak to me. One wonders why that is."

"You're drunk," she said. "Excuse me."

"No," Ben said, "I'm not," refusing to step aside so she could enter the ladies room. "You're going to have to talk to me eventually," he continued. "So far, I haven't made your life as difficult as I could."

"When are you going to get it through your head?" Harper said. "I have nothing to say to you. I don't know anything that could possibly help you."

"Well, why don't you give me a little bit of your precious time and we'll find that out for sure?"

"I don't think that will be necessary," she said.

As Ben started to say something else, a man came from his right and pushed him out of the way. Ben stumbled back a few steps startled.

"Get the hell away from my wife," Stephen Harper said. "You stay away from her."

Ben regained his bearings and focused on Stephen Harper. Bowden stepped between them and separated the two men. "Whoa, whoa," he said. "There's no need for any of that."

"I take it you're the husband?" Ben said in mock seriousness.

Stephen Harper wouldn't be deterred. "My wife doesn't have to put up with this from you or anybody else."

"Put up with what?" Ben asked.

"Put up with you."

Ben saw that people in the room were beginning to notice the altercation. He nodded several times. "Okay," he said holding up his hands. "I'll let it go for now. But you won't be able to avoid me forever. I'd think your wife would welcome the opportunity to spend a few minutes and dispense with any questions or concerns that I might have, but apparently not. It makes me wonder just what you folks have to hide." Ben smiled and raised his eyebrows at Bowden and walked away just as Libby and Fran arrived.

"Anything the matter?" Libby asked taking her husband by the arm.

"No, of course not. What could possibly be the matter?" Ben said.

As they walked away, he spotted Richard Seagram watching him from across the room. As the two men made eye contact, Seagram raised his glass and bowed in mock salute to his former student. Ben gave him a quick thumbs-ups behind Libby's back in return.

Half an hour later, as Libby pushed the SUV up to seventy-five on the outbound Eisenhower Expressway, Ben watched the buildings fly by, lost in his own thoughts. Was the killer there tonight? Was one of his classmates really a murderer? Or was it one of his former Professors? He didn't know and at that moment felt no closer to knowing than he had months before when he first read about Greenfield's death in the newspaper. Since then, they had gathered many more pieces to the puzzle that was the death of Daniel Greenfield, yet the pieces that he had didn't seem to fit.

37

Preparing for a trial, especially a big trial, always takes longer than you think, usually at least twice as long. That was a good rule of thumb, especially if you wanted to do it right. It was now late June and the trial was set for September 4th, the Wednesday after Labor Day. Ben felt confident that absent some unforeseen circumstances, the trial would actually start on that date. That left Ben with just over two months to prepare, through the heart of summer when everyone's attention span and motivation invariably waned, either because of the weather, summer vacations or simply LOI - lack of interest. They were behind schedule and Ben knew it. He had to kick it into gear or they would be in trouble come trial. He looked at his watch, got up from the conference table in the garage and walked back through the office to the kitchen, where he grabbed a cold Rolling Rock out of the refrigerator.

Walking back down the steps and through the short corridor separating the main part of the office from the garage, Ben was struck by the heat. Today, it was hot outside and even hotter in that small corridor, and it took Ben's breath away as he made the short walk from the main part of the office. A blast of cold air hit him as he opened the door to the garage and stepped inside. With the air conditioning cranked, it felt like a meat locker and Ben shivered as he sat down and put his feet up on the conference room table. Ben took a pull from the beer and grabbed a legal pad off the table to make some notes, a To Do List of sorts. He watched out the door as the first batch of commuters dragged across the parking lot in the late afternoon heat.

The list really consisted of two separate lists, one for Megan's case and another for the rest of his files. He started the second list first and quickly abandoned it. If he felt under the gun on Megan's case, he felt like he was hurtling off a cliff on his other files. The longer the list got, the more depressed Ben became until he finally ripped the page off the pad, crumpled it up and tossed it in the trash can then went back for another drink of his beer. He finally decided that he would devote at least one day per week to his other files through the end of July before the final push on Megan's trial began on the first of August.

He broke the trial preparation list down into several parts, beginning with legal research, then witnesses, documents, exhibits, experts and jury instructions. By now, they thought they had everything the State had and while the universe of documents was large, it was not insurmountable. Ben figured they had a pretty good handle on the documents with the possible exception of the grade reports and the exams Greenfield had been grading at or about the time of his death. They would be focusing more on those exams in the days ahead.

The list of witnesses, however, was still an open-ended mess, as were the exhibit list and the jury instructions. Yes, there was a lot of work left to do and the days to do it in were growing quite short indeed. Ben tossed the pad back on the table, stood and paced around the room. He stopped at the door and watched a few more commuters shuffle through the parking lot, a couple wearing jackets despite the stifling heat, apparently having misjudged the temperature when they left the house that morning. Then Nancy's voice came over the intercom. "I've got Ken on the phone for you."

"Put him through."

"Hey man, what's up?" Ken said.

"Oh, just going over the To Do List for trial."

Ken laughed. "Sucks to be you. Did you check out that Cub game last night?" The Cubs were in St. Louis playing a series against the Cardinals.

"No, I got home just after it ended. The bullpen blew another one?"

"Yeah. You got home that late? You're working too many hours, my friend."

"Someone's got to put money into Phil's pockets."

"Ain't that the truth. Say, I called because I've put together that stuff you wanted for the Motion to Suppress. I'll drop it in an overnight envelope for you."

"That would be great," Ben said. "I'll try and take a look at it or have Mark do it by the end of the week."

They talked for a few more minutes about the case, then more baseball before Ken signed off. A couple of minutes later, Nancy stopped down on her way out the door.

"So what'd Ken know?" she asked.

"Same old shit."

Nancy looked around the cluttered room, banker's boxes scattered around the floor and parts of two files spread across the conference room table. "It's really starting to look lived in out here," she said.

"Too lived in," Ben agreed, "with the amount of time I've been spending out here."

"Well, gotta go," Nancy said. "I was actually going to cook dinner tonight. See you in the morning."

Nancy left and Ben grabbed the phone to call Meg. She picked up on the second ring. "Your husband home yet?" Ben asked.

"No, not yet. I expect him soon though."

"Good. We can talk before he gets there. I've been thinking a lot about our witness list. Given that we may not have a lot of fact witnesses, and the likelihood that you won't be called to testify, we may need to call some character-type witnesses, you know, people who know you and can testify about your background, character, relationship with your family . . ."

Megan's laughter cut him off. "Relationship with my family? You mean Joe? I don't know how much you want to go into that."

"Probably not much," Ben said, "but under the circumstances, we may not be able to avoid it. In fact, we may want to think about calling him to testify, particularly if he knew you were having an affair a long time ago."

248

"He didn't know it was Greenfield," Meg said. "I think he figured that there was some brief relationship during that time frame, but that all changed when I got pregnant with Anthony. We didn't talk about it then and we don't talk about it now, even with what's happened."

"Right. What about other character witnesses?"

"Well," Meg said. "There's always Fran and Sally Renfroe, even though I know you don't think much of her."

"At least she's not as bad as she used to be."

"I wish you'd give her a break. She's changed from back in law school. Having a baby mellowed her out quite a lot."

"I'll take your word for that, although I suppose I could agree that I like her better as Sally Renfroe than I ever did as Sally Brzycki. I'll tell you what, I'll give her a call and see if she is even willing to do it."

"Oh, I know she is. She's already told me as much."

They talked for a few more minutes before Ben called Sally Renfroe. Megan was right. She was eager to testify and with her background as an attorney, probably would make a good witness too. Much as Ben hated to admit it, her status as a mother of a young son working part-time as a lawyer would also create a favorable impression in front of a jury.

"Why don't you make a list of things you'd want to say about Megan, how you came to know her, how your friendship has developed, stuff like that, and we'll get together at some point in the next few weeks either here or downtown somewhere and go over it. That way, we can see if we can create a direct examination out of it."

"No problem," Sally said. "I could come out there if you'd rather. My regular sitter can watch David if we need to meet. Whatever you need."

Ben hung up the phone and decided to give Sally Renfroe the benefit of the doubt. Even though she'd been far from one of his favorites while in law school, it seemed as though marriage and family life had made a new woman of her.

Ben spent the next couple of hours paring down his witness list and reviewing the possible witnesses who could be called by

249

Bridget Fahey and the prosecution. Satisfied that he had made a good start, Ben turned to the exhibits and reviewed a series of document summaries prepared by Dan Conlon and Brad Funk.

Meanwhile, his fellow lawyers and tenants in the building filtered out to the parking lot and went home. At seven-thirty, Casey Gardner stopped out and told Ben that everyone else had left the building. "You're it," Casey said. "I didn't lock the front. My car's out back."

"No problem," Ben said.

"You got Court tomorrow?"

"Who the fuck knows?" Ben said. He thought about it for a moment and then added, "No, I don't think so."

"Okay then, I'll see you tomorrow."

After Casey left, Ben stood and went back into the kitchen and got himself another beer. A little while later, Ben looked up and noticed the daylight outside beginning to wane. Another night he wouldn't be home in time to play catch with his son. He worked for another half hour, by now it was dark, and decided to pack it in for the day. He turned off the lights in the garage and walked to the front of the building, where he locked the front door and turned off the lights in the kitchen.

Then he went upstairs and walked directly into Phil's office and turned on the TV hanging from the ceiling in the far corner next to the window. He checked out the score of the Cub game. It was 4 to 4 in the top of the fifth inning. If he left now, he could get home in time to catch the last inning or two and maybe kiss the kids goodnight before they were entirely comatose. Ben watched for another minute, then turned off the TV, crossed through the French doors into his office and turned out the lights. He didn't even take his briefcase. Three minutes later, having shut off the remainder of the lights, set the alarm and locked the back door on his way out, Ben was in his car and ready to head home.

Upstairs, the Protector emerged silently from the hiding place in Phil's closet and tiptoed to the top of the stairs listening all the while for a hint of Ben's presence in the building. Had he left? Couldn't tell. The Protector couldn't believe it earlier when Ben strolled right into the office and turned on the television to check

250

out the stupid baseball game. They had only been a few feet apart. The Protector hid in the closet afraid to peer out for fear of being seen in the reflection in the bay window. Then Lohmeier had simply walked into his office, shut out the lights and taken off.

The Protector heard Ben go downstairs and it sounded like the door outside had opened and closed. Maybe he was gone. What could I do now? The Protector asked himself. Just unlock the door and leave. That was it. Just unlock the door and leave. But first, if he is gone, I could look through his office at will and even the conference room area as well. The Protector crept to the top of the stairs and listened. Nothing, not a sound. He must be gone. The Protector padded back through Phil's office and into Ben's office stopping at the first window to peek out of a crack in the curtains at the parking lot below. The car was gone. The Protector laughed aloud. "I'm alone," the Protector whispered. Still, I'd have to be more careful in the future. He almost walked right in here and found me. That could never happen again. That could ruin everything.

The Protector spent a few minutes rummaging through Ben's office, finding nothing of significance, before moving downstairs to the garage. As the Protector reached the bottom of the stairs and turned the corner, a slight clicking sound was followed by a loud BEEEEEP. Startled, the Protector lurched forward. What in the hell was that? An alarm? Have I tripped an alarm? The Protector looked wildly around in all directions as the beeping noise continued unabated. Up ahead on the ceiling, the Protector spied a white sensor about the size of a dollar bill, a red light in its lower right corner flashing. "Shit," the Protector said. The Protector moved quickly through the corridor and across the lobby to the front door peering outside for any signs of life anywhere. Unnoticed on the opposite wall and looking very much like a programmable thermostat, was the control panel for the alarm system. Seeing no one outside, the Protector unlocked the door and stepped out onto the porch. With the door shut, the alarm didn't seem so loud.

The Protector walked quickly down the steps and turned toward the parking lot. Rounding the corner in the general direction of the bar, the sound of the alarm grew fainter. You almost couldn't hear it from out here, the Protector thought. The Protector turned and looked back toward the garage - no one coming. Look like you belong. Then the Protector walked, never run, that would be too obvious, through the parking lot to the bar, climbing the steps and entering through the back door. The Protector stepped right up to the bar and asked for a gin and tonic, placing a five dollar bill on the bar. A moment later, the bartender, a burly man with an unusually large head and prominent jaw, returned with the drink and picked up the money. As the Protector took a sip of the drink, a squad car, with lights on, but no siren, passed by on Irving Park Road.

The Protector watched the squad car turn left and head back toward the law firm, swallowed, smiled and said, "Keep the change."

38

Ben grew suspicious after the tripping of the alarm, particularly since he had only left the building moments before. He confirmed that he had been the last one in the building, but insisted that he had locked all of the doors before he left. The Ithaca Police later said that the front door was unlocked and the building was empty when they arrived in response to the alarm.

A few days later, Ben and Mark sat in the garage talking about it with Ken, who had stopped in with some additional materials for the Motion to Suppress. Ken laughed at them. "You bozos haven't thought of the most important possibility. Maybe the alarm got tripped while someone was trying to get out, not while someone was trying to get in." Ben looked at Mark, who raised his eyebrows as if to say, "Could be." "You said you locked the front door, right?" Ken continued. "If that's true, maybe somebody was inside until after you set the alarm and took off. That happened to me a couple of times while I worked upstairs in your office," he said gesturing to Ben. "Guys on the other side of the building would leave and set the alarm without checking and not realizing that I was still upstairs working. I would come downstairs, get caught by one of the sensors and trip the alarm. Next thing you know, the Ithaca cops are here. One time, I realized that somebody had done it and I called to have somebody come over and turn the alarm off. I had to sit at my desk for about forty-five minutes so I wouldn't set the alarm off. You know, Phil gets pissed when that happens. The police charge for false alarms."

Ben nodded. "So I'm told."

253

He thought about the possibility of someone unknown being in the building with him the other night and didn't like the idea. Ken and Mark could read the discomfort on his face.

"Don't like the sound of that, do you?" Ken said.

"No, not really" Ben replied. "I don't think I'll share that one with my wife."

The defense filed a Motion to Dismiss and a Motion to Suppress Evidence, both basically designed to attack the evidence proffered by the State. The Motion to Dismiss the indictment never really stood much of a chance. Ben knew that, but filing it was just one of those things you had to do in a case like this. You couldn't just roll over and take it. The Motion to Suppress, on the other hand, was an entirely different matter. It focused on the small building blocks of the State's case, the individual pieces of evidence from which inferences could be drawn to plant the seeds of guilt in the minds of the jury. If enough of these building blocks could be knocked out or excluded from the trial, the State's case could very well collapse under its own weight, leading to a not guilty verdict or a directed verdict entered by the Court at the end of the State's case. Although this was an unlikely scenario, the dynamics of a jury trial were such that a lawyer could never know for sure which piece of evidence could become significant in the minds of the individual jurors. Therefore, the more bits and pieces you knocked out, the better off you would be.

The defense focused on three key pieces of physical evidence - the blood on the scarf, the hair and the fingerprints on the baseball bat. In ruling against the defense, Judge Wilson concluded that any arguments proffered by the defense went to the weight and sufficiency of the evidence, not to its admissibility. Although disappointed, Ben couldn't really disagree.

The defense enjoyed mixed results with the other evidence as well. Judge Wilson agreed that any mention of the paternity of Anthony Cavallaro should be excluded from the trial. This was likely a foregone conclusion once the results of the DNA tests had been learned. Conversely, the defense lost in its efforts to have certain phone records excluded from evidence, namely records of phone calls made from the law school to Megan either at her townhouse or her office at the Appellate Court. The defense reasoning revolved around the way the law school phone system routed and tracked outgoing telephone calls. The system did not trace outgoing calls back to a particular telephone in a particular location. For example, it was impossible to identify all of the specific calls made from the telephone in Daniel Greenfield's office. To the contrary, the calls could only be traced to a series of phone lines which handled outgoing calls from the law school building. Thus, the defense argued that anyone at the law school could have made those telephone calls. Nevertheless, pending the testimony at trial, Judge Wilson concluded that the jury should be entitled to hear the evidence and determine the appropriate weight to give it subject to the cross-examination by the defense.

On the drive back to the office, Ben and Mark were musing about the various rulings issued by the Court and their potential impact at trial. "My view is the blood was the key one," Mark said. Ben grunted in agreement. Mark continued. "I wish we had a way of proving that the blood came from his nose like she said it did and not from the wounds on the rest of his skull."

"Does that really make that much of a difference?" Ben asked.

"Well, sure it could. If you remember the pictures, the front of his face wasn't really caved in. All the damage was to the side and the back of his head."

"That's true. So what?"

"I don't know. It just seems significant, that's all. I don't think there was any blood that came out of his nose at the scene was there?" Ben shrugged. "I don't know," Mark said. "I'll check the file."

Mark's words percolated in Ben's head as he pushed the SUV up to eighty and flew past the Harlem Avenue exit. Lost in his thoughts of the blood evidence, Ben didn't notice when Mark began speaking again. There was something about the blood that didn't seem quite right. What was it? Ben turned the thing over and over in his mind as he drove. Mark could have been talking to himself because Ben didn't notice a word he was saying. Finally as the kernel of an idea dropped into place, Ben said, "Huh? What?"

"Hey," Mark said pointing, "you just missed the split."

255

"What?"

"You just missed the split. We needed to go to the right."

Ben looked up and realized what Mark was talking about. He had stayed to the left when the road split instead of going off to the right toward the office.

"God damn it," he said. "We'll just have to get off at Route 83 and head back north."

"What were you thinking about?" Mark asked.

"What do you mean?"

"You looked like you just thought of something."

"Yeah, I did."

When they got back to the office, Ben went upstairs, thumbed through his rolodex, picked up the phone and dialed.

A few seconds later, Dr. Stanley Liu was on the line. "What can I do for you, Mr. Lohmeier?" he said. Dr. Liu was the blood expert hired by the defense and one of the most renowned, and most expensive, blood and blood splatter experts in the world. To date, he probably felt underutilized by Megan's defense team.

"I think I have a project for you, Doctor," Ben said. "Do you have enough samples of the blood found on the scarf to do additional testing?"

"Why, yes, of course."

"And you have the results of the blood work supplied by the State?"

"Yes, I do."

"Good," Ben said.

39

"Fuck, this is boring," Ben moaned. He held up a stack of exam papers and gave them the evil eye. "I don't know how you could do this year after year." He tossed the papers on a stack on the conference room table.

Across the way, Mark laughed. "Oh, I don't know," he said. "It's not that bad. At least at the end of the day you get to assign grades to the arrogant fuckers."

"True enough, but what grades do you give them? I don't think I've read any good answers yet," Ben said. "He went to more trouble with these than I ever would have imagined. I always figured he just threw them down the stairs. The ones left at the top got A's, the ones at the bottom got C's. At least that's what everybody always thought."

"He did seem to put a lot of effort into it," Mark agreed, "but I can't figure out how he decided what to give credit for and what not to give credit for. I've got an exam over here with an 85 on it that didn't seem nearly as good as one with a 64."

Ben shook his head. "You've got to understand, he never actually practiced law. He was just a professor. He probably didn't know what he was talking about. You've been doing this shit for years and you do know what you're talking about."

"I'd like to think so. Check this one out," Mark said holding up a copy of an exam. "See the dark spots? I think this must have been blood. Several of these were found under him when he fell, like he had them in his hand when he got whacked."

"Probably stuffing them into his briefcase, right?" Ben said.

"It looks that way. This one seems to have been partially graded. I guess you could call it the final exam or the final final exam."

Ben shook his head again and stared at the exam Mark was holding. "What a shitty way to go," he said. "Of all the good things you could do in life, to be knocked off while trying to grade the exam of some arrogant little shit who probably thinks he's smarter than you are." Ben paused. "Do you think we were like that?" he finally asked.

Mark shrugged.

The two men sat in silence reviewing exams for a long while. Ben got up and went to the bathroom and then returned. As Ben pushed through the door into the garage, Mark said, "I didn't tell you. I went through Jason Hahn's final again the other day, yesterday I think it was."

"What'd you think?"

"Not too good, average at best. He probably got about what he deserved, not that you can tell with the way Greenfield graded papers. Another half a grade higher or so and I think he would've made the Dean's List, if my figures are correct. Had he gotten an A, he may have made Law Review."

"Really? Could he really have expected an A?"

"Who knows? You met him, he probably expects an A every time."

Ben thought about that for a minute and then asked, "Did we ever finish going through the grades to see who would get screwed by a bad final exam score?"

"Yeah, we did," Mark said. "Not much there really. There are only a handful of good candidates."

"Good," Ben said.

A little while later, they heard footsteps outside in the corridor and the door of the garage opened and Casey Gardner and Brian Davenport stepped inside. Ben looked at his watch. "It's only four forty-five," he said. "Where are you assholes going?"

Casey held up a cardboard ticket. "Republican Day, remember?"

"No," Ben said, "I didn't."

Republican Day was the biggest fundraiser sponsored by the Illinois Republican Party and it always took place on a Wednesday in the middle of summer. Everyone who was anyone in the Republican Party, and those who wanted to curry favor with them, either attended or bought tickets to the event. It included golf, which began early in the morning at various courses in the western suburbs of Chicago and culminated with dinner, drinks and speeches, not necessarily in that order, at a local country club. The guys in the office never played in the golf part of the event, you could be looking at an eight or nine hour round, but they usually tried to make it to the drinks part, which got going at about five or five-thirty.

"I think we have extra tickets upstairs," Casey said. "Phil really wants us all to make an appearance if we can. Funk's already not going so I was hoping you guys could go."

"What's up with Funk?" Ben asked.

Brian laughed. "I think his kid has swimming lessons."

Ben rolled his eyes. "You're kidding me."

"His wife pulled the leash more likely," Casey said.

Ben's head bobbed side to side as he mulled it over for a minute. "Okay," he finally said, "let's go. This shit will be here tomorrow. We aren't going to win the trial tonight anyway. I could probably use a few beers."

At twenty minutes to six, Ben walked across the parking lot toward the main clubhouse. Guests were milling about in small groups, drinking beer while music played over the loud speakers. Typically, much of the drinking and socializing took place outside, while dinner was served in one of the banquet rooms inside. The overcast skies of most of the day had given way to a bright sunshine and the temperature hovered in the low-eighties. Ben took a pair of sunglasses from his pocket and put them on. Since he didn't have Court today, he was dressed casually in a pair of khaki pants and an azure blue golf shirt. The air smelled like a summer barbecue, a mixture of grilling meat and spilled beer. Ben found Mark and Brian and headed over to a small hut where a couple of kegs were tapped. They each grabbed a beer and made the rounds.

259

Midway through his second beer, on his way inside to use the washroom, Ben ran into Karen Tilly, the Land Acquisition Manager for the Forest Preserve District. Good, Ben thought. He liked Karen. She was the kind of woman you could have a beer and bullshit with, without worrying about what you said. She was smart, attractive and had a good sense of humor. Ben could never figure out why she hadn't gotten married yet.

Ben introduced Karen to Mark and they talked for a little while. As she started to hand Ben another beer, she held it out and said, "I'll give this to you if you promise you're going to file the Spletzer case." She was laughing. Ben had been meaning to file the condemnation complaint on a series of parcels owned by a man named Dick Spletzer for a while now, but had never gotten around to it. He recoiled in mock horror. "When's the trial going to be over," she asked, "Christmas?"

Ben shrugged. "We should be able to get it on file by Christmas," he said, "maybe even Thanksgiving."

"Great," she said in a perky voice, "at least we have a timetable. Now we can drink."

She gave Ben the beer and pointed out another lawyer who did work on behalf of the Forest Preserve District talking to one of the District Commissioners across the way. The lawyer was known for being a little bit too pretty and for always being on the right side of the political winds. They gossiped about him for a few minutes until Ben's cell phone buzzed. It was Stan Disko.

"I've got something interesting for you on Angela Harper," he said.

"Do tell."

"It seems there indeed was a confrontation of sorts between the Harpers and Greenfield."

"You mean the husband?"

"Yeah, the husband. Apparently, despite what we've been told, the good professor did show some extra curricular interest in his colleague."

"What was her reaction? Did he complete the pass?"

"Not sure yet. I'm still checking, but my source tells me that the interest may not have been entirely unwelcome."

"Really," Ben said, "who's your source?"

"Can't say right now, but I'll keep digging."

"Good. Go for it. Keep me posted." Ben signed off and put the cell phone back in his pocket."

"What was that all about?" Karen Tilly asked.

"Can't say," Ben said. "If I tell you, I'll have to kill you."

She pinched his arm. "Come on, come on, tell me. Is it about the Law School Murder?"

"Yeah, it is."

"It sounded like good news," Mark said.

Ben put a finger to his lips and looked up at the sky in a thoughtful pose. "Well, let's put it this way," he said. "I just found out that the dead guy may have been hitting on one of his fellow professors despite protestations to the contrary."

"Ooh," she said, "sounds juicy."

"Could be," Ben said continuing. "And he may not have been entirely unsuccessful." More oohs and aahs. "We always assumed the two of them hated each other, or so everyone says."

"Maybe it was a love affair gone bad," Karen said. "You know, a lot of women like getting hit on. They look at it as good fun. It's kind of like the thrill of the hunt. It's usually the husbands or boyfriends who don't like it."

Ben nodded. He could understand that.

"Which one is it?" Mark asked.

"The one who won't talk to us," Ben replied.

Mark raised his eyebrows. "That is interesting," he said.

40

Ever since he had talked to Disko the night before, Ben couldn't get the whole Harper thing out of his mind, especially when coupled with Karen Tilly's comments about husbands and boyfriends and Stephen Harper's behavior at the reunion. He even called Professors Seagram and Makra at the law school, but they couldn't confirm anything. They were both surprised to hear of a possible link between Angela Harper and Daniel Greenfield, although Makra did say that he had witnessed Stephen Harper's temper on display a time or two in the past. Ben spent most of the day by himself in the garage letting things spin around inside his head while he tried to put what he knew into some perspective.

Ben often found it helpful to put what he knew and didn't know about a case in list or chart form, which made him focus on the big picture rather than on those facts or events that had been occupying most of his recent attention and that he couldn't get out of his head. He took a large easel from the corner of the garage next to the safe and pulled it out in front of the bookshelves behind the conference room table. He fastened a large white artist's pad to the easel using some two-inch binder clips and wrote notes on the pad using a black Sharpie.

He broke the notes down into categories, using one sheet per category, and flipped between sheets as he brainstormed. The exercise unleashed a torrent of built-up energy and Ben felt the adrenaline surging through him as his problem-solving mode kicked into full gear. He tried to distinguish between what he knew, what he suspected and what he didn't know at all. He created a timeline of events leading from 1991 when Megan first started seeing Greenfield all the way up to the present, searching for patterns, gaps, and connections that he had previously missed.

By six-thirty, he could feel his energy begin to wane and he decided to head out for a quick bite to eat. Forty minutes later, back in front of the easel, Ben stood trying to assemble the pieces of this complicated puzzle. After a couple of more hours of work, moving and re-moving pieces, massaging and tweaking others, Ben reluctantly concluded that he may already possess more of the pieces than he originally suspected. The holes in the narrative, from which he would weave the common theme that would form his defense, felt more like a lack of recognition, than a lack of information. There are more than enough pieces here, he thought.

He flipped over to a clean white sheet and wrote SUSPECTS on the top and underlined it. Then he made a list beginning with Sylvia Greenfield, followed by Joseph Cavallaro, Angela Harper, Stephen Harper, Nora Fleming and Jason Hahn. Below Hahn's name, he wrote the word OTHERS and then drew a line separating the first list from one additional name - Megan Rand. He stood before the list and studied it, his arms crossed, his left hand on his chin in a picture of intense contemplation. He stood there for a long time, his eyes going back and forth between the various names. Two jumped out at him. The first, Stephen Harper, displayed quite a temper in Ben's only encounter with him, a temper confirmed by Stan Disko's digging. Second, he kept coming back to the word OTHERS written near the bottom of the list.

Others, he thought, there had to be others, but who were they and what was their story? Drugs? That didn't seem likely. Greenfield was a small-time recreational drug user like so many other children of the 1960's. Nothing seriously pointed in that direction. Gambling? Same thing. His personal relationships? Now that made more sense. That brought him back to Sylvia Greenfield. They had a bad divorce to be sure, but from what Ben could figure, he was the more bitter of the two. She had gotten rid of him. Why would she kill him now several years after the divorce? Something would have had to trigger it and they hadn't come up with anything. On the other hand, if revenge was a dish best served cold, Sylvia Greenfield was plenty cold enough.

Then Ben thought of jilted lovers and their spouses. He looked at Nora Fleming's name. His gut told him no, but then again, she was in town at the time of the murder and knew her way around the law school. He took the Sharpie and drew an arrow next to Fleming's name and wrote, HUSBAND. A more likely candidate? He reminded Ben a little bit of Stephen Harper. Possible. But Andrew Scott wound up winning the prize. Nora had married him after all. Unless something came up and Greenfield wanted to get back together?

Ben stepped back from the names and paced around the garage. He walked over and spun the dial on the safe. After a moment, he climbed into the shoe shine chair and looked across the room at the list hanging from the easel. Hands in his pockets, he got up and walked over to the door as commuters veered off the sidewalk from the train station and cut through the parking lot on their way home from work. He watched them walk by, heads down and purposeful. The sun began to sink low off in the horizon. Ben turned and walked back to the conference room table, pulled out a chair and sat down amid the files scattered all around him.

Still, the names on the easel called out to him. Personal life and work life, he thought. The work life could only mean students and fellow staff members. How many law professors would be willing to get their hands dirty literally and figuratively by killing a colleague in his office? Most of them became professors of law in the first place because they didn't want to get their hands dirty practicing out in the real world. They could enjoy the cushy life on the outskirts of reality, never really jumping into the fray, yet close enough to feel part of it themselves. All the while, lording it over unsuspecting law students with the righteous air of expertise mixed with arrogance, wisdom borne of other people's labors.

That could explain the scene of the crime. Students and even some staff members might not know where Greenfield lived or maybe they were unfamiliar with his neighborhood and didn't feel comfortable attacking him there, but they would know the law school and how it emptied out during the holidays between semesters. Ben sat transfixed by the names for a long time before rummaging through a box and pulling out an expandable folder marked, "Jason Hahn." A while later, he pulled out a similar file marked, "Angela Harper", studying the contents the sixth, seventh or maybe tenth time.

Ben finished the last watery remains of a root beer poured hours earlier. He felt spent, drained, like a child's toy low on batteries. Everything seemed to work, just not as quickly as usual. He remembered reading somewhere, probably on the internet, that the human mind continually works on problems while sleeping, turning them over and analyzing them even as the needed rest refreshes and replenishes it. Maybe that's what I need, Ben thought, more sleep. Sensing a plan, Ben tossed his pen on the table, stood and arched his back, his hands on his hips. He stifled a yawn, then turned out all the lights in the garage and shut the door behind him. He walked upstairs and checked his e-mail one last time before grabbing his briefcase, shutting off the lights and coming back down.

He punched in the code setting the alarm giving himself a minute or so to finish locking up and get out of the building. He paused before hitting the final button on the alarm and tried to remember where he had parked. Out back, he thought, then hit the button, flipped up the lid on the control panel and walked briskly down the corridor through the copy room and out the back door. He locked the door with a key on his ring.

It was now completely dark and the lamp light standing in the grass beyond the parking lot was out. He still couldn't figure that out. Ben stepped off the back porch and down the five or six steps to the cobblestone walkway leading out to the parking lot. Just as he reached the corner of the building, he glimpsed something to his left and flinched, startled by an unexpected movement. Something black came at him from out of the bushes. He recoiled and fell back to his right, his left arm instinctively coming up. Something glanced off his wrist and struck him in the side of the head just above his left temple and Ben let out a, "Hey."

A figure clad all in black was on him now and swinging something, striking at him with a club or large stick. Ben tried to fend the figure off, but couldn't. In close, the figure, it had to be a man, smelled like a mixture of body odor, beer and cigarettes. He was swinging wildly now, catching Ben solidly on the left forearm, then his left cheek, then his forearm again, then with a knee into his ribs. Ben rolled on his back and tried to get his right hand up in front of his face. The blow to the ribs all but knocked the wind out of him and his left forearm burned with pain.

Ben grabbed the man's black shirt with his left hand and took another shot above the wrist forcing him to let go. He gasped for air as he struggled to protect his face. The blows came quickly, all aimed at or around Ben's head, but they seemed to lack the power of the initial assault. Ben lashed out with his left foot trying to kick the man in the groin and caught him weakly in the left hip. He caught the man more solidly the next time in the left thigh and the man grunted. Very few of the blows now got in solidly to Ben's head. He picked most of them off with his left arm causing searing pain to shoot down to his wrist and up to his shoulder.

Through it all, a raspy voice grunted at him through clenched teeth. Then Ben heard a noise - a scream, followed by more screams. Then footsteps. Someone was coming. Two commuters coming from the train station, a man and a woman, had seen the attack and had yelled out, "Hey you! Stop that! You stop! Stop!" and ran at them. Another man followed behind. The attacker stumbled off Ben, who tried to grab him by the legs, tripping him slightly. The man quickly regained his balance and tried to get away. He ran around the back of the garage, while Ben staggered to one knee, then up onto his feet. He threw his briefcase, which has been around his right shoulder the whole time, down to the ground and began chasing after his attacker. Ben stumbled over a shrub in the lawn at the end of the parking lot and fell hard to one knee. One of the male commuters overtook Ben in pursuit of the attacker and Ben followed him around the garage toward the other parking lot in front of the building.

Ben tried to keep up, but couldn't. The pain in his rib cage, coupled with the excitement of the moment made it impossible for him to catch his breath and he hobbled to a stop after rounding the dumpster in front of the garage. Up ahead, the commuter also slowed as off in the distance the attacker jumped into a waiting car and tore off into the night.

Ben dropped down to one knee and a moment later, the three commuters surrounded him, soon joined by several more. A man called 911 on his cell phone. The woman, a brunette in her mid-twenties, leaned down, looked at him and said "Jesus, what was that all about? Are you okay?"

Ben could feel the left side of his face swelling rapidly and his eye beginning to close, a hot liquid running down the side of his face, yet he looked at her and managed a weak smile. "Thanks to you guys," he said.

41

Ben sat in the examining room of the Alexian Brothers Medical Center and dabbed at his left cheek with the ice pack, now not nearly as cold as it had been earlier. Libby stood in front of him and looked down on him, a look of anger mixed with worry crossing her face. Once the Ithaca Police had arrived, they insisted on taking Ben to the hospital. Knowing he wouldn't be home for hours, Ben called his wife. Although he insisted that he was all right and that she should wait for him at home, Libby got her mother to baby sit, hopped in the car and hurried over to the hospital. When she arrived, the doctor on duty had just finished gluing a small cut above Ben's left eyebrow. "About two or three stitches worth," the doctor said.

She gasped when she first saw him. "Oh my God," she said. "Who did this?"

He told her the same thing he told the police. "I'm not sure. He was wearing a mask, a black tee shirt and black jeans. I even think he had black tennis shoes on. He may have been Hispanic, but I'm not sure."

"This must be about that damn case," she said.

Ben shrugged. "I don't know." Same thing he told the police. Truth is he did know. What he hadn't told the police, and what he wouldn't tell Libby either, was what the man said to Ben as he pummeled him.

"Leave it alone, leave it alone, leave it alone," spoken with a heavy Hispanic accent. Ben couldn't make it out at first, but literally had it beaten it into him so that he wouldn't soon forget it.

Ben didn't know whether a random assault in the middle of the western suburbs or his pending murder trial would cause more worry, but he chose to keep what the man said to himself, at least for the time being. In addition to the cut over his eye, now bandaged, more ice packs were wrapped around Ben's left knee and his left forearm, the latter of which had already been X-rayed, along with Ben's ribs and the left side of his face. The knee injury seemed the least significant of all, probably just a bruise sustained when Ben tripped and fell while trying to chase his assailant.

Once you got past the cut, Ben's face was probably just bruised too, although bruised enough that he would no doubt have one hell of a shiner. The arm swelled immediately and felt broken at first, but Ben had regained most of the use and feeling in his left hand, so that too might not be as bad as he first feared. Of his injuries, the ribs clearly felt the worst and sent a throbbing pain which radiated around his side to his back. The pain worsened whenever Ben breathed, which was difficult, and sharp pains like someone was stabbing him with a knife occurred whenever Ben tried to move too quickly or even breathe too deeply. He knew the ribs would be a problem for days, if not weeks to come.

Ben sat awkwardly in the chair, pitched at an odd angle trying to get comfortable. He felt like the Leaning Tower of Pisa. A few minutes earlier, a rugged looking nurse stopped by and gave him a small paper container with two Vicodin tablets inside, together with a small cup of water. The pain everywhere but in his ribs began to deaden a little as the Vicodin took effect. The ribs still ached like hell.

"Is it getting better?" Libby asked in a soft voice.

"A little bit," Ben croaked. He made a raspy wheezing sound whenever he breathed. As he sat there trying not to talk about the incident in too much detail, Ben kept hearing the gravelly Hispanic voice of his assailant playing over and over in his head. He could also just about smell the man's body odor and the alcohol-soaked breath. Libby could tell that he was thinking about something, but thought better of pressing him.

They sat in silence for several more minutes before a young doctor, Ben didn't even know his name, pushed through the privacy curtain and stepped inside. Ben studied him for a moment and said nothing. He didn't look old enough to be out of medical school, which didn't do much to inspire Ben's confidence. He wore a white standard issue doctor's coat over a yellow golf shirt and khaki pants, on which Ben noticed several drops of blood above the cuff on the right leg. Was that his blood? He didn't know.

The doctor held a series of X-ray sheets in his left hand. He flicked on an X-ray light on the wall and shoved three of the films into place. "Let's start with the knee," he said, a bit too enthusiastically, pointing at the screen with his right pinkie finger. "There doesn't appear to be anything structurally wrong from this X-ray. I think you just bruised it. If it doesn't get better in a few days," he said, "we might want to take an MRI. The one in the middle here is obviously the side of your head. No abnormalities indicated, which is good. You probably sustained at least a modest concussion, however. We'll give you a little handout on head injuries to look at, but the important thing is if you feel disoriented or nauseated, we might want to have you come in and take a CAT scan." Turning to Libby he said, "You should probably wake him up every couple of hours during the night to make sure he's all right."

Ben groaned. "Just give me enough of the god damn Vicodin and let me sleep."

The doctor looked at Libby as if to say not to listen to him.

"The film on the right," the doctor said continuing, "is your left arm. I don't see anything there either. You got whacked pretty hard and it's badly bruised and should be tender for a few days, but you seem to have the use back in your hand and wrist so I don't think it's broken."

He removed the three X-rays from the wall and slid in the last two. "These are your ribs. This one here on the left is the view more or less from the side, while the other one is a view from the rear." He pointed to a small dark spot on the second rib from the bottom on the left picture. "You see this here?" he said. "This looks like it may be a slight fracture. There is not much we can do for it except help you manage the pain. The course of treatment is

270

pretty much the same whether it's a fracture or not. Be careful with that area. I would minimize stretching, lifting, anything that could provide strain to your ribcage area. This will probably hurt for a while. Assuming all things go well, you should probably have a follow-up visit with your doctor in about a week to make sure you're healing on schedule. Other than that, I think you can go home, but I would let your wife drive. I'd probably also take tomorrow off, maybe the day after as well, unless you feel a lot better, which I wouldn't expect."

Ben struggled to his feet. "Just give me my Vicodin and let me get outta here."

It took another half hour or so before they finished with the doctor, the paperwork and all of the other stuff associated with a trip to the Emergency Room. He shuffled out to the car with a sample pack of Vicodin and a prescription for even more in his right hand. It hurt to walk and Ben moved very slowly across the parking lot. He pulled the door open to Libby's minivan and gingerly folded himself into the passenger seat. She slammed the door behind him.

It was now past midnight and the drive home was a pretty quiet one, which suited Ben just fine. He mostly gazed out the passenger side window into the vague middle distance as they made the trip home. Periodically, he sensed Libby looking over at him as if to make sure he hadn't lapsed into a coma. The events of the day swirled around in Ben's head as the minivan sped through deserted streets. Leave it alone, leave it alone, leave it alone. He couldn't get those words out of his head. What did they mean? Leave what alone? Did he know something and not know he knew it? Was he on the right track without realizing it? And who was it that attacked him? He didn't think it was the killer, that didn't feel right. It had to be a hired thug, he thought. There were more questions now, more than he had six hours ago looking at that easel in the garage. More questions, but no more answers, maybe fewer answers even. More for his mind to think about as he slept.

Soon they were home and Libby parked in the driveway. She ran around to help him out of the car, but he shooed her off. "I can make it," he growled. "I'm not an invalid yet."

Truth be told, the Vicodin had finally taken full effect and although the ribs still ached, everything else felt better. He felt fuzzy and out-of-focus, probably from the pills. He made his way up the steps and into the house finding his mother-in-law dozing on the couch in the family room. Rather than give her a fresh look at the evenings' horrors, Ben padded through the kitchen and went upstairs. In the bathroom, he struggled to remove his shirt and pants. He looked at himself in the mirror. His face was a mess. This must be about what a car accident looks and feels like, he thought. He popped another Vicodin, one for the road or at least the bed. How many was that? His brain was in a fog. He wasn't sure. He crawled into bed and drifted off to sleep before Libby even got upstairs.

Hours passed and Ben rolled over and opened his eyes. He immediately felt the ache in his left arm and a sharp pain in his ribs and back. It really had happened. His face and eye felt puffy, but didn't really hurt that much. Neither did his knee. His throat was dry. He pushed Libby's pillow out of the way to see the clock - five minutes 'til nine. "Holy shit," he rasped. He dragged himself out of bed and felt a little shaky. He started to call for Libby and then stopped. The house felt empty. Libby must have taken the kids and gone already. The ribs hurt worse standing up and the knee didn't feel quite as good either.

Ben walked into the bathroom and looked at himself in the mirror. If possible, he looked even scarier than the night before. His face looked swollen and puffy on one side and the area from his left cheek up into his forehead over his eye was beginning to turn a dark purple. A similar purple bruise began near his left elbow and extended down almost to his wrist. He slowly peeled off his shirt to reveal similar bruising in his lower left rib cage. He turned on the shower and brushed his teeth. Maybe it would feel better to be clean, he thought. He stood for a long time in the hot shower letting the water rush down his neck and soothe his back and ribs. When he got out of the shower, he felt a little better, but didn't want to look in the mirror. He dried himself off only with great difficulty. With the tenderness and bruising on the left side of his face, Ben decided not to shave. He laughed, which caused stabbing pains in his left side. It would probably give him a more rugged appearance.

He peeked out the window to check the weather and discovered a sunny cloudless day and bright blue skies. He carefully got into a pair of jeans, running shoes and a white golf shirt. On his way out, he grabbed a root beer from the fridge and called Nancy on his cell phone. "Are you okay?" she asked. "The Ithaca Police called this morning and said you were mugged outside the building last night. What happened?"

Ben took thirty seconds to fill her in and then asked whether Mark was in the office yet. Nancy told him that Mark had just arrived and Ben asked her to assemble the trial team for a meeting in the garage in a half hour.

They were all in the garage already when Ben arrived. As he pushed through the door, all eyes turned his way and there were audible gasps and jaws dropping. Ben gave a weak smile and hobbled over to the end of the table and sat down. Just as he started to say something, the door to the garage opened and Phil, Casey and Nancy came in.

Ben looked up and Phil said, "Holy fuck."

Nancy put her hands to her mouth and Casey said, "Look at your fucking arm," with an amazed look on his face. The others around the table had similar expressions.

Ben shrugged. "But you should see the other guy," he said.

"What happened to him?" Phil asked.

Ben grinned. "Not a scratch. He got away Scot free. I may have kicked him in the balls though. Obviously not hard enough." Ben shifted awkwardly in his chair. "The worst part," he said struggling to get his breath, "is that they think I have a cracked rib on this side. I think he caught me with a knee."

Ben briefly relayed the events of the evening as best as he could remember them. "Most of the damage was done in the first five or ten seconds or so," Ben said. "After that, it was mostly just flailing around until the commuters came and scared him off." Ben gestured to Nancy to shut the door. "Now," Ben said, "this doesn't leave this room. But yes, he said something which leads me to believe that it almost certainly relates to this case."

"What was that?" Phil asked.

"He said, 'leave it alone, leave it alone, leave it alone', whatever that means."

"He must think you know something or have figured something out," Casey said.

Ben nodded. "It sounds like it, but for the life of me, I don't know what it is we know or have figured out. The only thing I can think of is that maybe he thinks we know something or we do in fact know something, but either don't realize it or don't realize the significance of it."

"Or this is all bullshit and you were just mugged by some guy who just happened to be there waiting for you," Phil said.

Ben cocked his head to one side. "Maybe," he said, "and that's more or less what I told the cops because for now, I'd just as soon not let on what the guy said. So let's just leave it here. My wife doesn't even know and I don't want her to know for that matter. Are we clear?" Ben looked from one face to another.

They all nodded, even Phil, who said, "It's your call I guess."

Phil, Nancy and Casey left, leaving the trial team alone in the garage. Ben spoke to them about the things he thought needed to be done between now and the trial, coming up sooner than they wished. Ben knew from experience that what seemed to be a long way away would arrive in the blink of an eye. He divided up tasks and made sure that every part of the trial preparation was covered by someone who would thus accept responsibility for it.

The others felt an increased energy level and sense of urgency in their lead counsel in the wake of the beating, which would serve to focus them on the tasks that lay ahead. After he finished his pep talk, he didn't really intend it to be that, but that's how it turned out, Ben pushed away from the table and slowly rose to his feet.

"Where are you going?" Mark asked.

Ben's jaw was set and a determined look crossed his features. "I'm going out for a while," he said in a raspy whisper. "There's someone I need to see."

42

Ben found a spot on the street and parked. His destination was a couple of blocks away and as he hobbled up the sidewalk, he received an odd mixture of responses from passers by. Some looked away; others couldn't help but stare. He would have to get used to it.

Five minutes later, he pushed through the door into the reception area and limped past the receptionist down the hallway on the left. As he passed, she looked up, her eyes widening and jaw dropping, but saying nothing. Ben said over his shoulder, "Don't worry. I know the way. He may even be expecting me." Other staff members gave him similar looks as he made his way down the hallway. When he reached the end, a door opened and Joseph Cavallaro appeared. His look was much more restrained, but fairly similar to the others.

"What the fuck?" he said in a soft voice, not taking his eyes off Ben's face. Cavallaro stepped aside and let Ben pass, then closed the door behind them. Ben sat down on the couch and Cavallaro stood directly in front of Ben and looked down at him, his expression one of amazement. He studied Ben's face then looked down at the bruised and swollen mass that was Ben's left arm. His hand went reflexively to his mouth in a pose of studied concentration. The self-righteous arrogance so evident in previous meetings between the two men was now gone. Taken aback somewhat by Cavallaro's posture, Ben did not launch into the attack he had prepared on the drive downtown. Rather, he sat silently and watched Cavallaro assess his injuries.

Finally, Cavallaro said, "Tell me what happened." The words were spoken in an odd, almost concerned voice, a tone Ben would never have associated with this man. Perhaps he was scared for his own safety, Ben thought, or maybe even the safety of his wife and son.

"Don't you know?" Ben asked. It was the only part of his prepared remarks that he could get out.

"You think I did this?" Cavallaro asked pointing to himself. Cavallaro shook his head and turned, walking around behind his desk and plopping wearily into his chair. He looked across the room at Ben, his chin in his hand. Then he continued in a soft voice. "You must think a lot less of me than I'd ever imagined. Obviously, you've been hit in the head. When you're thinking clearly again maybe you'll come to your senses."

"I'm thinking very clearly right now."

Cavallaro shook his head. "No you're not. What made you think I would do such a thing?"

Ben cocked his head. "It seemed like your style," he said finally.

"Why? Because I'm Italian? All Italians are connected, is that it?"

Ben shrugged. "Not all."

"And not me either," Cavallaro said. His blood was rising and his face flushed. "I grew up in a neighborhood where that kind of thing was very possible. I knew people, sure. But I didn't want that kind of life for me or my family so that's why I went to law school and created all of this," he said gesturing broadly with his arm. "No, I could've taken that route a long time ago and many times since, but I didn't and I won't."

He almost sounded convincing. Then Ben thought, no, he's a personal injury attorney and a good one. He's paid to be convincing. That's part of his job.

Cavallaro looked at Ben again and laughed a humorless laugh. "Besides," he said, "if any of the friends you think I have had done this to you, you'd be looking a lot worse than you do right now. They would've broken your legs or worse or maybe picked on a family member. No, this doesn't look like that kind of maneuver."

276

Ben looked away into the vague middle distance thinking back on the attack. Maybe there was something to that. After the initial attack, the first few seconds, most of the blows were more or less just flailing away. He had said so himself earlier. The man hadn't seemed . . . what, fully committed to really hurting him. Not the way a mob enforcer would be, at least based on what he had seen on the *The Sopranos* and in the movies. Now he wasn't sure again. He looked back at Cavallaro, who sat studying him.

"You know I'm right, don't you?" Cavallaro asked.

"I'm not sure," Ben answered.

"Tell me what happened."

Ben replayed the scene as Cavallaro listened intently.

"Did the man say anything?"

After a pause, Ben told him. Cavallaro turned away and looked in the direction of a bookshelf across the room thinking. After another long pause, Ben asked, "If not you, then who?"

Cavallaro nodded and rose to his feet. "A good question," he replied. "Obviously, the killer, or someone hired by the killer. A random mugging would seem out of the question."

"Definitely," Ben said.

Cavallaro turned and faced him. "Do you know who did it? Do you know who killed Greenfield?" Ben shook his head. "You haven't figured it out?" Ben shook his head again. "The killer must think you have, or at least must think you're on the right track."

"I was thinking that too."

Cavallaro strolled over to the window and looked out in the direction of the Chicago River below. "You must know something," he said, "even if you don't realize it."

Ben sighed. His ribs ached. "The million dollar question is what," he said.

Cavallaro laughed again. "I can't believe you'd think I was behind this. Haven't you noticed that I've done exactly what you wanted me to do? Have I interfered at all?"

Ben shrugged. "Not lately. I figured you were getting pressure from your wife."

"Some maybe, but if I thought . . ." he stopped in mid-sentence. "It doesn't behoove me to undermine your efforts." He spoke calmly, almost matter-of-factly. "You have the complete and utter confidence of your client and I came to see that opposing you would only hurt me with her. Can't you see by now that I love my wife and son very much and will do whatever I can to keep them?"

"I suppose so, but love takes many forms and some people show it in ways that can be, well, counterproductive."

"Perhaps. But I want my family back. I've enjoyed having them back in my house and I want to keep it that way. The best way for me to do that is to help you make sure she is acquitted. As I said, she has complete trust in you and," he paused before continuing, "I can't say that her trust is misplaced. You know, at first I wanted a heavy hitter, someone with more experience. That's not a secret. But I've watched you over these months and I've had people in the courtroom every time the case was up."

"I've noticed," Ben said.

Cavallaro turned and looked at Ben. "You've done a very good job, you really have. You're committed to her defense in a way that not many people would be, even now."

Ben studied him, wanting to believe the words, but not trusting the man speaking them. After a long silence, Ben spoke. "We need a theme for the defense," he said.

"Yes," Cavallaro said, his eyes back down on the river.

"I'm not sure we need to prove who did it, but we may need to find a way to explain away the evidence. We may need to point in someone's direction." Cavallaro nodded. Ben continued. "We may need a fall guy."

Cavallaro nodded again. Without looking back, he said, "In my day, I think they called it a sap."

"Exactly," Ben said.

Cavallaro nodded again, his eyes still on the river. Then he slowly turned and locked eyes with Ben. "You do what you have to," he said.

Ben stood and nodded back. "I will."

As Ben turned to leave, Cavallaro said, "If you need anything . . ."

278

"Thanks," Ben said. As he walked out of the office, Ben shook his head. He didn't know what to believe.

43

Over the next several weeks, Ben and the rest of the team kicked it into overdrive and Ben actually felt they were in pretty good shape as the days left until trial dwindled to a precious few. Ben worked almost continuously during this period, stopping only for a long weekend in Michigan at the end of July where they attended the annual reunion of Libby's side of the family. The media reaction to Ben's attack exceeded all expectations and managed to even surprise Ben himself, which he didn't think possible. The attack transformed him overnight from an unknown young lawyer who was well-spoken but maybe in over his head to a brave gunslinger standing tall against all odds. Although Ben never publicly linked the attack to Megan's case, the media didn't need any help connecting the dots and pushed the story until the public was no doubt tired of hearing it. At home, Libby kept most of her concerns to herself, not wanting to interfere with or undermine Ben's efforts at such a critical juncture in the case.

Judge Wilson scheduled a final pretrial conference for Friday, August 16th, only nineteen days before the commencement of jury selection on Wednesday, September 4th. Throughout the summer, Judge Wilson encouraged the parties to engage in plea negotiations, and in order not to anger the Court, Ben reluctantly agreed to do so. Bridget Fahey's initial plea proposals were almost laughable and Ben dismissed them out-of-hand. They sought a sentence that may have actually exceeded what Meg could expect from the Court in the event of a conviction. Finally, two days before the pretrial, Bridget Fahey made her best offer to date - a guilty plea and fifteen years in prison. She could be out in about nine years with good behavior.

The death penalty was no longer an issue, Bridget Fahey having given that up at the gentle urging of Judge Wilson earlier in the summer. The Judge had made it clear that he didn't think the evidence supported capital punishment under the facts as he currently knew them. Truth be told, Bridget Fahey didn't really give up anything of substance in light of the moratorium on death sentences issued by the Illinois Governor a year or so before.

During a long and emotional meeting in the study at the brownstone, Ben and his client talked about the State's final offer and the ramifications for accepting it, and not accepting it. Finally, with tears beginning to roll down her face, her voice barely above a whisper, she said, "Tell me, what would you do if you were me?"

Ben hoped she wouldn't ask this question. He didn't want to answer it, yet he knew he would. He sat there for a long moment fighting back the feelings inside him. Then he said, "I'd fight."

"Good," she said squeezing his hands, "then let's fight."

In light of Meg's decision, the pretrial conference became something of an anti-climax, the press expecting something dramatic to take place that never materialized. Neither did the proposed jury instructions, witness lists and exhibit lists submitted by both sides generate any real fireworks. The only moment of any high drama occurred after the pretrial on the steps of the Courthouse when before a large throng of reporters, Ben said, "As we told Judge Wilson in his chambers earlier this morning, and have reiterated to State's Attorney Richard McBride and his assistant Bridget Fahey, Megan Rand Cavallaro will not under any circumstances enter a guilty plea which would require her to say she committed a crime she did not commit. To the contrary, Megan looks forward to this trial and the day when her good name is cleared once and for all."

Back in the office, the team worked to make those words a reality. With a week to go before the commencement of jury selection, Ben felt they had done just about all they could to prepare the case the best way they knew how. On the Thursday before Labor Day, Stan Disko walked casually into a large lecture hall at the Chicago College of Law, interrupting Angela Harper's first Constitutional Law lecture of the semester. "Angela Harper?" he said in a booming voice.

"Yes, what is it? Who are you?"

Reaching into his jacket pocket, he pulled out an envelope and with a dramatic flourish handed her the subpoena. "Consider yourself served," he said.

44

Friday, August 30th dawned hot and sticky and then got worse. Ben broke out in a sweat simply by walking into the office from the parking lot. The day had that last day before a long holiday weekend feel to it. Nobody wanted to get much work done and everybody was looking forward to the office closing early. The office of Schulte & Luckenbill typically followed the same general procedure. Phil would invariably get a jump on the long weekend first. He would be gone by noon if he bothered to come in at all. Today, he wasn't coming in. Everybody figured he was out playing golf somewhere. He would, however, call in just to make sure that the rest of the office hadn't abandoned ship. At some time after two, usually with heavy prodding from Nancy and Dianne Reynolds, Phil would say that they should close the office at three and people could go home.

Ben went upstairs and stuck his head in Nancy's office. "What do you think?" he asked. She turned in her chair and said. "LOI." Meaning lack of interest.

"Can't argue with that," Ben said. "When are we closing up today?"

Nancy shrugged. "Don't know yet," she said. "But I'm not gonna be here past three o'clock unless you absolutely, positively need something." She spoke the last words slowly and with emphasis giving him a look that said you better not.

Ben shook his head. "That's fine. You can probably leave at noon for all I care. I certainly don't anticipate anything."

After lunch, Ben convened a meeting of the trial team in the garage. Mark, Brad Funk and Dan Conlon sat around the conference room table, while Ben stationed himself in one of the barber chairs. This meeting was designed to explain how they would conduct the trial in the courtroom.

"No matter what," Ben said, "we will be professional in that courtroom at all times. We will be as cool as the other side of the pillow. Nothing that happens, good or bad, will ever show up in how we conduct ourselves. Not in our facial expressions or in our mannerisms. Nothing bothers us. We are unflappable. If at any point a juror looks over at any of us, that juror will conclude that everything is going exactly as planned, even if somebody testifies that they saw our client beating Greenfield over the head with the baseball bat."

Ben next spoke about the organization of the files. "We will look like a well-oiled machine at every moment. The defense table and our files will be neat and organized at all times. Dan and Brad, whichever of you is in the courtroom on a given day, will be in charge of the files. Mark, you will be in charge of the table. That means you'll be on your best behavior," Ben said pointing a finger at him. Ben knew of Mark's propensity for disorganization and sloppiness. This wasn't the first time they had talked about it.

Mark nodded with a laugh. "I know, I know. I'll do the best I can."

"No," Ben said, "you'll do better than that." Then Ben pointed to a stack of index cards on the conference room table. Half the cards were green, the other half red. "These cards," Ben said, "are the way we communicate during trial. I do not want us talking to each other while Court is in session. It doesn't look good in front of the jury and I can tell you Judge Wilson will not appreciate it. That's what the cards are for. If you have something you need to tell somebody, put it on a card. When one of us is conducting a direct or cross-examination, the cards are the way we communicate from the table to the person conducting the examination.

"If everything is going well and I haven't missed anything or left anything out, then you should have a green card showing at the end of the table, kind of like the green light on a stop light. That

284

way, I can glance over periodically and if the card is green, I know that you don't have anything you need to tell me. On the other hand, if there is a point I missed or that you need to tell me about, you write it on a red card and put it on the end of the table. Then I will know to walk over and take a look at the card to see what you wanted me to know. We need to make sure a green card is sitting there at the end of every witness. Any questions?"

They spoke for another twenty minutes or so about trial strategy and tactics. Then Ben looked at his watch - five minutes after two. He sighed and leaned back in the barber chair, his hands behind his head. "Look, I know I've been difficult at times over the past couple of months or so and I'll probably be difficult during the trial, but you should know I feel real good about our preparation. I'm confident that we're on top of things and that this is going to go as well as it can. Now is not the time to let up, but I think we've done a good job and should be proud of ourselves and remember," he said, breaking into a big smile, "this isn't the Bataan Death March. This isn't supposed to be torture. Sure, this is a big case, maybe the biggest case any of us will ever be involved in, certainly the most high-profile, but let's enjoy the moment if we can. Let's enjoy the satisfaction of hard work and a job well done. I know this is a shitty job sometimes. There's a lot of pressure and people don't like you. Despite all that, this is the best and most exciting part of our profession. Let's do our best, let's enjoy it and most importantly, let's win."

Ben stood. "Now I've got nothing really left to say. If you need to come in over the weekend to feel more confident, do it, but as far as I'm concerned, you guys can all go home right now. Try and have a good weekend." He turned to Funk. "Hey Brad, I'm going to meet Karen Tilly for margaritas at about three-thirty. You wanna go along?"

Funk shrugged. "Now you tell me," he said. "I'm supposed to take the family to my Mom's place in Indiana tonight, so I should probably get going. We'll be back late Sunday and I'll be in the office here on Monday."

Ben nodded. "Fair enough," he said. "Have a good weekend everybody."

Ben spotted Karen Tilly sitting under a green umbrella at a table at an outdoor Mexican café as he strolled up the sidewalk. She saw him too and they exchanged waves. A couple of minutes later, Ben had made his way through the interior of the restaurant and out into the Margarita Garden, as it was called. "How's it going?" he asked as he sat down. "It sure is hot out here."

She laughed. "That's why I got a table with a good umbrella." She nudged him playfully. "So I'm surprised you were available today with that trial coming up and everything."

Ben shrugged and looked around the area. It was only three-thirty and the place was beginning to fill up. People getting a head start on the holiday weekend. "I think we're about as ready as we're going to be," Ben said finally. "You can overdo the preparation sometimes. I think it's a good idea to get away from it for a day or two right before trial and try and refresh your batteries. Besides, the prosecution goes first, so we have a little bit less to do right off the start. Anyway, I'm surprised you were free too. No big plans this weekend?"

She scrunched up her nose and shook her head. "No, not really. I'm just going out on Sunday to visit the folks." Karen leaned over and said in a low voice, "I think we need to get some margaritas in us as soon as possible."

The aroma of grilled meat, vegetables and cilantro wafted out from the kitchen and Ben took a big sniff and looked around. "Something sure smells good," he said.

"I know," Karen agreed. "It's making me hungry."

The pitcher of margaritas came and hit the spot right away. Ben and Karen talked a little shop, but not too much, then they gossiped about their co-workers.

At five, Ben poured the last of the margaritas into Karen's glass. She took a sip, looked around and said, "So, without giving away any secrets, have you figured out who killed the guy yet?"

Ben shook his head. "No, I haven't. We have some ideas, but right now they're only ideas."

"I thought for sure you were on to something when they attacked you. By the way, everything looks pretty well healed now. You can't even really tell anymore."

"When you're ruggedly handsome, you can overcome a lot," he replied.

In fact, Ben was feeling pretty good. His ribs had basically healed, only a twinge now and then and you couldn't even really tell that he had needed stitches or that his face was badly bruised and swollen. A little time in the sun fixed that. The only real remaining symbol of the attack was a slight discoloration on his left forearm which hadn't fully disappeared.

"It's funny," Ben said shaking his head, "I swear I've got most of the pieces to the puzzle. I just can't get them to fall into place right."

She nodded thoughtfully. "I think sometimes you just have to look at things a new way, don't get so caught up in, I don't know, preconceived notions, I guess. Maybe you should just look at all the facts without drawing any conclusions. Don't assume you know anything. I think sometimes we can convince ourselves that something is true and then it becomes true, even though we don't really know that it's true. Do you understand what I mean?" Ben nodded. She continued. "I think that must have been true with some of those women you were telling me about. They must have convinced themselves that there was something there with him, when there really wasn't. They just didn't have the right perspective, that's all."

Ben took the last remaining nacho and stuffed it in his mouth, then took a drink of his margarita and thought about it for a minute. Maybe she had a point.

Ben and Karen left the restaurant at about five-thirty and Ben got home around six-fifteen. Libby had the grill going. "I've got small steaks for dinner," she said. Looking at him closely, she added, "How many margaritas did you have anyway?"

Ben raised his eyebrows. "Not nearly enough."

He went inside and Natalie ran up and greeted him with a big hug.

"Daddy, you're home early."

He picked her up and squeezed her tight. "Did you miss me?" he asked.

"Yes," she said.

"A little or a lot?"

"A lot."

"Good answer." He gave her a big kiss on the forehead.

"Daddy, are you going to have to go back to the office?"

"No, sweetheart, I'm not. I'm going to spend rest of the evening with you." And he did.

45

The heat and humidity that distinguished Friday gave way to much cooler and less humid conditions on Saturday. Ben met his father and his brother, Michael, for their first round of golf together of the year. Usually, the three tried to play together at least once a month during the golf season. Not this year. Too busy with the trial. Ben got home at about four-thirty and trudged upstairs to take a shower. He and Libby had dinner reservations downtown at seven with some friends and if he wasn't ready to go on time, she'd be all over him.

Ben was drying off after his shower when Libby pushed into the bathroom. "You sure got some sun today," she said giving him the once over with her eyes.

He acted wounded. "That's the best you can do when you walk in here and I've got nothing on but a towel is say, 'you sure got some sun today'?"

She raised her eyebrows. "Oh well."

Bryan and Helen Carlson arrived on time at six-fifteen and the two couples took the Carlson's Lexus SUV downtown to the restaurant. Libby Lohmeier and Helen Carlson had known each other since grade school and the two couples and their families frequently socialized, even taking vacations together from time to time.

The restaurant was a trendy eclectic spot in Lincoln Park and they left stuffed and satisfied, the beautiful warm day having transformed into a cool and comfortable evening. They walked down the sidewalk chatting about dinner and turned the corner heading toward the car when Ben, not looking where he was going, bumped into two men sharing an embrace. "I'm sorry, excuse me," he said stepping around them.

"No problem," one of the men said in a low voice.

As Ben looked back to once again acknowledge his indiscretion, something struck him as unusual, but he didn't know what. He stopped and studied the men for a couple of seconds from the rear as they rounded the corner and disappeared from sight. What was it? He couldn't put his finger on it.

Then Libby said, "Are you coming or not?"

Ben snapped back to reality, paused another second and then said, "Sure," and turned and caught up.

Later that night, in a small room with the door closed to keep the noise outside from intruding, the Protector sat on an old chair behind a small metal desk and pondered the beginning of the Greenfield murder trial. Would further action need to be taken? Had Lohmeier figured it out? No, he couldn't have. The beating may not have slowed him down much, but he couldn't have figured it out. He couldn't have. What of the other? What to do about the other? The Protector sat in that small room and thought about the future for a long while, the outside noise never intruding, then checked the time and went back to work.

46

Ben met with Meg the evening before jury selection began and found her much calmer than he had anticipated, even eager for things to get started. He sensed that she had come to terms with her situation and felt at peace with the road that lay ahead. Her husband, on the other hand, displayed none of the traits of a seasoned litigator and couldn't hide his nervousness and lack of comfort. Ben felt surprised that his attitude hadn't rubbed off on Meg, but was relieved that she seemed so ready for the trial to commence.

Ben took strength from her demeanor and when they met the media on the steps of the Courthouse on Wednesday morning, he conveyed her feelings when he said, "We've been looking forward to this date for a long time. As I've said in the past, today is the day Megan Rand Cavallaro begins to take her life back, her reputation back. We look forward to the impaneling of a fair and impartial jury of her peers, who will ultimately come to conclude what we have known from the first, that Megan is innocent. Thank you."

The final two jurors were seated the following Tuesday afternoon at about two o'clock. The final composition of the sixteen jurors and alternates seemed quite balanced and both sides appeared to get some of what they wanted. Of the sixteen, there were six men and ten women; seven were white and five black, three Hispanic and one woman from Korea. Once they had their sixteen, Judge Wilson thanked the rest for their service and adjourned for the day. "We'll start tomorrow with the State's opening statement at ten a.m.," he said slamming the gavel down and ending Court for the day.

On his way to Court the following morning, Ben tried to remember the last time he watched Bridget Fahey deliver an opening statement. Although he couldn't remember a specific occasion, he had seen her in action many times and knew that she would be well-prepared, thorough and probably quite effective.

Traffic moved fairly quickly and Ben reached the courtroom first, about half an hour early and only minutes before Dan and Mark. When the Cavallaros reached the courtroom about ten minutes early, Megan looked more nervous than before and her husband rubbed her shoulders as if to supply moral support. He and Ben exchanged nods. Meg wore a cream-colored blouse and a tan skirt, with simple pearl earrings and a matching necklace. She looked pure and innocent, like she belonged in a commercial for moisturizing lotion.

Bridget Fahey arrived only moments before Judge Wilson came out on the bench, followed by her gaggle of assistants. When Judge Wilson took the bench and everyone had found their seats, he turned to her and said, "Ms. Fahey, are you ready to proceed?"

She stood and said, "Yes, your Honor."

She remained standing as the Sheriff's deputy left to get the jury. As is proper decorum, Megan and her defense team also rose when the jury entered the courtroom and took their place in the jury box.

Judge Wilson turned and faced the jury. In his best professorial mode, he said, "We are now going to proceed with opening statements. One thing you should remember, the opening statement is not evidence and should not be treated as such. Rather, it is the lawyer's description of the expected evidence and testimony of witnesses. Nevertheless, you should listen carefully because it provides the road map for each side's case, what it expects to prove and even what it expects the other side to prove." He turned back to Bridget Fahey and nodded. "Ms. Fahey, you may begin."

Bridget Fahey rose and carried a file folder over to a rectangular wooden ledge in front of the jury box. She opened up the folder and took out her notes. She wore a charcoal gray suit and white blouse, with simple gold earrings and a matching chain. Her reddish hair was pulled back in a gold barrette. Ben thought she looked a little nervous. "Good morning, ladies and gentlemen. My name is Bridget Fahey," she said in a slightly uncomfortable voice. Her hands were clasped at waist level in front of her. "I'm the First Assistant State's Attorney for the County of Cook. I'm here today to present the People's case against the Defendant, Megan Rand Cavallaro. She has been indicted by a grand jury of your fellow citizens and charged under the Illinois Criminal Code with first degree murder in the death of Professor Daniel Greenfield, of the Chicago College of Law. The evidence will show that she committed this heinous act by repeatedly striking Professor Greenfield in the head with a baseball bat while in his office on or about December 28th of last year."

As she moved along, Ben sensed Bridget Fahey becoming more loose and comfortable and it showed in her presentation. Beside him, he could feel Megan growing increasingly uneasy over being portrayed as a murderer in open Court for all the world to see. Ben took a green index card from a stack on the corner of the table and wrote, "Stay calm" on it and slid it over to his client, who looked at it and nodded.

Meanwhile, Bridget Fahey continued laying out the facts as she saw them. "The relationship between the Defendant and Professor Greenfield began in 1989, when she enrolled as a student at the Chicago College of Law. Like all first year law students, the Defendant was assigned to a section consisting of about ninety students. The Defendant's section took Criminal Law during their first semester of law school in the fall of 1989. Daniel Greenfield was the professor of that course. Thereafter, sometime during late 1990 or early 1991, the Defendant initiated and ultimately began a more personal relationship with Professor Greenfield, a relationship which ultimately became a sexual one. The Defendant's affair with Professor Greenfield lasted for quite some time, finally ending before the birth of the Defendant's first child in the summer of 1992."

Ben's eyes narrowed slightly at the mention of Anthony's birth. While Fahey hadn't technically violated the Court's ruling prohibiting her from mentioning Anthony's paternity, she had walked right up to the edge and looked over the side. The implication was unmistakable. He looked up and Judge Wilson glanced briefly in his direction, occasionally a sign a Judge makes when he anticipates an objection. Ben made a split-second decision not to object, fearing that doing so might call more attention to the statement than it warranted. If she said anything else along these lines, however, he would be forced to object.

Bridget Fahey stepped away from the precipice. Ben maintained his outward appearance of serenity, as though he were listening to peaceful music or watching a movie. Fahey continued. "The Defendant's husband, Joseph Cavallaro, did not know about her affair with Daniel Greenfield."

Bridget Fahey was on a roll now and Ben watched as she picked up steam. "During the fall of 2001, contacts between the Defendant and Daniel Greenfield started up again. Phone records indicate several calls between the two in the weeks and months leading up to Daniel Greenfield's death. The Defendant even visited Daniel Greenfield at the law school. A security guard at the law school, Charles Powell, will testify that he recognizes the Defendant from seeing her during these visits around the date of the murder."

At these words, several heads in the jury box turned toward Meg and eyed her suspiciously. Exactly as Fahey intended. She went on. "On December 27th, the Defendant spoke to Professor Greenfield on the telephone, arranging a meeting for the following day. December 28th was a Friday, the last day the law school would be open for the year. It wouldn't reopen until January 2nd, the following Wednesday, five days later. The fall semester had ended a couple of weeks earlier, Christmas had just taken place and New Year's was only a couple of days away, so the law school was naturally quite empty. There would be few witnesses to worry about.

They met in Professor Greenfield's office. Whatever was said between the two, something went very wrong. The Defendant had reached the point of no return. While Daniel Greenfield was leaning over behind his desk, perhaps to put something in his nearby briefcase, the Defendant did the unthinkable. She picked up a baseball bat and struck him on the back of the head, somewhere behind and above his left ear. He fell. She struck him again and again and again, as many as ten to twelve times on the back of his head, crushing his skull and killing him."

Ben heard Megan inhale sharply, almost like a silent gasp, then hold her breath for a second or two before finally exhaling. He sensed her go rigid. He reached down and placed a reassuring hand on her right forearm and the tension seemed to ease somewhat. You could now hear a pin drop in the courtroom as all eyes were fixated on Bridget Fahey.

"After he was dead, the Defendant wiped down the bat, hoping to obliterate all of the finger prints, and wiped off anything else she touched in the office. She snuck from the room unseen and made her way back downstairs, where she left the building, probably through the back entrance, an entrance she would have known about from her days as a student. What she didn't know, is what she left behind and what she took with her." Ben saw several jurors lean forward. They were listening intently.

"At the scene of the crime, in Professor Greenfield's office, we found several blond hairs, which an expert will testify matched those of the Defendant. Also, we found two finger prints belonging to the Defendant, from her right forefinger and right thumb, near the trademark on the bat. In her haste, she had neglected to wipe the bat completely. Finally, prior to her arrest and in the brownstone she shares with her husband, we found a gray cashmere scarf, one used by the Defendant and the one she was wearing on that cold winter's day when Daniel Greenfield was killed. On that scarf, we found two drops of blood, the blood of Daniel Greenfield."

Ben could feel the tension in the room rising. Fahey was reaching her crescendo. "We will link the Defendant to Daniel Greenfield, first as a student, then as a lover. We will link them together during the fall and winter of 2001. We will link the Defendant to the law school and to Professor Greenfield's office, the murder scene. We will link her to the murder weapon. We will link her to Daniel Greenfield's blood. We will prove to you that Daniel Greenfield's blood is not only on the Defendant's scarf, but also on her hands. At the end of this trial, when all of the evidence is in, and we have linked the Defendant to Daniel Greenfield's murder, we will ask you for the only verdict justified by the law and the evidence. We will ask you to convict the Defendant. We will ask you to find Megan Rand Cavallaro guilty of the murder of Professor Daniel Greenfield."

47

When Court was back in session, Bridget Fahey called Professor Gordon Hyatt, who looked absolutely professorial in his tan summer suit. He testified about dropping by Greenfield's office to deliver some materials only to find him bludgeoned to death on the floor behind his desk. His testimony was interesting and while it displayed his cool demeanor and gentlemanly southern drawl, it was otherwise fairly unremarkable. After all, Ben thought, someone had to find the body. His direct testimony took no more than thirty minutes.

Ben's cross-examination was even shorter. Hyatt admitted that he had been present at the law school for a little while on the date of the murder, but had not seen either Meg or Greenfield. He also testified that he had never seen Meg and the Professor alone together, nor had he ever seen Meg act violently or even display any temper of any kind. All in all, Ben felt good about the cross-examination. He had begun to lay the groundwork for chipping away at the State's case and Hyatt had been cooperative and had not really provided any real damage.

Bridget Fahey's next witness was the medical examiner, Dr. Akhter. By now, the sun had risen high enough in the sky that it no longer shone through the windows behind the defense table. The odd reflections and shadows of earlier in the morning were now gone. Dr. Akhter took the stand after the lunch recess and walked to the witness stand seeming as though he did not have a care in the world, even nodding at Ben as he passed. Bridget Fahey took him through his educational background and extensive work experience with tedious detail. She went on somewhat longer than she needed to, though the point was unmistakably driven home - Akhter knew his business. Ben didn't disagree and let the testimony drag on for as long as Fahey cared to continue.

In describing Greenfield's fatal injuries, Akhter utilized charts, a series of carefully selected photographs agreed to by both sides after extensive argument prior to trial and even a life-sized model of a human skull. The photographs of the murder scene particularly worried Ben because of the graphic and horrifying nature of the carnage displayed. The murder was brutal and savage and the pictures could only serve to turn the jury against Megan, unless, of course, they concluded that a woman, or this woman in particular, could not have committed such an act. In the end, Judge Wilson let them choose from a dozen and a half or so different photographs of the murder scene depicted from various angles. Fahey ultimately chose to use about a dozen.

Doctor Akhter testified that the cause of death was blunt force trauma to the rear of the head caused by a baseball bat found at the scene. Toward the end of his testimony, Bridget Fahey displayed a thirty-four inch, thirty-three ounce Louisville slugger baseball bat autographed by Sammy Sosa. "Is it your testimony, doctor, that this bat is the murder weapon?" Fahey asked.

"Yes, Counsel, it is. The indentations made on the skull match the barrel of the bat." A few minutes later, Fahey displayed a gray cashmere scarf. The doctor pointed to small circular dots at one end of the scarf, about the size of a pencil eraser.

"Can you identify what these discolorations are?"

"Yes. They are blood."

"Were you able to determine whose blood?"

"Yes. The blood belongs to the deceased, Daniel Greenfield."

A murmur ran through the courtroom and Bridget Fahey sat down.

"I have nothing further, your Honor," she said.

Ben briefly took the medical examiner through some of his collection methods, then turned his attention to Professor Greenfield's blood. The witness testified that he had found a small amount of alcohol in the deceased's blood, probably from a drink at lunch on the date of his death. He also identified trace amounts of a common over-the-counter antihistamine. Ben walked back and picked up a document off the table. He looked at it for a few seconds and then gestured with it in the direction of the witness. "I've got your report here, Doctor. It appears from this report that you found some other things in Professor Greenfield's blood as well, didn't you."

"We did, yes."

Ben walked a couple of steps closer to the witness and paused as if reviewing the document carefully. The courtroom grew very still. "You also found marijuana in Professor Greenfield's system, didn't you?"

"Yes, we did. Trace elements of marijuana, yes."

"From your knowledge and experience, how many days before his death would Professor Greenfield have ingested that marijuana?"

"Approximately seven to ten days, given the levels in his blood."

"You also found traces of cocaine in Professor Greenfield's system didn't you?" Now the crowd murmured again. The doctor looked at him. "Doctor? Isn't that correct?"

"Yes, yes, it is."

"Based on the levels of cocaine found in the deceased's system, when would he have ingested same?"

"Roughly the same time frame, perhaps a week before his death."

Ben let the moment and the realization that Professor Greenfield was a drug user sink in to the members of the jury and the gallery, then turned and placed the report back on the counsel table, where Mark picked it up and put it in a pile. He turned back to the witness. "Doctor, you testified at some length about the nature and description of the wounds suffered by Professor Greenfield. In fact, you had diagrams, charts and photographs, as well as that model of a human skull." Ben shrugged. "Would it be fair to say that his wounds were confined to the rear quarter of his skull from approximately the left ear back around the rear of the skull?"

299

"Yes. I don't know whether I would call it the rear quarter, but the rear of the skull to roughly the section above the left ear would be about correct."

"Did he suffer any wounds to his face or the front part of his skull?"

"Only bruising associated with striking the floor and contact with the floor as a result of being struck in the rear of the head by the murder weapon, the baseball bat."

"So it is your testimony that Professor Greenfield was not struck in the face by the baseball bat, correct?"

"Yes, that's correct."

"And the source of the blood in the photographs, that blood came from the myriad of head wounds, isn't that right?"

"Yes, although some blood flow also came from his ears and his mouth as well."

Ben nodded and moved a little closer. "We've all seen the photographs of the murder scene," Ben said as he moved a little closer, his head down, his left hand on his chin as though in thought. His voice was low. "This was a pretty bloody scene, wasn't it, Doctor?"

"Yes, it was."

"There was blood on the carpeting?"

"Yes, there was."

"Blood on the wall behind the desk?"

"Yes."

"Blood on the credenza behind the desk?"

"Yes."

"Blood on the desk chair?"

"Yes, there was."

"Blood on the filing cabinet?" The witness nodded. "I need a verbal answer, Doctor."

"Yes, there was blood on the filing cabinet."

"There was also tissue from the skull and brain matter at these locations, isn't that right?"

"Yes, that's correct."

"And even bits of bone were scattered throughout the area?"

"Yes, that's true."

300

Ben moved even closer. He was standing directly in front of the witness now.

"Now Doctor, you testified about that gray scarf with the blood on it, two drops of blood, I believe you said."

"That's correct."

"And this blood matched the blood of the deceased, Daniel Greenfield, isn't that right?"

"Yes."

"Let's assume for the sake of my questions, that the person who committed this murder was wearing that scarf at the time of the murder."

"Okay."

Ben walked over to the bench and picked up one of the photographs showing Professor Greenfield and the bloody scene surrounding his body. He held it up in the general direction of the witness. "Given this bloody scene, wouldn't you have expected to find more than two small drops of blood on a scarf being worn by the killer?"

Doctor Akhter paused for a long time as if considering how best to phrase his answer. Bridget Fahey rose. "Objection, your Honor, the question calls for speculation."

Judge Wilson turned to Ben who was shaking his head. "Your Honor, this is a medical examiner with a vast amount of experience in crime scenes. He has more than enough experience and expertise to answer this question."

"I agree," Wilson said. "Objection overruled. You may answer."

Ben figured that Fahey knew the objection wasn't particularly well-founded, yet she made it anyway in an effort to give the witness more time to prepare an answer and perhaps hint at the answer desired.

The witness cleared his throat. "Perhaps," he said, "but it's hard to say for sure."

Ben grinned. "And given the amount of carnage in this scene," Ben said holding up the photograph again, "wouldn't you have expected the killer to have blood on his shoes?"

"Perhaps."

"His pants?" Ben was moving forward now, his voice rising.

"Probably, yes."

"His coat?"

"Perhaps."

"His shirt?"

"Maybe."

"And assuming he was wearing them, his gloves?"

"Yes."

"Did you or your office have occasion to examine any of those kinds of items belonging to my client, Megan Rand Cavallaro?"

"Yes, we did."

"Did you find any of the victim's blood on any of those items?"

"No, we didn't."

"Did you find any skull tissue or brain matter on any of those items?"

He shook his head. "No."

"Just those two little drops of blood on that gray scarf?"

"Yes."

48

Ben got home at about ten-fifteen only to discover Libby watching news coverage of the trial on television. She seemed almost giddy. "This is exciting," she said. "Everything was very positive. All of the experts, including that Stan Goldman guy on Fox, thought you did a great job. They had a lot of good things to say about her opening statement, Bridget Fahey's I mean, but they said you gained a lot of ground with the cross-examination of the medical examiner."

Ben dropped his briefcase and plopped down on the sofa beside her. She looked at him excitedly. "So, what did you think?"

He looked at the TV then at his wife and then back at the TV. "Can't we turn this off?"

"Don't you want to watch it? You're a celebrity."

He looked back at her, his head cocked, his eyes squinting. "You forget, Lib, I was there. I know what happened in the courtroom."

She sighed. "Okay okay," she said. "I've recorded most of it anyway."

He rolled his eyes. "Great."

"Seriously though, how did you think it went?"

"About how I expected. I figured her opening would be good and it was probably even better than I expected. Professor Hyatt wasn't much. Somebody had to find the body and he was the guy who did. The medical examiner went about as well as I could have hoped. They've got the blood, sure, but where's the rest of the bloody clothing? There should be some somewhere." He got up. "What did you have for dinner tonight?"

Ben took some grilled chicken out of the refrigerator and cut it up and put it on a salad. Then he grabbed a root beer and sat down in front of the television to eat. They tried to find something unrelated to the trial, much to Libby's chagrin, and settled on a rerun of *Seinfeld* and an episode of *The Sopranos* which Libby didn't particularly care for. She fell asleep during the show and Ben jostled her awake when it was over. She went upstairs at about ten minutes to twelve and Ben sat down on the couch for a while thinking about the case before joining her a half hour or so later. He knew there was still something he was missing, something that would make everything click into place in his mind. Try as he might, he just couldn't find it.

Ben got a good night's sleep, hopefully his mind was working overtime trying to piece the puzzle together, and got down to the Courthouse feeling refreshed and ready to go. The sun of the previous day had given way to clouds and cooler temperatures and the shadows so evident in the courtroom the day before were now gone. Mark hobbled in a few minutes later, apparently his knee was acting up, but happy with news coverage of yesterday's events. "A lot of good pub on TV last night," he said.

Ben shook his head. "Not you too. Libby wanted to watch that stuff when we got home. Isn't it enough that we have to live through it all day without watching it all night?"

Mark shrugged. "It's still fun to see."

"I guess."

After the jury was brought in, Bridget Fahey called Charles Powell to the stand. The tall, soft spoken, African American security guard for the law school ambled up to the witness stand wearing his best suit. Bridget Fahey took him through his background and experience working at the law school. He testified that he recalled seeing Meg at the law school on several occasions shortly before and around the time of the murder. This was consistent with what he had told Ben earlier. He also described the security system at the school, including the cameras.

On cross, Ben forced the witness to concede that he couldn't pin down Megan's visits to the law school to an exact date. He also stated that fellow staff members and professors possessed the pass cards which would enable them to go from the hallway outside Greenfield's office back into the library, a maneuver that might not be easily visible on the security cameras. Finally, the witness conceded that certain female professors, including Angela Harper, had inquired into the security procedures at the law school. Nevertheless, Charles Powell had identified Meg as having been at the law school around the date of the murder. Combined with the blood and the other evidence, this was something for the State to work with. Ben could only hope that he could create enough doubt to cause the jury to see things his way.

Bridget Fahey's next witness was her blood expert, who testified consistently with the medical examiner, Dr. Akhter. His primary conclusion was that the blood found on the scarf undoubtedly came from Greenfield and that it hadn't degraded to such an extent that he would say that it had arrived on the scarf a long time before the tests. Ben didn't do much with him on cross-examination, even his own blood expert conceded that the blood on the scarf was Greenfield's, so he let the man off the hook with a token cross-examination, rather than try and achieve something spectacular and fail in front of the jury.

The following day, Bridget Fahey led off with her expert on hair, a criminologist from the University of Chicago, who appeared overly devoted to his unusual niche in the field. Professor Byron Marks, a quiet looking man in his mid-fifties with a flop of brown hair falling in his face, looked uncomfortable in his navy blue sport coat, tie, gray pants and brown walking shoes. He described the science of hair evaluation and analysis, from root to stem, as though trying his best to bore everyone to tears. After a seemingly endless recitation on the differences between types of hair, with a peculiar focus on Oriental hair and African-American hair, neither of which was present here, he testified that three hairs found in Professor Greenfield's office were consistent with the samples received from the Defendant. Everyone seemed happy when his direct-examination concluded, especially the jurors.

Mark handled the cross-examination and sought to undermine the notion that hair analysis was a science in the area of criminology. His only real success came at the end of his cross-examination, when he asked, "Isn't it true, Professor Marks, that one cannot match hairs in the same way he or she can match fingerprints or blood?"

The witness fidgeted somewhat in his chair, looking off into the middle distance as if searching for the answer on a cloud floating by the windows to the courtroom. "Although the matching of hair," he said, "is not quite the same as matching blood or fingerprints, we can nonetheless state that a given hair is consistent with a known sample to a reasonable degree of scientific certainty."

The magic buzzwords, Ben thought. Mark strove onward. "Isn't it true that you found other hairs in Professor Greenfield's office that do not appear to you to have come from my client?"

"That's true. We found quite a few hairs that were consistent with hairs taken from Professor Greenfield himself. We also located three other light brown hairs that seemed to come from the same subject and two darker brown hairs which came from an entirely different subject. We also found one other blond hair that did not appear consistent with the Defendant's hair."

"So, in other words, you have at least three sets of other hairs that do not appear to have come, in your opinion anyway, from either the Defendant or Professor Greenfield?"

"That's correct."

All in all, a mixed bag, Ben thought. The blond hairs probably placed Meg at the scene of the crime, even if there may have been others there as well. Whether they thoroughly discredited the science or not, Ben couldn't tell.

The State's expert on blood splatters basically supported the testimony of Dr. Akhter, and established that Professor Greenfield was likely bending or leaning over next to his desk when he was struck with the first or the first couple of blows. Ben didn't really dispute this testimony and focused merely on the degree of splattering in his cross-examination.

"Given your testimony on splattering," he asked the witness, "and the amount of blood, tissue and brain matter found at the scene, can you reasonably expect that a person committing this crime could have escaped this scene without getting a significant amount of this material on their person and clothing?"

The witness paused and then said, "I'm not quite sure what you mean by significant, but I would say that the killer would have likely received some splattering on his or her person."

"A lot more than two drops on a scarf?"

"Yes, I would say so, but clothing could always be cleaned and, perhaps, disposed of somehow."

Ben got what he needed. He decided not to push it too far.

49

The toughest things about trial work are its relentlessness and its unpredictability. From the moment you begin a trial, it never lets up. Ben had lost ten pounds since the first of July on his slight frame and his regular suits started to feel loose on him. In order to keep from losing too much weight, he forced himself to eat even when he wasn't hungry, at times sucking down chocolate milkshakes rather than full meals he wouldn't be in the mood to finish. He slept fitfully, his mind working overtime, and after he showered, he pulled on an older suit that didn't feel quite so loose.

When Detective Scott Nelson walked to the witness stand, Ben felt an added electricity in the room and knew he faced one of those moments in a trial where he didn't quite know what was going to happen next. Nelson wore a tweed sport coat, a light blue shirt, print tie and brown slacks, and looked as much like a college professor as Professor Hyatt had days earlier. As always, he appeared soft spoken and earnest.

Bridget Fahey led the detective through an unremarkable description of the early stages of the investigation, from his first appearance on the scene through his conversation with the widow to his conclusion that Megan was a suspect in Greenfield's murder. Shortly before lunch, Fahey turned to the telephone records and asked, "Detective, from your review of these telephone records, did you find any telephone contact between the Defendant and Professor Greenfield?"

"Yes, we did. We found thirteen possible telephone contacts between the two from October 30, 2001 to December 26, 2001, two days before Professor Greenfield's death."

Fahey nodded and said, "When you say possible contacts, what do you mean?"

"A couple of things. First, we only know the telephone numbers attributable to both the Professor and the Defendant. We do not know necessarily who made the calls or who, if anyone, received them on the other end. Some of the calls are fairly short, only a minute or two, so perhaps the calls involved leaving messages, rather than speaking directly to the party on the other side. Also, the phone calls made from the law school do not come directly from an individual's phone line. Rather, they are routed through a central phone system. What that means is that phone calls to Professor Greenfield, for example, are recorded to his direct line number, while calls made by Professor Greenfield, show up on one of the outgoing lines available to the law school."

Bridget Fahey moved forward. "Thank you, Detective. Could you tell us how many calls were made to and from each particular location?"

"Of course," the Detective said.

Ben knew what was coming and would have to address the phone calls in his cross-examination. He was impressed that Fahey did not overreach by stating definitively that the calls made from the law school were made by Greenfield. Aware of the circumstances surrounding the phone system, she wisely chose to let the jury make that inference for her.

The Detective continued. "We were able to identify two telephone calls from Professor Greenfield's apartment to the condominium where the Defendant lives, or lived at the time. We found one telephone call from Professor Greenfield's apartment to the office where the Defendant worked. We found two telephone calls from Professor Greenfield's cell phone to the Defendant's condominium. We found three telephone calls from the law school to the Defendant's condominium. We found two telephone calls from the law school to the office at the Court where the Defendant worked, and we found three telephone calls from the

Defendant's condominium to the Professor's direct telephone line at the law school."

A murmur rose in the courtroom with these last words indicating telephone calls from the Megan to Professor Greenfield's office. Judge Wilson struck his gavel. "We'll have quiet," he said, "please continue." With his no-nonsense demeanor, whenever Judge Wilson asked for silence, he got it immediately.

Bridget Fahey seemed energized by the testimony and Ben studied her intently. Next to him, he could feel Meg begin to deflate. "Could you tell us, Detective," Bridget Fahey continued, "when these telephone calls began and when they ended?"

"The first of these thirteen calls took place on October 30th of 2001 and that was a call from the Professor's apartment to the office at which the Defendant is employed. The last four calls took place in late December. There was a call from the Defendant's condominium to Professor Greenfield's office on December 22nd, a call from the law school to the condominium on December 23rd, another call from the condominium to the law school on December 26th, and a second call on that date from the law school to the condominium."

Bridget Fahey nodded and continued. "Detective, can you tell the jury the length of these phone conversations?"

"Yes. Most of them were quite short, only a couple of minutes or so, with the exception of the December 22nd phone call from the Defendant's condominium to Professor Greenfield's office, which lasted approximately eighteen minutes, and the last call, on December 26th from the law school to the condominium, which lasted for twenty-one minutes."

Megan sighed and more murmuring rose in the courtroom only to be silenced by two sharp bangs of Judge Wilson's gavel. The sounds of the gavel echoed through the cavernous room and all was silent for almost ten seconds before Bridget Fahey continued.

She then turned her attention to the items found in Professor Greenfield's office after the body was discovered. "It seems apparent," the Detective said, "that the Professor had been in the process of grading final exams at the time of or shortly before his death. We found graded and ungraded exam papers on his desk, on the floor near the body and in his briefcase as well. In his pocket, we found a dog-eared note with the letter "M" on it and two telephone numbers, which later turned out to be the numbers for the Defendant's condominium and her office at the Appellate Court." Fahey tried hard to hide a smile. "We also found copies of old calendars dating back from 1991 through the present."

"What sort of calendars were these?"

"These were mainly appointment calendars, some of which had appointments scrawled in and other dates of apparent importance to the Professor written on them."

"Did you find a calendar for 2001 in his office?"

"Yes, we did."

"Was there any entry for December 28, 2001?"

"Yes. The word 'meetings' was written in, with no name or time."

"Did you find anything else in Professor Greenfield's briefcase?"

"Yes, we did. We found a series of cases and law review articles on the field of advances in DNA analysis. From subsequent conversations with others, we learned that Professor Greenfield was apparently researching DNA, presumably in the context of criminal matters."

"You say presumably in the context of criminal matters?"

"Yes, because we did not find any notes or drafts of any articles written by the Professor himself. We only found the research."

Fahey then went through each of these documents in detail, from the note to the research, introducing them all into evidence. By now, it was almost twelve-thirty and Judge Wilson decided to adjourn for lunch until two p.m.

When Court resumed, Bridget Fahey completed her direct examination of Detective Nelson. "Detective, did you ever have any occasion to speak with the Defendant regarding Professor Greenfield?"

"Yes, we did. On several occasions, we spoke to the Defendant at her condominium and also once at the station, which was recorded."

"What did she tell you?"

"She told us first that although she knew Professor Greenfield as one of her teachers in law school, she had no personal relationship with him of any kind other than professor/student. She also told us that she had not seen, heard from or spoken with the Professor in many, many years, perhaps not even since graduation. Finally, she denied having a sexual relationship with the Professor and denied knowing anything about the circumstances surrounding his death."

Fahey then went through the laborious process of playing back the tape of the interrogation performed by Detectives Nelson and Cole of Meg at the station. "Are you telling us," the tape spat, "that you have never had a personal relationship with Daniel Greenfield?"

"Yes, I am. My only relationship with Professor Greenfield was as his student." Meg's voice on the tape sounded shaky and unsure.

"Did you ever have a sexual relationship with Professor Greenfield?"

"No, never."

A few minutes later. "Have you ever been inside Professor Greenfield's office at the law school?"

"Not for many years. I may have been in there years ago when I was a student to talk to him about class or something, but not since then, no."

The tapes went on for a long time, Meg's hesitant voice and repeated denials made Ben feel somewhat uncomfortable and caused Meg to look down at the table. He slid a card toward her. "Look calm" was written on it. She nodded and tried to pull herself together, without complete success.

The jury paid rapt attention to the sound of Megan's voice on those tapes, and Fahey let them play on and on, beyond the time her point was made, filling the courtroom with Megan's often quavering voice. Then with a dramatic flourish, she turned off the tape recorder. "Detective," she said with all the solemnity she could muster, "did you ever learn that any of these statements made by the Defendant were untrue?"

The Detective nodded. "Yes, we did," he said. "We learned she had a sexual relationship with Professor Greenfield from Samuel Dorlund, another professor at the law school."

Ben was on his feet. "Objection, this is hearsay."

Fahey knew it was coming. "Your Honor, we would ask that you allow it in light of the fact that Professor Dorlund will so testify later in this trial."

Judge Wilson nodded. "I'll allow it for the time being, pending Professor Dorlund's testimony. Should he not so testify, Mr. Lohmeier, you may renew your objection at that time."

Fahey continued. "Did you ever learn any of the other statements made by the Defendant were false?"

"Yes. We learned that the Defendant had been inside Professor Greenfield's office, the scene of the murder, when she originally said that she hadn't."

"How did you learn this?"

"We learned it when we identified her fingerprints on the murder weapon, the baseball bat, and when we matched hair found at the crime scene to the Defendant."

Ben thought about objecting, but held his tongue. Despite the fact that Nelson's statements were technically inadmissible legal conclusions, he figured that Judge Wilson would probably allow them. Moreover, Ben knew he could probably address the evidence better in his own case, as well as in his closing argument.

"Did you learn it any other way?" Fahey continued.

"Yes. When we found the victim's blood on a scarf owned by the Defendant."

Bridget Fahey walked slowly to her seat as Scott Nelson's words hung in the courtroom like a shroud over the freedom and future of Megan Rand Cavallaro.

Ben rose to his feet and offered the Detective a slight smile. "Good afternoon, Detective Nelson." He wanted the jury to see that he bore no animosity toward the Detective and that, if anything, the Detective was merely misguided, not malicious. The he picked up a file and moved out from behind the counsel table and toward the center of the courtroom. He stood there for a moment, then held the file up and said, "I have those telephone records you were speaking about earlier today with Ms. Fahey. You said you identified thirteen calls that could have taken place between Professor Greenfield and my client, isn't that right?"

"Yes, that's right."

"Of those thirteen calls, isn't it true that five of them came from the law school to either my client's condominium or the office where she works at the Appellate Court?"

"Yes, that's right."

"And you can't tell for sure who made any of those five calls, can you?"

"No, not for sure."

"Because the way the phone system works and the phone records are gathered, those calls could have been made from any telephone within the law school?"

"I believe that's right, yes."

"And of the remaining eight calls, three more were directed to my client's office at the Appellate Court, isn't that right?"

"Yes."

"Those calls too could have been made to anyone at that location, isn't that right?"

"I suppose that's possible."

Ben paused and moved closer to the witness. "And of all those thirteen telephone calls you identified, only two lasted longer than two minutes, isn't that right?"

"Yes, that's right."

"And the others could have been just one party or another leaving a message?"

"That's probably true."

Ben looked at the telephone records for a minute then continued. "Isn't it also true that Professor Greenfield was a member of the Reunion Committee for the 1992 graduating class at the law school?"

"Yes, he was."

"Isn't it also true that my client was a graduate of the law school in 1992?"

"As you were yourself, yes."

314

"And my client was also on that Reunion Committee, wasn't she?"

"Yes, she was."

"There were other members of that Committee as well, weren't there?"

"Yes."

"How many?"

"I believe about eight to ten."

"Some of those were also Professors at the law school, weren't they?"

"Yes, I believe there were four other Professors besides Professor Greenfield."

"Would you find it unusual for one member of a Reunion Committee to contact another?"

"Perhaps not, but your client and Professor Greenfield knew each other more than just as members of the Reunion Committee."

Ben nodded and moved even closer. "So you say. But you really don't have any evidence whatsoever as to what was said in any of those telephone conversations, do you?"

The witness looked at Ben for a long moment then said, "No, I suppose we don't."

"The parties in those telephone conversations could very well have been talking about the Reunion Committee."

"Yes, I suppose they could have."

Ben stood before Detective Nelson as though he were calculating something in his head. Then he continued. "So, really, all you've got for sure is three calls from my client's home to Professor Greenfield's office, only one of which took longer than two minutes, isn't that right?"

"I wouldn't exactly put it that way."

"No, of course you wouldn't. Regarding that Reunion Committee, didn't Professor Dorlund tell you that he gave Professor Greenfield a packet of materials regarding the Reunion Committee?"

"Yes, he did."

"Now you don't think the Reunion Committee was a motive for murder, do you?"

"No, I wouldn't think so."

"Didn't he also tell you that a list of all the Reunion Committee members with their telephone numbers was included in that packet?"

"Yes, he did."

"You never found that list in Professor Greenfield's personal effects, did you?"

"No."

"Not in his office, or in his briefcase, or in his apartment either?"

"No, we never found it."

"Do you think maybe the killer took it?"

Nelson paused as though considering the question. "It's possible," he finally said.

"Any reason why the killer would take it?"

"I don't know."

"You never discovered that my client had it, did you?"

"No."

"You never found any notes on that research you say Professor Greenfield was doing either, did you?"

"No, we didn't."

Ben walked over to the side of the courtroom where various pieces of evidence already introduced in the State's case sat on a table. He picked up a baseball bat wrapped in plastic and grabbed it by the handle, moving it back and forth as though testing it for his next at bat. "You say this is the murder weapon, don't you?" he asked holding it up.

"Yes, that's the murder weapon."

"You know this because the medical examiner was able to match this bat to the wounds on Professor Greenfield's skull, isn't that right?"

"Yes, that's true."

Now Detective Nelson looked a little curious as Ben waved the bat slightly as though standing before home plate. "This is one of Sammy Sosa's actual baseball bats, isn't it?"

"Yes. I understand that it was one of the Professor's prized possessions."

316

"In fact, this is Sammy Sosa's autograph right here on the barrel, isn't it?" Ben asked indicating with his forefinger.

"It's supposed to be his autograph, yes."

"This is a big bat," Ben said, swinging it slightly, "kind of heavy."

"Objection," Bridget Fahey said, "there doesn't appear to be any question here. Mr. Lohmeier appears to be living out some childhood baseball fantasy."

"Get on with it Mr. Lohmeier," Judge Wilson said. "Objection sustained."

Ben waved the bat back and forth again. "This is no fantasy. This is a bat used by a professional baseball player, one of the best in the world, isn't that right?"

"Yes."

"And it's a pretty good-sized bat too, isn't it?"

"Yes, I suppose so."

"And what you want all of us to believe is that that woman over there," he turned and pointed at Megan, "picked up this large baseball bat and used it to kill a grown man, isn't that right?"

"Yes, that's right."

Ben said, "Huh," shook his head and made a face of disbelief, then walked toward Detective Nelson and handed him the bat. "Here," he said, "take this for a minute." Nelson took the bat. "There was also testimony earlier in this trial about finding my client's fingerprints on this bat."

"I'm aware of that, yes."

"Why don't you show us where those fingerprints were, if you know. You can stand up if that makes it easier."

Detective Nelson held the bat awkwardly, then looked around as if for assistance. He looked up at the Judge, who nodded and said, "Go ahead. Stand if you like."

He rose slowly to his feet and stood before Ben holding the bat. Ben looked at him, his arms crossed. Then he pointed at the bat and said, "Now, I believe you folks testified that there were two fingerprints belonging to my client on that bat, isn't that right?"

He shrugged. "Yes, two of your client's fingerprints."

"Anyone else's fingerprints?"

"There were several of the victim's fingerprints on the bat as well, but no one else other than those two people."

"Those fingerprints allegedly from my client, they were from her right hand, isn't that right?"

"Yes, I believe so."

"There were no fingerprints from her left hand?"

"No."

"Can you show us where those two fingerprints were?"

Detective Nelson studied the bat for a few moments and then pointed at it with his right hand, holding it about twelve inches from the end of the handle with his left. "I believe the thumb was here and the forefinger was over here," he said indicating.

Ben pointed at the bat again. "Why don't you go ahead and put your fingers on the bat in approximately the position you say that my client's fingerprints were left."

Nelson now looked very, very uncomfortable. He looked around for help, but none was forthcoming. He placed his thumb on the top of the barrel of the bat near the trademark, and the forefinger underneath on the bottom.

"Now take your left hand off the bat." Nelson did so. It was obvious that the bat was much more difficult to handle with just one hand. "I see that the Sammy Sosa autograph is now facing up toward you, isn't that right?"

Nelson looked down and shrugged. "Yes, I guess it is."

"So that may be about where one would hold the bat with his or her right hand if looking at Sammy Sosa's autograph, isn't that true?"

"Objection," Fahey said, "calls for speculation."

Ben laughed. "Your Honor, I think the witness has enough experience with looking at things that he can tell how someone would hold an object and look at it."

There was laughter in the courtroom. "I think Counsel makes a good point, Ms. Fahey. Objection overruled. You can answer."

Nelson looked like a man who didn't want to hold the bat any longer. "I suppose if you were to look at the autograph, you could hold the bat this way."

Ben nodded several times, perfectly at ease. "Now, you're not suggesting that my client held the bat with just those two fingers in her right hand and that's how she repeatedly struck the Professor in the head, caved in his skull and ultimately killed him, are you?"

"No," Nelson said somewhat awkwardly, "not necessarily. It's just that these two fingerprints were left on the bat, that's all. She could very well have wiped off her remaining fingerprints."

"Such as, say the fingerprints from her left hand?"

"Yes." Now Nelson felt better.

"Okay then. Go ahead and put your left hand on the end of the bat, down near the handle." Nelson did so. "It's easier to hold now, isn't it?"

"Yes, it is."

"Now it almost looks like how you'd hold the bat if you were going to bunt the baseball, doesn't it?" Ben said with a grin.

"Yes, I guess it does."

"Yet you still have your right forefinger and right thumb in the areas where you found my client's fingerprints?"

"Yes."

Ben paused for a long moment as though studying the Detective, his eyes squinted, head tilted to the side, arms folded across his chest. Then he cocked his left eye and pointed an inquisitive forefinger at the Detective. "Now, if you were going to kill a man with this bat, kill him by hitting him so hard and so many times that you crushed the back of his skull, do you think you'd be bunting, or would you swing away?" There was laughter in the courtroom, and Ben gave the Detective a sarcastic grin, met with narrowed eyes.

Bridget Fahey rose and shouted, "Objection, Your Honor." Ben turned and raised his hand in mock apology. "I'll withdraw the question," he said, returning to his seat. But the point had been made.

50

Sylvia Greenfield looked like a cross between a business executive and movie star when she strode purposefully down the aisle and toward the witness stand. Her posture perfect, her head erect, she displayed cool confidence and just a hint of blue-blood arrogance. She wore a dark gray suit and white blouse, her frosted blond hair swept back behind her ears displaying gold oval earrings. Everything was put together and accessorized perfectly. She took her seat on the witness stand and smoothed out her skirt, leaving her hands folded on her lap. She gave Bridget Fahey the slightest of cool smiles indicating that it was now appropriate to begin, and Fahey questioned her briefly regarding her marriage and children before turning her attention to the reason for their breakup. She told the Court essentially the same thing she told Ben months earlier at her home - the marriage fell apart when she couldn't put up with her husband's infidelity any longer.

Ben watched carefully from his spot at the defense table. He found Sylvia Greenfield's demeanor very curious, much like it had been the day he had spoken to her at her home. She spoke in a detached way, almost as though she were describing events that had occurred to someone else, rather than herself. He wondered if she could really be this unemotional, or whether this was simply a strange façade. In any event, it was clear to Ben that the appearance of being treated badly hurt Sylvia Greenfield as much as the actual mistreatment itself.

Bridget Fahey didn't elicit any real specifics. It was as though the marriage had simply ended after a time, almost like the expiration of a driver's license or credit card. The questioning went on in this strange detached manner for fifteen minutes or so, without any particularly relevant testimony coming out. Then Fahey asked her about her last communications with her former husband.

"I last saw Daniel in late September when he stopped by to visit the girls on our eldest daughter's birthday."

"Can you describe that meeting?"

"It was rather ordinary. I was only there a few minutes before I left to go out to dinner with a friend. I didn't think they wanted any unpleasantness between their parents, so I left."

"Did you speak to him again after that occasion in late September?"

"Yes, a couple of times. The first time was around Thanksgiving. Daniel was never happy with how things took place around the holidays because the girls always wanted to stay with me and my family, rather than visit him. He generally took that out on me and assumed that I urged the girls to take that position, which of course I did not. I spoke to him a couple of times after Thanksgiving, once in early December and again about a week before Christmas."

"Can you describe that first conversation for us?"

"Daniel was very angry. He told me that he felt I wouldn't let him see the girls over the holidays and he didn't want to sit home alone in his apartment while we celebrated. The conversation only lasted a few minutes, but it was quite unpleasant."

"Describe the second conversation for the Court."

"Well, his mood was much better than it had been before. He was almost arrogant. He said that the time was coming when I wouldn't be able to control his access to his family like I did then. I didn't know exactly what he meant and said so. He said that I would find out soon enough."

Ben leaned forward in his chair. Where was she going with this? Mark slid a green card over to him with one word on it - "What?" Ben wrote, "Don't know" on the card and slid it back.

"Did you ever ask him what he meant?" Bridget Fahey continued.

"No. Frankly, I didn't want to speak to him anymore. So I just let it drop."

"Did you ever find out what he meant?"

"No, I'm afraid not."

Bridget Fahey looked at Judge Wilson and said simply, "I have no further questions, your Honor." As she walked back to her table, she gave Ben a quick glance out of the corner of her eye, apparently searching for some reaction. She got none.

Ben pushed away from the table and rose slowly to his feet. He eyed the witness. "You won't always be able to control access to his family. That's kind of a curious thing to say, don't you think?" he asked.

She shook her head. "I don't know."

"You don't know whether you think it's curious?"

"I suppose it may be somewhat curious."

"You thought it was curious at the time, didn't you?"

She cocked her head. "I suppose I may have."

"Is that a yes or no?"

She looked annoyed. "Yes. It's a yes. I thought it was curious."

Ben nodded and advanced slowly toward the witness. "Did you view that statement as some kind of threat?"

"No."

"Why not?"

"Daniel would never threaten me, at least not physically."

"What about in other ways?"

"No, not particularly. I just figured he was trying to get a reaction out of me."

"Did he do that a lot?"

"Of course, isn't that what lawyers are good at?" She smiled coldly and murmurs of laughter erupted in the courtroom.

Ben smiled and nodded taking the hit gracefully. "Point well taken," he said. "Now, let's talk about your husband's infidelities. When was the first time you learned your husband was unfaithful to you?"

She paused and looked out toward the gallery as though to locate the memory. "I don't know," she said finally, "a couple of

322

times over the years I probably had my suspicions, given Daniel's position and all those young female law students around, but I never really pursued the issue, probably because I didn't want to believe it. I didn't first start taking it seriously until about ten years ago."

"Ten years ago?" Ben said. "Did you say anything about it to your husband at the time?"

"No. I don't think I ever said anything about it until probably five years ago. I didn't want to think about it. Then it really became an issue when the students accused him of improper behavior."

"Did your husband ever admit to having relationships with female law students?"

"No, he didn't. He always denied it, but that didn't mean that we both didn't know it was true."

"How did you know it was true?"

"Mr. Lohmeier, you just know."

Ben nodded and left it alone. He still didn't know what to make of Daniel Greenfield's last comment and also didn't know quite how to pursue the matter. Finally, he decided to give up and asked, "Before your husband's death, had you ever even heard of my client, Megan Rand Cavallaro?"

She looked directly at Meg, her cold eyes suggesting a feeling of marked indifference, rather than anger or contempt. "No," she said finally, "I had never heard of her until I saw her name in the papers and heard it on television."

"Before you came here today, had you ever seen my client, Megan Rand Cavallaro?"

Sylvia Greenfield gave Meg one last cold glare. She shook her head. "No, not in person. I'd only seen her on television after she was arrested."

"So you never saw your husband with my client?"

"No, never."

"I have no further questions."

Bridget Fahey offered no re-direct and Sylvia Greenfield stepped down from the stand and walked briskly down the center aisle of the courtroom and right out the door. As the door closed behind her, Judge Wilson ordered a brief recess.

While people scurried about to get a drink of water or head to the bathroom, Ben sat in his chair and turned to face Mark. He knew he hadn't gotten anything out of Sylvia Greenfield, but then again, he didn't think she offered any damaging testimony either, save for the odd comment allegedly made by her husband that she would no longer control access to his family.

The final witness of the day was Samuel Dorlund. As he passed the counsel table, he gave Ben a smirk which Ben took as a warning of things to come. He appeared to be sweating in his best blue suit, blue Oxford shirt and red-print tie. As he climbed into the witness chair, Dorlund nodded at Judge Wilson, whom he'd known for many years, then sat down and looked out at the courtroom with a smug expression on his face.

Bridget Fahey looked up and took the witness through the preliminaries. As Ben watched, he felt an eerie sense of uneasiness in the pit of his stomach. He never particularly liked Professor Dorlund, didn't trust him now, and wouldn't put it past him to say something that wasn't true.

"Tell us," Fahey continued, "how did you know Daniel Greenfield?"

"Daniel was my colleague at the Chicago College of Law for more than twenty years. He was also my best friend."

Slowly and methodically, Bridget Fahey took Samuel Dorlund through his background at the law school and his relationship with Daniel Greenfield before moving on. "At the time of Professor Greenfield's death, were you involved with a committee planning for a reunion of the 1992 graduating class at the law school?"

He nodded. "Yes, I was."

"Was Professor Greenfield also involved with that Reunion Committee?"

"Yes, he was."

"Was anyone else in this courtroom a member of that Committee?"

"Yes," he said gesturing in the direction of the defense table, "the Defendant, Megan Rand Cavallaro, was also a member of the Committee."

"Did you ever speak to Ms. Rand yourself about the committee?"

"No, I don't believe I did."

"Was Ms. Rand ever a student of yours during law school?"

Dorlund shook his head, his right arm resting casually on the ledge of the witness stand. "No, I don't believe she was. But I do remember her as a student at the law school during that time."

"Did you ever have any other occasion to meet her?"

"Yes, I did. I met her on several occasions in Daniel Greenfield's office."

"Did you know what she was doing there?"

He shook his head. "At first, I assumed she was just there because she was another student. I later learned that they were having a relationship together."

"A sexual relationship?"

"Yes."

"Was she still a student at that time?"

"Yes, she was."

"Did you ever tell anyone about this relationship?"

"No, I should have, but Daniel was my friend and I didn't want to get him in any trouble, so I didn't."

"How did you learn of this relationship?"

"Eventually, Daniel told me that he was having a sexual relationship with her, but I could tell by the way they acted together that something was going on between them."

Ben thought about objecting, but figured it would be futile. Besides, he didn't want Dorlund testifying about the details of how they looked at each other or what they may have said so he left it alone. He could feel Megan cringe next to him. Just hold it together, he thought.

Fahey continued. "Do you know how long this relationship lasted?"

"I believe about six months or so."

"Was Ms. Rand still a student when the relationship ended?"

325

"I believe so, yes."

"Do you know whether Professor Greenfield had any contacts with the Defendant after the relationship ended?"

"No, I don't believe so. Not until recently anyway."

"What do you mean by recently?"

"Daniel mentioned to me not long before he died that he had spoken to her."

"Did he tell you what they spoke about?"

"No, he didn't. He just said he was happy to talk to her and told me how much he still cared about her."

Ben eyes narrowed. Somehow this didn't ring true.

"Did Daniel Greenfield tell you anything else about the Defendant?"

"He just said that he looked forward to seeing her again at the Reunion. He even wondered whether she was still available." Ben didn't like the way that sounded in front of the jury. "Other than that," Dorlund added, "he didn't say anything directly about her."

"Did he say anything indirectly?"

"Yes. Right before he was killed, he spoke to me about possibly getting back together with an old flame. We had recently been talking about the Defendant, so I assumed . . ."

Ben rose to his feet and cut him off. "Objection, your Honor. His assumptions aren't important. This is nothing more than speculation on the witness's part."

Judge Wilson didn't wait for a response from Bridget Fahey. "Sustained."

Bridget Fahey moved closer to the bench and began to say something, but reconsidered. Instead, she turned back to the witness and asked, "Do you know whether Professor Greenfield was working on any special research projects before he died?"

"Yes, he was," the witness said. "He was doing a substantial amount of research on DNA and paternity. I originally believed it related to his work, perhaps he was writing an article on the subject, but I eventually changed my mind."

"Why was that?"

"In talking to him, I became convinced that he had personal reasons for wanting to know about DNA and paternity."

326

"Objection," Ben said again. "This is more speculation without any foundation whatsoever."

"I'll agree with the part about foundation," the Judge said. "Ms. Fahey, lay a better foundation if you want to get into this kind of thing."

Ben didn't like where this was heading and wanted to cut it off immediately. "Your Honor," he interjected, "I think we need to be heard outside the presence of the jury."

Judge Wilson eyed him for a minute and then nodded. "Very well, let's go out here in the corridor. The court reporter is also directed to come."

Ben looked over at Bridget Fahey, who showed no reaction. He then glanced at the jury and saw puzzled and concerned looks throughout. Normally, Ben didn't like to interrupt the trial and ask to speak to the Judge outside of the jury's presence because it tended to offend the jurors and make them wonder what was being discussed behind their backs. In this case, however, he saw little choice, particularly in light of the direction in which the questions seemed to be heading and the prior ruling which precluded Bridget Fahey from getting into questions surrounding Anthony Cavallaro's paternity.

Ben followed Bridget Fahey out the door and into the corridor leading to Judge Wilson's chambers. A moment later, the court reporter maneuvered her machine and chair out into the small space so she could transcribe what was being said. Judge Wilson waited for her to get set up, then turned to Ben and said, "Okay, Counsel, what's on your mind?"

"Your Honor, it appears from where this questioning is heading that Ms. Fahey is attempting to get the issue of paternity in through the back door. As I'm sure you recall, long before this trial began, you granted our Motion in Limine which barred any evidence regarding the paternity of Anthony Cavallaro, my client's son. Ms. Fahey is trying to get at the issue of paternity without mentioning Anthony directly, despite the fact that the implication is obvious. She can be talking about no one else. I let it go in her opening statement because it was a rather indirect reference and I didn't want to call more attention to it than was necessary. Now, however, she is clearly trying to circumvent your ruling and present the issue of paternity when we all know full well that Anthony Cavallaro is Joseph Cavallaro's son and not Daniel Greenfield's. She is trying to make it appear as though my client had a motive for killing Professor Greenfield to keep something quiet that isn't even true."

Judge Wilson gave a stern and thoughtful look, then turned to Bridget Fahey and said, "He has a point, Ms. Fahey. I've ruled that paternity isn't relevant and should be barred. What are you trying to do here?"

"Your Honor, I'm not really trying to circumvent your Order, but I think the issue of paternity is relevant. Yes, it's true that we learned that Anthony Cavallaro is not Daniel Greenfield's child, but that really isn't the point. The point is what everyone may have thought they knew at the time of Daniel Greenfield's murder. Daniel Greenfield may very well have believed that Anthony Cavallaro was his child and acted accordingly. The Defendant, your Honor, may have also suspected that her son may have been Professor Greenfield's child and not known for sure.

"Either way, she may very well have been motivated to keep Daniel Greenfield quiet about the affair, assuming her husband didn't know, and we believe he didn't know, and also to keep him from pursuing the paternity issue. Also, I'm sure she didn't want her son to learn that Joseph Cavallaro was not his real father."

"Judge, this is ridiculous," Ben said.

But then Judge Wilson held up a hand. Ben fell silent and watched the Judge consider Bridget Fahey's words. He thought for several moments and then turned back to the Prosecutor. "What's Professor Dorlund going to say?"

"He's going to say that he saw no evidence that the DNA and paternity research that Professor Greenfield was working on had anything to do with any article. He's going to say that his conversations with Professor Greenfield led him to believe that the research was personal, and not work-related. He's also going to say that Professor Greenfield told him that he had just found something out that would make a significant difference in his personal life."

"What was that?" the Judge asked.

Fahey spoke quickly and intensely. "He will say that he doesn't know for sure, but that Greenfield's comments led him to believe that Greenfield thought that the Defendant's child was his."

"You've got to be kidding me," Ben interrupted.

"Hold on, Counsel," the Judge said with another raise of his hand. Ben was incredulous. In his mind, this was made up out of whole cloth, with no facts to support it. It also constituted the worst kind of blindsiding at the last minute.

Fahey continued clearly excited. "Judge, we believe the jury can reasonably infer that Professor Greenfield suspected that the Defendant's child was his and that she acted in order to silence him."

Judge Wilson finally turned back to Ben. "Now you can tell me what you think," he said.

"Judge, there is no basis for this whatsoever. We know the issue of paternity is settled. Anthony Cavallaro is Joseph Cavallaro's child. The rest of this is all made up. It's all just speculation out of nothing, out of thin air."

The Judge looked thoughtful. "If I do reconsider the issue of paternity, of course, you would be allowed to put into evidence the fact that a paternity test was taken and the child was shown to be Joseph Cavallaro's. That discounts their theory right there."

"Sure it does, Judge, but they have no real proof that any relationship ever took place. It's not like anyone can come in here and say they saw them having sex. They're just trying to dirty her up without any evidence of paternity whatsoever. They needed a motive and now they've gone and made one up."

"I wouldn't go that far, Counsel," the Judge said. "It is circumstantial and I would agree it's speculative, but there are pieces of evidence that do support it. I'm not sure that the jury can't make that inference. You can certainly take steps to disprove it."

"It's awful hard to disprove a negative, Judge."

"Mr. Lohmeier, there are a lot of ways to disprove a negative. There are a lot of ways for you to attack this evidence if you so choose. I think on reflection that Ms. Fahey's right. I'll allow the testimony subject to your objection. Now let's go back inside."

The Judge made it clear that the discussion was over and his ruling would stand. Ben shook his head and remembered to put on a brave face when he returned to his seat. Bridget Fahey strutted her way back into the courtroom, not even trying to conceal her feelings over the Court's ruling. Ben, on the other hand, appeared stoic, but tried to maintain a calm air of indifference.

When he sat down, Judge Wilson was just coming through the door back into the courtroom. Meg leaned over and said, "What happened?" into Ben's ear. He turned at her and shook his head telling her to be quiet.

When the court reporter was back in place, Judge Wilson addressed the jury. "We've had a brief conference outside your presence to decide some evidentiary issues which were originally raised before this trial began. The lawyers have made their arguments and I have made my ruling. We are now ready to proceed. Ms. Fahey, you can continue."

Before Bridget Fahey could continue, Ben rose to his feet and said, "Your Honor, for the record and in front of the jury, I would like to renew my objection to this whole line of testimony. The issues that Counsel is raising, and the inferences she is seeking to draw from them, are both irrelevant and improper and should not be admitted. As such, the defense demands a continuing objection to this whole inquiry."

Judge Wilson looked down at Ben, a surprised and very irritated expression on his face. He cocked his head and said with a tone of astonishment, "You demand such an objection, Counsel?"

Ben never expected to put himself in this kind of position with this judge, but he did not back down. He returned the Judge's glare with one of his own, filled with anger and contempt for the ruling. Abandoning his long-held belief that he would never show that anything bothered him in a courtroom, Ben stared back at the Judge and said, "Absolutely. I think we're so entitled."

Judge Wilson raised his chin and looked at Ben for a long time, then he nodded and said, "Very well. The defense has a continuing

330

objection over this line of questioning. Now, Ms. Fahey, you may continue."

"Back before we were interrupted," Fahey said with a sly grin, "you were telling me about conversations you had with Professor Greenfield shortly before his death regarding his personal life."

"Yes," Dorlund said looking even more smug than before. "He told me shortly before he was killed that he'd found out some new and exciting news about his personal life that would change his life forever. He also told me that he hoped to possibly get back together with someone he had seen before."

"Did he tell you who?"

Dorlund shook his head. "No, he didn't."

"As we discussed briefly before, you are familiar with research that Professor Greenfield was conducting on DNA and paternity?"

"Yes, that's correct."

"To your knowledge, was Professor Greenfield drafting an article or writing a book with respect to those topics?"

"I assumed so at first, but then I changed my mind because I saw no evidence of him drafting anything with respect to those topics. I came to believe that he was only researching them for his own personal use."

"What do you mean by that?"

"I think it related to the exciting news in his personal life that he spoke about."

Ben rose. "Objection, your Honor. This is all speculation."

"Overruled."

Bridget Fahey moved in for the kill. "Professor Dorlund, looking back on everything you know now, based on all these conversations with Professor Greenfield and your knowledge of him as his best friend, do you have an opinion about what the significant events in Professor Greenfield's personal life may have been?"

"I do."

"Objection, your Honor," Ben said as he rose to his feet again. "This calls for speculation and a conclusion on the part of the witness. This is not directly related to any testimony whatsoever.

He's merely giving an opinion and that's not proper in this circumstance."

"I'll allow it."

"I think Daniel Greenfield believed that the Defendant's child was his."

Several gasps were heard in the courtroom and a commotion took place as several reporters rushed out into the hallway. Judge Wilson banged his gavel and said, "I expect there to be order in this courtroom. Everyone quiet please."

Meanwhile, Bridget Fahey smiled sweetly at the witness and said, "Your Honor, that's all I have for now."

Ben stormed from his chair, not bothering to hide his anger. Judge Wilson looked down and said, "Would you like a brief recess before your cross-examination, Mr. Lohmeier?"

Ben shook his head. "No," he said and kept charging. Not waiting for the Judge to respond, Ben tore right into Samuel Dorlund. Ben stopped about ten feet short of the witness box and pointed his index finger directly at the Professor.

"Professor Dorlund," Ben said, his contempt for the witness clear, "you and I have spoken about this case on several occasions over the past months, haven't we?"

"Yes, I believe we have."

"We spoke several times at the law school, didn't we?"

"Yes."

"We spoke in your office on more than one occasion, didn't we?"

"Yes."

"We also spoke in the cafeteria at the school?"

"Yes."

"And we've even run into each other in the hallways from time-to-time, haven't we?"

"Yes."

"We talked about the Reunion Committee, didn't we?"

"Yes, we did."

"You told me how Professor Greenfield expressed an interest in serving on the Committee with you, didn't you?"

"Yes, I think so."

"You told me how you had the materials for the Committee copied for him, didn't you?"

"Yes."

"You told me that you gave him a list with the names and phone numbers of all the members of the Committee on it?"

"Yes, that's true."

"We talked about Professor Greenfield's relationships with students, didn't we?"

"Yes, we did."

"We talked about Nora Fleming and how you knew Professor Greenfield was having a relationship with her at the time, didn't you?"

Dorlund hesitated. "I think so," he finally said. "I'm not sure I knew her name . . ."

"Of course, you didn't tell anyone at the law school about that relationship with a student, did you?"

"No, I should have, but I didn't. Daniel was a friend and . . ."

Ben cut him off. "We also talked about your little problem with law students and how they accused both you and Professor Greenfield of inappropriate behavior, isn't that right?"

"I believe we spoke about that as well, yes." By now Dorlund was fidgeting in his seat and looking increasingly uncomfortable. Ben did not hesitate and moved closer and closer to the witness, his voice rising, his anger visible for all to see.

"We talked about Professor Greenfield's relationship with his wife, didn't we?"

"Yes."

"We talked about his relationships with fellow professors at the law school, didn't we?"

"Yes."

"We talked about his attraction for students, make that female students, didn't we?"

"Yes."

"We talked about possible suspects in this case too, didn't we?"

"Yes, I believe we did." Dorlund's watery eyes darted from Ben back toward Bridget Fahey and even occasionally up toward the bench.

Finally, Fahey broke in. "Your Honor, we object. Counsel isn't so much questioning as badgering the witness."

Ben shook his head and glanced up at the Judge. "Your Honor, this is cross-examination," he said. "I'm entitled to great leeway, particularly in light of your ruling."

The Judge nodded. "Objection overruled."

Ben moved closer and now was standing directly in front of the witness box.

"We even spoke about how you wanted to make sure the person who killed your best friend was caught and punished, didn't we?"

"Yes, we did. That's what this trial is all about, isn't it?"

"Move to strike, Your Honor," Ben said.

"Granted," Judge Wilson said. "Professor, you know better than that. Stick to answering the questions."

Dorlund nodded meekly and Ben continued to savage him.

"That's it, isn't it? You think my client did it and you want her convicted, don't you?"

Dorlund seemed to regain his footing for an instant. "Of course I think she did it. She can't get away with this."

"That's why you're saying these things, isn't it?"

"I'm saying them because they're true."

"During those conversations," Ben said, "the conversations that took place before all this paternity baloney got in the media a few months back, you told me that the only way you thought my client ever had a relationship with Professor Greenfield was because he told you about it years later, isn't that right?"

"I think so."

"Before that time, you never told me about seeing my client in Professor Greenfield's office, did you?"

"I don't recall."

"You didn't tell me that Professor Greenfield told you he had a relationship with her back when it allegedly took place."

"No, I didn't."

"You never told me anything about changes in Professor Greenfield's personal life."

"I don't remember. It may have slipped my mind."

334

"Don't remember?" Ben bellowed, "Did you or did you not tell me about those alleged changes."

Dorlund stared at Ben for a moment. "No," he finally croaked. "You never told me . . ."

Bridget Fahey interrupted. "Objection, Your Honor. What he told Counsel isn't relevant."

"This is impeachment, your Honor," Ben shot back. "I'll get on the witness stand myself if I have to."

Judge Wilson nodded again. "Objection overruled."

Dorlund now appeared to be sinking into his seat. Ben continued. "You never told me about your theory that Greenfield wasn't really working on a law review article, did you?"

Dorlund paused. He was still looking around for help. "No, I don't think so."

"You never once mentioned that Daniel Greenfield believed that Megan Rand's child was his, did you?"

"No." He paused again. "I don't believe it came up."

"You certainly didn't bring it up, not like you did today, did you?"

"No. I don't think I did."

"You only mentioned a relationship between Greenfield and my client after this paternity stuff hit the media, isn't that right?"

"I don't specifically recall the exact date."

"You don't? Let me refresh your recollection. Do you remember my coming to your office about as angry as I am right now?"

"I seem to."

"Do you recall trying to blow me off and head to class in order to avoid talking to me?"

"I don't know if I did that."

"Do you recall that I had to threaten you with dragging you into Court to talk about these things on the record with the whole world watching in order to get you to talk to me?" Dorlund hesitated, then looked away in the direction of the prosecution's table. "Do you remember it or do you not?" Ben demanded.

"I seem to recall something like that," he said in a small voice.

"And only then did you come back and sit down and talk to me about Megan Rand and what you say you knew about her alleged relationship with Daniel Greenfield."

He nodded and mouthed the word before finally saying it aloud, "Yes."

"During all these conversations, did I ever ask you for anything but the whole truth?"

"I don't recall."

"Wouldn't you recall if I had?"

"I suppose so."

"That's the same thing you swore to give in this Courtroom, isn't it?"

"Yes."

"But even then, after all that, you never mentioned to me at all, not during any single conversation, this idea that Daniel Greenfield thought that my client's child was his own, did you?"

Dorlund shook his head only slightly. Then he whispered, "I don't remember."

"Not once."

Dorlund looked away. "No, I don't think so."

Ben stood there and faced him for a long time, his feet apart, his hands on his hips, looking as though he couldn't decide whether to strike Dorlund or spit on him. Dorlund finally looked up at him somewhat defiantly, and Ben held his gaze until Dorlund looked away. Then Ben said, "No, of course not." He paused again, his eyes boring into Dorlund. "When did you and Ms. Fahey cook this up?" he finally said.

Fahey was on her feet in an instant. "Objection!"

"Withdrawn."

And the cross-examination was over.

51

The prosecution rested their case-in-chief later that week and Judge Wilson gave each side until the following Monday to file concurrent briefs regarding the Defense Motion for a Directed Verdict. A directed verdict means that notwithstanding the evidence presented by the State, a reasonable jury could not conclude beyond a reasonable doubt that Megan was guilty, and a not guilty verdict would be entered and she would go free. It's almost like saying, "So what?" at the end of the State's case. Ben recognized that he had a better chance of being chosen Miss Congeniality than getting a directed verdict, but he and the team went through the formality nonetheless.

As expected, Judge Wilson dutifully considered the evidence and the briefs and denied the Motion. In the meantime, Ben's explosion in Court was the talk of the TV pundits and legal talking heads. Some praised his cross-examination of Dorlund as among the best they had ever witnessed, while others deemed his display of anger inappropriate and likely unpersuasive before the jury. Ben knew that despite his thorough dismantling and humiliation of Dorlund, the seeds of paternity had literally and figuratively been planted. The idea was now in the minds of the jury and try as he might, Ben would not easily remove it. Every time the jurors looked at Megan, Ben thought, they would look at her with a question, wondering whether she believed the child was Greenfield's and to what lengths she would go to keep the question of paternity, and maybe even the relationship itself, from her husband and son.

For her part, Megan expressed her support for Ben's outburst and genuinely seemed moved and appreciative of his desire to fight so hard on her behalf. Ben noticed a sense of serenity in her on the eve of the defense opening, as though she had come to terms with her lot in this trial and was ready to accept her fate without hesitation. Ben and Mark spoke with Megan for a long time on Tuesday evening, with Ben's opening scheduled for the following afternoon. They discussed the various aspects of the defense, which witnesses they intended to call, and even broached the possibility of calling Meg to testify. She seemed more willing to testify now, but Ben told her that he preferred to take a wait-and-see attitude and did not want to call her unless absolutely necessary.

"There are too many pitfalls associated with cross-examination," Ben insisted.

Ben stayed around the office for awhile after Megan and Mark left, putting the finishing touches on his opening statement. Judge Wilson had a hearing he needed to attend to in the morning, so Court would not resume until one-thirty in the afternoon, giving Ben a little extra time in the morning to do some necessary polishing. He got home in time for a nice meal and some quality time with his kids.

The following afternoon, Judge Wilson looked down at him and said, "Mr. Lohmeier, are you ready to proceed with your opening statement?"

"Yes, I am," Ben said coming to his feet. He stood behind his client, his hands on her shoulders and began. "Ladies and Gentlemen of the jury, as you know, my name is Benjamin Lohmeier, and I am proud to represent my friend and client, Megan Rand Cavallaro." He patted her once more on the right shoulder and moved out from behind the counsel table and walked slowly to the center of the room. He carried no notes of any kind.

"On or about December 28th, 2001, Daniel Greenfield drove downtown to finish grading the final exams taken by the students in the Criminal Procedure class he had taught for many years at the Chicago College of Law. He had meetings scheduled that day as well. We know this because there was a notation to that effect in his appointment book. Unfortunately, we don't know who the meetings were with. As you might expect at a school of this type during the holidays, the Chicago College of Law was pretty empty on December 28th. There were very few people there, few people coming and going, and as far as we can tell, Daniel Greenfield's floor was empty, save for Professor Greenfield working alone in his office grading those final exams.

"Sometime on that fateful day, most likely in the afternoon, Daniel Greenfield had one or more of those meetings, probably with the person who murdered him. During the course of this meeting, while Professor Greenfield was bending over to put something in his briefcase or maybe pick something up off the floor, the killer picked up the Professor's prized possession, an autographed Sammy Sosa Louisville Slugger and struck the Professor on the back of the skull, above and behind his left ear. The Professor collapsed to the ground. The killer struck him again, and again, and again, and again, as many as ten to twelve times, crushing the Professor's skull and killing him. Bits of skull, tissue and bone painted the walls, the shelves, the desk, the floor and the filing cabinet of Professor Greenfield's office. Blood was everywhere."

The jury sat transfixed as Ben described in calm, measured tones the death of Daniel Greenfield. He paused, eyeing the jurors carefully, then continued. "Then the killer left him there, carefully fled the scene, and probably escaped around the corner and through the door into the library. From there, the killer returned to the 9th floor and out through the front of the library, down the elevator to the first floor and out the back entrance, unseen by Charles Powell, the security guard on duty.

"That Friday night, December 28th, the law school closed for the New Year's holiday. It reopened five days later, on January 2nd, 2002. Professor Gordon Hyatt was one of the first people back in the building that morning, he too seeking to finish grading final exams. Sometime in mid-morning, Professor Hyatt stopped by Professor Greenfield's office to drop something off, only to discover his colleague dead on the floor of his office. The police were summoned. The security cameras examined. They were useless. Their seventy-two-hour capacity, known only by a few, was too short to reach back to the time of the murder.

"We are here today because the State believes my client, Megan Rand Cavallaro, a well-respected member of the legal community, a former Hearing Officer in child custody matters, a clerk for an Appellate Court Justice, committed this heinous act. Nothing could be further from the truth. The State's case is based largely on a couple of drops of blood, a few strands of blond hair, two fingerprints and the story of a man who said one thing right after his best friend's murder, then something altogether different the other day in this courtroom."

Ben shook his head slowly as though the mere thought of it sickened him. "All of these elements, the fragile underpinnings of a faltering case, are easily explained." Then Ben briefly laid out a simple outline of the defense case before concluding, "In this country, in courtrooms just like this one," he said looking around the ornate courtroom and gesturing at its wide expanse, "courtrooms large and grand and courtrooms simple and small, juries make promises. You made promises when we selected you. You said you'd wait until you heard all the evidence, all the testimony, before you made up your minds. You said you'd make the State prove its case beyond a reasonable doubt."

He gestured in the direction of Bridget Fahey. "We chose you because you made those promises. We know you'll keep them. That's all Megan asks. That's all she needs."

When he finished, Ben looked into the eyes of each juror, one by one, looking for the affirmation that this promise would be kept. Then he nodded once and sat down.

52

Ben and Mark sat in the garage trying to convince themselves they hadn't forgotten anything. Brad Funk had left about half an hour earlier and Dan Conlon was on his way out the door now, so it was just the two of them amidst a sea of paper, scattered files and a couple of empty pizza boxes. Ben leaned back in his chair and plopped his feet up on the conference room table while sipping the last remnants of his watered-down root beer. He looked across the room. There, in front of the bookshelves, stood the easel with the poster paper and Ben's notes scrawled all over it. Some of the notes dated back to that night a couple of months earlier when Ben had hoped that seeing the pieces in front of him could help him assemble the true picture of Daniel Greenfield's death.

Over the following weeks, additional notes, ideas and thoughts had been added, but the picture didn't seem any clearer now than it had been then, or even clearer than it was on the day Daniel Greenfield was found laying dead in his office. Still, Ben thought that most of the pieces were there and hoped that something would click in his head and allow him to see what really happened.

Mark stuffed some papers into a file and looked up to see Ben studying the easel on the other side of the room. "What?" he said.

Ben shook his head. "I don't know . . . nothing." He paused, then said, "Do you ever think we'll really know what happened?"

Mark didn't hesitate. "No, I don't. And to tell you the truth, if we get a not guilty, I don't give a shit if we ever know."

"Yeah, I guess," Ben reluctantly agreed. "I'd still kind of like to know though. I'd like to know who did it and why." He paused. "I'd also like to know who had me beaten up."

Mark stood and hitched up his pants. Unlike Ben, who had lost weight during the previous several months, Mark seemed to be putting it on with astonishing ease. He was one of those guys who handled stress by eating. Mark turned and looked at the easel. "What I'd like to know," he said, "is what Bridget Fahey has up her sleeve for rebuttal."

Ben stood and nodded. "That would be worth knowing," he said.

Mark laughed. "My view is arguing last is worth everything, or at least almost everything. I've heard some big-time criminal defense lawyers say they would give up reasonable doubt if they could just argue last. Anybody who has ever been married knows that arguing last is the key."

"Yep," Ben said.

"That's why wives never give it up," Mark added.

Ten minutes later, after clearing away the remnants of their dinner and packing up for Court, Ben and Mark headed home. Since the attack on Ben, they tried not to leave one person alone at the office at the end of the day. The last two guys would typically leave together, and they'd call ahead of time to let the Ithaca Police know they were leaving. That way, an Ithaca squad car cruised the parking lot as the last of them left for the night. The police also helped keep the media away.

Libby was surprised to see him when he got home. "You're home kind of early," she said. "Just in time for bath."

Ben heard feet on the stairs and then his daughter, clad only in her underwear, turned the corner and ran straight toward him and jumped into his arms. Ben scooped her up and gave her a big hug and several kisses on the head. Then he carried her upstairs for the bath and bedtime ritual that he had missed so many times in the previous weeks. It was ten-fifteen before Ben got back downstairs, grabbed a beer from the refrigerator and ambled into the family room where Libby was watching television.

Libby clicked the pause button on the Tivo and tossed Ben the remote. "How far did you get today?" she asked. "I've been busy and I haven't been watching the news shows."

"The opening and we did the blood splatter guy."

"How'd that go?"

"The opening was good. It was shorter than Fahey's, but I thought it was pretty good. Mark said it was good, so we were pretty happy with it. The blood splatter guy did okay. He testified that there was a big mess and whoever did the whacking probably got quite a bit of blood and other shit on him. Of course, we knew all that. Bridget Fahey didn't do too much with it, probably because he really didn't disagree with her guy. We're trying to undercut the idea that Meg could have done it and only gotten two drops of blood on the scarf."

"Unless, of course, the scarf was wrapped all the way around her neck," Libby said.

"Shh," Ben said. "Thank God you're not on the jury. Don't even suggest ideas like that. Somebody may be listening."

They watched TV for awhile, and Ben even checked out a few minutes of Geraldo talking about the trial. Good reviews on his opening statement. That felt good. Libby went upstairs about midnight and Ben clicked off the lights and the television and plopped back down on the couch for a few minutes. The only light in the room came from the small fish tank on the table in the corner. Ben watched the two goldfish float lazily in the water. He thought back to what Mark said in the garage about not ever finding out who killed Greenfield. He hoped that wouldn't be the case, but figured that it was probably true.

The hardest part about criminal trials is the unknown and the unknowable because they planted the seeds of doubt that could eat you alive. Maybe Mark was right, Ben thought, maybe a not guilty would be good enough. Ben thought about Bridget Fahey's rebuttal case. He knew she must be keeping something in reserve to hammer him with in rebuttal. Give up reasonable doubt to argue last? There might be something to that. Ben got up, walked over to the fish tank, said, "Goodnight fish," clicked off the light on the tank and went upstairs to bed.

The following morning, as Ben entered the courtroom, Stanley Disko caught up with Jason Hahn in the locker area at the law school. "You have now been served," he said after Hahn took the trial subpoena from his hand.

Hahn responded with a string of expletives in imaginative combinations that even Disko had to appreciate. "You kiss your mother with that mouth? If you have any questions about the subpoena, why don't you call Professor Harper. She's in the same boat as you," Disko said over his shoulder as he left the locker area. He nodded to the onlookers on his way out. One more good story for his memoirs.

Back in Court, Stanley Liu took the stand, a small Asian man whose parents emigrated from Taiwan in the mid-1950's. Stanley was born two years later, and at age forty-five, was one of the foremost blood experts in the United States. He looked fidgety, a crooked grin crossing his face. He wore an ill-fitting tan suit and had a mop of uncontrollable black hair that flopped down in his face and he frequently pushed it away with one hand.

Mark conducted the direct-examination and deftly led Liu through his background and considerable experience. Ben watched carefully as Mark questioned Dr. Liu about his evidence collection methods and data analysis techniques. He saw the jury paying careful attention to Dr. Liu's testimony. From the defense table, he could get a better perspective on how the testimony was being viewed and processed by the individual jury members whom he could not watch and certainly not study while conducting an examination himself.

Despite his somewhat quirky demeanor, Dr. Liu was an engaging witness and one to whom people seemed to instinctively want to listen. Mark turned his attention to the blood found on Megan's scarf. "Dr. Liu," Mark said, "did you ever have occasion to examine the gray cashmere scarf which has been introduced into evidence as Exhibit 15?"

"Yes, I have, in some detail."

"As you know, two drops of blood were identified on that scarf, isn't that correct?"

"Yes, that's correct."

344

"Were you able to identify anything else on that scarf?"

"Yes, I was. There were two different types of hair on the scarf. First, there were several blond hairs."

"What about the other hairs?"

"Those were hairs from a different subject, more coarse, some black, some gray. Our further analysis indicated that those hairs likely came from Joseph Cavallaro."

"What conclusions, if any, did you draw from that analysis?"

Dr. Liu looked serious. "I concluded, of course, that both Ms. Cavallaro and her husband occasionally used that scarf. It is my understanding that there were two identical matching scarves, both gray cashmere."

"Did you find anything else on the scarf?"

Dr. Liu nodded. "Other than the blood, we found traces of what we identified as women's makeup, at least two different kinds of perfume and men's cologne."

"Did you draw any conclusions from this?"

"Yes. This confirmed our previous analysis that both the husband and the wife frequently used this scarf."

"Objection, your Honor," Bridget Fahey said as she stood. "We object to the use of the word 'frequently'."

Before the Court could rule, Dr. Liu turned and looked up at the Judge. He said, "Your Honor, sir, may I explain my use of the word 'frequently'?"

Judge Wilson looked startled, then said, "Sure, go ahead."

"When I say the word 'frequently', I use that word because of the quantity and different sizes of the male hairs found on the scarf. From that I conclude that not all of the hairs got on the scarf on one occasion. Furthermore, that quantity of hairs would be unusual for just one or two uses. Hence, I believe that the scarf was used by both parties on numerous occasions."

Judge Wilson nodded. "Objection overruled," he said.

Bridget Fahey frowned and sat down. Mark put his head down and shuffled toward the witness. He had kind of an "aw shucks" manner that didn't always make him appear to be the smartest lawyer in the room, but juries found him appealing. Ben suppressed a smile. Mark continued. "Dr. Liu, did you ever have an occasion to perform any analysis of those drops of blood found on Exhibit 15?"

"Yes, I did."

"What sort of analysis did you conduct?"

"Well, the first thing I did was test to confirm whether or not the blood actually came from the victim, Daniel Greenfield. I did this by checking the blood on the scarf against a known sample of Professor Greenfield's blood."

"What did you determine?"

Dr. Liu shrugged. "I determined that the blood on the scarf did, in fact, belong to Daniel Greenfield."

Ben saw several puzzled looks on the faces of the jury. They were apparently expecting something more explosive. Mark nodded several times and moved on. "Did you conduct any other tests on the scarf?"

"Yes, I did. We looked at the blood samples themselves to determine whether there were any other elements or compounds present in the blood itself."

"And what did you determine?"

"We determined that there were small quantities of an over-the-counter antihistamine, traces of marijuana and traces of cocaine contained in the blood."

Mark looked a little surprised. He scratched his head and asked, "Isn't this similar to the conclusions drawn by the witnesses for the State?"

"Yes. Similar, but not the same."

"What do you mean, not the same?"

"In our analysis, the traces of antihistamine and marijuana found in the blood on the scarf were somewhat similar to the amounts found by the prosecution's witnesses. However, our analysis turned up a much greater concentration of cocaine in the blood on the scarf than was found in the blood analysis done by the prosecution."

Now Bridget Fahey looked puzzled.

"What conclusions, if any, Doctor, did you draw from these test results?"

"We concluded that the blood on the scarf came from Professor Greenfield's nose, not from his head wounds. In other words, the blood came from a nosebleed."

Ben saw expressions of enlightenment on the faces of several jurors and more murmuring could be heard from the gallery. Bridget Fahey jumped to her feet. "Objection."

Judge Wilson looked down at her and didn't answer. He appeared to be waiting for a basis for her objection. Mark turned to face her, also anticipating some sort of response. Fahey stood there, her mind spinning while she tried to come up with an answer for the Court. The best she could come up with was, "There's an inadequate basis, your Honor, for this conclusion. It is not supported by the evidence."

Judge Wilson shook his head. He didn't even bother to turn to Mark. "Objection overruled." Then he looked at Mark and asked, "Do you have any more questions, Counsel?"

Mark shook his head, "Nope, Judge, not at this moment," he said. Then he ambled back to the defense table, not even concealing a grin.

Judge Wilson turned back to Bridget Fahey and said, "Your witness, Counsel."

She stood at the prosecution table and looked down at her notes trying to gather herself again. Then she looked back up at the Judge and decided she better get on with it. "Dr. Liu," she began, "what is the basis for your conclusion that the blood on the scarf came from a nosebleed?"

"Several factors," the Doctor said calmly, "the first of which is the presence of a higher concentration of cocaine. As was indicted in the autopsy, Professor Greenfield exhibited some damage to his septum area, where there was also evidence of recent bleeding and blood coagulation. This is a symptom of cocaine use, with the drug having been ingested through the nose. Because of that, it could be expected that there would be excess cocaine residue present in the nasal canal. When the nose bleeds, that excess cocaine residue would show up in the blood coming from the nose as an increased concentration of cocaine in that blood. These increased concentrations would not occur in blood taken from other parts of the body, including from the head wounds. Also, as you have undoubtedly seen from the photos of the Professor's injuries, the damage to his skull was in an area confined to that area above and behind the left ear ranging through the rear portion of the skull. There were no wounds to the face or specifically to the nose."

Not exactly what Bridget Fahey was hoping for. She tried to rebound by questioning the Doctor on his background. "It's true, isn't it Doctor," she said, "that you are not a trained pathologist?"

Dr. Liu cocked his head. Then he nodded. "Yes, that's correct."

"Nor are you an expert in head wounds, are you?"

"No, but I can tell when a victim doesn't have any wounds to part of his head."

Fahey looked down at her notes for a long time and Ben sensed that she had no real way to attack his conclusion. Any attack on that would likely have to occur in her rebuttal case. Now that she was in a hole, she decided to stop digging. Looking up at the Judge, she said, "That's all I have for this witness, your Honor."

After lunch, Mark put on the defense expert on hair, who testified that hair could not be matched to a specific individual in the same manner as blood or fingerprints. Rather, it could only be properly concluded that a given hair was generally consistent with those samples taken from a particular subject. DNA could not be taken from the hair itself, but rather required the presence of blood or flesh such as a skin tag. This typically occurred when a hair was plucked or pulled out, not when it simply fell out. Thus, attempts to match a few strands of hair to a specific individual were a problematic undertaking at best.

They didn't complete this testimony until after lunch on Friday. It was almost three when Ben rose to call his next witness. Judge Wilson looked at the clock on the wall and turned to Ben and asked, "Mr. Lohmeier, do you have a good idea about how long it will take to conduct the direct-examination of your next witness? I don't want to interrupt your examination to adjourn for the week."

Ben considered the question for a moment and then decided to call Sally Renfroe, who would provide character evidence on Megan's behalf. He knew her testimony wouldn't take that long

348

and the cross-examination would not be that extensive either. He looked at Judge Wilson and said, "Unless you have a preference for adjournment, your Honor, I could call a witness that we should probably be able to complete this afternoon."

Judge Wilson nodded and looked in the direction of Bridget Fahey. "Ms. Fahey," he said, "is that okay with you?"

She rose and nodded. "That's fine, your Honor."

Then Ben said, "The defense calls Sally Renfroe to the stand." The clerk called her name and Sally rose from near the back of the courtroom and made her way to the aisle, turned and walked confidently past the counsel tables to the witness stand.

As she took the witness stand and raised her hand to be sworn in by the clerk, Ben stood at the defense table reviewing his notes. He saw movement out of the corner of his eye and looked toward the back of the courtroom, only to see several people entering and leaving. He recognized one or two of them, whether from repeated appearances in the courtroom or somewhere else he didn't know, then turned back to Sally Renfroe.

Then it hit him and he stopped in his tracks. In his head, Ben could hear the little clicking noises of the pieces beginning to fall. He looked back in the direction of the gallery, then back at the witness, then up to the Judge. He glanced back at his notes as the clicking grew louder and louder, the pieces of the puzzle finally at long last falling into place.

He stood there transfixed, right in the middle of the courtroom, as the realization that he knew the identity of the killer of Daniel Greenfield hit home. All the pieces were in place now. He knew what happened. He knew who the killer was. Or at least he thought he did.

He looked down at the counsel table, trying to figure out what to do. He tried to focus. He heard voices. His mind was racing now. How should he handle this? What should he do? The voices grew louder. Finally, out of the corner of his eye, he saw Mark knock on the table slightly. He turned and caught Mark's eye, his eyebrows raised, a worried look on his friend's face. Then he heard the voices again.

"Mr. Lohmeier, Mr. Lohmeier." It was Judge Wilson. Ben turned back toward the bench. "Mr. Lohmeier, are you ready to proceed?"

He looked up at the Judge and tried to gather himself. "Just one moment, your Honor. I didn't think we'd get to Ms. Renfroe today, so I just need a moment to get things together."

"Okay," the Judge said, "let's get on with it."

"In just one moment." Ben turned and faced Mark. He appeared to fiddle with some files sitting on the corner of the counsel table even though he and Mark both knew that they had nothing to do with Sally Renfroe's testimony. He looked back at Sally Renfroe and nodded. He made up his mind. "Your Honor," he said, everyone in the courtroom looking at him and now a little curious, "in looking at the time, given that it's Friday afternoon, I'm not sure it's a good idea to begin Ms. Renfroe's testimony after all. Although I'm confident I could get through her direct-examination in a reasonable amount of time . . ." he fumbled for his words. "I think Ms. Fahey might be rushing through her cross-examination if we were to try to finish with this witness today. Also, I'm sure that the members of the jury would appreciate getting out a little early on a Friday afternoon. So, with the Court's indulgence and Ms. Fahey's indulgence, I would suggest that we adjourn now and pick up with Ms. Renfroe on Monday."

Judge Wilson gave him a look that seemed to suggest that Ben should have known this earlier, but eventually he nodded in agreement and said, "Ms. Fahey, any problems with that?"

"No, I think that's fine, Judge," she said rising, giving Ben a puzzled look.

As the jury left the courtroom with two Sheriff's deputies, Mark leaned over to Ben and asked, "What the hell was that all about?" in a voice barely above a whisper. Megan also gave him a strange look.

Ben shook his head. "Nothing. I can't tell you now. I'll tell you later."

Now Mark looked even more confused. "What?"

Ben cut him off with a wave of the hand. "I said I can't talk about it here," Ben said firmly. Ben grabbed his friend by the

350

forearm and looked straight into his eyes. "Do you understand me?" he said slowly.

Mark had seen that fire in Ben's eyes before. Something was up. "Sure," he said nodding, "we'll talk later."

Ben could feel his heart pounding. Nervous energy surged through to his fingertips. Even his knees were shaking. He didn't know what to do.

After Court was adjourned, Ben watched Sally Renfroe climb down from the witness stand and walk over to the defense table. He didn't want to look back at the gallery. He stared at her trying to size her up. When she reached them, she shrugged. Ben tried to look casual. He thought everyone could see through it. "I'm sorry for putting you in that position," he said to Sally. "I didn't initially intend to call you today, but I knew you were here and your testimony wouldn't take so long, so I figured, what the hell? Then I got to thinking that I wouldn't get it done today and, well, you saw what happened."

She nodded. "That's okay. Monday is just as good as today. I better go catch up with Peter," she said gesturing toward the gallery.

Ben followed Sally with his eyes as she headed for the railing to meet her approaching husband. Ben and Peter Renfroe made eye contact and the other man nodded. Ben nodded back, forced a smile, then quickly looked away.

Ben turned his back on the Renfroes and exchanged some small talk with Meg, Mark and Dan, all of whom seemed to think he had behaved strangely. He strained to seem normal and relaxed, while his insides were bursting with the fact that he may have solved the case. I have to be right, he thought. It all fits. It all fucking fits.

Ben walked down the steps to the media throng trembling with excitement, his hands visibly shaking. He balled them into fists and led Mark, Meg and Joe Cavallaro to the microphone. He didn't have time for this, he thought, but he couldn't just blow them off.

"We think the case is proceeding very well," he said with nervous smile. "I think everyone, probably yourselves included, is glad to get out a little early on a Friday afternoon. With that, I

351

hope all of you have a nice weekend, and we'll see you back here on Monday."

Turning back to his colleagues , Ben gestured in the direction of the street. They all seemed a bit surprised that his remarks had been so short. Nevertheless, they all moved on, grateful to get out of there. The reporters also seemed eager for the weekend to arrive.

Ben and Mark were soon separated by the dispersing crowd. Ben could see his friend's lumbering gait disappear among the crowd of reporters crossing the street in the general direction of their parking lot. Joe Cavallaro caught Ben's arm. "I need a quick word," he said in Ben's ear.

I don't need this! Ben screamed inside his own head. Don't they realize I know who did it? He nevertheless gave Cavallaro a couple of minutes of his time while people milled all around them. Ben kept looking at his watch, his impatience clear to everyone. Finally, unable to contain himself any longer, Ben cut Cavallaro off in mid-sentence. "Look," Ben said, "I don't mean to interrupt you, but I have to go. I've got something I need to do at the office and it's really important."

Cavallaro looked startled. "Oh, sure," he said. "You go ahead. Do what you have to do. Call me later."

Ben didn't wait for Cavallaro to say anything else. He simply nodded to Meg and took off for the car.

Within five minutes, Ben was maneuvering the SUV down the alley toward 26th Street and pulling his cell phone from his pocket. He dialed Mark. He needed to talk this out. He had to make sure he was right, that his logic made sense. No holes. The call went quickly to voicemail. Ben slapped his phone closed and slammed it down on the seat next to him. Mark didn't have his phone on again. "God dammit! Now what?" he said. He reached the intersection and had to make a snap decision – the Stevenson Expressway or the Eisenhower? Ben looked at his watch. It was already almost four, on a Friday afternoon no less. Neither choice was a good one. He picked the Eisenhower since he was heading back to the office and drove off in that direction.

The arterial streets were clogged with Courthouse traffic and Ben inched northward toward the Expressway. His mind continued to race with possibilities and he tapped his fingers non-stop on the steering wheel. He thought of Nelson and tried to remember his cell phone number. The detective hadn't been in Court. Although Ben didn't really have any proof in support of his growing conviction that he finally had the pieces of the puzzle in place, he knew how they could get it. How would Nelson react to Ben's theory? Ben thought he could be convinced. Sure, Ben had been hard on him during cross-examination, but Nelson knew the lay of the land. He had been around long enough. He knew how things worked. It wasn't anything personal.

Ben couldn't remember the number and knew he hadn't programmed it into his phone. It had been a long time since he had called Nelson, probably since Meg's arrest. He knew he had it at the office, he couldn't remember quite where at the moment, maybe buried somewhere on his desk.

Fifteen minutes later, he still hadn't reached the Expressway. He tried Mark again. Still nothing. Between the traffic and Mark, he thought he was losing his mind. Then he called the office. Nancy picked up.

"Nance, it's me," Ben said. "I need to talk to Funk."

"He's not here," Nancy replied. "He left a few minutes ago."

Ben thought for a second. "Okay, then give me his cell phone number."

She did. "Are you on your way back here? Do you need me to stay?"

"No," he said too quickly and too loudly. He didn't want that. He wanted everyone out of there. "I mean, I'm fine. It's Friday. Go home. Send everyone home. Everything's fine. Good day today." He didn't want to let her in on it yet. He still hadn't figured out exactly what to do.

She laughed. "Good. I didn't want to stay anyway."

Ben signed off and tried Brad Funk's cell phone. More voicemail. Why couldn't he get in touch with anyone?

He set the phone down just as he reached the ramp for the Eisenhower. It was just as he expected, a parking lot.

Ben crawled west on the Eisenhower, the setting sun burning into his eyes and giving him a headache. All the while, his mind worked overtime. The more it spun around in his head, the more he knew he was right. He tried weaving in and out of traffic in order to get to the office faster, but eventually gave up when the same cars kept pulling up alongside him. He tried Mark and Funk a couple of more times each, growing alternatively angry and frustrated in the process. He needed to get back to the office now. He needed to come up with a plan, a good one, before it was too late. Before it was too late.

53

By the time he finally reached the office, it was 5:30 and he was a wreck. But he knew what he wanted to do. He ran into Nancy in the parking lot. Hers was the only car left. Good.

"It took you all that time to get here?" she asked looking him over. "You look like shit. Traffic must've sucked."

He shrugged. "It did. I thought you'd be gone by now."

"Casey called in with a rush letter at 5 o'clock."

"Figures."

"No shit. Are you sure you don't need anything?" she said while shaking her head no.

He managed a weak laugh. "No, I'm good."

"Are you guys going to need anything over the weekend?" Her head was still shaking.

"No," Ben said trying to put her off, "not a thing. We should be fine. You go ahead. Have a nice weekend."

"Everyone else is gone," she said over her shoulder as she headed for her car.

Ben stood on the back steps of the building and watched Nancy get into her car and drive away before unlocking the door and going inside. He moved quickly to the front lobby to disengage the alarm and then walked immediately out to the garage to look through the files.

He pushed through the door to the garage, flicked on the lights and stuffed his keys into the pocket of his overcoat. He dropped his briefcase on a chair and looked around the room trying to find the file he needed. The bulk of the files used for trial had been locked in a storage room at the Courthouse for safekeeping. Judge Wilson kept the only key. It was much more convenient to do that than to schlep the files back and forth every day. There were just too many of them.

As he looked around the room, boxes and files and documents stacked everywhere, Ben wondered if he had outsmarted himself and left the files he needed at the Courthouse. He doubted it. They probably had ten copies of everything. He just had to find it. He found his backup witness files in a box under the conference table, pulled them out, and thought back to Dorlund's testimony. That prick, Ben thought, may not have been completely full of shit after all. He may have been closer to the truth than even he realized.

His heart pounded and his fingers trembled as he searched for the right file. He didn't find it in the first group, but found it back in a box under the table. He laughed out loud as he opened it and walked over and sat in one of the barber chairs to study the contents. He felt like a kid on Christmas, the excitement and anticipation building. He knew he was right. He just had to be. He looked across the room at the notes and posters that had been mocking him for so long. The timeline. He studied the timeline. Then he snapped his fingers.

His phone buzzed. He looked at the display and recognized Brad Funk's cell phone number. He opened the phone and started in on Funk, eager to talk to someone. "Where the hell have you guys been? I've been trying to get in touch with you and Mark ever since I left Court and nobody answers their fucking phones."

Funk started to answer. "Sorry, but …"

Ben cut him off. "Never mind that. I figured it out. I think I know who did it. I think I know how and I think I know why. It came to me out of the sky right in the middle of Court. Well, not exactly out of the sky, but I did figure it out. I'm sure of it."

Funk was stunned. "What? Who? Tell me everything."

"It was the Renfroes. At least one of them, or maybe both of them. You see, Bridget Fahey was right. Dorlund was right. At least almost right. They had the right basic theory. They just had the wrong people, the wrong defendant."

"I don't get it," Funk said. "Tell me what you mean."

"Look, here it is." He got to his feet and starting pacing the room. His voice quivered as he told his tale. "I think that Fahey's basic theory of the case is right."

"What do you mean?" Funk interrupted. "We already know that Joseph Cavallaro is the father of Megan's son."

"Yes, we do," Ben agreed "but listen, that doesn't mean that Greenfield didn't father someone else's child, or least think he did."

"Okay."

"Remember how everyone on the Reunion Committee seemed to have that list of all the other members of the Committee except Greenfield? Remember how we never could find Greenfield's list, not in his office, his briefcase or at his apartment?"

"I remember."

"We could never figure out why Greenfield of all people didn't have that list like everyone else did. We figured that there had to be something on that list, or least Greenfield's copy of it, notes or something, that implicated the killer in some way, that caused the killer to steal it to protect himself, or herself. I think we were right. I also think that Bridget Fahey is basically right. Greenfield got killed because he fathered someone else's baby, or at least he and the killer thought he might have, and the killer didn't want to find out for sure. So Fahey's version of the case is basically correct, except that Megan Rand Cavallaro wasn't the right woman. So let's ask ourselves, who else is on that Committee with a child about the right age?"

"You mean Sally Renfroe."

"Yeah, I mean Sally Renfroe. Her son is just a little younger than Megan's, meaning she got pregnant not long after Megan did, probably while we were still students. I haven't done the math, but I'd bet I'm right. Let's assume she was screwing around with Greenfield at about the same time as Megan, or maybe a bit after. From what we've heard about Greenfield, he wasn't going to leave his wife, not willingly, and he wasn't going to commit to someone else. He had a long relationship with Nora Fleming later on and he wouldn't commit to her even after he was divorced so why would he commit to Sally when he was still married? He wouldn't and she

357

probably knew that. Maybe they'd slept together a few times or maybe they'd slept together just once, it doesn't matter. She gets pregnant and knows she's in trouble. What does she do?"

Ben was on a roll now, the words shooting out of him like a geyser. "She decides to keep the baby. Any other decision wouldn't make sense. She's from Nebraska or someplace. Anything else just wouldn't do. In the old days, they'd send her off somewhere until the baby was born. They don't do that now. Besides, she had the bar exam to worry about. Now she needed a cover for the pregnancy. She turns to Peter Renfroe and they get married. One or the other of them told me that they've been friends forever. So she's desperate and she turns to him and he agrees to marry her and raise the kid as his own. So that's what they do.

"Everything is hunky-dory until this Reunion thing crops up. Remember, Greenfield wasn't originally on the Committee, but Sally Renfroe was. She got Megan to join, maybe as a buffer for Greenfield once he joined, maybe not. Then Greenfield looks at the list, sees who is on it, and starts thinking. Maybe he found out about the kids. He's got a lot of time to think about that now that his wife left him. At least two of the women on the Reunion Committee were women he'd previously slept with, maybe more for all we know. Remember, he was doing all that research on DNA and paternity and the legal aspects of them. He wasn't doing that for a law review article, he was doing that for himself. He looked at Megan and Sally, remembered their past history, did the math, and figured out that he may have a child out there that he didn't know about, a son no less. He starts poking around and gets killed because of it."

Brad Funk whistled into the phone. "That's some theory. So you're saying that Sally Renfroe killed Greenfield."

"Sally or Peter or both. Dorlund may have had it just about right. Greenfield may have thought he fathered Megan's son, or maybe Dorlund assumed he was talking about Megan because he knew of their relationship, and he didn't know about Sally and Greenfield. Maybe Dorlund misunderstood. Maybe Greenfield was talking about Sally all along." Ben shook his head and sighed.

"Anyway, I should've thought of Sally earlier. That was my fault. When I first saw the Committee list, I didn't know she was married and had any kids. I didn't think about anyone having an affair with her. I always thought she might be a lesbian, to tell you the truth. By the time I realized all that, my view of her had been filtered through Megan's perceptions. They were friends and Sally wanted to help out any way she could."

"She has been awful eager to help out," Funk agreed. "She did volunteer to be a witness."

"And Peter Renfroe has been very interested in the case too. Sure, I guess he and Sally are friends of Megan's, but he's been in Court all the time. I don't know why I didn't think of it earlier. He was in Court today. That's what made me put it together."

"I don't understand," Funk said.

"I saw him out of the corner of my eye when Sally was taking the stand. Something clicked. A few weeks ago, right before the trial started, I was downtown going out to dinner with Libby and some friends. I was rounding a corner and I bumped into these two guys. They were together, if you know what I mean. I didn't get a really good look at them - who pays attention to everyone they run into on the street - but I remember that it bugged me at the time. I thought I recognized one of them, but they rounded the corner so quickly it was like they didn't want to be seen. I sort of put it out of my mind. It wasn't that important. But now, I'm pretty sure that one of those guys was Renfroe. I got a glimpse of him out of the corner of my eye today just like I did that night on a street corner and it all started clicking into place—Greenfield, Sally, Peter, Megan, Reunion Committee, murder. And then when Court adjourned, he looked at me and I looked at him and I think we were both thinking the same thing. Hell, the way I acted in Court, everybody in the room knew that something was going on. I had a brain cramp right there in front of everyone. Only it wasn't a brain cramp, it was a revelation, and I think Renfroe knows it, or least suspects it. I could tell by the way he looked at me."

"If that's true," Funk said, "then he's on to you. You have to get a hold of Nelson right away."

Without thinking, Ben had climbed up into the shoeshine chair, and was leaning over, elbows on knees, talking to Funk. "I tried, but I couldn't find his number. I must have it here somewhere. I thought of calling Nelson right away. I've tried calling Mark, over and over, but there's no answer."

"His phone is probably off," Funk said. "You said you have Nelson's number here. Where's here? Where are you?"

"At the office. I'm out in the garage. I just got back. Everybody's gone. I've been going through the files and ..." Then Ben heard a rattling sound, then a small knock and he jumped. His heart was pounding more than ever now. He looked around and there, outside the door to the parking lot and waving at him, stood Sally Renfroe. "Jesus Christ," he said into the phone, "she's here."

"What? Who's there?"

"Sally. Sally's here. She's standing outside waving at me. I've got to go."

As Ben rose to his feet and closed the phone, he could hear Brad Funk yelling on the other end of the line. Forcing a smile, Ben tucked the cell phone into his coat pocket with his car keys and walked over to the door. Sally had stopped waving, but her smile was as big as ever. "I figured you were coming here," she said loudly through the door. "I thought I'd take a chance."

54

Ben looked down at the deadbolt lock, took a deep breath and flicked it open. He didn't know what else he could do. He pulled the door open, stepped aside and Sally walked in. She took off her coat and laid it on one of the barber chairs. He closed the door behind her and locked the deadbolt. Sally turned, still smiling, and said, "You know, I followed you almost all the way out here from downtown. I didn't realize it was you right away, but eventually I figured it out. It seemed like you were trying to weave in and out of traffic, but then just gave up. I figured you were in here so I walked around from out front. You must not have heard me at the front door."

Ben shrugged. She got that right. "I didn't," he said. It felt like his stomach was rolling over, and he struggled to appear casual. "So, to what do I owe the pleasure?"

"Like I said, I was more or less following you without really trying and I figured that you were coming out here to the office and I thought, as long as you are out here, and I was heading in this general direction myself, maybe we can go over my testimony one more time to make sure I have it down. What do you think? Unless you're in the middle of something." She looked around the cluttered room as though searching for something.

Ben studied her. He didn't see any hint of calculation on her face. Was this legit? He didn't know what to do, but knew that he had to do something, either go along or get rid of her, but he had to do it now. Careful not to turn his back to her, Ben took off his overcoat and placed it on the chair next to hers. He smiled again and said, "I'm not sure you need any more practice, but we can go through it one more time if that would make you feel more comfortable."

"Great," she said, "I would really feel a lot better if we did that. I don't want to screw anything up."

Ben cleared a space at the near end of the conference table, pulled a copy of her direct examination from a file in his briefcase and they took seats opposite each other, Ben facing the door. Although the garage temperature was fairly cool, Ben could feel trickles of sweat rolling down his back from his hairline back behind his ears.

After the first time through, Sally looked up and said, "I have to use the bathroom. It's right out there in the hall, isn't it?"

Ben was startled. This was it. This was the moment he'd been fearing. "Sure," said rising to his feet. He pointed out the door toward the main part of the office. "It's right out there once you get through the hallway."

Sally got up and left. Ben watched her not knowing what to do. He thought about making a break for it, but figured he wouldn't have gotten too far if she were actually planning something. He paced the room and a couple of minutes later, she returned, ready to go through her testimony again. Ben looked at her, trying to read her mind. She looked sincere. He sat down and they continued.

Sally's direct examination was relatively short, and by seven, they had gone through it twice, made a few small changes, discussed cross-examination and generally felt comfortable with things. She would make a pretty good witness, Ben thought.

Ben forced himself to remain calm, not an easy task, and when they were through, Sally wanted to make small talk. Ben tried to put her off without appearing rude.

"Well," she said after a moment, "I'm just happy to help Megan out. I think from what I've seen, the trial is going very well so far. You guys are doing a great job."

Ben rolled his eyes. "Thanks. I just hope you're right."

He ushered Sally to the front door, they said their goodbyes, and she left, Ben closing the door behind her. He watched her go down the stairs, turn and head for the front parking lot.

Ben knew he wanted to get out of there in a hurry, but he also wanted to find Scott Nelson's cell phone number. He reached the door to the copy room, stopped and looked through it out toward the garage. He thought he remembered the business card with Nelson's phone number sitting on his desk next to his phone. He turned and headed down the curving hallway toward the stairs that led to his office. Just as he reached the stairs, Ben heard a noise and froze. What was that? Was that the natural creeks and groans of a hundred-year-old house? Or was it something else? Someone else? Just nerves, he tried to convince himself. He heard it again. The problem with a house like this is that every floorboard creaked and no steps were silent. After a while, you get used to it. But Ben's feet weren't moving. He was standing still.

Keeping his feet stationary, Ben turned his upper body and craned to look back down the hallway. The way it curved kept him from seeing very far. He couldn't see as far back as the lobby, or even the copy room. He looked in the reflection of the windows facing the courtyard—nothing. Across the courtyard, he could see people eating dinner in the pizza place.

Ben felt his knees shake as he considered his options. All the exits on the first floor were behind him, in the direction of the sounds. He looked up the stairs into the darkness and then back out in front of him. One of the renters had an office just up ahead, but that would undoubtedly be locked. The stairs to the basement were just around the corner. The basement consisted of two or three small rooms from the turn of the last century, complete with a leaking stone foundation and God knows what else. Although there was nothing down there in the unfinished space but shelves and storage, Ben thought he might be able to hide down there. There might be tools or something down there he could use as a weapon. He hadn't been down there in over a year, maybe two and couldn't remember seeing anything useful. He knew there was a door from the basement to the outside that opened into the parking lot. He took a couple of seconds and racked his brain and couldn't remember ever seeing that door opened. He didn't want to get trapped down there. No, that would be a mistake. They might not find him until spring. He shook his head, turned and started creeping up the stairs. He felt the skin on his arms prickle.

Ben took the steps two a time, trying to be as deliberate and quiet as he could. Some of the steps creaked anyway and he winced with every sound. The stairway was a long, narrow tunnel of fourteen steps, which made it difficult to hear any noise coming from below. Ben reached the landing and looked left toward Phil's office. Where could he go? There was that hidden closet in the back of Phil's office, however, there was no escape from there. There was no time to detour into his own office to get Nelson's phone number. He just needed an escape plan. He turned and leaned over so he could see all the way to the bottom of the stairs—still nothing. He looked into the office to the right. There was a storage closet in there, really more of an attic than anything. He hadn't been in there in years either and couldn't remember how big it was or if it had an outside entrance onto the roof. No, he could get trapped in there too.

Then he saw the balcony through the window of the office. That's where Nancy smoked her cigarettes. He could sneak out onto the balcony, then either shimmy down or jump down to the ground below. He felt around the pocket of his pants. Damn, he thought. His car keys and cell phone were still in the pocket of his overcoat, which was sitting on one of the barber chairs in the garage. Had he locked the outside door to the garage when Sally came in? He couldn't remember. He had to either make it to the garage to get his car keys or make it to the bar next door. He'd be safe at the bar with all those people around. He just couldn't stand here waiting for the killer to arrive.

Ben moved slowly into Debbie's office and made his way to the door leading outside. He reached down and eased the deadbolt open. His hands were shaking. Now he felt cold. He tried to pull the door open as quietly as he could, but the pressure pulled the screen door back against the door jam making a slight slamming sound. He pushed through the screen door. Once outside onto the balcony, he turned and placed the door silently back into place.

He could smell the remnants of the cigarettes dotting the giant urn that Nancy used as an ashtray.

Ben put both hands on the rickety railing and pushed slightly. It gave a little, too much, he thought. He looked down at the sidewalk below. It was much farther down there once you started thinking about jumping. If he jumped out far enough, he might be able to catch some grass. If he jumped out too far, he could land in the small, stone fountain Jim Schulte had put in for "ambience." He spotted a gutter to his left, but would that hold his weight? Not likely. Off in the distance, Ben heard the rumbling of a train approaching. He looked out toward the tracks beyond the parking lot and a gust of wind blew through his hair. It was almost completely dark now, the only lights emanating from the garage and the streetlights scattered around the property. He felt weak in the knees. He was scared.

Ben took a deep breath and started to go over the rail when the window behind him exploded showering him with glass and blowing out a hunk of rail were Ben's right hand had been a moment earlier. He went to his knees and heard footsteps pounding. He leapt to the screen door to hold it shut just as Peter Renfroe jerked the inside door open and tried to push his way outside. Renfroe was a much bigger man and he had the momentum. The screen door quickly gave way as Ben's feet skated beneath him. Renfroe screamed and piled through the door.

Ben saw the gun in Renfroe's right hand and clawed at it as the larger man rolled over him. Ben got a grip on Renfroe's thumb and pulled it toward him with all his strength trying to loosen Renfroe's grip on the weapon. Renfroe screamed again. He tumbled over the top of Ben and the gun came loose. The two men scrambled for it like football players diving for a fumble, the gun bouncing hard on the wooden planks of the balcony.

Ben landed on it first, the butt of the gun pressing into his side. He couldn't get his hands free because he was busy fighting off Renfroe's charge. Then the gun slid free. Renfroe launched at it with his left hand and Ben blocked him with his right knee. Just when it appeared that Renfroe might have the gun within reach, Ben swung his leg around and swept it under the railing and over the side. Renfroe made one last desperate lunge for it like a sprinter leaving the starting gate. As he dove over Ben's midsection and toward the railing, Ben bucked his legs and kicked at Renfroe's body with his feet, sending the Protector crashing into the damaged railing. Renfroe scrambled to hold on. Ben kicked at Renfroe again, until the wood splintered and finally gave way, Renfroe screaming and flailing his arms as he somersaulted headfirst toward the sidewalk below.

Ben heard, but did not see, Renfroe hit the ground with a large crack. Gasping for breath, shards of broken glass biting him in his side, Ben rolled over to the edge of the balcony and peered down at Renfroe's body laying still on its side, one leg bent awkwardly beneath him. Renfroe did not appear to be breathing. Ben couldn't see the gun.

Ben pushed himself to his knees, then to his feet. The screen door hung on one hinge, swaying gently in the breeze. He looked at it, then back down at Renfroe's body below. He looked dead. How could it all come to this? A dead husband and father down there on the walk. All this because he didn't want anyone to know the truth. Ben stretched his back and felt a stabbing pain in his side, just like he did the night he was attacked a couple of months earlier. He looked down and saw a small shard of glass sticking out of his shirt. It was poking him in the side. He gently pulled it out and dropped it in a pile of broken glass before pulling the door open and going inside.

As he walked downstairs, Ben took inventory of his parts. He felt a trickle down the right side of his face, touched it and looked at his fingers – blood. He felt more small cuts on his face and was sure he had a couple on his back as well. His right hand was scraped pretty good too. His knee felt a little funny as he came down the stairs, but all in all, he had emerged okay, certainly better than he could have. Certainly better than Renfroe.

He walked through the copy room, reached the door to the outside and stopped. The hallway to the garage, where his keys and cell phone were located, was to his immediate right, but Ben figured he'd better find the gun just in case. Rubbing his jaw, he pushed through the door to the outside and saw Renfroe rolling onto his right foot, his left leg dragging behind him, the gun on the ground right in front of him. "Shit," Ben said and jumped back as it registered. He couldn't believe it.

Renfroe had heard the door open. He looked to his left, saw Ben and grabbed the gun, firing wildly in Ben's direction as he fell over onto his side. Another window shattered above Ben's head and off to his left. Ben barely heard it over the roar of a freight train now rolling by the building. Ben ducked back inside the building and Renfroe fired again. More glass shattered behind Ben and he burst through the doorway and ran out toward the garage, slamming the door behind him. That was at least three shots, Ben thought as he ran. How many more did he have? He locked the door even though he knew that would only hold Renfroe for an instant.

Once back inside the garage, Ben searched for a weapon of his own. He scanned the walls. The buffalo head and horse's rear end were of little use at the moment. Then he looked up toward the ceiling. There, on one of the beams crossing through the center of the room, hung two Civil War-era infantry sabers. Ben jumped on one of the chairs, then atop the conference room table, and yanked at one of the swords. It was fastened tightly and wouldn't come off at first. Finally, Ben wrenched it free just as he heard Renfroe's lumbering footsteps in the hallway outside over the sound of the passing train. He turned back toward the door as Renfroe hit it for the first time. Renfroe hit the door a second time and a third time before the door finally gave way and he barreled into the room, gun drawn.

Ben leapt from the table and swung the sword over his head at the instant Renfroe crashed into the room. But Renfroe saw the attack coming and turned to shield himself while trying to get off another shot. Ben's blow caught the Protector on the shoulder, forcing the gun down and the shot harmlessly into the floor. Although the sword was not sharp, it was heavy and dealt a powerful blow. Ben swung it again like a left-handed hitter attacking a high outside fastball. Renfroe ducked out of the way, his right arm coming up to protect his head, and Ben caught him solidly on the right bicep, the sword bouncing down his arm, the gun flying out of his hand and skidding across the floor.

The strength of Ben's blow forced Renfroe's weight over onto his damaged left leg and he toppled over onto his side. Ben immediately went for the gun. He tried to get around the fallen Renfroe, who swung around and kicked at Ben with his good leg. The kick caught Ben in the hip and sent him reeling into the corner of the table, knocking some of the wind out of him. Renfroe kept at it, swiping Ben's legs out from under him with another kick. Ben went down onto Renfroe and the two men wrestled and fought on the floor. Renfroe tried to wrest the sword away as Ben jammed his elbow into Renfroe's neck. As they struggled, Renfroe's gun was kicked under a nearby rolltop desk.

They fought over the sword, Ben on top and the Protector thrashing beneath him. Although Renfroe was the bigger and stronger man, Ben had greater leverage and eventually managed to wrest the sword from Renfroe's grasp, the latter seeming to let go. In doing so, Ben fell back against a couple of bankers boxes. He quickly scrambled to his feet and raised the sword over his head, only to discover the reason that Renfroe had given up so easily.

Renfroe rolled over and pulled himself up to a sitting position. In his right hand, he held the gun. Ben froze. "Drop it!" The Protector screamed. Ben looked around searching for an alternative, finding none. Renfroe was at least ten feet away and had the gun firmly leveled at Ben's chest. It wasn't a tough shot and Ben was too far away to get a jump on him. "I said, drop it," Renfroe repeated. Ben paused, then placed the sword gently at his feet, never taking his eyes off of Renfroe. "Nice try," Renfro said. "That's too close. Kick it away toward the door." Ben did so and backed slightly away from Renfroe in the process. He wanted to get around the conference room table if he could, to get something between himself and his pursuer.

The Protector was on to him, however, and wagged the gun at Ben as he pulled himself to his feet. Ben stopped. Renfroe sneered. Covered in sweat, his hair matted with blood from an oozing wound on the side of his head, his left leg apparently almost useless, Renfroe looked more like a wild animal than a man.

"You're pretty tough little shit, aren't you? Greenfield wasn't nearly this tough."

Ben tasted blood and wiped at his mouth with the back of a fist. "Greenfield probably didn't see it coming, did he?"

"You think you know all the answers, don't you."

"Enough of them. Greenfield figured it out too." Ben said.

"He had an idea, let's put it that way. Fat lot of good it did him."

"When did Sally first begin sleeping with him?"

"Not sure exactly. Probably around the same time as Megan. Then, obviously, for a time afterward."

"Just long enough afterward," Ben interjected, "for her to get pregnant with his child." It was a statement not a question.

The Protector nodded. "Yes. At least that long enough, but not much longer. He decided he was through with her by then, before he realized that she was pregnant with his child, with his son. But that doesn't matter now, does it?"

"No, I guess not."

Renfroe paused, suddenly lost somewhere in the past, remembering. Ben glanced around trying to find something that would help him. He inched a little bit further back.

Renfroe started speaking from his memories. "That's where I came in. Sally and I had been friends for a long time and when she was pregnant, she didn't know where to turn, except to me. She was scared. I told her that I would marry her and raise her son as my own, and I've done that. He is my son now, not Daniel Greenfield's. I'm proud to be married to her, and I'm proud to be David's father. Sally is my best friend in the whole world, and she's done more for me than anyone else ever could."

Ben said nothing. He just looked at the other man. They endured a nervous silence, Renfroe still seemingly lost in his memories. Finally, Ben said, "Then Greenfield started figuring it out. What happened? Did he find out she had a son when she joined the Reunion Committee?"

Renfroe snapped back and Ben regretted speaking. "Something like that. Actually, I think someone mentioned to him a couple of months before that they had run into Sally and that she

369

had a nine-year old child. Eventually, he must have started wondering."

"And what about Megan? Look what you've put her through."

"I think he may have wondered about her too. She was on the list."

"Yes, I've seen the list," Ben said. "It's funny though, the police never found Greenfield's copy. I suppose you took it?"

The Protector nodded. "Yes. He had some notes written on it about both Megan and Sally, notes that were very incriminating and might very well have proved that he knew that Megan's son was not his own, and that David . . . well, you know that already. I thought I could reason with him, but that didn't work. He wanted a paternity test, a DNA test. He was obsessed with having another family, with having a son, and once he thought that our son might really be his, he wouldn't let go. I tried to reason with him. I didn't want to kill him, but I knew I had to do whatever it took to protect my family."

Ben nodded. "And the bat, that was a convenient weapon?"

Renfroe looked at the gun. "I had the gun with me at the time," he said holding it up, "but the bat was just sitting there, and I had already looked at it and we had even spoken about it briefly, so when he leaned over to put some exams in his briefcase, I hit him." Renfroe paused, his eyes remembering. "He fell to his knees, then I hit him again, and again, and again. The first sound was loud, almost like hitting a board with a hammer, but then as I crushed his skull, I could hear it and feel it in my hands. I don't know how many times I hit him. I saw on TV that they said ten or twelve times. That may be right, I don't know. When it was done, I left. Through the library as you guessed."

Ben noticed that Renfroe was breathing very heavily. His leg must be killing him. "You knew about the security cameras?" Ben asked.

"Yes. I had made a number of visits to the law school and had even spoken to the security guard, your Charles Powell, on a couple of occasions. He told me about the time limit. I think he just assumed I was another student because I always had a backpack with me. I had longer hair back then too. I actually looked like a

370

student. I went back throughout the second semester in the spring so that he wouldn't get suspicious. I even saw you there. That was amusing. You were working so hard trying to figure out what happened and I was right there in front of you watching you the whole time. I hadn't met you yet."

Ben stared intently at Renfroe, looking for an opening. "Why did you have the guy attack me?"

"I just wanted to shake you up a little, make you think you were on the right track and didn't know it. Keep you from looking in my direction."

"I didn't really know anything at the time," Ben said.

"I know that. I'd been here in the office on numerous occasions. I looked through your files." He gestured proudly toward the boxes on the table. "I was keeping close tabs on you the whole time."

"You're the one who set the alarm off," Ben said.

Renfroe nodded and sneered. "Yes, that was me. You got out and locked up before I could leave the building. I had no choice. I simply slipped out the front door, walked over to the bar and disappeared into the crowd. No problems. I even have a key. Took it from one of the secretary's desks. They shouldn't leave stuff like that lying around where anyone could take it. The only thing I didn't have was the code to the alarm system."

"Who beat me up anyway?"

"A busboy at my restaurant. He was going to go back to Mexico anyway, so, you know, I slipped him an extra five hundred bucks to do a little job for me and then leave a week or two early. I told him you disrespected my wife. He understood. No one will ever find him."

Ben nodded.

"Now you answer a question or two for me," Renfroe said, "now that you know everything."

"Sure, go ahead." Ben wanted to keep Renfroe talking as long as he could.

"When did you start to figure it out?"

"Something may have clicked when I saw you on the street that night. But then again, I didn't get a really good look at you and you got out of there so fast, it didn't really register. I knew I recognized you from somewhere. I just didn't know where, and since I had a lot of things going on at the time, I didn't put it together. Something about today though, changed that. I saw you and everything clicked into place. I thought I knew what happened and who did it. At first, I thought it might be Sally, but then I realized that Sally really has changed over the years since her son was born. She wasn't the same person she was in law school, the same bull in a china shop she used to be. That left me with you." Ben paused and continued looking at Peter Renfroe. "And here you are."

Renfroe scowled. "Enough talking," he said. "It's time to get this over with."

Ben heard a soft sob, followed by a gasp. He and Renfroe simultaneously looked back toward the door to the main part of the building. Sally Renfroe stood there, tears streaming down her long face and onto her coat. "No, Peter," she whispered in a choked voice, "it's already over."

55

Renfroe shook his head emphatically. "No, I can't stop now. I can't give up. I can't leave my family now. No, I just can't. I vowed ten years ago I would protect you and David and make sure everything would be okay, and I have protected you and I'll keep protecting you. It will be okay. I'll fix this!"

Sally moved toward him, her arms outstretched, her face pleading. She spoke softly. "No, Peter, you can't do this. You have to put the gun down."

Peter Renfroe was facing his wife now, his back to Ben. Ben moved further to his left and now the table was directly between Renfroe and himself. Ben wanted to give Sally a chance to get the gun away from her husband, but wanted to give himself a chance to jump Renfroe if Sally proved unsuccessful. He kept inching further to his left.

Peter Renfroe kept shaking his head as Sally approached, the gun still raised. She stopped about three feet from him, her arms still outstretched. Tears continued flowing down her face and she spoke in almost a whisper. "Honey, we can get through this, but you have to put down the gun. There can be no more killing. Not because of me. You don't have to do this. It will be alright. I'll help you. Just put the gun down."

The Protector seemed shocked at her words. He looked at her as though she didn't understand why he did it in the first place and why he had to do it now. He scrunched up his face in an angry mask. "No. I can't turn back now. I can't. Don't you understand? You must believe me. I did this for you, for us, for David, for our family. Now stand back and let me finish this now."

Sally didn't stand back. She started moving forward again. "Peter, I love you with all my heart, but you can't do this. You just can't."

The Protector couldn't believe what he was hearing. Just as Sally reached him, he screamed and pushed her to the floor. "Don't you see I did all this for you?" He wanted to make her understand. Now he was crying too. He turned back toward Ben and pointed the gun at Ben's chest. Ben raised his hands. Sally screamed.

Suddenly, a blast rocked the garage. Ben dove behind the table. A second blast slammed into the safe behind him. He heard a thump, a moan and another blast. Something hit the floor. Then, a couple of seconds later, one final blast. The sounds boomed like a cannon in the confines of the garage. The blasts deafened him. His ears rang. He couldn't hear. The acrid smell of gunpowder filled the air. Ben lay on the floor behind the table as still as possible.

The smell of gunpowder grew stronger and Ben looked up and saw wisps of smoke floating over him. Trying to remain as quiet as he could, Ben rolled and looked back under the table toward where Peter Renfroe had been standing. Gazing through the legs of the table and chairs and around bankers boxes, Ben saw a body crumpled a few feet from him, its arm outstretched. He vaguely heard Sally's screams as though they were coming from miles away. Ben got to his knees and moved around to the corner of the table. He saw the outstretched hand less than three inches from an automatic pistol lying on the floor.

His ears still ringing, no signs of movement, Ben slowly pushed to his feet. Peter Renfroe lay motionless on the floor. Sally lay over her husband sobbing. Behind them in the doorway of the garage, a .45 caliber pistol raised, smoke wafting from its barrel, its owner staring transfixed at the body on the floor, stood Brad Funk.

"Brad," Ben said not knowing how loudly he was talking. He still couldn't hear himself. No answer. "Brad," he said again, this time louder, trying to get over the sound of Sally's wailing. Still no response. "Funk," he screamed. "Funk," he screamed again. Then a sliver of recognition and Funk's eyes slowly moved and met his. "It's okay," Ben shouted, his hands out in front of him as though trying to slow traffic. "Put the gun down. Put the gun down now."

Slowly, Funk nodded and lowered the gun about a foot, then another six inches. It was still pointed in the general direction of Renfroe on the floor.

"Be careful," Ben said. "Don't shoot me. It's okay." Ben inched forward and slid the gun further out of Renfroe's reach with his foot.

Gradually, Funk seemed to be regaining his senses. It was as though someone had slapped him in the face and he was beginning to come to.

Ben moved forward and looked closely at Renfroe's body. Sally cradled him in her arms and held him as she cried, her body heaving with each breath, but she could do nothing for him now. Blood began to seep from beneath him and cover the front of her clothes. Ben watched the blood trickle off of her left knee and puddle on the floor. There was no doubt this time. Shot three times, Peter Renfroe, the Protector, was gone.

56

Two hours later, Ben and Brad Funk sat in the lobby drinking their second beers. By then, Mark had joined them, having finally been located at home, summoned by Ben to serve as Funk's attorney in the event that there were unexpected problems with the police. Funk had fired three shots, the first of which struck Renfroe in the back, staggering him, but allowing him to get off a single shot as Ben dove to the floor. Funk's second shot dropped Renfroe and his third, fired with Renfroe laying on the ground and reaching for his dropped gun, finished him.

Ben called 911 and the Ithaca Police were there within minutes. Shortly thereafter, he found Nelson's cell phone number in his office and called him as well. Detectives Nelson and Cole arrived about an hour later, and they were out in the garage now conferring with the Ithaca Police, who had taken control of the crime scene. Ben did not allow Funk to talk to the police until Mark had arrived. Rather, he explained what happened since it had been Funk, not himself, who had fired the fatal shots. By now, Funk had fully regained his senses, yet the impact of what had occurred was certainly not lost on him.

Ben sat sprawled at one end of the church pew, his feet up, sipping on his beer and occasionally holding the cool bottle against one of the cuts, scrapes or bruises that covered his face. Brad Funk sat in one of the rocking chairs, while Mark took the other. Funk shook his head and took another long drag from his beer. "It's like Clint Eastwood said in that movie."

Ben nodded. "It's a funny thing killing a man . . ." Ben said.

376

"Yeah," Funk replied.

Ben looked at him thoughtfully. "But Brad, you didn't have choice. He was going to kill me for sure, and if he knew you were in the office or if he had heard you, he would have hunted you down too. He might even have killed Sally."

Funk nodded. "I know that. I did the right thing, but it's not what you expect when you see it on TV or in the movies."

"No," Ben agreed, "it's not."

They heard footsteps in the hall and Detectives Scott Nelson and John Cole joined them. Cole leaned against the receptionist's desk and Nelson took his hand and swung Ben's feet to the floor and sat down on the pew next to him.

Ben winced and held his hand to his side. "What? You're not going soft on me now, are you?" Nelson asked.

Ben shook his head. "Funny. I think I caught another one in the ribs sometime during the fight. Same spot as before, God dammit." Then Ben looked at Funk. "Not that I'm not grateful, but where in the hell were you and why did it take you so long to get here?"

Funk shrugged. "You won't believe this, but I was at the pistol range doing some target shooting. I got here as fast as I could." Ben looked at him sideways and Funk held up his hand and said, "I swear." Then he shook his head. "This was a lot different," he whispered.

All fell silent. They could hear the evidence technicians murmuring off somewhere in the distance. "Sure is," Detective Cole said after a minute. Funk looked down at the floor.

"My ears are still ringing a little bit," Ben said.

"You know," Nelson said, "I'm pretty impressed with how you fought him off. He was a pretty big guy."

Ben smiled ruefully. "Yeah, I did okay for a while," he said tipping his beer toward Funk. "But if Sally and then Brad hadn't arrived, I'd be dead. At the end, he was the guy holding the gun."

Nelson offered Ben a slight grin. "Still ... anyway, you'll be happy to know," he said, "that I just got off the phone with Bridget Fahey." Ben raised his eyebrows and Funk looked up at the Detective. "I told her that her case against your client just went to

377

shit. I told her who did it and that he was dead and that her case was dead too."

"How'd she take it?" Ben asked.

"Not too well, as you might expect," Nelson said, his grin widening. "But what the fuck is she going to do? It is what it is. Between you and me, I think she knew it was going downhill anyway."

Mark got up from his seat, moved over to Ben and extended his hand. Ben shook it. "That's not going to do anything for her political career," Mark said with a laugh.

"Who said an ill wind doesn't blow someone some good?" Nelson added.

Ben looked over at Funk. "Brad, you get the job of calling Phil and explaining how you shot up the office."

Funk grinned. "He'll probably make me pay for the damage. Hey, none of my shots missed. I didn't even damage anything."

"I, on the other hand," Ben said, "get to call Megan and tell her she just got the rest of her life back." He looked at his watch – almost ten-thirty. "I think she's probably still up. It's probably worth a phone call."

Nelson looked at Cole and said, "Pretty soon this will be all over the television."

"Probably already is," Mark said.

They all nodded, and no one said anything for a minute or two. Then Ben looked over at Nelson and asked, "What are you going to do about the paternity issue? Greenfield's dead. Does anybody really have to know? Do we have to put the kid through all that on top of this?"

Nelson sighed. Cole looked at him and shook his head. "That is a good fucking question," Nelson said, clearly not relishing the prospect.

They all thought about unintended consequences for a moment. "Mark, my friend," Ben said, breaking the silence, "tell you what, why don't you go into the kitchen and bring us each back a beer and we'll talk it through. In the meantime, does anybody want to hear my closing argument?"

CPSIA information can be obtained at www.ICGtesting.com
Printed in the USA
LVOW061634210312

274166LV00001B/246/P

9 781470 108366